LIFE CLASS

LIFE CLASS

JENNY NEWMAN

Chatto & Windus

LONDON

Published by Chatto & Windus 1999

2 4 6 8 10 9 7 5 3 1

Copyright © Jenny Newman 1999

Jenny Newman has asserted her right under the Copyright, Designs
and Patents Act 1988 to be identified as the author of this work

First published in Great Britain in 1999 by
Chatto & Windus
Random House, 20 Vauxhall Bridge Road
London SW1V 2SA

Random House Australia (Pty) Limited
20 Alfred Street, Milsons Point, Sydney
New South Wales 2061, Australia

Random House New Zealand Limited
18 Poland Road, Glenfield
Auckland 10, New Zealand

Random House South Africa (Pty) Limited
Endulini, 5A Jubilee Road, Parktown 2193, South Africa

Random House UK Limited Reg. No. 954009

A CIP catalogue record for this book
is available from the British Library

ISBN 0 7011 6887 0

Papers used by Random House UK Limited are natural,
recyclable products made from wood grown in sustainable forests;
the manufacturing processes conform to the environmental
regulations of the country of origin.

Typeset in Janson by SX Composing DTP
Printed and bound in Great Britain by
Creative Print and Design, Ebbw Vale

Contents

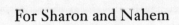

For Sharon and Nahem

Gentleman's Relish

It was Mam who dreamt up the scam in the convent parlour. 'It's a lucky break, Mo,' she says, perched on the armchair like a battered sparrow. 'The old man's got a lot of money in his back pocket.'

I think of the blocky, muscle-bound Archdeacon who shares my love of sport and likes to boast about his glory days as a prop forward. 'Then I wish he'd divvy up. Our roof's leaking in fifteen places.'

'He's always had a soft spot for you,' says Mam, who's the Archdeacon's cleaner. 'He'll give you some money if you ask him nicely.'

'I can't ask him at all, because I'll be stuck in the kitchen. Mother Wilfred's the one who'll show him round.'

My Superior is a woman of steep dark spirituality who never panders to the visiting clergy, and least of all to her old enemy, the wily, power-loving Archdeacon.

'That's a pity,' says Mam, nibbling her biscuit. 'He doesn't take kindly to starchy women.'

'It would go against her conscience to butter him up.'

'Even if her nuns have blue noses and eat blind scouse every night?' Mam's words take the chill off the cold parlour air. 'You may be a nun, Moey – but you're a woman too, and you know the way to a man's heart. With a good tea your Mother Wilfred could wind the old boy round her little finger.'

I think of Wilfie's arthritic pinkie, and feel doubtful.

'It's worth a try,' urges Mam, who has a Dingle woman's fighting spirit. 'Make him Gentleman's Relish butties and his favourite coffee layer cake. That should do the trick.'

'Gentleman's Relish?'

'A sort of posh people's fish paste.'

'We're too skint for that kind of tea.'

At that Mam gives a mysterious smile, puts on her hat and coat, and hurries off down the path.

Two hours later she reappears with a plazzy bag bulging with butter, eggs, coffee, flour, almonds, Belgian chocolate, Darjeeling, white bread, and a little white pot of Gentleman's Relish. 'For tomorrow afternoon,' she says, laying out the packets on the parlour carpet.

I stare in panic at the door. Mother Wilfred's study is just across the hall and she could walk in at any moment. 'Where did you get all this?'

Mam looks smug. 'I nicked it from the old boy's larder.'

'That's a sin,' I say lamely.

'No it's not,' replies Mam optimistically, 'because he'll eat it anyway. And besides, he's getting a pot belly.'

I shove the ingredients into the bag, wishing I could make her take them back, but not wanting to hurt her feelings. 'Where shall I tell Mother Wilfred I got the chocolate – and the Gentleman's Whatsit?'

'Tell her they were donated by a grateful parishioner,' says Mam. 'It's right enough,' she adds, rising to her feet, 'and a special tea will make all the difference – you mark my words.'

On the Feast of All the Faithful Departed I rise as usual while the Choir nuns are still asleep, and open the baize door into the high school. It's the bleak blue hour before dawn, so I switch on the florries in the school gym and tie on my apron. Mother Wilfred thinks to punish me with housework but to me drudgery is a joy, and my love for the convent building stretches up to its attics and down into its bowels. My early-morning sleepiness vanished, I polish the windows, sweep the floor and rub the shiny brown suede of the vaulting-horse. Its racy energetic smell takes me back to PE lessons at school, so I hitch my habit above my knees and jump on to the spring-board, wondering if I could manage a thief vault.

'Still unladylike and immodest, Sister Maureen?' My Superior glares at me from the doorway. As a girl I was caught with a condom in class and kicked out of school; and Mother Wilfred, who has a mind like a deep-freeze, will never forget.

As she strides towards me with her rosary clacking I pull down my skirt and try not to think of the condom, borne between her fingers to her study desk, where it lay between us like a rubber teat. Then I drop my gaze to her lace-ups, shiny and hard as a man's, and now parked in front of my scuffed ones.

'The Archdeacon is coming today,' she says, looking so grey with worry that I long to tell her about the coffee layer cake and fish-paste sandwiches. But she'd ring him at once and make me give it all back.

'He'll be wanting to see the school.' She runs a finger

along the top of the horse then inspects it for grime. It's spotless, and for a second I think she's going to admit it. But no, her praise might make me vain. She turns to stare at yesterday's scuff marks and the wafers of trodden gum. 'You must scrub this gym floor till it's immaculate.'

By immaculate she means cleaner than the Archdeacon's rectory floor which should be scrubbed by my mam more often than it is. But Mam says floor-scrubbing's a waste of time, because no man ever notices what he steps on. While a bubble floats from my bucket and bursts on Mother Wilfred's toe cap, I kneel down, dip my brush in the suds and get to work, willing the bell to ring for Matins. When its twelve strokes toll at last she squeaks off to chapel, leaving me to get up from my knees and keep watch through the window.

Within two minutes she's crossing the courtyard with her Choir nuns in her wake: Ursula, Bosco, Kevin, Brigid and Elisabeth, all mincing along with the snooty expressions of women absolved from housework, and each one knowing they're the cream of St Cuthbert's, founded, as it says in our Holy Rule, to give the daughters of the bourgeoisie a higher goal than domesticity. This explains why the Divine Office always clashes with the busiest times of the household day.

The chapel door shuts behind them and Wilfie's cracked contralto floats across the courtyard.

Crushed bones shall rejoice before the Lord.

Which means nearly half an hour for my forbidden baking. With my duster tucked in my belt I slam the springboard against the wall and tug at the curled-up matting. Its handle parts from the lumpy old horsehair which flops on the floor like a failed Swiss roll, but for once I don't stop and mend it. If Mam knows the Archdeacon as well as she thinks, we'll soon get the money for another mat.

The Visitation

Mother Wilfred enters the parlour with her face set, followed by the Archdeacon who brightens a bit when he sees me spreading the cloth. The Visitation's ended half an hour early, a sure sign it's gone badly.

The Archdeacon lumbers up to me and grips my hand. 'Now then, my dear – what chance Everton wins the cup?'

I stare down at his blotchy old paw in its bracelet of gristle, not wanting to admit in front of Wilfie that I follow the sports news. 'I don't know, Father.'

'Then let me tell you the Blues are in for a pasting.'

It's a view I'd like to contest, but Wilfie's pointing crossly at the half-laid table. I carry on arranging the cutlery while the Archdeacon rotates towards the hearth, sees that it's empty, then lowers his bulk into the only armchair. 'Winter's early this year.'

Mother Wilfred pulls out a wooden stool. 'We don't feel the need for a fire.'

I wish that she'd tell him the truth, that we have no

money for fuel. Like many men who love power the Archdeacon also loves to be generous, and would soon send us some sacks of coal.

He pulls out a large white handkerchief and blows his nose energetically. 'You nuns have such wonderful circulation.'

'Of course if you're feeling the cold I could ask Sister Maureen . . .'

'Please don't light a fire on my account.'

His tone's so snappish that I excuse myself at once and hurry to the larder where I slice the white loaf so thin you could read a newspaper through it. Then I pile on the Gentleman's Relish, brew a pot of Darjeeling and load the tray. Crossing the hall I can hear the two voices, the cold and the gruff, batting back and forwards like a ping-pong match: ancient rivals who'd die rather than give in. Not wanting to pick the wrong moment, I pause outside the parlour door, resting the tray on my hip.

'I've been watching your nuns teach all day,' the Archdeacon is saying testily, 'and intellectually they're below par.'

If Mam was in there she'd jolly him along, and make him see that he's being silly; but, never one to pass up a challenge, Mother Wilfred steps straight into the ring. 'We've been educating the girls of Liverpool since our foundation – and very well educated they are too.'

'Maybe,' comes the Archdeacon's growl, 'but you're running at a loss. It's time you learnt to be business-like.'

'I hardly think that nuns—' says Mother Wilfred.

The Archdeacon cuts across her. 'Your only chance is to go comprehensive – and then you'll get State aid. I can match what they give you for each pupil.'

'That would mean going co-ed.'

'Exactly so,' says the Archdeacon. 'And boys' minds need stretching. It's high time you got some graduate nuns.'

His voice has an angry ring. I raise my right hand and knock.

Mother Wilfred opens the door and beckons me inside. I long to break the icy silence with a joke, but am put off by the way she's glaring at the pile of triangular sandwiches with their crusts extravagantly cut off.

'That looks a very fine spread.' The Archdeacon's eye roves greedily over the tray. 'The best ever, if I may say so.'

My eye's drawn through the window to the street at the Archdeacon's back, where a wild-haired figure is wielding a can of Heineken like a monstrance. As I watch, it swivels round and starts waving the can at the convent.

'Help yourself, Father,' says Mother Wilfred, rising to pour his tea.

The Archdeacon's mottled hand impounds a sandwich while I place the coffee layer cake in the centre of the table, watched by the figure now peering at us through the rhododendrons. Then, as the Archdeacon raises his cup to his lips, it lobs the can of Heineken at the window.

'What's that?' he cries, splashing his lapel.

'There is no need to be alarmed,' says Mother Wilfred with a touch of scorn. 'It's a regular occurrence these days.'

The Archdeacon puts down his cup and revolves across the room.

'Fuck the Pope,' caws a voice as the Archdeacon stares anxiously at his top-of-the-range Vauxhall Cavalier.

'Who is it?' he cries.

Clutching its coat around it, the figure aims a kick at the car door then bobs off down the street.

'Some down-and-out,' replies Mother Wilfred who knows as well as me that it's Heather March, a frequent visitor to our back doorstep. 'Drink your tea, Father, before it grows cold.'

'You nuns should get out of Toxteth.' The Archdeacon picks up his teacup again. 'It's growing dangerous.'

'St Cuthbert's has always been here,' says Mother Wilfred. 'If the Good Lord wants us in Toxteth we have nothing to fear from a few hooligans.'

'Me mam says there's trouble brewing with the police,' I say to them both. 'Only the other night —'

'And who should know better than your mam?' says Mother Wilfred coldly. 'And now, Sister Maureen, if you'll kindly leave us alone...' She rises to her feet and, under the guise of handing me an empty plate, moves my coffee layer cake just out of the Archdeacon's reach.

He casts a concupiscent glance at the chocolate filling which is oozing on to the doily. 'You'll soon be as good a cook as your mother, Sister Maureen.' He turns from Mother Wilfred to give me a wink, then lunges across the table at the fattest slice. 'She'll be glad to hear about this very excellent tea.'

The Annunciation

For a long time the afternoon quiet is disturbed only by the thump of Sister Pious's zimmer from the infirmary overhead, and the shifting of coke in the Aga. And then I hear the parlour door open, and the Archdeacon's voice in the hall. 'Great changes afoot!' he chuckles as Mother Wilfred draws back the bolts. 'Very great changes.'

I'm expecting her to question me straightaway but she strides off to the grotto instead, leaving me to wash up in peace. I'm beginning to think that the last two days were a dream, and our life in St Cuthbert's will carry on as always, when I empty the teapot down the sink.

And there it is against the porcelain: a pattern of big black leaves, clear as an ABC.

At first I try not to look. Ever since the rainy afternoon when she caught me scrying for Sister Gonzaga, Mother Wilfred has made us buy tea-bags, dusty and over-priced.

'Fortune-telling is a sin,' she scolded me. 'The future is

God's business, not ours. And what's more' – she looked at me with disdain – 'it is a tinker's habit.'

But the leaves of the Archdeacon's Darjeeling are long, dark and perfect for reading; a rich people's tea, though the rich don't know how to scry. I try to stave off temptation by reaching for the tap – but how to ignore the future when it's written by Fate at the bottom of my sink?

After checking the corridor's empty I take a deep breath and steady myself against the draining board. Then the rest of the kitchen fades away while my eyes are drawn down, down to the tea-leaves which are larger than life and blacker than crow feathers against the white of the sink. But before I can make out their shapes the sound of the school bell slices the air. On the far side of the wall schoolgirls are shrieking at the bus stop, and the pattern jumbles and turns to mud, leaving me peering down the plug-hole. Not knowing if the omens were good or bad, I swoosh the tea-leaves down the sink and put away the Spode. It's the end of afternoon school and time to start cleaning the classrooms.

I breathe in the smell as I hurry down the corridor: Germolene and chalk dust from the Choir nuns, carbolic soap and sweat from the lay sisters; cabbage from the kitchen, incense from the chapel; an airborne casserole of all we are. Sister Elisabeth's classroom smells of sulky teenagers and half-eaten packets of crisps. The radiator's cold ribs are jammed with litter by Elisabeth's chilly and resentful pupils. I wish that she'd remove it – but she sits on the dais all day beneath her chosen picture of Jesus preaching in the courtyard of His friend Lazarus. Jesus clearly prefers Mary who sits idle while Martha does all the housework.

It's while sweeping the parquet that I feel the first subtle shift in energy – and then comes the clump of boots down the empty corridor. Wilfie says there's no such thing as ghosts, and to see them is the sign of a lower-class background. Gripping my broom in one hand and the dustpan in the other, I struggle for the second time today to fight down my superstitious nature; but a few seconds later the door creaks open and shut, and I see from the corner of my eye a shimmer in the air above the step and a smudge of lay sister's serge. Then the air grows warm with the smell of sweat, starch and carbolic soap – a sure sign of the Holy Army.

As they gather round to watch me sweep, I can sense rather than see their serviceable serge habits and the heavy boots on their feet. Lay sisters like myself, they spent their lives polishing the prie-dieux at which the Choir nuns prayed and the toilets on which they sat. Now they're all dead, but instead of staying in Heaven with their hands folded they haunt the corridors they used to clean while the Choir nuns are at prayer.

At the head of the Holy Army is Sister Carthage who cooked school dinners when I was a pupil and was summoned to class when any girl threw up or wet her knickers. In life she was often heard to grumble about the lay sisters' lot, and in death she has kept her fists like hams and beetroot face which is now, I sense, staring at some pieces of loose parquet, which jiggle beneath my broom like wonky teeth. At the weekend, I promise her, I'll take them out to number, polish, glue and replace.

I'm halted by a polite cough, and look up to see a neat figure: Sister Elisabeth, smooth and posh, who went to finishing school as a girl and, as she often reminds us, has studied Fine Art in Rome. Though she entered the order before I did, her eyebrows always look as though they've just been plucked. At the sight of her debutante's smile even Carthage seems abashed, bobs humbly and disappears with the other lay sisters, their clay feet clumping towards the kitchen.

'What were you muttering about?' asks Elisabeth.

I start stumbling out a reply and then check myself. Elisabeth comes from a grand house in Cressington Park where people wear dressing-gowns, have life insurance and watch BBC2. It doesn't matter what she thinks.

'Mother Wilfred wants to see you when you've finished cleaning my classroom.'

'What for?'

'Have a guess.'

I remember Wilfie's glare when I carried in the tray, and my heart fills with cold water. Knocked off, half-inched, robbed, dropped off the back of a lorry – all the dirty old words from the Dingle sidle back into my head. I can tell from Elisabeth's smug smile that she knows, but instead of pumping her with the questions she longs to knock back, I kill the ball and keep on brushing.

She looks disappointed then carries on anyway. 'It's something to do with the Archdeacon.'

'What are you lounging round here for?' I snap.

'I'm waiting because I was told to wait,' she says with a little yawn. 'Wilfie wants us both together.' She picks up a wet cloth between thumb and forefinger and begins swabbing at the mahogany window-sill. Her hands are small and useless with concave nails. At night after lights out I hear her nail file rasping like a cat's tongue.

'Don't!' I snatch back the cloth. 'That should be done with a duster.'

She nods towards the bedraggled garden where the Superior is pacing up from the grotto, her rosary beads swinging. 'You should be getting ready for Wilfie,' she says with a shrug, 'not worrying about dusters.'

Giving us an angry stare the Superior carries on to the back door while I wonder why Elisabeth's involved.

My thoughts are broken by a yapping noise which sounds like lapdogs, and then I see them high above Wilfie's head. As a child I used to watch for them with my dad: Barnacle geese flying in from the high Arctic to winter by the Mersey. Necks outstretched and wings flapping, they beat across the first pale stars of evening, gabbling companionably. Still worried about deceiving Wilfie, I ache at the sight of their brave and ragged chevron.

Elisabeth is staring into the garden. 'Gardeners are supposed to like order,' she complains, ignoring the geese. 'You should have pruned those roses.'

As the birds disappear into a sky the colour of raw turnip I return the broom to its closet, remove my apron, straighten my veil and head for Wilfie's office.

'Wait for me,' calls Elisabeth who has a Choir nun's gait, slow and dignified.

Together we pass the rows of empty classrooms, push through the green baize door and turn down the cloister.

Elisabeth taps on Mother Wilfred's study door and then, without waiting for a reply, enters the room and plops to her knees in front of the big oak desk.

Knowing better than to enter without permission, I hover in the doorway.

'Come in, come in,' barks the Superior.

I kneel down beside Elisabeth, my heart pulsing like a goose's wing.

'I've prayed for an hour about this,' Mother Wilfred pauses to stare at us both over her half-moons, 'and can only hope that I've come to the right decision.'

Perhaps Wilfie's phoned the Archdeacon and got my mam sacked. Cleaners have no patron saint of their own, so I beg the Holy Army to protect her.

'You may look up, Sister Maureen,' says Mother Wilfred. Normally so composed, she sounds tired and almost hesitant. 'As you know,' she continues, 'the high school is not doing well – will you stop fidgeting, please – and the Archdeacon is forcing us to join the comprehensive system. That will mean admitting boys – and he seems to think we aren't qualified.'

Boys in the school with their cricket and football – games that no other nun knows about! For a wild and joyful moment I think Wilfie's asking me to be their coach.

'But the Archdeacon sat in on our classes today,' Elisabeth pipes up. 'He must know how well we teach.'

I note that the wood of Mother Wilfred's desk is starved and needs polishing. 'Paper qualifications seem more important these days,' she says to the crown of thorns she keeps by her blotter. 'And besides,' she carries on, 'the Archdeacon wants you to apply to the university.'

I'm startled by the voice of Elisabeth, pitched high with indignation. 'You mean Maureen as well as me? But that's not possible!'

As usual with Choir nuns, they're acting as though I'm not present.

'That is the Archdeacon's wish.' Mother Wilfred's eyes are pale as a starling's eggs. 'He has made it a condition of his support.'

'But Sister Maureen is too superstitious – and she comes

from the Dingle – she'll make us a laughing stock.'

'Her A level grades are nearly as high as yours, Sister Elisabeth. And as St Cuthbert's is almost bankrupt I have no choice.'

'Do you mean,' I gasp, 'that I'll have to get a degree?' I think of my sister Lorraine who went to college with her head high and came back a year later, defeated. Then I wonder why the Archdeacon, who's always been kind, has decided to torture me in this way. 'Elisabeth's right,' I blurt out. 'I can't do it. The O'Shaunessys hate study.'

Mother Wilfred smiles as though she knows what I do when the Choir nuns are in school: drink tea with the down-and-outs at the back door and listen to the sports news with the transistor hidden under a tea towel. 'O'Shaunessy or not,' she replies, 'you must get a degree for the good of the order.'

'But the housework,' I say desperately. 'Who'll take it over?'

'I could go to university on my own,' puts in Elisabeth, 'or else Sister Brigid could come with me instead of Maureen. She's always wanted to go to —'

'That is not possible – and you know why not as well as I do.'

Elisabeth gives me a sidelong glance, then says to Mother Wilfred with a little shrug, 'Well – at least I shall have the chance to look at some paintings.'

'And who told you what to study?'

'I thought art – because that's what I teach —'

'The Archdeacon wants you to enrol for an English degree.'

'But it's Sister Brigid who teaches English – and I teach Art. I've studied in Rome —'

Favourite as she is, Elisabeth's dangerously close to being offside and Mother Wilfred looks ready to show her the yellow card. 'You are going to university for the greater glory of God and not,' the Superior pauses emphatically, 'for love of your subject.' She makes it sound like one of the seven deadly sins.

Wrong-footed for once, Elisabeth can only stare back in silence.

I think of my coffee layer cake, pulled out of the Aga this morning with so much hope. 'So what shall I study?' I ask, my throat tightening.

Mother Wilfred shoots a glance at Elisabeth whose eyes are swimming like a hurt kitten's. 'The Archdeacon wants you, Sister Maureen, to study art history.'

I've always believed that if I hit the right stations in life God would show me the way forward and, like a tough but loving coach, pick me up if I fell short. Now I am not so sure.

Turning her head, Elisabeth looks at me as though for the first time. Then, at a sign from the Superior, she takes two application forms from the desk and hands one to me.

Too shattered to ask any more questions, I slip it inside my pocket.

'Be it done unto us according to Thy word,' say Elisabeth and I in chorus as we rise to our feet.

G-O-N-Z-*Aga*

Sister Gonzaga, the convent cook, sits at the table and sighs. I glance at her doughy old face, thumbed by sixty years' hard work, and wonder if she's troubled by the cauliflower rotting on the dresser. Her sense of smell went years ago, so it's unlikely. But she's possessive about her kitchen with its mouse droppings, sour milk and blocked drains, so while she's around it's best not to interfere. When she takes her afternoon nap I'll pitch the mouldering vegetable on to the compost heap.

With hands like tubers she fumbles through the plazzy bags and elastic bands she hoards in her kitchen drawer while I strip a cabbage of its outer leaves. Behind her is the Aga, stencilled as a joke by a long-ago novice with the first four letters of her name. G-O-N-Z-*Aga*. She it was who first welcomed me to St Cuthbert's, making me cups of cocoa when I pined for the Dingle and warming my chill spirits like the ancient stove at our backs. It's seemed part of her personality ever since.

By the time she finds her knife I've shredded the first vegetable and started the second. Chop, slice, hack, chop, slice, hack. Despite the blunt blade my board is already stacked high. Then the old cook sighs again so I slacken my pace, not wanting to hurt her feelings. But the knife speeds up against my will.

'You're martyring that poor cabbage,' she tells me. 'What on earth's the matter?'

'Nothing.'

'Just tell me the truth,' she says, firm in her belief she can solve my problem even if she might not choose to.

'I'm unhappy.' Chop, slice, hack – my words keep time with the knife. 'Unhappy and angry at being uprooted.'

'Uprooted from what?' she says in mock amazement.

I poke my knife at the kitchen cupboards. 'The cooking and cleaning. I want to stay here.'

A lay sister and mystic, Gonzaga's often reluctant to knock her opinions into shape. 'No woman should love housework to excess,' she pronounces at last. 'Especially not a nun.'

'Because of Holy Detachment?' I name Mother Wilfred's favourite virtue.

'Because we should learn to put our feet up.' Gonzaga contemplates the slimy cauliflower with satisfaction. 'Once, dearie, I used to glory in hard work, but now I'm near death I have bigger things on my mind.'

If that's her attitude, I think, I shall spend the afternoon scouring her kitchen. Then I remember the Holy Army haunting St Cuthbert's when they could be sitting on a cloud with their hands folded, and decide to spend my free time filling in that application form.

Before I can share this resolution with Gonzaga, Sister Brigid appears on the threshold. Known as the convent bookwork, she's a rare sight at this end of the house.

'Have a cup of tea.' I wave at the simmering kettle. Brigid and I grew up in neighbouring streets, and our mothers were always in and out of each other's kitchens.

Brigid steps back as though I have muddy paws. You'd never guess that she, like me, was born not just in the Dingle but in the Holy Land at its heart. Ever the obedient nun, she never refers to David Street, Isaac Street, Jacob Street or Moses Street – the four lovely streets sloping down to the river. We are the Brides of Christ, says our Holy Rule, and united in His love. Talk of our backgrounds can only divide us.

'Come for a cookery lesson?' asks Gonzaga sardonically. 'Maureen can show you how to chop cabbage.'

Brigid hesitates for a second then picks her way across the tiles. She is, as Gonzaga often says, a typical Choir nun, turning incompetence into a sacrament. 'Why ever should I learn how to cook?'

At eighty-one Gonzaga still has the smile of a cheeky teenager. 'Because you'll have to help out when Maureen's at her studies.'

Brigid stares down her nose at the old cook. 'What on earth do you mean?'

'Haven't you heard?' chirps Gonzaga. 'She's applying to the uni.'

'Sister Maureen?' Brigid says incredulously, then turns towards me. 'Can this be true?'

Looking into the sallow face with its eyes the colour of greaseproof paper, I'm tempted to answer back. And then I remember her hopes of university as a girl, abandoned to enter the convent. 'Um – yes,' I confess, as though I've committed a crime.

'Why did nobody tell me?' croaks Brigid, clutching the edge of the table.

Gonzaga prods at a chunk of cabbage. 'Because they knew what you'd say.'

'But why choose you, Maureen?' Brigid blunders on. 'Why not send one of the teaching nuns?'

'It was the Archdeacon's idea.'

'He should have chosen Elisabeth or – or me.'

'He *did* choose Elisabeth,' Gonzaga chips in, 'so you'll have to make up for the both of them.'

'They're sending that – that tell-tale to get a degree,' Brigid's face turns yellower than ever, 'while I'm stuck here in St Cuthbert's?'

'Why do you call her a tell-tale?' I ask.

Gonzaga shoots Brigid a warning glance.

Brigid shuts her mouth then opens it again. 'It's not fair,' she gasps. 'I'm cleverer than you, Maureen – and far cleverer than Elisabeth.'

'That's enough boasting,' snaps Gonzaga. 'Just give us your message, then go.'

'Your parents are waiting in the parlour,' she says to me sulkily.

'What do they want?' I ask, afraid it's bad news. They're only allowed to see me on the first Sunday afternoon of every month – a rule they don't like but usually daren't ignore.

'I didn't ask.' Brigid ties on an apron. Now she'll have to finish the chopping.

I shrug and turn to go. Brigid's never had time for my mam and dad. Far too resigned to their lot, she used to say. Now it's her turn to resign herself, I think, with a tweak of spite. Pushing her pained expression from my mind I hurry towards the parlour.

My parents are sitting one on either side of the empty fireplace with their heads turned towards the door, two little people in big chairs.

'So the Archdeacon liked his tea,' says Mam, looking pleased with herself. 'He phoned me last night with your news.'

Sometimes I wonder who's in charge of my life: God, my mam, Mother Wilfred or the Archdeacon. They all like to play their part.

My dad gets up to kiss my cheek. He's the same height as Mam and six inches smaller than me. His snub nose and freckles, both of which I've inherited, give his face a cheerful look at odds with his personality. As always when visiting St Cuthbert's he's wearing his shiny blue suit as a mark of respect for the nuns – a waste, in my view, as they never come near him. Under it is one of the shirts bought by my mam, drip-dry because she's too busy ironing for the Archdeacon.

'And how's my girl?' asks Dad. Though he tried to stop me from entering the convent, he's prouder of me now than anyone and boasts about me to all his mates. It was my Clothing that did it – me dressed up as a bride and the choir singing *Vene Sancto Spiritu*. Like most men from the Dingle he's a sucker for a white wedding.

'Your dad nearly collapsed when he heard you're applying to the uni,' says Mam.

'I probably won't get in.'

'Just as well, if you ask me,' says Dad. 'Them students know nothing about the city – just settle here like a plague of bloody locusts and stop the rest of us getting to the bar at last orders.'

'Don't let him put you off,' says Mam.

'I'm afraid she'll end up like our Lorraine.'

'Don't be daft, George.'

'I'm not daft,' says my dad. 'I've seen one of me girls crack up – and I don't want it happening again.'

'Lorraine's a worrier.' My mam gives a glance at Dad's pleated brow. 'But Mo's like me – she takes life in her stride.'

'I used to take life in me stride,' says Dad, 'but now I know better.' Once Dad was a bold young squaddie who'd lied about his age to get enlisted. After being invalided out of the war, he took a job as an ambulance driver. He'd expected danger in the trenches, but had never seen the carnage of everyday life. Fingers severed by deck chairs, steak stuck in the oesophagus, throats sealed with wasp bites: he lost three people in his first month, and it knocked the optimism out of him.

'How's our Lol?' I ask, hoping to distract him.

'She spends most of her time moping,' says Mam. 'Us O'Shaunessys don't take to being rejected.'

'She could get a job tomorrow if she put her mind to it,' says Dad who thinks Lorraine's been spoilt by her taste of university.

'Get her to come and see me,' I say. 'I'm beginning to feel out of touch.'

Dad looks doubtful. 'She still feels bitter. First her best friend Brigid a nun, and then her kid sister.'

'Are they going to make you a Choir nun, our Mo?' As usual, Mam tries to make Dad look on the bright side.

I picture myself with snobby high-school pupils and my heart sinks lower than ever. 'I hope not,' I tell her, 'because I don't want to teach.'

'What has want got to do with it?'

'Sometimes I think you'd have made a far better nun than me.'

Mam looks smug. 'What course are you doing?'

'Art History – and I've told you already: I probably won't get in.'

'Of course you will if you put your mind to it. The Archdeacon says that they want local students.'

As always when Mam starts quoting the Archdeacon Dad shrinks in his chair and looks liverish. Ever since she got her job at the rectory he's felt overshadowed by the pushy, vigorous cleric. 'Just a bit too full of himself,' he grumbles to his small, meek-looking friends from the Sacred Heart Men's club, 'telling us married fellers when to put a knot in it.'

'We'd best be going, Mo,' he says now, straightening his tie. 'We've only got permission for a short visit.'

I kiss him on his bald patch and give Mam a hug. 'Don't you go worrying about me. You know I always come out on top.'

After closing the front door my first thought is to stop Gonzaga, who has trouble with her dentures, from boiling the cabbage to a pulp. But the kitchen corridor is blocked by Brigid's stiff figure. I stand against the wall to let her pass but to my surprise she beckons me into the butler's pantry – a little room whose name has stuck from the old days when the house was owned by a Liverpool merchant. Her expression's so intent that for a moment I'm reminded of the schoolgirl I used to adore.

'So you'll soon be filling in your application form,' she says, fixing me with her greaseproof eyes.

'Worse luck,' I reply with a grimace. 'I'll see it as a penance.'

'A penance?' Her nose turns sharp enough to peck with. 'When other people long for the chance?'

'I'll make a mess of my interview on purpose,' I say to her sallow face. 'It'll be easy because I know nothing. Then Wilfie will send you instead.'

For a second she looks too shocked to reply.

'I know it's disobedient,' I race on, 'but you love study and I'd rather stay here.'

'Mother Wilfred would never send me,' she says, her face pinched with thwarted ambition.

'Why not?' I ask nosily.

'I'm not allowed to tell you.'

'What on earth do you mean?'

Now that she's conquered her temper Brigid's a model nun, and would do us credit at the university. But her face has gone so gloomy and awkward that I bite back my next question. And then, before I can say anything friendly, she turns her back, tugs open the door and bolts away down the corridor.

The Bosco Song

Brigid and I go back a long way – longer than either of us cares to remember. As a girl I adored her but when she tried to deny the past and me with it my love turned to resentment. It was my first taste of human betrayal – otherwise known as putting God before your pals, as I now realise people sometimes have to. Even though I've forgiven her long since, our friendship has never recovered.

Like me and my big sister Lorraine, Brigid once won a scholarship to St Cuthbert's High School for Girls where the three of us stood shoulder to shoulder against the world of white starch and good breeding and most of all against Sister Bosco, a red-faced nun with a bluff soul who wanted to break our spirits. A frustrated missionary, she saw the Dingle as darkest Africa and us scholarship girls as the great unwashed. On fire with the zeal for souls, she hacked her way through our glottal stops and converted our vowel sounds.

'Now is your chance to r – ay – se above your backgrounds.'

Bosco tried to teach us deportment and elocution and when to use butter knives and fish slices, and, most of all, how to despise housework – lessons which Brigid, I sometimes think, learned all too well.

But in those days Bid was a rebel, refusing point-blank to sit up straight and lose her scouse accent. I loved my big sister Lorraine but I loved Biddy even more for her way with words and for not bossing me about and most of all for the unladylike rhymes of her Bosco song:

> *She tries to make us middle class*
> *She's got a poker up her arse . . .*

Even the women of Isaac Street looked shocked. Three convent girls marching abreast, singing rude songs about the nuns. None of us cared. Still stinging from our daily round of humiliations we'd mimic Bosco's stiff walk and genteel accent. 'Dingle Girls Rule OK!' I'd shout through a burst of healing laughter. Hadn't Lol chalked it on the back of the bike shed?

We got used to the nuns. Bosco remained a tyrant but the others were bearable in their place, like the Way of the Cross or fish on Fridays. A restless, leggy Second Former, I excelled at sport and domestic science, two subjects which luckily the nuns despised and left to the lay staff. Brigid and Lorraine, bent on escape from the Dingle, entered the Upper Sixth and began to work hard.

Then, one misty day in November, Brigid announced her vocation. Lorraine ran indoors sobbing and swearing while I hung around on the pavement, sick to my stomach. Our Number One Dingle girl was a traitor. Soon she'd be one of them with a stiff back and mincing ways. And just when she'd promised to go to university with our Lorraine.

'I can't do it, Mo. I have a vocation,' she told me the next day, her small hand inching into the pocket where she kept her rosary beads. 'It's ineluctable.'

I was unfazed by the long word because in those days she often had me running to the dictionary. 'But you were so keen to get a degree – keener than our Lol. She'll never manage without you.'

'Lorraine will soon find a new friend down south,' said Brigid. The rosary beads clicked like ill-fitting false teeth.

'A new friend down south?' Only that morning Lol had threatened not to go. 'You must be joking.'

On her last night in the world Brigid gave me her little wooden rosary.

It had belonged, she told me, to the Irish nan she'd never met. Remembering Lorraine's tear-stained face, I flung it to the back of my wardrobe the moment Brigid was out the room.

Brigid was sent to the Mother House in France while Lorraine went to university on her own, grew homesick and failed her first-year exams. The trouble with Brigid started two years later, when she came back to St Cuthbert's to teach.

My English teacher had been kind old Sister Kevin who always gave me high marks. But instead of being impressed by my Holy Land ghosts and dockside tragedies, Brigid stared in dismay at my blotted exercise book. 'This is baby work,' she said. 'It's time to study some real writers.'

Her slouch a thing of the past, she stood at the board and drilled us in Shakespearean tragedy. Try as I might, I couldn't concentrate. Thanks to perfect girl-to-girl marking within the twenty-five-yard line our hockey team was heading for victory. I wished it had been soccer but Mother Wilfred said that football for girls was an abomination before the Lord and would never be played at St Cuthbert's.

By the end of Brigid's first week there were bags beneath her eyes. Sorry for her despite myself, I disobeyed Lorraine and spoke to her after school. 'Are you coming to the match, Sister?' It was an effort to use her new title. I secretly hoped she'd admire our lovely black and gold strip as we buzzed like hornets round the goal posts. Wasn't she, like me, from the Dingle where everyone was sports mad?

She laid her red pen on top of the desk. 'It's time you forgot about games,' she said, her face longer than the Mater Dolorosa's on the wall above her head. 'You could be top of the form if only you'd try.'

Try to be top of the form? When I was both coach and captain of the First XI and had scored more goals than anyone else that season? The Archdeacon himself had heard of our success and was coming to watch the final against Denver Street C. of E. He'd once played rugby for Orrell and longed, so he'd said to my mam, for a Catholic team to win the cup.

At ten o'clock the next morning the whole school turned out to cheer us on. In the front row sat the muscle-bound Archdeacon in his astrakhan coat, following the game intently, his head flung back as though in ecstasy. He was flanked by the St Cuthbert's nuns, uncannily composed among the yelling crowd. Mother Wilfred, Sister Bosco, Sister Ursula, Sister Kevin, Sister Julian – hating success and sport in equal measure but obliged by the Archdeacon to shiver in the March wind. His face turned red as a turkey-cock's when I scored the winning goal but for me the victory was incomplete. As I held the cup in the air my eyes searched the stand for Brigid, hoping she'd appear at the last minute. But no, she told me in the Monday lesson, she'd had more important things on her mind.

I was hurt, and too much of a baby not to show it. Refusing to join in the class reading of *Hamlet*, I spent the lesson drawing up plans for our next practice: dodging, dribbling, open stick tackles. I was only halfway through when Sister Rigid, as I'd started to think of her, strode down the aisle and snatched up my notebook.

'Knocking a greasy ball round a field!' she sneered. 'You should stop wasting your time.'

Her constipated face said it all: for her, wasting time meant anything physical. Hardening myself against her, I folded my arms and stared out of the window. She was a very young nun and could, I sensed, be made to lose her rag.

'Look at me.' She put her face so close to mine I could see the zits on her forehead from the bad convent diet. 'It's time you remembered your manners.'

Still staring out the window, I hummed the tune of the Bosco song.

> *She tries to make us middle class,*
> *She's got a poker up her arse.*

I knew from Brigid's reddening face that she remembered the words, and the air around us wavered and seethed as she struggled to fight down her temper.

Hoist on your own petard, I thought.

But the novitiate had taught her self-control. Instead of hitting me as I'd hoped she blundered back to her desk and groped for her book. 'Insolent girl,' she said, the colour fading from her cheeks. 'I wash my hands of you.' It was a victory for her, of a sort, and she drove it home by ignoring me for the rest of the lesson.

From then on I needled her every day – chipping away at her self-esteem, trying to make her falter. The rest of the form followed suit and her discipline, shaky to start with, grew steadily worse. Then one day I nicked a condom from Lorraine's handbag and took it into English. In my view boys were made by God to be beaten at football and the condom was not for me but Selena Hastings, the class swot, who was already sleeping with her boyfriend. I could have given it to her at break – but it was more fun passing it from hand to hand under our desks.

'Bring that here,' ordered Sister Rigid as everyone called her by then.

When we took no notice she darted across the room and tried to prise it from my grasp. Having already passed it to Linda Renucci I spread my hands in a gesture of inno-cence. With that, Sister Rigid's temper snapped at last and she slapped me across the cheek.

I've won, I thought, staring into her shocked yellow face. But it proved to be an own goal. 'You're an impure girl and a typical O'Shaunessy,' said Mother Wilfred when she heard what had happened. I could have told her the con-dom was for Selena but the O'Shaunessys have never grassed anyone up and never will. My reward was getting kicked out of school.

The worst part was telling my mam. 'How could you?' she gasped, her face white. Sick with regret I thought of her struggle to buy me the right blazer, summer dresses (two), boater, gabardine, velour hat, tunic, tie, blouses (5), gym shorts (2 pairs), socks (winter, brown, 5 pairs; summer, white, 5 pairs; gym, white, 2 pairs, hockey, grey, 2 pairs), shoes (outdoors, lace-up; indoors, sandal), hockey boots, plimsolls (white), Aertex shirts (ditto); swimming costume (regulation), all from the most expensive shop in town. The endless textbooks and music books and raffles and geometry sets and jumble sales and school trips and hockey sticks and most of all her pride when I captained the school team.

It took me two years to get back on my feet. Spurred on by the Archdeacon, I worked in Woolies by day and studied at night, getting my A levels in ten months flat. I also took up football and played centre half for the Catholic Women's team. One day I was rooting in my wardrobe for an old pair of shorts when I came across Brigid's rosary beads and allowed myself to wonder how she was getting on. A new batch of scholarship girls had told me St Cuthbert's was going downhill. Sister Julian, the Head of English, had left under a cloud, the school was short-staffed and discipline was growing lax.

That night I said the rosary for the first time since being expelled, beginning of course with the Joyful Mysteries. First comes the Annunciation and I pictured the Angel Gabriel landing on Mary's roof in a flurry of pigeon feathers. It was peaceful, sitting up in my bedroom with the worn old beads in my lap. A working woman's prayer, I thought to myself, the fingers keeping busy while the mind ponders on.

First I prayed that I might put things right with Brigid, which seemed unlikely. Mam and Dad blamed her for what had happened to our Lol – and besides, she was locked away in St Cuthbert's where I never went. My fingers moving automatically from bead to bead, I prayed next for Lorraine, that she'd forget about her failed exams and recover her fighting spirit. I hated seeing her slumped round the house all day, reading women's magazines and wrecking her health with cigarettes. Finally I prayed for the women's football team. Our fullbacks were weak that year and half the team hadn't yet learnt to tackle.

No sooner had we won our first match than I began to fear I had a vocation. No Angel of the Annunciation for me, just a sense that something was lacking from my life – it was difficult to know what. I longed to be a professional footballer, but there was no chance of that in the women's game. My A levels were easily good enough for PE college but then all I could do was teach, and I didn't fancy spending my life coaching younger players from the sidelines. At a loss, I stayed with my job in Woolies and prayed for something to happen.

Outside work I poured my pent-up energies into boshing the opposition, and wellied the ball into the net every week – but my team-mates didn't back me up. In spite of our success, three of them got pregnant and others would cry off training just because it turned frosty. All of them, sad to say, preferred being with their husbands or boyfriends, and no one would try and outrun me for the ball or practise flying tackles till every ligament hurt and then do an hour's circuit training. By the time we'd won the regional cup I'd grown bored with outstripping other women and living with my brains in my feet. I wanted a way of life to which I could bring all of me, one where I couldn't dominate so easily. There was only one such life I could think of, and the thought of it wouldn't go away.

Unlike the Mother of Our Lord, I greeted God's news with horror. Surely He couldn't be asking me to give up sport and become a nun? I asked the Archdeacon in Confession. Like a good doctor he listened carefully to my symptoms. Yes, he said at length, I think He might. I knew why he sighed on the other side of the grille. If I entered St Cuthbert's it would be the end of Catholic Women's Football.

For the next few weeks I had a queasy time of it. By day I prayed that God would change His mind. Hadn't I everything to live for? PE college if I wanted it, then a good career and a lifetime of sport. By night the St Cuthbert's nuns gathered round my bed: Sister Bosco, Sister Brigid, Sister Kevin, Mother Wilfred, ranged against me like a jury. Keep out, they whispered through pale lips. You are not wanted here.

Then slowly I grew used to the idea. Perhaps, as the Archdeacon had suggested, God really saw me as special and wanted me in His team, never to be expelled again. I began to think I'd been wrong about Brigid. Being a nun wasn't a cop-out, I decided, stowing my football boots on the top shelf. It was the best and noblest game, lasting not just the length of the match but your whole life through. Each new day sharpened my vision of the future and brought my prayers into focus. While my former team-mates got injured, grew old and muscle-bound, I would be going from strength to strength in God's service.

One morning over a cup of tea in the kitchen I gave my news to Mam. Drawn by nature to the dangerous and difficult, she took it even better than I'd expected. 'I've always begged Our Lady for a daughter a nun,' she said with her eyes shining, 'and at last she's heard me prayer.' She paused to stir in two spoonfuls of sugar. 'But we'll have to break it gently to your dad.'

I'd hoped he'd be glad to see me escape from the Dingle with its drunkenness, dole queues and lifelong struggles with the never-never, but Mam shook her head. 'He'll be gutted, you mark my words. Look what happened when Lorraine left home.'

She refused to give him the news till Everton had just beaten Spurs and he was bound, she assured me, to be in a good mood. She proved over-optimistic. His face dark with anger, he did what every other man in the street would have done and peeled off to the Welly Vaults.

When he came back bladdered at chuck-out time, my mam pointed me towards the stairs, but I didn't budge. Dad and I had argued a lot in the past. Now was the time to concede defeat – and disarm the opposition while I did it, like all the best players.

'You were right and I was wrong,' I told him as he lurched towards me. 'Women's football has its limitations. I'm tired of coming second to a load of men.'

He listened with the sweat breaking out on his forehead while I went on to say that convent life had a lot in common with sport: its teamwork, its self-discipline, its commitment to excellence and sense of a goal.

At that he slapped me as hard as he could on the cheek and called me all the silly bitches going. Then he put his head in his hands and cried. 'Wasting your life with a gaggle of bloody nuns,' he sobbed, his eyes clouded with the Welly Vaults' bad ale, 'when you could have stayed with us and been a games teacher.' With that he staggered upstairs to the lav.

I made Mam and me a cup of tea and went to bed, knowing Dad would come round in time. After all, I would be living just across the park, and would pray for him every day. And wasn't I making it up to my mam for being expelled? For the next few weeks I soared high as a kite, and wasn't brought down even by an interview with Mother Wilfred. 'Your soul has been tarnished by your love of sport,' she told me in the cold convent parlour. 'As you are unfit to take charge of the young I have decided to make you a lay sister.'

'Spiteful old cow,' said Dad. 'No daughter of mine is spending her life as a skivvy.'

Though disappointed herself, Mam stopped him from making a fuss. It wasn't difficult. A Dingle man and a cradle Catholic, he was secretly in awe of the frosty-faced nun who'd once caned him for swearing in Sunday School.

As for me, I felt happier than ever. I'd dreaded being stuck in a classroom all day, and like any sportswoman I had studied the League Table of my new calling. It was there in the Gospel according to Matthew: *Many that are first shall be last; and the last shall be first.* What better way of becoming a saint than by scrubbing the floors of those who'd expelled me?

But soon I was struck by a contradiction. 'What if I grow too proud of being humble,' I asked the Archdeacon, 'and lose my high place in Heaven?'

At that the Archdeacon just laughed and said that if anyone could pull it off I would, so I pushed my doubts aside till my last week in the world when I began to worry about meeting my old teachers. They were so refined, so self-controlled, so very austere. Would they ever accept an O'Shaunessy, even as a lay sister? Most of all I worried about Brigid. After all, we'd parted on bad terms and I hadn't even said a proper goodbye.

I needn't have bothered.

'Welcome to St Cuthbert's,' she said with a subdued smile. Though no longer stern or hostile, she was nothing like the spirited girl I'd known in the Dingle. 'Let me show you the community room.'

Her genteel behaviour made me more ashamed than ever of the brat I'd once been, and at first I was happy to hide behind the Rule which forbids any mention of home. But I soon saw that Holy Obedience had little to do with Brigid's changed manner. Once so sure of her views, she now seldom offered an opinion; and while her fellow Choir nuns chattered in recreation she stayed silent night after night, her head bent over her sewing. Even her face, in girlhood so easy to read, had grown heavy, pale and secret.

'What's happened to her?' I asked Gonzaga. 'She never used to be like this.'

The old nun faltered for a second and then sighed. 'A Choir nun's life isn't easy,' she said. 'It takes some of them that way.'

I thought of Wilfie, Bosco, Elisabeth and Ursula – all so very strait-laced. 'But no one's as mopey as Brigid,' I persisted. 'Something else must be wrong.'

Gonzaga frowned and laid her finger on her lips, which put a stop to my questions for the time being.

But it didn't stop me from worrying about Brigid. Over the next few months I tried to get close to her again, giving her all my news from the Dingle and confiding in her whenever I could, in the hope that she'd trust me in return. It didn't work. Though she listened patiently to my stories she never let anything slip, and her face stayed yellow and closed as ever.

The Sorrowful Mysteries

There are signs of disturbance in the Holy Army – weird clatterings and bangings overhead, as though they're dropping metal buckets in Heaven. Longing to ask them about my future, as I sweep I strain for the clump of boots. But the ghosts stay away for days and then, when they do appear, they stand in a row looking stiff and vanish when I turn to face them, as though scared of giving me advice. Without their encouraging presence I no longer sing as I work, or feel I'm on top of the job. Meanwhile damp spreads along the walls and paint flakes like dandruff from the ceilings, as though the building misses its ghosts even more than I do.

One Sunday afternoon in December I pull out my rosary and head for the garden. Instead of filling in my application form as instructed by Wilfie, I've put it off for the past four weeks, not knowing what to write in the little white boxes and too proud to consult Elisabeth. I should go straight to the community room and ask her now – but after washing up in the dank old kitchen I'm longing for some fresh air. This morning I dozed off in chapel and dreamt I'd missed the closing date. 'You've brought ruin on St Cuthbert's,' shouted a shadowy Mother Wilfred, spindly and hoarse, 'you stupid, brazen child.'

Struggling to ignore the sore throat that's stayed with me all day, I tramp past the brown-robed statue kneeling before the grotto: St Bernadette Soubirous, the ignorant, sharp and unshakeable peasant who had eighteen visions in a single summer yet never got beyond elementary school. I'm scared of higher education, I say to her, scared of being rejected, and even more scared of being accepted.

The sky overhead is yellow with sulphur from the refineries upriver, and though it's only four in the afternoon, the lights are coming on in the tower block at the back of our garden wall. It went up five years ago and the Choir nuns call it an eyesore. An invasion of privacy, they say, lips pursed, and an insult to our Holy Rule. But I'm cheered by the lighted squares, and the sight of the busy women running from room to room.

From Sefton Park comes the sound of the Sunday League, where Dad and his mates will be watching Dingle Rail play a team from the North end. I'm straining to hear the chants of the supporters when Elisabeth appears at my elbow. The Choir nuns are taking more notice of me these days – as though I'm almost one of them.

'Have you finished that form yet?' she asks and then, when I say nothing, she adds, 'The closing date is Tuesday.'

I should be grateful for the warning, but can't help wishing that the Archdeacon had chosen Brigid and me instead. Though prim, Brigid does at least come from the Dingle and would understand how I feel. Or better still if Wilfie had sent Brigid and Elisabeth: both of them Choir nuns, and keen to get on.

And then I remember the words of Our Blessed Lady. Be it done unto me according to Thy word. I turn to the convent at once, leaving Elisabeth to follow in my wake.

'Why the bad mood?' she twitters. 'It's a chance in a million.'

It's all very well for you, I think, retracing my footprints across the frosty grass, with your doctor father and brother Timmy already an art historian.

'Art history is easy,' she persists on reaching the community room door. 'You just have to look at pictures. I'll have to read lots of books.'

Desperate to shake her off, I barge down the aisle between the old oak desks with their white china inkwells and brass hinges. On reaching the back row I slam down the seat of my desk, raise the lid and start rooting for my form.

'Don't you want to be a student?' asks Elisabeth, sitting down beside me.

'I've got A levels but no O levels,' I remind her. Although I try to sound downcast, it's been a secret source of hope for weeks. 'They can't possibly accept me.'

Elisabeth leans back in her chair. 'Of course they will,' she says expansively. 'You're twenty-six years old – a mature student.' She gives me a glance from the corner of her eye, as though to add, mature in theory.

'I know nothing about art history.'

Elisabeth sounds unconcerned. 'That department is desperate for good students. Timmy says so.'

'What do you mean, good?'

'Hardworking,' returns Elisabeth promptly. 'They know

nuns are extra conscientious and they'll snap us up, you'll see – that is, if we catch the post.'

I stare down at the form with its list of baffling questions. 'What can I put for hobbies?' I ask, able to remember nothing apart from football, gym, tennis and hockey.

'I put fossil-collecting and flute-playing,' says Elisabeth. 'Now please stop fussing about details. What matters is the interview.'

Which I shan't be attending, I decide, scrawling '*Haven't got any*,' across the place for O levels.

'No, Maureen, not in biro,' exclaims Elisabeth. 'This is meant to look neat.'

I drop the biro back in my desk and unscrew the top of my fountain-pen which leaks watery ink over my fingers.

'Don't look so gloomy,' says Elisabeth as she seals the envelope half an hour later. 'I myself shall coach you for the interview.'

For the next few days she's as good as her word: so good that she never leaves me alone. 'Stop day-dreaming,' she chirps, popping up where least wanted, while I'm listening out for the Holy Army or trying to switch on the sports news – or, on one occasion, washing the kitchen floor. 'You must learn to use your eyes,' she trills at me.

I reach for my mop and blot out her muddy footprints while she hoists herself on to the kitchen table. 'Just look at the red of those tiles,' she warbles, gazing at the floor as though she wants to kiss it. 'Pure Ugolino di Nerio.'

'Oo-go who?' I say rudely, then remember I'm supposed to respect all Choir nuns. 'What did you say the artist's name was?'

'Ugolino,' replies Elisabeth, pointing to a picture above the dresser.

I read out the title. 'Jesus opens the eyes of a man born blind.'

'That's just a reproduction,' says Elisabeth, swinging a well-shod foot. 'There's a real Ugolino in the Walker.'

My thoughts skitter back to the only time I've been to the gloomy old art gallery: a community outing when Mother Wilfred made us all close our eyes whenever we passed a nude. I couldn't see what was so special about the place. For me winter afternoons at Everton were special as the players in their beautiful azure strip floated like shadows across the turf, and the smell of hamburgers and onions made my eyes water.

Elisabeth jumps down from the table and straddles a chair with her elbows on its back like a presenter on *Blue Peter*. 'Your mind's wandering again,' she tells me, then starts to describe another painting by that same artist while I stare at the figure of the blind man bent over his stick, full of humble trust before Jesus, who seems to be poking him in the eye.

Old pictures mean nothing to me, I want to cry, and never will. But Elisabeth, her face rapt, rises from her chair to describe curves and flesh tones and the room in the Uffizi, wherever that is, where the original hangs among other works of the High Renaissance, all glowing like jewels against the gallery walls. She's a good teacher – fond of the sound of her own voice and sure that what she says is important. 'So you see,' she concludes with a little smile, 'painters were beginning to celebrate the flesh in a new way.'

It's a polished performance and as an act of humility I force myself to smile and meet her gaze. Where my eyes are the same muddy grey as the River Mersey, hers are a

Mediterranean blue, and wide and bright as the day when I was a Second Former and she, a seventeen-year-old dressed by Biba and Mary Quant, enrolled in the Sixth Form and voiced her surprise at the backwardness of St Cuthbert's girls in general and us Dingle girls in particular.

'I wish she'd stuff off,' Lorraine would say to Brigid and me, her beehive nodding angrily. 'Boys don't like her dowdy old clothes.'

'Supercilious cow,' Brigid would nod back. 'Looking down her nose at us all.'

But when the brainy Brigid Murray became a Choir nun, Elisabeth was obliged by the Holy Rule to forget her sister's Liverpool roots and learn respect.

When the bell rings for Office Elisabeth rolls her blue eyes heavenwards. 'What a shame!' she cries, clasping her hands. 'It's so gorgeous to talk about art.'

I nod, wondering if I'll ever prefer pictures to housework. Then she turns to go and the shabby old kitchen heaves a sigh of relief.

'Soon you'll be singing office instead of saying your rosary,' she adds, popping her head round the door.

'Maybe,' I reply. Elisabeth's manners are so perfect it's hard to tell if she's being ironic.

'Not maybe, certainly. Mother Wilfred told me so.' With that she swings off down the corridor, humming a snatch of plainsong.

As the click of her heels dies away I become aware of a faint scratching – a mouse in the skirting-board like as not. I'm looking in the cupboard for a trap when the sound starts again – but this time I can tell it's on the outside. I stare at the window, where a sea fret clings to the glass, but it's blank. When the scratching grows louder I know it's a fingernail on woodwork. Flinging open the back door I see a battered figure on the step, a felt hat crammed on its head and straw hair sticking out round its ears.

'Heather March!'

Once she was a housewife in Moses Street, proud as any woman of her scrubbed doorstep and white nets. When her husband died she got sick and fell behind with the never-never. They wanted to put her in a council home but she took to the streets instead, sleeping in Sefton Park on summer nights and by winter in the cathedral crypt. Then she disappeared down to London and came back two players short of a squad and happy to beg for her daily bread.

'How's it going, Sister?' Heather, who claims to have had a vocation, is greedy for scraps of convent gossip.

'Better than ever,' I say untruthfully. 'What about yourself?'

She stares at the small wooden cross round my neck. 'Me life has been cursed by me failure to answer God's call.'

'Would you like a sarnie?' I ask with a glance over my shoulder because Wilfie has forbidden me to feed the down-and-outs. Our community, she says, has barely enough for itself.

Heather nods, continuing to stare. 'I hear yer trying to get in to the uni.'

I stare back, wondering how she found out. Not from my mam and dad, who haven't seen her in years, nor from the Archdeacon, whom she can't abide. I could ask her outright but it would be pointless because she never answers a straight question.

'I'll make you a sandwich but you must take it away with you,' I say, hacking some meat off a scrag end. Tonight the community will be making do once again with blind scouse.

While I fill Heather's battered tin mug she munches on her sarnie. 'I saw Sister Julian-that-was the other day,' she says, fixing her eyes on my face.

Sister Julian, whom I remember from school, left before I joined the community. Aloof and sarcastic, she was, in my view, no loss to St Cuthbert's.

'They say she's got a new job,' adds Heather, plucking a worm of mutton from her false teeth.

'Maybe.' I've never been able to understand people's fascination with ex-nuns and am beginning to feel bored. At least Julian keeps well away from St Cuthbert's – unlike other ex-nuns who can't find their niche in the world and keep turning up at the convent.

'And how's Sister Brigid?' asks Heather, popping her dentures into her cheek. 'Still moping about —'

'That will do, Heather.' Gonzaga, surprisingly light on her feet for a heavy old woman, has appeared at my side. Pushing past me, she grips Heather by the elbow, bundles her down the steps then cries out as Heather dashes her tea down her habit.

'I want to stay with you,' caws Heather who has dropped her sandwich. She scoops it up and pokes out the gravel. 'I was born to be a holy nun!'

Without stopping to wipe her habit Gonzaga climbs back up the steps, slams the door shut and stands against it, her doughy face paler than ever.

'What's the matter?' I ask. It's the first time I've seen her rebuff a down-and-out.

Still panting a little, Gonzaga turns away, her face closed. 'If Heather March turns up again, you call for me.'

'But you were having a nap!'

'Then call for Columba.'

'Why?' I ask, beginning to feel angry. Gonzaga sounds more like Mother Wilfred than the chatty old lay sister whom I love.

'Because I say so.' With that she bends over and begins to riddle the Aga. Its iron raking puts a stop to any more questions and I'm left hurt and dissatisfied to ponder yet another mystery of convent life.

On Three Different Sorts of Sin

'A second demand from the lecky!' says the postman, brandishing an envelope with angry red letters. As usual he's arrived while I'm scrubbing the front step, so I pause while he jams back the brass flap and drops the mail into the wire cage. It would be more than my life's worth to take it from him myself.

He doesn't stay long: bills for Mother Wilfred, a pastoral letter from Maria Goretti, a thin blue envelope or two from across the water. The St Cuthbert's nuns are mostly old with few living relatives.

'Thanks, Bob. Better news tomorrow, if you don't mind.'

Then Sister Columba, the old portress, takes a small key from her belt, unlocks the cage, removes the letters and trots down the corridor to Mother Wilfred's study. Although censorship went out with the Vatican Council fifteen years ago, Wilfie hasn't seen fit to discourage her. Instead she nods distantly as Columba lays the letters on her desk, then carries on writing.

Sometimes, after the portress has bowed and left the study, the Superior picks up her letter knife and absently slits one or two envelopes.

'She doesn't know she's opening them,' explains Columba, her little face flushed. 'It's forgetfulness.'

'Funny that it's always the letters one would least like her to read,' murmurs Elisabeth who receives more post than anyone else.

'That's pure coincidence – because she doesn't read them. She told me so herself,' says Bosco.

The rest of us say nothing – but we know that things are better in other convents. Elisabeth has told us how the Roman community lives on the tenth floor of a block of flats. In the kitchen is a fridge filled with cans of Coke, and each nun has a transistor on her bedside locker. You can use the telephone whenever you want and help yourself to stamps. Elisabeth claims to have written to Maria Goretti complaining about Wilfie's behaviour but hasn't yet had a reply. As for me I'd rather tackle our Superior face to face, but so far haven't dared.

After posting the application forms I keep an anxious eye on Bob's deliveries, but when the weeks pass without any crested envelopes I start to feel hopeful. Our applications might have been late or got lost in the post. Or Elisabeth and I are too old, more like, and not nearly clever enough.

By the start of the new year I reckon we're out of danger. 'It's the Lord's will,' says Gonzaga as we stoke the Aga one night. 'He's keeping you here to help us.'

The windows are etched with frost as we walk down the cloister to Compline, where Mother Wilfred offers a prayer of thanksgiving that our community will remain intact.

The only one not to join in is the irrepressible Elisabeth. 'Take no notice of Wilfie,' she whispers behind her hand. 'We'll be called to interview any day now.'

I glance at her strained face and eager blue eyes. 'Ursula says the interview date has passed.'

'Impossible! They're desperate for good students – Timmy says so, remember?'

The next day after lunch I go to the staff room as usual to serve coffee. I'm setting out the cups, their handles all facing the same way and a teaspoon in each saucer as instructed by Mother Wilfred, when Elisabeth appears at my side. 'Isn't Mrs Tarn like Hendrickje Stoffels?'

On seeing my blank look she points at the rosy-cheeked French teacher bent over her marking. 'Rembrandt's second wife and most famous model.'

'I know nothing about Rembrandt and luckily I'll never have to.'

I'm loading the trolley with used crockery when Columba trots into the staff room with a white envelope. At the sight of the blue crest I slop a cup of cold coffee on the carpet. Too anxious to search for a cloth, I watch the portress track across the room towards me. Then I see with relief that there's only one envelope, and Elisabeth is stepping in her path.

But Columba dodges past her. 'No, dear – it's for Sister Maureen.'

'Is there nothing for me?' cries Elisabeth.

'No, Sister – nothing at all.'

'I'm sorry, dear,' says Columba as she hands me the envelope. 'Mother Wilfred opened it by accident.'

Sisters Ursula and Bosco hurry to our side where they're joined by Mrs Tarn, Miss Vavasour the games teacher and

Mr Bethany the music teacher: old convent-school hands who've devoted their lives to St Cuthbert's.

'A letter from the university!' Mrs Tarn claps her hands.

'Go on, child – see what it says,' says Ursula, forgetting about decorum in the excitement.

Dear Miss O'Shaunessy, I read out loud and then stop. They can't be writing to me.

'For goodness' sake, girl, spill the beans,' urges Miss Vavasour who's cheered me through a thousand hockey matches and feels licensed to be familiar.

'Is it a rejection?' asks Elisabeth.

'I have an interview on Tuesday.'

Elisabeth blinks. 'What about me?'

'I don't know – there must be a mistake – I can't believe it.'

'I'm glad one of you got good news,' said Columba, her head cocked to one side like a robin's, 'but it should have been both.'

'It's preposterous,' says Elisabeth. 'Sister Maureen knows nothing about art, she'll never . . .'

As her voice tails away I look round the little ring of faces, noting Mrs Tarn's amused glance and the sympathetic, bloodshot gaze of Miss Vavasour. Whether her sympathy's for me or Elisabeth I'm too gobsmacked to tell.

'They've probably offered Sister Elisabeth's place to a long-haired layabout,' says Mr Bethany, plucking at his cardigan.

Bosco gives him a withering look. 'Sister Elisabeth will be accepted without interview. She is after all a Bavidge.'

'Well done, Sister Maureen,' says Elisabeth bleakly.

'Sock it to them, Sister Moey,' says Miss Vavasour, her leathery cheeks creased into a smile. 'They won't know what's hit them when you pitch up.'

'I'll bet they'll be surprised by your nun's gear,' says Mr Bethany.

'Nonsense, there are plenty of nuns at university,' says Miss Vavasour.

'Not dressed like district nurses.'

'I've got to prepare a special topic,' I say, rereading the letter. 'I'll have to start straightaway.'

'Don't get too competitive,' Ursula warns me. 'You must learn to be yourself.'

'She's most herself when she's most competitive,' says Miss Vavasour, who alone among the staff religious and secular approves of my true nature.

'The bell has gone.' Mother Wilfred bears down on us like an angry referee. 'It will be awkward if Sister Maureen gets in and you don't,' she says to Elisabeth as the rest of the staff disperses. 'Very awkward.'

'I applied to a different department,' says Elisabeth who has come back from the ropes with who knows what effort. 'There may be a letter for me in the next post.'

Mother Wilfred ignores her. 'I can't think why they chose Maureen and not you. You must ask them next week.'

'You mean I have to go with her to interview?' Elisabeth's mouth droops.

'She is younger than you and needs a chaperone.'

'But I'll look out of place.'

'It's a sin to worry about how things look,' barks the Superior, 'the sin of Human Respect.'

'I can't go into the interview room,' protests Elisabeth. 'It's not allowed.'

'There's no need to hang about.' Mother Wilfred suddenly remembers my presence. 'You may take the cups back to the kitchen.'

I joggle my aluminium trolley through the door and down the corridor through crowds of snobby high-school girls returning to class. Though I serve their dinners every day, not one of them smiles or says hello. On reaching the green baize door to the convent I pause for a moment to check no one's around, then trundle on down the main school corridor. I should ask Elisabeth for help with my special topic but that posh little voice sets my teeth on edge.

Rolling past the row of classrooms I curse the loose parquet for rattling the cups and saucers, and half expect Bosco to poke her head out of a door and ask me where do I think I'm going. Though I dust the library twice a week I've no reason to be here in school hours so I check the corridor again, park my trolley by the wall and dart inside.

This was the billiard room of the Liverpool merchant, and the librarian's desk is beside the disused cue rack. Since Julian went there's been no librarian, and as I expected the room is empty. Even so, I have an uneasy sense of being watched while consulting her Sellotaped plan. Everything's near to hand because the library is, as the Archdeacon often remarks, far too small even for a girls' school. The art history section is between the mullioned windows overlooking the park. *A–F, G–Q, R–Z*. Each shelf is labelled in Julian's bold italic. But the shelves themselves are empty.

My first feeling is relief – now I won't have to bother swotting. Absolved from effort, I can turn up for my interview in five days' time, fail, and return to my life as a lay sister. I roam the nearby alcoves out of duty to see if the books have been misplaced, then return thankfully to the bare shelves. It seems like a gift from God, a sign of His pleasure in my hidden life.

Then it occurs to me: I dusted the shelves this morning,

as always on a Thursday. In particular I remember plucking a crisp packet from a misplaced book on Picasso, then lodging it next to Pirandello. The books have disappeared since the news about my interview.

I remember Elisabeth's shaken white face – but she heard the news the same time as I did. Then I think of Brigid, sallow and envious. She wasn't there when I opened my letter but could easily have heard from Wilfie, then nipped into the library.

I'm shocked to discover that I want to get hold of the books – want to very much indeed. It's not my fault, I think, gazing out at the lads playing football in the park. I'm an O'Shaunessy, and put on my mettle by a setback. No longer thankful for the missing volumes, I feel the urge to get out on the pitch and win, not just to be best but to be seen to be the best. I'm wondering what I should do about my special topic when the Angelus bell reminds me that the morning's almost over and my trolley, with its cargo of dirty cups, is still parked outside in the main corridor.

And then I see it, an outsize book with splodges of colour on its jacket, almost hidden behind the bottom shelf. *Auguste Renoir: His Life and Work*. Dropping to my knees I haul it towards me and start flicking through the pastel-coloured pages.

It's forbidden to take books from the library – but the temptation to disobey has slipped between the goal posts of my mind and is bobbing round in the mud. The Rule wasn't designed for lay sisters so I've often ignored it in the past – giving food to the down-and-outs under Wilfie's nose like a latter-day Robin Hood.

But now I'm not acting for the down-and-outs or even for the Choir nuns and their precious school. I know it from the tightening of my muscles as in pre-match nerves, and the sense of constriction in my lungs: I want to succeed for no one but my vainglorious, competitive self. Not knowing the patron saint of interviews, I pray for advice to the Head of the Holy Army.

When her potato-shaped top half appears through the frosted glass door I know that she's heard my prayer – but she fades from sight as I spring to my feet, and I realise with dismay that she'll never enter the library. Standing undecided with the book in my hands, I see another, taller figure approach the frosted glass, and I slip the book under my cape. Although Ursula must have noticed my trolley, an expression of wonder flits across her equable, horse-like face. 'Sister Maureen! Such a rare visitor! What can I do for you?'

'All the art history books have disappeared.'

'Have they, dear?'

The one book that hasn't disappeared is poking out from my cape, but Ursula seems not to have noticed. 'I'm invigilating the Sixth Form Mocks,' she whispers though no one else is present. 'The devil soon finds work for empty hands.' From the librarian's desk she picks up scissors, backing paper and a book with a torn cover, then treads her way back to the door and closes it softly behind her.

Before anyone else can appear I dive for my tea-trolley, hide the book under a tin of Jacobs Cream Crackers and trundle towards the kitchen. Gonzaga is at the Aga boiling a pan of carrots. I long to show her my find but she looks too hot and cross. I hurriedly unload the trolley, splashing my habit with milk as I pile the cups into the sink. Then I wait till Gonzaga's back is turned, slip the book under my arm and dart out of the kitchen.

The attic has been subdivided into a row of cells each

with its own door and wooden partitions. It is out of bounds in the daytime – in case lazy Choir nuns or tired lay sisters are tempted to lie on their beds and sleep. But I want to look at my book – and besides, my habit is smelling of milk and should be changed. I open the tome the moment I reach my cell but am rightly punished for my disobedience. There's nothing here for a special topic – just the briefest of introductions, then page after page of cow-like women with nothing better to do than sit round the house all day with no clothes on. Their flesh is unhealthily soft, their hips wide and their faces blank and self-indulgent – the sort of women who've never had to work in their lives. How can this be called great art, I think angrily, when all they need is more exercise?

I shove the book under the clean towels in my wardrobe and begin changing my habit. Only when it's dropped to the floor do I notice the tang of sweat from my armpits – the result, I'm sure, of my nervous half-hour in the library. I peel off the rest of my clothes, fill the basin with warm water, then pick up my old habit. I'm about to pitch it in the laundry basket when a hand mirror clatters to the floor.

It's a little girl's mirror, its plastic stencilled with a peeling bouquet of pink roses and frosted with imitation quartz. I found it this morning in the First Form cloakroom, put it in my pocket for safekeeping and forgot it till this moment. I check it's not broken then raise it to look at my face. Snub nose, freckled skin and eyes of Mersey grey: it hasn't changed since I saw it last. It's an Irish face, an O'Shaunessy face, with wary eyes and a hint of defiance in the chin; but not, I think sadly, the face of a university student.

We're meant to wear dressing-gowns when we wash but after showering naked as a teenager in dozens of different changing-rooms I've never bothered, not even as a novice. After my hot and sweaty morning I pause for a second to enjoy the draught from the skylight on my bare skin and then, on impulse, angle the mirror on to my breasts then downwards over my body.

My belly, I'm glad to see, still looks hard and flat as an athlete's. I wonder if I get into the uni will my hips spread and my waist thicken like Renoir's women? Most of my life has been spent on the move – sweeping, cooking, polishing, running up and downstairs to the infirmary. Even my rosary is said walking in the garden. Holding the mirror in my right hand I run my left hand over my breasts – the only bit of my body that used to hurt when hit with a football. The nipples are erect in the cool air and to my surprise I feel a tweak – then a queasy tug in the pit of my stomach. It's not a feeling I like, and I put down the mirror at once and wring out my flannel.

'Sister Maureen! It's time to serve dinner,' calls Gonzaga, her heavy tread on the bottom stair.

'I'll be down in five minutes,' I shout, then shove the mirror under my towels with the book on Renoir.

An irregular motion of the flesh – that's what my sin is called in the Catechism. It's the result of three separate acts of disobedience, all of which I shall confess to the Archdeacon. But I shan't tell him about touching my breasts because he's known me since I was a child, and would feel embarrassed. And besides, I'm in no danger from sex and never have been. Sex leads to getting pregnant and varicose veins and lifelong servitude in the Dingle, all the things I never wanted. Thanking God for my escape, I put on my habit, adjust my veil and hurry down to the dining-hall.

The St Cuthbert's Madonnas

Mother Wilfred looks up the moment I open the library door. I should have checked before bringing back the book – but who'd have guessed she'd be sat here when her Choir nuns are at Vespers? Sliding the volume under my arm, I cross the floor and hover awkwardly in front of her desk beside the empty art history shelves.

Her eyes fix on the book which is poking out from my cape. 'You had no right to take that.' Lunging across her blotter, she pulls it towards her. It falls open at a seated nude with a dreamy face. One hand is clasping her knee, the other resting lightly between her legs.

'But I need to prepare my special topic – and all the others have disappeared.'

Wilfie's normally pale cheeks are blotched with red. 'It was my duty to remove them,' she croaks, her hand beating at the page with its milk-white flesh, 'because most of them are obscene.' Snapping the book shut, she lays it face down on the desk. *Me, I paint with my penis.* The words jump out at us from the back cover, printed so large I can read them upside down. *A painter who has the feel of breasts and buttocks is saved.*

'Saved!' gasps Mother Wilfred, jabbing the book into a drawer. 'What could a man like that know of salvation?'

I scan the bare shelves behind her head. 'Couldn't you give me something about animals or – um – landscapes?'

Though Mother Wilfred stares back angrily she makes no reply, and for a second I wonder if she's at a loss. After all, the Archdeacon wants graduates: if we fail to get in to the uni, St Cuthbert's will be starved of funds.

'There's no need to be looking at books,' she says at last, taking a key from her belt and locking the desk drawer, 'when we have better pictures on our very own walls.'

'Whereabouts?' The only painting I can think of is the one in the kitchen, pointed out to me by Elisabeth.

'In the top corridor,' replies Wilfie with a glint of triumph, 'which you are supposed to clean twice a week.'

I remember the row of frames, because the curly gilt leaves are tricky to dust; but the pictures themselves I've ignored, mainly because I prefer the Dingle way of slapping colour on the wall in wallpaper. 'Who are they by?' I ask.

'The masters of the Renaissance. And they are all great paintings – great *devotional* paintings, I might add. You may stand in front of them now, and pray for help with your interview.'

Dismissed, I make my way up the stairs. I've never liked the infirmary corridor with its cold white walls and frosted windows which stop us looking down into the park. Today the corridor's empty, but sometimes two crabby old invalids, Sisters Pious and Placid, hobble up and down with their rosaries clacking against their zimmers.

No matter how much I polish the glass, the paintings always seem flyblown with the prayers of sick nuns. Looking at them closely for the first time, I see that they're not real paintings at all but copies snipped out of magazines. They're of a dozen different Madonnas – posh Madonnas on couches, prim Madonnas in churches, Madonnas posing in palaces or perched on pointy-looking rocks. They're mostly pale and blonde and in much richer clothes than the real-life Mary would have worn; and they're all giving soppy smiles as they cradle their babies' bare bottoms.

I stare at a picture of a peevish Christ child struggling out of his jacket, his chubby white legs spread. I saw plenty of boys' willies as a girl when we changed to go swimming at New Brighton. Unlike my big sister Lol who shrieked and giggled or Brigid who turned away with pursed lips, I thought they were nothing special – just hard to protect in the penalty wall.

Now, more than ten years on, I find myself staring at a Christ child's penis – it seems rude to call it a willie – popping out like a frozen prawn. I learned about the Incarnation in school, and know that Our Lord took the body of an ordinary man – but why put this funny little worm of flesh in what Mother Wilfred calls a devotional painting? Even a Renoir would be better than this.

In the next picture by – I peer at the handwritten label – someone called Masaccio, the baby's private parts peek out through a wisp of cloth. Then comes a Botticelli where a little boy fights to open his mother's dress and after that a Raphael with the child lunging at the Virgin's nipple. All are naked apart from a halo.

How can Mother Wilfred, who objects to female nudes,

expect me to pray to these lustful, fleshy infants? This must be a test, to see if I'm modest enough to be trusted at interview.

My eyes drawn on against my will, I wonder why none of the babies need nappies. Three more frozen prawns and I'll go and tell Wilfie that these paintings are – what did she say about Renoir? That these paintings are obscene.

I'm mouthing the word the way she did, as though spitting out a piece of gristle, when I hear her heavy tread along the corridor. 'I see you're finding plenty to look at,' she says, breaking the rule of silence.

I watch her arthritic forefinger trace a line on the greenish glass. 'I'll polish it tomorrow.'

'Don't worry about that now.' Far from testing for dust, Mother Wilfred appears to be caressing the Christ child's pudgy flank. 'I'm glad you like my sweet little babies.'

Sweet little babies – these lardy, jumbo-sized infants? I try to look blank as she bends her face to my ear. 'Something wonderful has happened this term,' she says, her voice gone all thick and chocolatey. 'One of my Fourth Formers has become a mother.'

Can this be the Mother Wilfred who kicked me out of school for bringing in a condom? It's a sin to criticise a Superior even to yourself, so I'm struggling to blot out the contradiction when my eye's caught by a muscle-bound Christ child tweaking his mother's nipple, too sure of his Godhead to be troubled by his total nudity. His fierce little gaze meets mine, as though willing me to get with this tough new game and learn how to win it. It's several seconds before I realise he looks uncannily like the Archdeacon.

'How shall I know what to say at my interview?' I cry out as Mother Wilfred turns to go.

'You may stay here and pray to that sweet little infant Jesus,' says the Superior with a serene glance at the blocky, red-faced baby. 'If he wants you to go to university, he will tell you what to say when the moment comes.'

Liverpool Renaissance

When me mam appears at the front door her hair's permed tight from an afternoon at Maison Gwlady's, and I can tell from her flushed face that she's got something important to tell me.

'You're going to get in,' she announces. 'You will, and that stuck-up Elisabeth won't.'

'*Sister* Elisabeth,' I snap. I love Mam next to God and Our Lady, but no outsider gets away with insulting another nun. 'And anyway, how do you know?'

'I consulted Madam Imelda.'

'Hush up, Mam. Fortune-telling's a sin.'

'I know that – but Imelda did it for free.'

'Then it won't come true,' I say.

Mam's stopped listening to ferret in her shopping bag. 'Your dad wants you to have this.' She produces a fountain-pen with a silver top in a presentation case. 'It's for tomorrow,' she says, clearly believing I'm in for some sort of written test. Her voice croaks, as it always does when she's being especially generous. 'It'll give you the edge on them other students.'

As usual when Mam and me look as though we're going to cry, one of us cracks a joke. 'No wonder I'm competitive with you for me mam.'

'You've got to be a fighter round here,' she replies, 'otherwise you go under.' She pats her tight new curls. 'If you have a degree you won't ever have to get your hands dirty.'

I can never convince her that I enjoy what she calls drudgery because I do it for God and not for a man.

Mam hands me a postcard of Paddy's Wigwam, with a message on the back. *Imagine your interview's a game of football*, reads the Archdeacon's scrawl, *and throw your heart and soul into it.*

'Tell him I'm St Cuthbert's number one striker so I know how to chase a lost cause.'

'How can it be a lost cause?' Mam looks reproachful. 'The whole street's praying for you – even your dad.'

'And what about Lol?' I ask as Mam picks up her bag. Although my big sister hates nuns and dodges her visits to St Cuthbert's whenever possible, I secretly feel hurt that she hasn't even sent me a card.

At that Mam darts forward again to squeeze something small and hard into my palm. It's the lucky black poodle Lorraine kept on her desk in exams. As she failed her first year I feel a bit uneasy slipping it into my pocket but do it anyway out of loyalty.

When Mother Wilfred beckons me into her study the next morning it's clear from her clouded face that, unlike Mam, the Archdeacon and Madam Imelda, she takes a dim view of my prospects. 'Remember that everyone has to fail sometime,' she says impressively.

I nod, wondering if at long last she's forgotten I was kicked out of school. Like most of the Choir nuns she seems to be in two minds about my interview. They want the Archdeacon's money all right – and another teacher would come in handy, even if it's only me. Yet their polite smiles and shaking heads tell me I'm not the right type, and that I'm better off as I am. An O'Shaunessy in university? I can hear them thinking. Wonders will never cease.

'Do be careful, my dears,' says Gonzaga as Elisabeth and I put on our capes. She's been listening for years to delivery men on the back step and is a mine of city myths and legends: about pickpockets working the buses with false arms, men dressed as women offering lifts, murderers with axes hidden in Adidas bags on the back seats of their cars, and thieves riding the roofs of the underground trains, ready to climb through the windows between stations.

As we pull back the front door I whisper a prayer to the Holy Army, who have stayed away all week. I want them on my side, but the air round my head stays empty. And then, as we walk down the path, I give a last glance over my shoulder and see them at the attic window, smiling down to wish me luck, with Carthage's broad face at the end of the row.

'Who on earth are you waving at?' asks Elisabeth as I trip over a stone. 'For goodness' sake act normally – at least for this morning.'

Soon the bus is jolting us towards the university while I stare through its grimy windows. Liverpool has changed since I was a girl. Ford Cortinas are rusting in the gutters of Granby Street and the new bollards at the end of the road make it look even more like a ghetto. The pavements are covered in litter, and receivers dangle like broken arms in the shattered phone booths. Some houses on the Boulevard have collapsed while others stand like rotten teeth, their walls daubed with wobbling graffiti. NF. GOD BLESS OUR POPE. MAN UTD. TROOPS OUT and a mysterious A in a circle.

Had it not been for Elisabeth sitting beside me, calm and clear-eyed, I would have jumped off the bus. 'Tell me what to say about those Madonnas in the top corridor,' I say, wishing I'd asked yesterday.

'They're nearly all from the High Renaissance,' trills Elisabeth as we speed towards a bus stop. At the head of a long queue a black man in a woolly hat sticks out his hand.

'When was that?'

Elisabeth grips the seat in front as the driver accelerates past the black man. Though still not called to interview, she seems more cheerful than usual and almost excited by her trip to the uni. 'Between 1500 and 1527.'

'What makes it so special?'

'As I've told you already, it's the quality of the flesh that's important,' she continues in her high, clear voice, unaware of the twirly staring rheumily across the aisle. 'Flesh. Painters were beginning to glorify it in a new way.'

I think of the muscle-bound Christ child. Obedient to Mother Wilfred, I prayed to Him for a quarter of an hour last night, averting my eyes from His curly willie. No wonder nothing happened. 'It's not fair,' I say aloud to Elisabeth. 'You should have applied to read art history, not me.'

Elisabeth gives a sweet, sad little smile. 'God is testing me to the limit, Sister Maureen. That is how I know that He really, really loves me.'

The art history department occupies all four floors of a Georgian house on a square in the middle of the university precinct. Twenty minutes early, we hang around on the pavement. On the ground floor is an office with secretaries answering phones and bustling between desks. It's term time and students are passing up and down the steps in chattering groups. Every now and again I glance at the tall sash windows on the first floor, half-expecting a professor to lean out and shout, 'Please go away! You have no business here.'

Poised as ever, Elisabeth follows my gaze. 'That used to be Timmy's room. The one above belongs to Cynthia Fothergill – and the big room over the front door is Professor Canterville's.'

I glimpse a wall of book shelves, an Anglepoise and some spider plants on the window-sill and shiver as the February wind cuts across the square. There's no sign of any other candidates.

As the Victoria clock tolls its ten strokes we obediently climb the steps and present ourselves in the office. We know from my letter that a Dr Palfrey is to give a short lecture before the interviews begin at ten thirty.

'Miss O'Shaunessy?' A woman with the plumped-up breast of a pouter pigeon is staring crossly at Elisabeth. Unfamiliar with the use of my surname, I take a few seconds to answer.

'You're late,' she snaps. 'Dr Palfrey is already on the podium.' She ticks my name off her list and turns to Elisabeth. 'You'll pick up your – er – friend later.'

'Certainly not. I'm staying with Sister Maureen.'

'That's not allowed,' says the secretary. 'It's candidates only.'

I flinch, knowing that Elisabeth is bound by Holy Obedience to do as Mother Wilfred has instructed; and that my own embarrassment arises from the sin of human respect. Fixing my eyes on an overflowing in-tray I remind myself that it doesn't matter how we appear to lay people, who know nothing of our Holy Rule. All the same I hope that Elisabeth will go away.

'I'll stay with Sister Maureen,' she says again.

The woman shrugs, clacks down a corridor and opens a big oak door, leaving us to follow in her wake. 'Mrs Bossy Boots Dagnall,' whispers Elisabeth. 'Timmy couldn't stand her.'

'There's two more here, Dr Palfrey,' says the secretary to a young man sitting on a podium. 'I did tell them it was candidates only.'

To my horror we're standing at the front of a lecture hall, facing rows of chattering students. I take in a long, white-walled room with oak desks and high windows, a bit like a retreat house. Unlike nuns, who would have filled the front pews first, the students have all crowded to the back.

Dr Palfrey gestures at the front row but Elisabeth shakes her head and smiles at the assembled students as though they've been waiting for her to appear. Then she prods me in the ribs and, when I fail to move, strides to the back. I wish I was a hard man like Tommy Smith who could take on the Kop and win. But I'm not, so when faced by this polite little crowd just four rows deep I take fright, lurch after Elisabeth, then grab her by the elbow and shove her at the nearest row.

'Budge up!' she says to a girl in a cashmere coat. The girl slides obediently along the row and for the first time I see the point of being like Elisabeth. Cool as a cucumber, my mam would have called her, and not a bit ashamed of her worn old habit with its calf-length skirt and nurse's veil. Not wanting to sit on my own in another row, I squeeze in beside her and plant my right foot in the aisle.

I glance round at the other candidates. They're mostly the same age as the Sixth Formers at St Cuthbert's whom I serve every day with school dinners. But them I can subdue with a glare or a wave of my ladle – whereas these look down their noses at us. All I can see is snooty smiles, clear skin and the sort of long shiny hair you get in shampoo ads.

'I say, Sasha,' cries a girl in front to another sitting beside her, 'are you going to Bernard's cockers p?'

It's unfair, I think, with a grimace at Elisabeth. They'd all know where I'm from the moment I opened my mouth, while I know nothing about them – except that they're rich.

My grimace is not returned because Elisabeth's listening intently, her mouth curving into a smile. Then she leans forward and taps the girl called Sasha on the arm.

'Not Bernard Tallant-Smythe?' she asks her.

The girl swings round, her blonde mane flicking my cheek. 'Actually, yes,' she shrieks. 'Do you know him?'

'Yes, ackshy,' breathes Elisabeth, her voice even farther back than it is at St Cuthbert's. 'I used to go to dancing-class with his big brother.'

I stare at the podium where the young man is flicking languidly through his notes. He's tall and lithe with a sportsman's figure; though I guess from his elegant clothes that he'd prefer cricket to football and enjoy the back page of the *Observer* more than *A Question of Sport*.

'That's Piers Palfrey – Timmy's replacement,' says Elisabeth, dragging her attention away from her new friend. 'He's a seventeenth-century man.'

Too anxious to ask what that means, I gaze round the room until I become aware of a girl watching us from the other side. She's neatly dressed in a crisp white polo neck and with smooth hair under an Alice band. 'Isn't that Nathalie Steen?' I shout to Elisabeth above the rising chatter. Nathalie was in last year's Upper Sixth and used to leave most of her dinner at the side of her plate because it was too fattening. Just seeing her across the room makes me smell the mashed potato and greasy gravy. She believed she had a vocation but Mother Wilfred told her she hadn't, on the grounds that she was a bookworm.

Before Elisabeth can reply the lecturer rises to his feet and the noise drops miraculously. On seeing his white, well-shaped hands tremble slightly as he arranges his notes, I realise with surprise that he must be my age or even younger. While I pull my new fountain-pen out of my bag, he introduces himself and begins to speak: about lectures and seminars – five a week of each – and options and core courses: Impressionism and Expressionism, Formalism and Modernism and lots of other isms I've never heard of. It's like a sermon, I decide, beginning to feel at home; not on hellfire and damnation but some obscure point of theology, with the black-suited Dr Palfrey as a scholarly young priest.

As I flick over a page in my notebook I become aware that Elisabeth's frowning and shaking her head. Glancing down the row I see I'm the only one taking notes and, feeling crushed, return my pen to my bag.

By the time I've calmed down the lecturer has changed tack. 'We know how clever you all are,' he's saying, 'and that some of you have had very good offers from Manchester —'

I prick up my ears when he mentions our rival – a city

with posh shops, pricey restaurants and two overrated football teams. The girl called Sasha sighs noisily and begins flicking through a prospectus. In front, a boy begins whispering to his neighbour.

'But Liverpool is a far better town for art than Manchester,' continues Dr Palfrey with a special smile for the whisperers. 'Here we have a celebrated Georgian quarter, more galleries than anywhere else in England outside Kensington, and more students per capita than any other place in Europe.'

Though I like him for praising Liverpool I can't help feeling he sees a different city from the one I grew up in. Watching his fervent young face I wonder what he'd make of the down-at-heel people we saw in the Boulevard this morning, or the Wellington Vaults with its smell of smoke and Jeyes' Fluid.

'Besides having a major orchestra, four theatres and two great cathedrals, there's a . . .' he pauses 'thrilling night life, and some of you might have actually seen our two famous football teams – even if only one of them ever wins anything.'

I suppose he means Liverpool, I think, suddenly losing sympathy. Has no one told him about Everton's unbeaten run of nineteen games? He shouldn't joke about what he doesn't know.

His voice rises over the ripple of laughter. 'If you want to see the city, at its best, go down to the Pier Head and take a ferry. Then you will view our famous waterfront as it was meant to be viewed – from the river. And on your return, visit our commercial quarter and admire the grand old buildings modelled on the princes' palaces of the Florentine Renaissance.'

While my mind wanders round the sooty old banks and offices, Dr Palfrey puts down his notes and steps in front of his lectern. 'But Liverpool, you know, does more than trade on its former glories.' He raises a slim white hand. 'There's another renaissance going on – the renaissance of art history. Though it is new, and has yet to gain its inter-national reputation, our department is young, energetic, and highly selective. From all of you here we can take only ten – not just because we are choosy but because we like to know our students personally.' He pauses to run his eye over us. 'We give one-to-one tutorials, go on trips to studios and galleries, drink together in wine bars and eat in restaurants.'

Dr Palfrey's smile suggests he is offering us a treat. But I've never been to a studio, wine bar or restaurant, and am still trying to decide which sounds the most alarming when Mrs Dagnall reappears with a clipboard. He favours her with a smile, then gazes earnestly round the room. 'We already have in our department some of the best scholars in England, and our job this morning is to spot the scholars of the future. To you I say: come to Liverpool and develop your potential. I promise you won't regret making us your first choice.'

He's finished, and the audience cheers and claps with an inappropriate air of relief. The interviews are about to begin.

David and Goliath

'You'll be interviewed by Dr Palfrey himself,' says the pigeon-chested Mrs Dagnall.

By the time we reach his office there are gales of laughter coming from inside. Elisabeth puts her ear to the door, listens intently for a few seconds, then springs back when a young man in a three-piece suit strides out, waving an umbrella.

'Don't worry,' she says to me as he clatters down the stairs. 'He's been rejected.'

'Next!' comes Dr Palfrey's voice.

'Just keep calm,' says Elisabeth, 'and answer what you can.'

Leaning back in his chair with his legs crossed, Dr Palfrey has the unmistakable air of someone who's never been put down or discouraged, not even as a boy. Too nervous to look him in the eye, I stare at his hands, which are resting on the desk. A button is missing from his white shirt, and his jacket, though of good quality cloth, is a little frayed at the cuffs. His hands themselves are bony and pale as a Choir nun's. 'Two sisters for the price of one!' he says, rising to his feet.

'I should be doing art history,' says Elisabeth, stepping forward, 'but I've been told to apply to the English Department.' She sticks out her hand. 'Elisabeth Bavidge – Timothy's sister.'

'Timothy? Oh, you mean Beaver Bavvers.' He runs an appraising eye over Elisabeth's figure. 'How's he getting on at the Met?'

'Not the Met, the Frick,' corrects Elisabeth, 'where he's started making his mark.'

She begins to chat about the galleries she knows in London and all the painters with whom she's on first-name terms, and Dr Palfrey's so impressed he's forgotten all about me. I should be relieved but to my surprise I feel put out. Stepping to one side and folding my arms, I stare pointedly round his study at the little fireplace with the row of blue and white coffee cups on its mantelpiece, the heaps of papers on the table, and all the walls full of shelves, and wonder if he dusts all the books himself or if he has a cleaner to do it.

'Well,' after a few minutes he catches my eye, 'we'd better begin the interview.' He moves a stack of files from the battered armchair and pulls it forward for Elisabeth.

She gives him a dazzling smile. 'Interviewees aren't normally chaperoned. Why don't I wait outside?'

'If you wish,' says Dr Palfrey with what sounds like a hint of regret.

'But – but shouldn't you —?' I stammer. 'Aren't you —?'

'I have one or two things to sort out,' she explains kindly.

She must have a good reason for this outright defiance of

Mother Wilfred, and I'm so busy wondering what it is that I fail to notice that Dr Palfrey has moved to his side of the desk, and is pointing me to the opposite chair.

'It's perfectly safe to sit,' prompts Elisabeth, looking back from the doorway.

Though I do as she says at once, I don't feel the least bit safe. From his sharp eyes and clever smile I know Dr Palfrey's going to make me look a wally. On the desk between us is my application form with its blot in the middle, and at the bottom a line of somebody else's handwriting which I try to read upside down as he pulls on a pair of wire-rimmed spectacles and stares at it for a few seconds.

Luckily he seems less bothered about my knowledge of art than my reasons for becoming a nun. Normally I'm rude to Nosy Parkers but today I feel too nervous, so I tell him more than he could ever want to know about growing up in the Dingle and the roots of my vocation.

'I suppose,' he says when I come to a halt, 'that it's the little things you miss the most.'

Glad not to be asked about art history, I ramble on obligingly about my craving for fish and chips, and the absence of hot-water bottles and the *Brookside* omnibus. It's an answer out of stock, and I'm almost disappointed that he swallows it whole. The things I miss are grander than that, like the smell of beer, sweat, and mown grass at the first match of the season, and the crowd rising to its feet as one whenever there's a goal. But there's no time to tell him that now because he's waiting to speak.

'And what sort of people are your parents?'

Remembering his enthusiasm for Liverpool, I tell him that they grew up in the Holy Land, like their parents and grandparents before them. By this time I know I'm talking too much but can't help careering on to my parents' struggle to keep Lol and me at St Cuthbert's, Lol's success at A level and her sudden return from the uni. Letting my eyes stray to the shelves I'm cheered by a row of Wisdens, and tell him how I used to play for the Catholic Women's football team, neatly skipping past my expulsion from school and lack of O levels.

At the mention of sport he opens his mouth to speak – but after ten years of never mentioning the past I'm gabbing so fast he can't get a word in edgeways. I race on to my life as a young nun, stressing the two bits I think will interest him most: my single visit to the Walker Art Gallery, when Mother Wilfred told us to close our eyes every time we passed a nude, and the contemplative side of convent life.

'You must all be mystics,' he says when at last I pause for breath, 'after so many hours on your knees.'

'I don't pray on my knees,' I reply. 'I pray as I sweep.'

He presses his fingertips together to make a cathedral. 'You mean you're not a proper nun?'

'I'm a proper nun all right – but not a Choir nun.'

His nails are perfect ovals, so smooth they must have been manicured. 'How bizarre!'

Don't be so snooty, I want to reply, but am scared of wrecking my chances. If only I could explain that lay sisters too can be mystics – but I don't think he'd understand.

He tilts back in his chair and fixes his gaze on the ceiling. 'And whereabouts is your convent?'

'On the edge of Sefton Park, opposite the Palm House.'

'Not that ostentatious Gothic monstrosity with the pseudo-Jacobean spires?'

I glare across the desk at his tilted chin. 'It's a beautiful old building.'

Settling back in his chair he smiles politely at my form. 'I see you don't have art A level.'

It would be disloyal to explain that Mother Wilfred wants me to do art history as an act of penance so I listen in silence as the After Eight clock on his mantelpiece chimes the half-hour. My interview is now over – with what result I've no idea.

'I suppose that I'd better ask you a question – just for the record.' From his desk he picks up a statue about twelve inches high. 'Which is your favourite period in art?'

'The Renaissance,' I say, because it's the only one I can think of.

'Then you'll probably recognise this.'

The statuette is of a naked man, and he hands it to me face down. No nun should ever look at such an object, let alone clutch one round the midriff in the presence of a layman, and the colour flames up my face as I stare at the small round buttocks.

'What can you find to say about that?' the tutor is asking me.

Despite his silky manner I know that this is power play and that it's time to raise my game. Acutely aware of his gaze, I will myself to stop blushing, then turn the statue face up. It's of a curly-haired young man with a muscular torso and huge hands, one of them clasping a stone; and – I can't stop the thought from darting through my brain – his penis is even smaller than a Baby Jesus's.

'Surely you've seen him before?'

My grip tightens round the torso. He looks like a stuck-up public schoolboy, sure he'll be chosen for the First XI.

How can I have seen him before, I want to yell back, when I've never been out of Liverpool in my life?

Instead I beg the Holy Army of lay sisters for inspiration, but they must be flummoxed, too, because nothing comes to me except the ticking of the clock and Dr Palfrey's sigh as he starts to shuffle his papers. I remember that from all the candidates today they're accepting only ten, and know with a surge of disappointment that I won't be one of them.

After a few more seconds Dr Palfrey stands up. It's a signal the interview's over so I too rise to my feet, still clutching the little statue. Reluctant to call it a day, I take a last look at the proud-faced young man with the assessing stare and the stone clasped in his hand. Only now that it's too late does it come to me who he is: my favourite character in the Bible. Like many a good footballer, he took on someone stronger than himself – and won.

'This is David from the First Book of Samuel!' I say as I turn to go.

The tutor sits down again with a smile, and fixes his eyes on mine. 'And when do you think it was made?'

Fifteen hundred BC? Nineteen hundred AD? I loom awkwardly over the desk.

Then the blocky baby Jesus flashes into my mind, his cheeks dark with exasperation. You've been told all you need to know, he snaps, lifting a podgy knee. Act like a Number One Striker.

Knowing the best goals are scored under the worst pressure, I take him at his word and measure the space between the posts. The right words are there in my mind, if only I can reach for them. Then, not quite knowing their source, I mouth them one by one into the air. 'This is the work of the

Florentine High Renaissance, 1500–1527.'

'And how,' Dr Palfrey presses on, 'do you know that?'

Because Elisabeth told me so on the bus is the truthful answer – but I'm on a roll, so I kick it straight into touch. Plonking the statue on the desk where it faces Dr Palfrey, I look fearlessly down at its taut white buttocks and muscled frame – a sportsman's body if ever I saw one. 'I know from the quality of the flesh,' I tell the tutor. 'Artists were glorifying it in a new way.'

For once Dr Palfrey is sitting up straight. 'You know rather more than I thought, Sister Maureen.' His words roar in my ears like applause as I march to the door. 'Congratulations, you have won yourself a place. I shall see you in October.'

The girl in the cashmere coat is waiting on the chair outside the door; but as I cross the landing I see Elisabeth dart through the foyer. I run down the stairs towards her, desperate to start boasting.

'Guess what!' I cry.

On seeing Mrs Dagnall hovering by her office door Elisabeth puts her finger to her lips, then bursts out as we run down the steps. 'I went over to the English department while you were at interview,' she says, clearly very pleased with herself. 'That's why I didn't come in with you – it was my only chance. I told the prof who I was and how Wilfie wanted me to read English, and he said my application form must have been overlooked but he'd see to it straightaway. He said I might even be able to transfer to art history at the end of my first year. I've got in, Maureen, I've got in.'

So Imelda was only right about one of us. Is that because she's working class and can't read Elisabeth's psyche – or did Elisabeth twist her fate by being so pushy? 'I knew you'd get in,' I say to her truthfully.

She's so thrilled by her news that we've reached the bus stop before she stops talking about herself.

'He didn't mention art till the end of my interview,' I tell her, too proud to show that I'm hurt.

'And did he ask you a difficult question?' says Elisabeth as though I come from the soft school.

'He gave me a statue of David to look at.'

'That was by Michelangelo,' she smiles as a bus rounds the corner. 'I saw it on his desk.'

'How do you know?' I ask, impressed.

'Everyone knows Michelangelo's David. It's the main icon of the High Renaissance.'

'When was it made?'

Elisabeth has stopped listening. 'Don't tell Wilfie he showed you a naked statue,' she says anxiously, 'or she'll murder me for leaving you without a chaperone.'

As I grope in my pocket for the bus fare, my fingers touch Lol's lucky black poodle, and I remember how Elisabeth sneered at my sister's tight skirts and backcombed hair.

'Piers meant to help you by choosing a Biblical figure,' she says. 'I'm sorry you didn't recognise it.'

I fight back a quiver of laughter.

'At least you won't have to see Dr Piers Superior Palfrey again,' she adds as she flags down a bus.

'Oh, but I will,' I say with a wicked surge of pleasure, 'because I got in too. He told me at the end of the interview. From next October I'll be seeing him every day.'

The Rambling Rector

A bin bag in one hand and a gardening glove on the other, I scoop up the empty Heineken cans from the back lawn while Columba scrubs out a rude word chalked on the grotto. This morning we got an unexpected letter. As a reward for getting Elisabeth and me into university, Maria Goretti's sending two replacements from South Africa – and they're flying in to Manchester at this very moment. Sister Xavier's a lecturer and Sister Bertilla's a nurse in need of a rest cure.

'We should have got more notice,' says Mother Wilfred, shoving the letter back in its envelope. She spots a polystyrene tray from the Chinese chippy in the middle of the lawn. 'You had better dial me a taxi,' she tells Columba with a cross face. 'And you, Maureen, can pick up that litter. It creates a bad impression.'

As the taxi rattles her off to the airport, the tired old convent breathes a sigh of relief. It's the first real day of spring and the kitchen door is standing open. Inside,

Gonzaga can be heard riddling the Aga, and from the community room comes the sound of Ursula practising a new hymn on her guitar to the tune of 'I am the Walrus'.

Putting down my bin bag I watch the sooty pigeons peck at a rosary of crumbs scattered this morning – the down-and-outs of the bird world who have to make do with St Cuthbert's stale bread and scrubby grass. The garden is smothered in weeds, and most of the roses are turning to briars. Coming from Moses Street where everyone makes do with a back yard, I don't feel too bothered. Gardens are for rich suburbanites who are happy only when they're walled in. As for me, I sympathise with the scallies who climb in at night to spray their tags and dump tinnies on our lawn. Even the plants seem to be on the scallies' side: the buddleia has invaded the top rows of brick, making the wall easier to scale. My dad could rebuild it in a morning if Wilfie would let him, but she's sworn never to allow a man into the enclosure.

Though I should be helping Columba, I let my eyes stray to the block of flats where a woman in jogging shorts waters her window box. It's enough for her, I decide, and should be enough for us – especially with the park just over the road, with its tennis courts, bowling greens and lads knocking footballs about the grass . . .

'The secateurs have gone from the garden shed.' Columba's voice, gone high with anxiety, cuts across my thoughts.

Someone's been lifting things from St Cuthbert's, coming over the wall at night and helping himself to odds and ends. Not the scallies, I feel sure, who'd never bother nicking secateurs, garden gloves, a ball of green twine – but someone who wants us unsettled.

'It's strange,' says Columba as I hurry across the grass, 'because none of the locks have been forced.'

'Maybe they got in during the day.'

'But one of us would have noticed.'

'All the same, we'd better keep the shed locked.'

'They were good secateurs,' says Columba sadly. 'Now we'll have to manage with the kitchen scissors.'

I sneak the scissors from the dresser drawer when Gonzaga's not looking, then hurry back to the garden, rejoicing in the fresh and loamy air and the white of the pear-tree blossom.

'I know it's Holy Obedience,' I say as Columba snips the dead shoots, 'but it's a pity we have to cut them back.'

Columba straightens her back. 'But it's Grand National Day – we always do the roses.'

'It's just that they look so stunted.'

'We've got to tidy up for the newcomers.'

'That might be them up there,' I say as a plane speeds out of a cloud. In it I imagine two gingerbread women, their faces burnt by the African sun and their eyes growing wide at the thirty-nine convents of Liverpool, surrounded like stately homes by their spreading lawns.

'It's heading the wrong way,' says Columba, pointing the scissors. 'The airport's over there.'

While she carries the dead shoots to the compost heap, I turn to the convent and allow my eyes to linger on its crumbling masonry and old sash windows. Since noting Dr Palfrey's scorn for its Jacobean-style front, I've begun to study the back where the softer, darker brickwork is broken up by a fretwork of drainpipes and is, as Dr Palfrey would say, less . . . ostentatious.

'You've stopped working again,' says Columba. 'I hope

you aren't going to turn idle when you're a student. You're not nearly so handy about the place as you used to be.'

I bend down to gather the last of the pruned twigs. 'From now on I'll work like a slave.'

'It's too late,' says Columba. 'They're here.'

Mother Wilfred is pacing towards us, the new nuns in her wake. These are no sunburnt missionaries. Sister Xavier is the palest woman I've ever seen, with sandy eyebrows and invisible lashes. She's nearly as tall as Mother Wilfred and her feet, clad in white stockings and sandals, are large and splayed. Sister Bertilla, who scarcely comes up to her shoulder, is short, broad and black.

'So English women are not answering God's call,' says Xavier to Columba and me, as though holding us personally responsible. When we fail to reply she stares at the grass, as though wanting to graze it.

Glad of my gardening gloves, I snatch up a used condom I've spied at her feet and then, blushing furiously, drop it in the bin bag while Wilfie turns to her hastily. 'You will be a light shining in the darkness.'

'In the past England sent us many priests and nuns,' says Xavier, 'and now she is short of labourers in her own vineyard.'

While Xavier looks solemn, Bertilla, far from being the burnt-out religious I expected, seems permanently on the brink of laughter. 'Let's hope that England is truly grateful, my sisters,' she says in her chuckling voice. 'I've heard you don't always welcome immigrants – especially black ones.'

I want to say that there is no racism in Liverpool because black and white live happily side by side, but feel unexpectedly shy in the presence of these strangers.

84

'Why is it,' says Xavier after a pause, 'that there are no more English vocations?'

'Today's girls are given too much freedom,' replies the Superior with a glare at Bertilla. 'They have never learnt to be selfless.'

Instead of keeping quiet, like most people who've been glared at by Mother Wilfred, Bertilla chuckles again and plants her hands on her hips. 'I like your garden,' she says with a glance at the overgrown flower beds.

'That's good,' says Mother Wilfred more coldly than ever. 'We need someone to tidy it up.'

The light turns pale as though about to drown us in skimmed milk, and Xavier draws her shawl round her arms. 'In Jo'burg today it's seventy degrees.' Her accent is thin and pained as though someone is pinching her nostrils. 'When may I see the classrooms?'

She picks her way after Mother Wilfred towards the school. 'Xavier used to be one of those hippies,' explains Bertilla. 'She lived on raw wheat and it tore out her stomach lining. Now she can't put on weight – so we call her Sister uNowanga.'

'The old nuns are longing to meet you,' I tell Bertilla, pulling off my gardening gloves. It's a lie. Only this morning the ailing Pious swore that she'd never trust a foreigner. Goodness knows what she'll say on discovering that Bertilla's black.

'All in good time,' says Bertilla. Her voice is strong and deep as though she's not afraid of being overheard. 'First I'll take a look at these sick little bushes.'

Swaying her solid hips, she strolls ahead of us across the grass while Columba shoots me a puzzled glance. I can only shrug back. I like Bertilla's friendliness and the way she opens her mouth without waiting to hear what people think. Though sure of herself as any Choir nun, she's kind and friendly like a lay sister. But I can tell she's already offended Wilfie, and feel worried by her casual manner. She doesn't know what Wilfie's like when crossed, or the penances she can dish out.

Bertilla points at the bush Columba's just finished pruning. 'What do you call this?'

'That's a rose,' offers Columba.

'I know it's a rose! I mean, what kind of rose?'

'Grace Abounding,' replies Columba. 'Mother Wilfred's favourite.'

'Impossible,' says Bertilla. 'Grace Abounding is a bush and this is a climber. What are its flowers like?'

'Cream to start with, fading to white.'

'Probably a Rambling Rector,' replies Bertilla, 'one of my favourites.'

'So we could let it climb?' I ask hopefully.

'Ai, Maureen, you'll get me into trouble with Mother Wilfie,' says Bertilla, not looking too bothered about it, 'and I've had trouble enough in my life.'

'What do you mean?'

'Let's just say that I don't want to cause a disturbance.'

'Mother Wilfred won't notice what you do in the garden – as long as you act polite.'

'In a few years the Rambling Rector would reach the top of the grotto.' Bertilla sifts some soil through her fingers which are delicately tipped with pink. 'The earth here is good, very fertile.'

'That's why things need cutting back,' says Columba anxiously.

'Ag, don't you know that roses long for the wild? You can

meddle with them for years, but they go their own way in the end.'

'How do you know all this?'

'I spent three years of my life in Queenstown, the rose-growing capital of South Africa.'

'If we leave the other roses unpruned,' I say, catching Bertilla's enthusiasm, 'they'll grow smaller and less . . . ostentatious – and we could let the suckers trail over that flower bed.'

'That would be bad for the . . .'

'Their berries would be good for the birds,' Bertilla's strong deep voice drowns Columba's light one, 'and if we left that patch of nettles it would bring the butterflies.'

'A charm of goldfinches feeds on those thistles.' Columba is looking hungry and hopeful, like a chick poking out of its shell. 'That is, when I forget to dig them up. And a tawny owl lives in that tree.'

'*umZwelele*!' hoots Bertilla. As her voice rings round the garden a face appears at the infirmary window. It's old Sister Pious, her features tugged into a disapproving knot. 'In South Africa we have nonnetjie owls – but no tawny owls.'

'*umZwelele* tu-whit tu-whoo.' Columba, who hasn't seen Pious, echoes Bertilla's hoot. 'He sings on the roof during Compline.' She clouts the Rambling Rector with the side of her spade, then swings round to face Our Lady who's staring down sadly at the graffiti on her plinth. 'Do you think she'll mind about the weeds?'

'She'll like them better.' By now Bertilla's laugh is so loud that it's hard to believe no one's banged on the window to stop her. 'Why did she appear to little Bernadette on a rubbish heap in the veld?'

Far from being offended, Columba looks happier than I've ever seen her. 'We could plant a butterfly border with mustard, nettles and red valerian. Our Lady would love to see more butterflies.'

'And I could use the mustard and nettles in the infirmary. Ai, but we could work wonders with all this space.'

'I don't think that Pious and Placid will eat mustard and nettles,' I say but the others are too excited to listen.

'We could plant vegetables and sell them cheap to the people in the tower block,' says Columba.

'Then they might stop throwing their frenchies over the wall,' chuckles Bertilla.

'There's rain on the way,' I warn them as the poplars begin to rattle their downy white underleaves against the sky.

'But it's only just stopped,' says Bertilla. 'Your nice spring day didn't last.'

'They never do,' replies Columba as the pear tree rains down its blossom. She picks up a red feather and sticks it in her veil. 'But never mind – it's time for tea. Have you ever eaten strawberry jam?'

'Yes I have, Sisi.' Bertilla starts laughing all over again. 'Have you ever eaten *phutu*?' Ignoring Columba's puzzled face she links her arm through hers as they hurry towards the back door, leaving me to follow with the bin bag and kitchen scissors.

Holey Poverty

Lorraine teeters into the convent parlour, slots in a No. 6 before she's even sat down and aims the match at the empty grate. She's the same height as our mam but where Mam is spare Lorraine is plump with a pink face and showy figure and clothes so loud they need volume control. Or did. She's gone drab since I saw her last and thin as a stray cat.

'Mind where you flick your ash,' I tell her. What with term starting tomorrow it'll be days before I can sweep the parlour.

'*Mind where you flick your ash,*' she mimics in a bossy little voice then adds sarcastically, 'That's sound, that is, *Sister* Maureen.'

I shut up at once and look for a saucer. I'm worried about my big sister, worried about her chewed nails and hair gone lank with failure. Only her shoes are the same – the highest heels you can buy with tiny little bows on the back.

'Friggin' hospitable.' After balancing the saucer on the arm of her chair, she rubs at a scorch mark on her sleeve.

She says it's being on the dole that's done her head in.

'I'll soon be a student,' I say into the silence.

'At least you'll be close to home.' In a fit of daring Lorraine went to study in Sussex, which is further south than any O'Shaunessy has ever gone. 'If you can call this place home,' she adds, huddling into her jacket. It's the first week in October and far too early to light a fire.

'My interview was a piece of cake,' I say, wanting her to look pleased.

'My interview was a piece of cake an' all,' says Lol, who like Everton this season is low on verve.

'And then what happened?' I ask though I know from her pinched white face that she doesn't want to talk about it.

'Then I got to mix with a load of little snobs and we didn't see eye to eye.'

'In what way?'

'In every way – me politics, me accent – even me clothes.'

'Get on with you!' With her royal-blue polo-neck sweater, white boots and red hot pants, Lorraine used to look like a model.

She shakes her head. 'I was dressed from the wrong catalogue,' she says, adding in a posh accent, 'Your skirts are too short and *far* too tight, and why are they all in *Crimplene*? Not,' she goes back to her normal voice, 'that I wanted to look like them in their stupid Jaeger.'

'You should have all worn the same gear – like footballers signed up for the one team.'

Lorraine's little yellow finger knocks at its cigarette. 'Worse still was me accent. At first they thought I was putting it on so they began doing it too, asking if I knew John and Cilla. I wanted to be friends so I played along but underneath I couldn't stand their bad imitations and smug bloody faces. I'd have felt better if they'd meant to be cruel but they thought it was funny. In the end I lashed out and said I didn't know John bloody Lennon because he was posh and went to Quarry. And besides, his Liverpool accent was nearly as phoney as theirs.

'"No need to get uptight," said one of them, giving me a funny look. From then on they had it in for me. "Hello whack," they'd say whenever they saw me – in lectures, in the union, everywhere. Their stupid voices nearly drove me spare. I didn't tell Mam and Dad in case it upset them. Now I wish I had – it would have saved Mam's feelings in the end.'

'How does Mam come into this?' I ask nervously.

'Well, you know she's got this sixth sense when one of us is unhappy.'

I nod, remembering the novenas, postal orders and weekly food parcels – as though Sussex was a war zone. But our mam isn't one to solve things by remote control. It was before I entered the convent and I remember the long hot Friday we spent making pies, scones and fruit cake. Then the next morning Mam put on the turquoise suit with a fur collar that she'd bought for Auntie Eileen's wedding and boarded the early coach with a suitcase in one hand and in the other a plazzy bag full of home baking.

'There was a kitchenette at the end of our corridor in hall,' continues Lol without looking at me, 'and Mam saw it was in a mess. Which it usually was because none of them lazy little cows could be arsed to clean up. And I wasn't going to be their skivvy.'

I see our Lol tottering out of the kitchen with her head high, and the amused faces at her back.

'Mam began washing up – she'd even brought her apron

and rubber gloves.' Lol's voice has gone harsh and crude, a sure sign she's about to hit something painful. 'She'd nearly finished when one of the little cows came in and dumped a load more dishes on the draining board and told her to do them. She thought Mam was the cleaner.'

I laugh – and then remember that Mam *is* a cleaner. 'So what did she do?'

'Sad to say she carried on washing up, because she thought they were my friends. But I could see she was upset and then I got upset too because I can't stand it when she acts the martyr.'

I nod. On off days Mam models herself on Jennifer Jones in *The Song of Bernadette*, with lots of sighs and long-suffering looks. I remember her coming back from Brighton a day early but apart from saying Lol was OK she stayed tight-lipped.

'Why didn't you tell one of your teachers?'

'You mean the lecturers? Fat lot they cared.'

I remember Dr Palfrey's questions about the Dingle – as though it was a foreign country – and wish I hadn't been so gabby. Struggling to change the subject, I take a small packet from my pocket. 'Your lucky black poodle worked wonders.'

'Sometimes I think Mam and you need your superstitious heads looking at.' Lorraine pitches the dog into the bin then looks at her watch. It's the longest she's stayed at St Cuthbert's since she left school. 'I've only told you all this so you'll be prepared – after so long away from the world.'

You get snobs in the convent too, I want to reply, but don't because it would be disloyal. And besides, there's no need. Didn't Bosco teach us both elocution?

Lorraine is staring at my long brown skirt. 'That stupid

old habit won't help. What happened to your new look?'

'It got old and wore out and we've no money for more material.'

'Holey poverty,' says Lorraine.

It's her first attempt at a smile so I force myself to smile back – but privately I detest the yards of extra serge which hamper my stride and have to be looped up before I can start cleaning. Instead of the calf-length skirts and short veils adopted by the order in the 1960s, we're back in our old-style habits. Only our headgear is different, because the white starched coifs have been squashed out of shape in storage. But the waist-length brown veils have survived and are now tied at the back of our necks by two tapes.

It started with Bertilla and Xavier. Their white African cotton was too thin even for what Xavier calls the execrable English summer; but there was no money, said Mother Wilfred, for thicker cloth. Then Xavier, zealous in her new role of school librarian, went to inspect the art books which Wilfie had stowed in the attic, and spotted the yards of brown serge abandoned after the Vatican Council.

'There's a lot of wear in these habits,' she told the Superior, fingering the dusty cloth. 'Why don't we use them?'

Mother Wilfred seemed pleased by the suggestion and agreed to put it to the community during Chapter.

'A good idea,' said Kevin with a glance at her varicose veins. 'We look like a bunch of frights.'

Gonzaga, Pious and Placid nodded complacently, having refused to change their habits the first time round on grounds of age and infirmity.

'And,' said Bosco with a glance at Elisabeth and me, 'our student nuns will be modestly clad.'

'We can't traipse round in floor-length habits,' said Elisabeth with a grimace. 'We'll look out of place.'

'Out of place!' snorted Mother Wilfred. 'You'll be more in place than anyone else. Scholars have dressed like that since St Hilda's day.'

'It goes against the new spirit,' countered Elisabeth. 'Maria Goretti will have a heart attack.'

'And who appointed you to speak for Mother General?'

Elisabeth looked mutinous but said nothing and Wilfie was beginning the Hail Mary which signalled the end of Chapter when Bertilla cleared her throat and spoke. 'I won't be wearing that old habit, Mother Wilfie.'

'It's a question of Holy Poverty,' replied Mother Wilfred with an astonished glance at the African nun, who was sitting with her legs crossed and one arm hooked over the back of her chair. 'We have no money to buy you a new one.'

'Then I'll stick with the white,' said Bertilla, 'even though it's as cold as charity in this place.'

'This is not South Africa,' replied Mother Wilfred impressively. 'We do things democratically here – which means a majority decision.'

Bertilla gestured at Gonzaga, Pious and Placid. 'Then why did the old ones stay with the long habit?'

'Sister Gonzaga suffers from neuralgia, and the short veil would have left her neck exposed to draughts. As for Sisters Pious and Placid, they joined us when their retirement home was closed down. They have a long history of service, and it is our job to make their closing years as peaceful as possible. Now please sit modestly, Sister Bertilla. This is a convent, not a shebeen.'

I, who have never dared speak out in Chapter, stared in admiration at the black nun. Though her eyes were a little more watery than usual, her arm remained hooked defiantly over the back of her chair. 'I too believe in democracy,' she was telling Mother Wilfred, 'but I can't remember being consulted.'

The Superior looked taken aback, and for a moment it seemed as though she was going to give in. Then she cast a glance round the room. 'Very well,' she smiled, 'we can consult everyone now. All in favour of the old habit please raise their hands.'

Up went the hands of Kevin, Bosco, Brigid, Xavier, Pious and Placid.

'There,' said Mother Wilfred to Bertilla, 'a majority decision.' And that was how it went. Bertilla and Elisabeth voted against. Ursula was at a parents' meeting. Gonzaga, Columba and I had no vote at all, being lay sisters.

'Perhaps you'll pull through where I didn't,' Lorraine says to me now as she hauls herself to her feet. 'You're tougher than me, despite your flaky ways.'

'Me, flaky?' I protest, glad Lorraine doesn't know about the Holy Army of lay sisters or how I pray to St Bernadette that Everton will beat Man Utd.

'Anyone who wastes their life in a convent is flaky.' Lorraine shivers as she looks round the pale green walls, grown shabbier than ever since her last visit.

I wait till she's putting on her coat then scoop the black poodle from the bin and slip it in my pocket. 'Eternity is spent with God,' I tell her, 'so it makes sense to spend this life —'

'Don't give me that crap,' she cuts in. 'I heard it too often from Bosco. And yes, I saw you grovelling in the bin when you thought my back was turned. Maybe the uni's a good idea after all — knock a bit of sense into you.'

'Or maybe I'll knock a bit of sense into the uni.'

'Then you'd better stop acting airy-fairy and learn to play their game.'

I'm longing to ask what their game is so I can start practising straightaway. But a glance at her taut sad face changes my mind, and I follow her in silence as she teeters towards the door.

The Big Match

I was going to take a last-minute look at my book list but Lol's visit has made me feel edgy – so edgy that I iron my best veil, then darn a hole in my sleeve and shine my shoes. My success at interview was a fluke, I think, spitting into the dried-out polish. Worse still, I know nothing about art history and by cheating my way in have kept out someone cleverer. Tomorrow is my day of reckoning.

Only when my shoes shine like conkers do I put them back on and prowl up and down the corridors, hoping for a sign from the Holy Army. But all I can hear is the clatter of Ursula's Remington, and an early owl hooting in the pear tree. I drift on to the back lawn and, as the lights come on in the tower block, think how nice it would be if someone there was doing Art History. I'm wondering if Dr Palfrey will remember me, and if the posh girl who spoke to Elisabeth has decided on Liverpool, when I glimpse a movement in front of the grotto, and sense rather than see a white shape: the ghost of a long-dead lay sister, perhaps, risen from the grave to wish me luck, and now floating towards me across the grass.

'*Vuka*, Maureen! What are you doing?' Bertie's rich warm voice engulfs me.

'Er – I'm saying tirrah to the back garden.'

'You sound as though you're off to Jupiter,' replies Bertie, planting her spade in the earth.

'I'm scared they'll test me on me holiday reading.'

Bertie places her hands on her solid hips. 'Go and do something straightaway, then you'll feel better.'

'I'd rather help you lock away your tools. It's nearly dark and—'

'Maureen – *hamba!*' Grabbing me by the elbows, Bertie propels me to the back door.

Through the frosted glass of the community room window I can see the shapes of the Choir nuns bent over their marking. With Bertie's eyes on my back I march towards them across the grass.

The Choir nuns look up in surprise when I open the community-room door, because normally I come in here only to darn their stockings. Trying not to feel self-conscious, I slip down the aisle to the back row, raise my desk lid and gaze at the fountain-pen bought by Mam and Dad, and beside it my brand-new notepads, pencils and textbook, *An Introduction to Art History*. The Archdeacon has given Elisabeth and me a book allowance, and though most of the titles cost more than a week's groceries I made myself buy this one slim paperback.

With hands made meaty by years of housework I prise it open and weigh down the pages. Whatever the price of study, I'll have to pay it: for the sake of my sisters and their high school, for Mam, Dad and the Archdeacon, and most of all for Lorraine. With her ashy little voice still echoing in my ears, I swear I'll show the world I can make it, and that Dingle girls don't always wilt under pressure.

But the spine of my new book cracks before I've started, and some of the pages spring loose. The Choir nuns' backs, broad and identical under their veils, seem to stiffen reproachfully. Ahead of me is Sister Kevin, towering over a pile of exercise books. She sighs as she turns a page, while Bosco harumphs into the air and Ursula clucks back from the far side of the room: a group of dotty old teachers who've been together so long they've got their own language.

Feeling sinfully lazy without my mending, I stare at the first page. *Chapter One: The Art Forms of Antiquity*. But my concentration is shattered by the crash of the door and the stamp of feet down the aisle. Then a dustpan and brush are slammed on top of my book.

'If you must let that sister of yours smoke in the parlour, you could at least sweep up her ash.'

'I'm sorry, Sister Brigid — I meant to but —' The dustpan is smudging my brand-new book.

'Please will you shift your feet.'

It's not a question but an order and I'm about to answer back when I remember her tight hurt face on hearing I'd been accepted.

'Will you shift your feet?' she says again.

'Be quiet, dear,' says Kevin. 'We're trying to do our marking.'

Brigid leans on the desk with one square-tipped hand and with the other nudges her broom into a pile of dust which scatters under my feet. Her mother was a cleaner like mine, so she knows how to goad me with slovenly work.

'I'll do that,' I offer. To clean well you have to throw your heart and soul into it.

'I've been told you've got to study.'

'That's not my fault.' My voice has risen so high that Kevin looks up for a second time.

Brigid bends over her broom with a cross face while I try once again to focus on my book. But the words skid away as I read. I'm not up to it, I want to cry. Lol was brighter than me and got better A levels. If she failed, what will become of me? Five minutes later Brigid slams out of the room and I too give up and go to bed, where I dream of being chased by a giant Michelangelo's David with a cricket bat in his hand.

By the morning I'm so nervous that I almost wish I was Elisabeth, who climbs on the bus to the uni as though it's the most normal thing in the world.

'God, this place is a dump,' she says, glancing through the window at the Boulevard. I follow her gaze to a lime-green Capri rusting in the gutter, but feel too nervous to reply. If only we were doing the same subject, but the English Department is in a different building, and we spend our day in separate queues – for our major subject, our minor subject, a union card we'll never be allowed to use, a book-shop voucher and a library card. I'm only seven or eight-years older than my fellow students but it feels more like a hundred, as though the weight of St Cuthbert's is on my back, and all the anxious hopes of my sisters.

'Hello,' I say, first to one student and then another. 'I'm Sister Maureen.'

But instead of replying they either giggle or answer politely then turn away. Only once in the library do I catch sight of Elisabeth, chatting to a student in clever, understated clothes, while I hover on the edge of the crowd like an anonymous brown bird.

'How did you get on?' Columba is waiting for us by the front door, her eyes bright as a mother hen's.

'It was tedious,' I tell her, 'tedious and lonely.'

'Maureen will feel better when her seminars begin,' Elisabeth puts in. 'It's difficult, being a fresher.'

The bell has gone for the end of school and the Choir nuns are in the refectory, where they ask about our day over bread and jam.

'It was the greatest possible fun,' Elisabeth butts in again. 'Luckily I get on well with young people.'

'Not too well, I hope.' Mother Wilfred peers over her half-moons. 'You must keep a distance between you and them. You are in the world but not of it.'

'Yes, Mother.'

From the way Elisabeth smirks and lowers her eyes, I know she's no intention of obeying. She is in her element at last – hobnobbing all day with her own kind. As for me, I find it easy for once to obey Wilfie, and spend the rest of the week without speaking to a soul.

The only person not to troop down to the basement coffee bar at the end of Friday afternoon, I read the notices on the board while waiting for Elisabeth. As my eye travels down a list I thank God for all the student societies: Real Ale Soc, Disco Soc, Sex Soc, Netball Soc. At least I can try to catch up while the others enjoy themselves. I'm wondering what Soc Soc can possibly be when Elisabeth saunters through the main door.

'What's up?'

A stocky boy with blond curls has appeared by the

noticeboard. Though he, like me, said nothing in our seminar this afternoon, he's looking cheerful and unabashed.

'Let's go home,' I whisper to Elisabeth.

Elisabeth turns towards the basement steps which are lit by a lurid orange light like the mouth of hell in a miracle play. 'It's pouring with rain,' she says. 'Why don't we go for a cup of tea?'

Two girls, one blonde, one chestnut-haired, stride past and run down the steps, their pageboys bouncing on the collars of their matching camel coats. Although the chestnut-haired girl is also in my seminar group she doesn't even glance in my direction.

'I don't want to go down there. And besides, I've no money.'

'I'll pay,' said Elisabeth. 'I saved my bus fare by walking in on Tuesday.'

'We don't have permission,' I remind her, with another glance at the blond boy, who seems to have moved closer.

A lay sister should never correct a Choir nun – as Elisabeth reminds me with a warning glance. 'Wilfie doesn't know our timetables yet – we can do what we think best.'

The girl called Sasha swings by in the sort of raincoat advertised in front of stately homes. 'You'll feel better when you've made a few friends,' says Elisabeth.

'I don't want to make friends,' I reply as Sasha runs down the steps with a wave. A shriek of laughter rises from the bottom, to be drowned by the throb of the juke-box. 'I want to – learn.' I really mean that I want to catch up on art history while my fellow students waste their time – but I'd never admit that to Elisabeth.

'The best students learn from discussion,' she tells me, moving towards the steps. 'Timmy says so.'

'But these are art history students. You should be learning from English students.'

'I'm trying to help you fit in. Come on, I'll introduce you.'

While Elisabeth joins the queue at the counter, I look round for somewhere to sit. There are no free benches, only a corner booth already occupied by three girls who spring to their feet as I sit. The noise level's no higher than in the Welly Vaults so why, I wonder, does it grate my ears? At least half the people in the room are smoking – not No. 6's like Lorraine's but the kind of long white tube seen in colour supplements. The ventilator fan flaps intermittently, failing to dispel the reek of tobacco, damp wool and French perfume.

Sasha is nowhere to be seen, but at the table across the aisle the two pageboys are flirting with a hook-nosed man. 'Hamish, you're so sweet!' squawks the blonde. 'Isn't he a riot?' the chestnut screams back, then looks round the room as though expecting applause. Soon they're joined by a tall man in a green quilted waistcoat who grumbles about the Liverpool weather. And so it goes on from table to table. No matter how stupid, each remark is made at full volume so that everyone has to hear it.

For the first time in years I'm feeling homesick – not for St Cuthbert's but the Dingle with its chip shops, docklands and corner pubs. I remind myself how I always hated the Welly Vaults with its frowsty seats and the shoving round the bar at last orders. But it has to be better than here, I decide, as another braying vowel sound pierces the air. At least the voices in the Welly don't get on your nerves, because they intertwine with things beyond themselves: the crash of waves on the sea wall at the end of the street, the ships' sirens on the estuary, and most of all with each other, making one harmonious roar, like the noise from the Kop on a winter afternoon or the fabulous sound of . . .

'Cheer up!' says Elisabeth. 'You look like Job on his dunghill.'

I wonder how I'll cope with three long years.

'We had a terrific discussion about Joo See today.' She slaps down two cups. The tea, I can tell, is made with tea bags, and flecks of powdered milk are floating on the surface.

'Joo See?'

'*Julius Caesar*. The tutor said I showed insight.'

'Lucky you.' Earlier that afternoon I had my first seminar with Dr Palfrey, determined after interview day to guard my runaway tongue. I needn't have worried. He only smiled at me once, and seemed far more interested in the chestnut pageboy and her family home in Orvieto.

Elisabeth's reply is drowned by a record on the juke-box – a loud, rough number I've never heard before. *Don't stand so, don't stand so, don't stand so close to me!* caws the singer. Which is ironic, because no one's standing anywhere near us. Across the aisle the girls who moved when I sat down are greeting the boy with blond curls. Polystyrene cup in hand, he stares for a second at the empty seats opposite us, then gives us an apologetic smile and squeezes in beside the girls. Other students are crowding round the serving-hatch, the juke-box and even flowing through the doorway and up the steps. On the far side of the room I can see Sasha detaching herself from her group and moving towards us.

'I say,' she smiles down at Elisabeth, 'aren't you a friend of Bernard's?'

'That's right.' Elisabeth smiles back. 'I'm Elisabeth

Bavidge – now Sister Elisabeth. We spoke on the day of Sister Maureen's interview.'

'So you're not reading art history?'

'No – I'm doing English, worse luck.'

Sasha's silk scarf is covered with horses' heads linked by little chains and stirrups. 'I wouldn't say that. This isn't a terribly good department. I applied to Manchester but didn't get the grades.' She glances at me as though I'm a ketchup stain then turns her attention back to Elisabeth. 'Are you coming to the Freshers' Conference?'

'What's that?' I ask as Elisabeth shakes her head.

'A Fresher is a First Year – like you,' says Sasha as though I'm an idiot, 'and the Freshers' Conference is a series of student events.'

'What about?' I ask, anxious not to fall further behind.

'They're not *about* anything.' Sasha's little horses stare down their noses at me. 'There's a trip on the Mersey ferry, a pub crawl, a cheese and wine party and a rock concert.' She waves a bunch of tickets. 'Tonight there's a disco – for people to get to know each other.'

'We nuns can't go to that sort of thing, worse luck,' says Elisabeth.

I remember my teens when I used to dance every Saturday in the Beverly Hills ballroom till my legs ached. 'It's not worse luck,' I blurt out. 'It's part of being a nun.'

At that the horses' heads glaze over completely, as though left in a bed by the Mafia.

'Oh well, another time.' Sasha drifts back to the far side of the room.

The smoke from her St Moritz is lying on my tongue like a dirty blanket. 'There won't be another time,' I call after her but my words are drowned by a peal of laughter from the chestnut pageboy.

Elisabeth adjusts her veil, which has slid to one side during the afternoon. 'How can you be so rude?' she asks reproachfully. We rise to our feet and begin pushing our way towards the steps. 'Sasha is young and bright and she's come to live in your city.'

The rain is now heavier than ever and my shoes are beginning to let in the wet. 'Sasha couldn't care less about *my* city,' I say, aware I sound just like my dad. 'She'd have gone to Manchester if she'd had the chance.'

'That's not a mortal sin,' says Elisabeth as we head for the bus stop. Just as we reach the back of the queue there's a squeal of tyres by the kerb. A battered Morris Traveller stops beside us and the curly-haired boy from the coffee bar leans across the passenger seat to wind down the window.

'You live by Seffie Park, don't you?' His voice is pleasingly broad and Northern. 'Fancy a lift?'

'How do you know our address?' I ask, moving towards the car.

'My big sister used to go to St Cuthbert's – before your time, I should think.'

'Aren't you going to the disco?'

'I wish I was, given the weather.' The boy jerks his thumb towards an Adidas bag on the back seat. 'But I've arranged to go pot-holing.'

'If you could drop us off,' I say, opening the car door, 'that would be great.'

The boy pushes the front seat forward and tips his Adidas bag on the floor. The handle of a pick-axe is poking out through the zip. 'One of you will have to sit in the back.'

'Sister Maureen,' cries Elisabeth from the pavement, 'what on earth are you doing?'

'Climb in,' I call from the rear seat. 'We'll be home in time for tea.'

'Thank you so much,' Elisabeth chirps at the boy, 'but here's the 86. It goes quite close to our convent.' Without waiting to see if I'll follow, she moves with the queue to the waiting bus.

Muttering an apology, I back out of the car. Though the boy's smile is broad his cheeks are pink – but whether from anger or amusement I can't tell.

'There was no need to be rude,' I snap at Elisabeth as his car rattles off down the road.

'That's rich, coming from you!'

'He was only being friendly.'

'We can't accept a lift from an unknown man.'

'Just because he doesn't wear a Burberry,' I retort as we shuffle to the top of queue. 'He's a student – and a Catholic at that.'

The bus is full. Its doors swing shut with a *whumph* and it pulls away from the kerb. I stare down the road through a veil of rain. There are no more buses in sight.

Advent

Bosco is teaching me how to become a Choir nun. On the first Sunday in Advent my brown serge will be swapped for a woollen habit and Mother Wilfred will hang a silver cross and chain around my neck. What with custody of the eyes, parlour manners and deportment, lessons on how to converse with the visiting clergy and my old bugbear of elocution, a Choir nun's life is harder than I thought.

'Cheer up,' says Columba as I sit sewing my new habit. 'It's supposed to be an honour.'

I touch my wooden cross with its rough brown cord. 'I'd rather keep my Second Division strip – like you have.'

'See it as a reward for talent,' says the old lay sister. 'You've been promoted.'

Though I try to smile back I'm scared that I'll be redundant. When I was a lay sister the Choir nuns depended on me to cook, clean, haul the old ones in and out of bed, and do all the other things they couldn't do or didn't want to. Now Bertilla has taken over the cooking and nursing; which is nothing, she says, compared with running a dispensary in Soweto. I see with a twinge of envy that her chores get done at record speed, leaving her plenty of time to dig her vegetables, chat to the down-and-outs and tend to the old ones.

The rest of my duties have been divided among the others, and even Brigid is learning to sweep and dust. Early in the morning I sometimes glimpse the Holy Army at the window, watching me follow Mother Wilfred across the courtyard. I'd like to wave but am too aware of Bosco's eyes on my back, so I file into chapel with the others where we warble the Divine Office in funny little voices coming out of our eyebrows.

What fight I have left is knocked out of me by the uni. The girl with the chestnut pageboy has less to say for herself these days, and I've got to know that the boy with the Morris Minor is called Toby Smart, and a girl with shorn hair is called Hannah Youel.

Unlike the others, I've now read all the books on the list and bring notes to every seminar. But whenever I make a comment they pause a second, smile politely, then carry on as though nothing's happened.

If only it was a football match with lots of mud, yelling and collisions – then I'd cut them all off at the ankles. As it is, their tactics are so refined they're impossible to follow. At the end of each seminar, when they all disappear to the coffee bar, I go to the library and wait for Elisabeth. I begin dreading Monday mornings and the sight of the other students, but when I confide my feelings to Wilfie she says she hopes I now see that competition is the devil's work, and when will I learn to accept my limitations? I'm not limited, I want to shout back – just handicapped by me background.

'See a seminar as a conversation,' advises Elisabeth as we sit in the Catholic Chaplaincy, watched suspiciously by students in anoraks and what she calls Cornish-pasty shoes. 'A conversation between equals.'

Elisabeth's kinder now she knows that I'll soon be a Choir nun, but still she misses the point. 'It's because they won't stop yakking,' I try to explain, 'so I never know when to butt in.'

Elisabeth picks one of Gonzaga's doorsteps out of her lunch box, grimaces, and flicks a bit of raw onion into the bin. 'Why on earth not?'

If she wasn't so blinkered I'd envy her, pumped up as she is by class and self-assurance. 'Leavin' aside de problem of me scouse accent,' I lay it on extra thick to hide my embarrassment, 'I can never pronounce dem foreign names.'

'You'll learn in time,' says Elisabeth airily. 'Everyone does.'

I know now that it's Michelangelo not Michael Angelo, and Renaissance with the stress on the first syllable – but a new word pops up every seminar.

'Wait till they move on to something you know about,' Elisabeth takes a neat bite out of her sandwich, 'then disagree with them – politely, of course. Academic arguments can be fun.'

I'm in the sort of mean sour mood that I'd once have cured by a punishing run in the rain followed by an hour's circuit training. On my way to the afternoon seminar I dodge into the Students' Union and when no one's looking open the door of the empty gym. It's the best equipment I've ever seen and it's sad I'll never be able to use it. Wondering why my fellow students seem to prefer the coffee bar, I carry on to Dr Palfrey's room. Today's topic is something I have strong opinions on – Catholic versus

Protestant art – and I'm determined to give it my best shot. If that doesn't work I shall go to the Archdeacon and beg him to send Brigid in my place.

'Oh God! I mean, oh gosh! I'm so sorry,' says Toby who's accidentally snagged my new veil on the zip of his Adidas bag.

'Please don't worry.'

His fair-skinned young face turns puce and he hangs back against the wall till I've chosen a seat.

My skirt's so bulky it gathers round my feet as I sit and fans out on either side so I can hardly blame the others for leaving those chairs free. While Dr Palfrey selects a book from his shelves Vicky, a redhead with a clever London face, whispers to Hannah, the student with the shaved head, and Toby and the chestnut pageboy swap lecture notes. Then Dr Palfrey takes his place and the seminar begins.

He kicks off by saying Protestant art is central to the Northern European tradition, and looks round the room with an encouraging smile. I'd like to agree with him but can't. In the Dingle we prayed for the conversion of Protestants, and Mam had to ask permission from the Archdeacon to attend the funeral of the Ulsterman who'd married my auntie. I remember the altar bare without its tabernacle, and the meaty disapproving faces. However can I be expected to appreciate their art?

Hannah is the first to speak, telling us how she once hitch-hiked to Amsterdam where she visited the Rijksmuseum every day for a week. Soon the others start chipping in with knowing remarks about the Dutch, whom they all seem to admire. You've got to be joking! I want to retort. I've looked at their paintings in the library – page after page of big fat burghers.

The central heating is on full but instead of turning it down or opening a window Dr Palfrey takes off his jacket and hangs it on the back of his chair. The students in their T-shirts and jeans look at ease, but in a habit designed for stone cloisters I'm starting to swelter.

'So who knows about Catholic art,' says Dr Palfrey with a smile in my direction, 'and how do you suppose it differs?'

'I'm afraid I find it rather sentimental,' chirps the chestnut pageboy with a little wriggle. 'All those highlights and low lights.'

I may not like the pictures at St Cuthbert's but they have to be better than anything Dutch. Jesus curing the man born blind, Jesus preaching in the courtyard of His friend Lazarus – even Mother Wilfred's Madonnas: at least they're about something important. I'm waiting for Dr Palfrey to put the pageboy in her place, when to my surprise he starts agreeing with her.

'Catholic art can be rather nacreous,' he says with another smile in my direction.

Feeling like a lone defender in the face of two strikers, I remember Elisabeth's advice: it's OK to tell them I disagree. But I've forgotten what the pageboy said, and don't know the meaning of the word nacreous. As though sensing my wish to speak, Dr Palfrey holds up his hand in the middle of a statement from Vicky.

'Protestant art is last,' I say loudly and wait for them to come back just like my dad would in the Welly Vaults.

'That's fighting talk.' Dr Palfrey sounds like a man who can take any ball in his stride, no matter how badly delivered. 'Has no one got an answer for Sister Maureen?'

Hannah examines the toe of her shoe while the others look as though someone's made a rude noise. Then the pageboy begins talking to Dr Palfrey about yet another artist I've never heard of, and the conversation closes over my head. The room grows hotter than ever and for the rest of the hour I sit in silence while the sweat soaks my serre-tête and runs from my armpits to my waistband. And then, while the others stand chatting outside, I blunder across the road to the library.

After plucking a book from the shelves I sit down, open it, then prop my head in my hands. It's the unhappiest I've ever been — far far worse than when Everton lost the League Cup to Villa by one goal after three final matches and extra time. I try praying to the Holy Army but know that they have no clout in this alien, snobby world. Raising my head, I see the students from my seminar group sit down at the next table without even a smile in my direction. Toby chooses the chair beside Vicky then lays a broad red hand on the back of her neck while she ducks her head and simpers. Even though I've never wanted a boyfriend this show of affection makes me feel lonelier than ever, and it's a struggle to focus on my book. We've already been given our first essay topic: three thousand words on the Dutch painting of our choice. Now Vicky and Hannah are show-ing Toby the catalogues they've doubtless picked up in the galleries of Europe. Watching their bright young faces I know for sure that I'll never stick this out.

Whatever Mother Wilfred says and no matter how dis-appointed my mam and dad, I shall write to the Archdeacon tonight and tell him I've had enough. Wondering when Elisabeth will arrive so we can get back to St Cuthbert's, I become aware of a slim figure wandering past the stacks with some books tucked under her arm. As she crosses the floor towards us I see that she's middle-aged, and wait for her to tell off the whisperers at the next table. But to my surprise she pulls out a chair and sits down beside me.

'Sister Maureen, isn't it?' With her auburn hair and chiselled nose she looks vaguely familiar. 'Dr Palfrey told me you were in his tutor group.'

Remembering how I've just made a fool of myself, I stay silent.

'He said you were finding it tough.'

'I'm packing it in,' I tell her with a sense of relief.

'I thought nuns were supposed to have guts.' The green-grey eyes are watching me keenly.

What does she know about nuns? And why does everyone feel they can give me advice? 'It's not a question of guts – it's a question of wasting three years and a lot of money.'

With her left hand, which is small and ringless, she strokes the right sleeve of her bright angora. 'Believe me, Maureen – I mean, Sister Maureen – it can be done. I was a working-class student, and I know.'

She still looks naggingly familiar – like a long-lost figure from my childhood. But where would I have known a woman whose clever shingle must have cost more than a cleaner could earn in a week?

'Come to my room tomorrow.' She gathers up her books with a smile. 'I can give you some tips for your essay.'

Perhaps Dr Palfrey has sent her to help me, knowing I'm not up to it. 'I'd rather do it on my own,' I tell her, 'or I'll feel a cheat.'

'As long as you do it.' She touches me lightly on the wrist. 'I'll see you in my workshop next term. In the meantime, come and talk if ever you feel like quitting.'

'You know all about me and I don't even know your name.'

She extends a hand too soft and white ever to have done housework. 'Julia Mulcahy.'

'But what should I call you?'

'Julia, of course.'

She pushes back her chair, looking fine-featured, sure of herself and totally unlike anyone I've ever called by their first name.

'I don't think I could.'

'Then call me Ms Mulcahy or Dr Mulcahy or whatever you like but come and see me, eh?' She pronounces the z in her title so I could never mistake it for Miss, but in her fuchsia-pink jersey and black velvet jeans she doesn't look like a women's libber.

I watch her trim figure bob towards the door while Toby starts leafing through a pot-holing magazine and Hannah chats to Vicky until a postgraduate in a hand-knitted jumper tells them to shut up.

'I want no derivative work,' Dr Palfrey has warned us, 'so don't go rummaging through the critics. Choose the painting you like best and respond to it unaided, as fully and humanly as you can.'

I begin that evening by looking round the high-school classrooms, but as I expected there's not a single Dutch painting. In the convent, too, they are all Spanish or Italian. *Highlights and low lights and acres of nacreous flesh*, I murmur, staring at Wilfie's Madonnas. Having looked up the word nacreous I'm beginning to see my tutor's point.

But my heart sinks further when I open my library books. Much as I long to succeed, I can't help jibbing at the veal-faced burgomasters, and by Compline I'm no nearer finding the right picture. Knowing it's disobedient, I borrow a torch from Bertilla and pore over yet more artists after lights out, while tiredness spreads through my brain like a tumour. Stiff with cold I wake with the rising bell, my books scattered across the coverlet and my mind blank.

'I don't know why you bother,' says Elisabeth at the bus stop. Having finished her own essay on *The Faerie Queene*, she's now telling everyone that course work is easy.

'You've had the chance to study in Rome,' I say as the 86 speeds round the corner. 'I want to catch up.'

'Then you'd better hide that torch,' says Elisabeth as she flags down the bus. 'Wilfie thinks you're not getting enough sleep.'

Ignoring the warning I continue to work after lights out for the rest of the week, and wake each morning with eyelids like sandbags. Then, when I've almost despaired of finding the right picture, I come to one I like: of a woman with a high forehead and shiny blonde hair by a follower of Cuyp.

She gazes out boldly from centre canvas, a pair of skates dangling from her hand and one high-arched foot on a footstool before a glowing fire. There are no smirking suitors, no tankards or lutes or black and white floor tiles, and her dress is not of brocade but a plain blue fabric.

At last I've found a real woman, I think with a surge of elation, a woman of energy and independence, as different as possible from the fleshy, house-proud burgesses. She's not in a parlour but a mountain hut, with a frozen lake and some evergreen trees through the window.

There's no time left to respond 'fully and humanly' so I disobey Dr Palfrey and consult the introduction. By the seventeenth century, it seems, the Dutch had lost the art of making green, so used to mix yellow with lapis lazuli.

Although Van der Huygen used more pigments than any other artist of his time he was poor, and like many people I know made do with shoddy equipment. For example, he must have resorted to smalt instead of lapis then mixed it with yellow lake pigment, which is why, I discover, the leaves outside the little window have turned blue, and the woman's skirt is so thin in places that the carpet shows through.

Headachy with exhaustion I hand in my essay next morning, aware that Vicky's, Toby's and Hannah's have already been marked and returned. During the seminar two days later I watch Dr Palfrey to see if he's read my work, but he gives no sign. I've resigned myself to waiting for my mark till after Christmas, when I meet him on the stairs at the end of the afternoon.

'Ah! Sister Maureen. Where's your chaperone?'

'In bed with a sore throat,' I reply, remembering too late that no nun is supposed to utter the word bed in a man's presence.

'She looks just like that brother of hers,' Dr Palfrey says thoughtfully, 'which is a pity, because I can't stand Beaver Bavvers – not since we were students, and he had me gated for spending a week in Venice.'

I long to tell him that Elisabeth's known among the lay sisters as the convent sneak. But that would be a gross act of disloyalty so I stare in silence at his paisley waistcoat.

'Why not come to my room for a cup of coffee?'

I hesitate for a second because in no circumstances should a nun go to a man's room unchaperoned – even if he's a tutor. I then wonder if I should ask Mrs Dagnall to sit in, but am put off by the thought of her icing-sugar claws poised over her notepad.

'Don't look so worried,' says Dr Palfrey. 'I only want to return your essay.'

I've worked far harder than Elisabeth so I should at least get a ß, like she did, maybe even a ß+. How surprised they'd be at St Cuthbert's if a one-time lay sister did better than a Choir nun. I follow Dr Palfrey to his office where he lays his bulging briefcase on the table and gestures at one of the armchairs.

'Coffee?' he asks, and without waiting for a reply pours some sticky-looking beans into a blue and white grinder with a picture of a windmill on the front. It's the first time I've seen anyone make coffee this way and it looks complicated and fiddly. Watching him turn the little handle, I wish we could settle for instant and talk about my essay.

He tips the grounds into a jug, his movements deft as a sacristan's. 'What did you think of it?' I burst out.

'Think of what?' he says, filling a kettle at the sink.

'My essay,' I croak back.

'It shows potential,' he replies, 'but you should have chosen a domestic interior.'

I remember the whey-faced burghers and their wives. 'I hate domestic interiors,' I shoot back, my voice sharper than I intended. 'They're all about owning things.'

Far from looking offended, Dr Palfrey smiles as he tips the boiling water into the pot. 'So what should art be about?'

For a moment I can't think – but then I remember the pictures at St Cuthbert's. They may be nacreous but at least they stand for something. 'Great art should tell a story – a story that leads us to higher things.'

Dr Palfrey points to a poster of a burgher's wife with a tray of tankards. 'Aren't you missing the joy of domesticity?'

I think of the effort it must have been to polish all that pewter. 'That isn't domesticity, that's just a – a dream of it.'

'But surely you can see that it's beautiful.'

The little room is filling with the smell of coffee. 'I've taken a vow of poverty,' I tell him, 'and that means not bothering with earthly possessions.' As though I had anything to renounce, I think, seeing a smile flit across his face. My home was even poorer than St Cuthbert's and its artwork would have given my tutor a heart attack.

He takes my essay from his briefcase and places it on the table. 'Surely by comparison with all that' – he waves a coffee strainer at the burgher's wife – 'your world seems rather straitened?'

'But I thought you approved of convent life . . . . at my interview . . . you seemed quite interested —'

'Interested? I was riveted! That story you told about the funny old nun in the Walker!'

No wonder Wilfie wants me chaperoned, I think, stricken. And I still haven't found the middle ground between sitting mute and giving myself away. 'I don't want to come to any more seminars,' I say to Dr Palfrey. 'Nobody listens to what I say.'

He hands me my coffee as though it's a cup of medicine. 'You can sound a little bigoted,' he says gently as I take my first sip, 'always a problem with religious people. Part of university is learning from others – which brings us back to your essay. You should have done as you were told.'

'But the woman I chose is Dutch. And she isn't bothered about owning things.'

'I didn't intend to say this, Sister,' Dr Palfrey gives an embarrassed little smile, 'but the woman in your painting is not Dutch – and she's a high-class whore.'

'Haw?' I grope for the meaning of a word I know but have never before heard spoken, then feel myself blush furiously. 'How do you know?'

'You can tell by her footstool. It's a seventeenth-century trope.'

I remember the high-arching instep posed on the yellow brocade, and the broad bold stare. 'I had no way of knowing.'

'But you picked up on one thing.' Dr Palfrey smiles again, and sips his coffee. 'Pieter van der Huygen was an Italian Catholic who adopted a Dutch name to peddle his work at the court of Queen Anne.'

'I worked far longer than the others.' My breath is coming in bursts as though I've been winded. 'And yet I've blown it.'

'Nonsense,' says Dr Palfrey. 'It's just that your taste is unformed.'

'You mean that it's bad.'

He shakes his head. 'Taste can be cultivated, which is one of the reasons why you're here. You can write me another essay before Christmas, but this time you must fall in love with all things Dutch: from Haarlem seascapes to peasant cowscapes, right down to these little blue and white coffee cups and the smell of Douwe Egbert.'

Aware of a desire to cry, I swallow hard. Christmas is the busiest time at St Cuthbert's with the convent to clean, the floors to Ronuk, dinner to be cooked for the down-and-outs and the crib to be made. I'll never find time to write an extra essay.

'What's wrong, Sister?' says Dr Palfrey.

Before I can explain there's a rap at the door and for a second I hope it's Ms Mulcahy, come to check how I'm getting on. But no, it's Mrs Fothergill who pokes her head into the room. A lecturer on the French Impressionists, she's built along the same lines as the Renoir models in the library book; but instead of looking languorous she teeters in with a swirl of flower patterns and a fox fur over her shoulders.

'Very familiar, this,' she says, 'in a tête-à-tête with your nun!'

'I'm not his nun,' I retort.

Mrs Fothergill ignores me. 'It's time, Piers.'

'Good heavens!' Dr Palfrey glances at his clock. 'Sister Maureen and I were having a talk about Dutch art.' He stands up and closes his briefcase.

'*Cara semplicità, quanto mi piaci!*' Mrs Fothergill punctuates her lectures with snatches of opera in her wobbling soprano. Although I don't understand the words she's just sung I can sense her hostility.

Dr Palfrey reaches for the coat on the back of his door. 'We're off to the early showing of *Last Year in Marienbad*,' he explains as I gulp the rest of my coffee.

'Take your essay, Sister Maureen,' he adds as I pick up my bag. 'It will be a good foundation for the next one.'

Avoiding the eye of Mrs Dagnall, who is locking up the office, I stuff the essay into my bag as I hurry through the front hall, aware of the other two chattering down the stairs behind me.

Only when I'm on the bus do I look at each page in turn but there's no sign my essay's been read until the end.

C+(+).

I read and reread the mark in the hope that I've got it wrong.

Shows potential it says underneath.

The Pride of Life

Having wangled permission from Wilfie to visit the sick, Bertilla now spends most of her afternoons in Toxteth. At first she felt she didn't fit in. 'The people here don't respect me,' she said, her bright eyes watery. 'I arrange to meet them and – hau – they never turn up.'

'That's often the Liverpool way,' I tell her. 'Bad buses – and not being on the phone . . .'

When I reach St Cuthbert's that afternoon she's trudging up the path ahead of me, still wearing her thin white habit despite the December wind.

'What is the matter, uMoey?'

'Nothing, really.'

'Rubbish – it's not nothing.' She shifts her bulging shopping bag to her left hand and opens the door with her right. 'Nobody cries over nothing.'

'I only got a C for my essay.' I try to pass off the news with a laugh which comes out like a startled yelp.

'Don't let it upset you, *ntombi*.' Bertilla follows me

across the hall. 'Tutors often make mistakes.'

'Then why do I have to go to the uni?'

'*Ithi ingahamba idle udaka.*'

I stare at her round brown face, wondering why every-thing's going over my head these days.

'When a chief travels he may sometimes have to eat mud. Which means you must take things as they come, my baby.'

'I'm not very good at that.'

'You'll feel better when you've had some tea.' Bertie lays her broad palm on the small of my back and propels me towards the refectory. As usual, the big aluminium pot has been placed by Gonzaga in the middle of the table, and I head for it straightaway; but my hand wobbles as I line up my cup and saucer and my head feels as though it's been butted.

'Tip that stuff back.' Bertie is rummaging in her shop-ping bag. 'I'm going to make you some rooibos.'

'Rooibos? What's that?'

'A special tea grown in the Cape.' She plucks out a twist of silver foil. 'Just the thing to put you right.'

As Mother Wilfred takes her place at the head of the table her eyes fix on Bertie who's dashing some leaves into my cup. Even bigger than Darjeeling and perfect for scry-ing, they fall at once into a bold black pattern.

Mother Wilfred stirs in her chair. 'Where did you find that tea, Sister Bertilla?'

The African nun clearly hasn't heard about the embargo on tea-leaves. 'Mr Gopal gave it to me,' she says, splashing in the hot water.

The teaching nuns are drifting in from school. While they help themselves to bread and jam, I carry my cup to my Choir nun's place near the top of the table. With Wilfie so close I'm far too nervous to scry; and besides, my powers might have been zapped by my years as a nun.

But a leaf, long and dark, has floated to the top of my cup and bobs there for all to see; a sign so strong that everyone must know its meaning – even Mother Wilfred, to judge by her expression. Someone's coming into my life – a man, by the look of it, and soon. Trying to look unconcerned I carry on sipping the rooibos, but the giant leaf brushes my lips, and the heat from the tea starts fanning my cheeks.

I'm reaching the bottom of the cup when Elisabeth, still nursing her sore throat, comes down from the infirmary. 'What's the matter with you?' she croaks with a glance at my face.

I drain the last drops of rooibos and push away the cup. 'I got a bad mark for my essay.'

'You should take no notice,' says Elisabeth with a look of amusement. 'Piers Palfrey has a second-class mind – Timmy says so.'

'The pride of life,' Mother Wilfred muses to no one in particular.

We all listen respectfully. Our Superior's way of making her opinions known is as easy to read as the tea-leaves.

'The pride of life? What is this?' breezes Bertilla, cutting a slice of bread.

'It's – er – a kind of vanity,' says Wilfie, who is not usually asked to explain herself. 'A thirst for success in the eyes of the world.'

'But Sister Moey is a student. If she fails, she will be thrown out, hey?'

'All this fuss about a low mark is excessive,' pronounces Mother Wilfred with a glare.

'uMoey's been overworking, na?' says Bertilla. 'Believe me, I know the signs. We need to show Christian charity. A cup of rooibos, anyone?'

'She'll have us eating grass next,' says Bosco.

'And now, Sister Maureen,' says Wilfie, wiping her mouth with her napkin, 'you may go straight to your cell and fetch me that torch. No wonder Our Lady has not been blessing your work.'

That evening I start flicking again through my library books while Bertie sits winding bandages and Brigid, in the desk beyond, is attacking her marking.

'What is your essay about?' asks Bertie.

'The Dutch,' I say tersely, not wanting to discuss it in the presence of Sister Rigid who, I notice, has raised her head from her work.

'The Dutch! I don't trust 'em,' says Bertie. 'Our oppressors in South Africa are descended from the Dutch.'

'That's irrelevant,' puts in Brigid bossily. 'The Dutch have produced many masterpieces.'

'Maybe they did.' I close my books and ram them inside my desk. 'But I haven't found any.'

'So what does your tutor say you should do?'

Bugged by her nosy manner, I try to make light of what happened. 'He wants me to fall in love with black and white floor tiles . . . and tankards . . . and blue and white coffee cups.'

'Only a man could expect you to fall in love with a pile of washing-up,' snorts Bertie. 'We nuns have bigger things to think about.'

Brigid looks as though she wants to disagree, then thinks better of it, lays down her red biro and hurries from the room. A few minutes later she's back, clutching a shabby-looking tome. 'This book on Rembrandt was left in my classroom.' Her normally reined-in manner has given way to an urgent, almost pleading tone. 'It might be of use.'

Though touched by her gesture the last thing I want is Rigid Brigid to muscle in. 'Thanks very much – but I don't really like Rembrandt.'

Instead of being put off, she sits down at the next desk. 'But you should!' she says. 'Just look at this self-portrait.' She shows me an old man in a night-cap, awkward and perky at the same time. 'Isn't he the spit of me mam?'

I stare back in surprise. Brigid never speaks to anyone about her mother, a rude old woman who spent most of her life in the Welly Vaults and died when Brigid was a novice.

'Dr Palfrey says that Rembrandt is a bourgeois.'

'Nonsense,' says Brigid, propping the book on my desk. 'Just look at that battered old face.'

Bertie stares at the picture over our shoulders. 'A lot of people round here look like him, not eating, neglecting themselves – just beaten by life. Hau, but it gets me down sometimes.'

'They don't all stay beaten,' says Brigid. 'Some people fight back.'

She sounds a bit like the Brigid of old who made up the Bosco song and refused to learn elocution. 'Perhaps I could write about that portrait,' I say with a burst of hope, 'and prove Rembrandt was working-class.'

'Prove he was *populist*,' Brigid corrects me. 'You can't really call him working-class.'

'Maybe not,' I concede, 'but I'd still like to prove some-thing.'

'Once a Dingle girl, always a Dingle girl,' says Brigid, cracking a rare smile. 'Awkward to the end.'

While she gets on with her marking I comb through the introduction and footnotes then sit planning my argument, pleased to find out that Rembrandt van Rijn was a miller's son who probably converted to Catholicism before he died.

Knowing goal-scoring opportunities usually come awkwardly and under pressure, I struggle over the next few days to carve out time for a first draft. At first I dash down my thoughts anyhow like I did in my last essay; but Brigid takes time off her school work to teach me to marshal my facts. Soon, like a fullback in Kenny's army, I know how to make my argument boot neatly from one paragraph to the next. And then, when I flop into bed at eleven, Brigid stays downstairs to catch up on her marking.

'It's good of you to help,' I say the next morning, struck by her tired face.

'It's the best time I've had in years,' she replies, picking up my script. While I work on my main ideas she looks over what I've written, correcting the spelling mistakes and helping me highlight my strongest points. This time I don't bother with critics' notes about dating and pigmentation but look longer at the painting itself, trying once again to respond 'fully and humanly'. To my surprise there's a lot to write about: the bold use of chiaroscuro, the tilt of the chin and the ragged clothes – a world away from the simpering burghers. Best of all, the forehead is defiant and the rheumy old eyes have an honesty which I hope mine will have when I'm an old nun. I may be broken down and out of fashion, they say to me, but I, like you, had the courage to follow my star.

On the last morning of term Brigid reads my finished essay with a tight smile of approval. I slide it into the carrier bag from Mr Gopal's that I use as a briefcase and set out for the university. For the first two hours I check footnotes and then, at 11.45, I meet Elisabeth outside the library.

It's time for one of my new duties as a Choir nun, the petit examen, or midday examination of conscience. Every fault committed over the last twenty-four hours is recorded in the notebook I now carry in my pocket, to be confessed at the Choir nuns' Chapter.

Together with Elisabeth I march up the cathedral ramp past a concrete tower the colour of dirty yoghurt and in through the big glass doors. After we've knelt in front of the Blessed Sacrament and made the sign of the cross, I thank God for my sister, Brigid, and the subtle, awkward gifts He's given her; and then I let myself daydream for a few last seconds about the essay nestled in my bag. This time I know I'll do well – maybe even better than Elisabeth who's made much of her ß grade.

But when I glance at the neat profile bent beside me in prayer I feel guilty for vying with another human being, and a sister in religion at that. Was Mother Wilfred right when she said my soul was tarnished by love of sport – or was it my proud competitive nature that drew me to sport in the first place? Either way I'm bad at coming second. Pulling out my notebook I sigh and write: (1) *The Pride of Life.*

But even after an Act of Contrition my thoughts drift back to my essay. Thanks to Brigid I can be proud of its strong, wide-ranging argument – but can it be wise, I wonder, to take on my tutor in the very first term? Tommy Farr, Joe Bugner, Freddie Mills – all were destroyed by tackling the big boys. I reach for my notebook again and write: (2) *Vainglorious behaviour.*

A whispering gaggle of schoolchildren heading for the high altar snag my mind back to the present. Under the draughty lantern at my back they begin practising for the evening's carol concert.

Away in a manger, no crib for a bed
The little Lord Jesus lays down his sweet head

Over a hundred of them are crammed into the centre pews but the poor acoustics turn their song into a sickly bleat which makes me wish I was back in the convent kitchen, listening to carols on the radio. With another sigh I write down a third fault: *Lack of Recollection.*

It's while closing my notebook that I'm struck by the mural over the altar. I first saw it as a child when the cathedral had just been finished, and me dad and his mates came to jeer at the barmy modern art. From then on I ignored it – a meaningless abstract painting that had nothing to say to people like me. Now, like the man born blind, I've been granted the gift of sight, and it's clear that the diagonal yellow stripes are sheaves of wheat, and that those sheaves represent the Eucharist – and yes, that blue above them is obviously the sky. How could I not have seen it before?

But unlike the man in the Gospel who praised Jesus for his cure, I'm not helped by my new vision. It was better in the old days when I never even noticed the slanting forms or worried about what they meant – just poured out my heart to God and Our Lady. Discouraged, I cast my eyes downwards and write: (4) *Forgot custody of the eyes.*

The bones in my knees are digging into the hassock and my thoughts swoop and dive like pigeons in the dome above. Why has the time started to drag, I wonder, as I squint at Elisabeth's watch. It raced while I wrote my essay, and instead of clock-watching I was startled by the bell and had to snatch an extra five minutes – which reminds me of yet another fault. (5) *Failure to answer the chapel bell.*

One thing is plain as I look through my notebook: all today's faults have sprung from art history. But the failings, though bad enough in themselves, are minor compared with another fault lurking beneath – a fault too serious to write down, especially with the prying Elisabeth kneeling at my elbow.

I know now that art history's important, and that Dr Palfrey's an ace tutor – elegant in midfield with remarkable touch and control. But I've been trying too hard to impress a man – and a layman at that. I was warned by the big brown leaf that bobbed round my cup of rooibos: though Wilfie thinks it's the devil's work, scrying can sometimes be helpful.

As the schoolchildren start snuffling their way towards the exit I slide my notebook into my bag where it lodges beside my essay. Next time I shall mortify myself, and deliberately aim at a lower mark. That way I'll prove that my work is for the greater glory of God.

Elisabeth gives a cat-like sneeze, makes the sign of the cross and picks up her carrier bag. It's time to begin the afternoon.

Above the cathedral a flock of racing pigeons hurtles towards the waterfront, the bonny white bird in front breasting the current. Christmas trees are piled high on the pavement outside the greengrocer's but instead of looking festive they remind me of sacrificial offerings. I'm wondering why I'm feeling so gloomy, when I spot the hoarding outside the newsagent's: JOHN LENNON SHOT DEAD IN NEW YORK.

Eternal rest grant unto him, O Lord. I know that the poor man's soul is no dearer to God than anyone else's, and that we nuns shouldn't care about pop stars, but he's always been my favourite Beatle, and he grew up in the same street as my Auntie Eileen. Even though I'll have to note down my sin of superstition, I can't help feeling his death is a terrible omen.

While Elisabeth returns her library books I trudge on to the art history department. It's ten past two when I enter the foyer but there are no seminars this afternoon and the heating has already been turned down for the vacation. Trying to stop my soles from squeaking on the lino, I tiptoe across the hall.

'Dr Palfrey isn't in,' says a voice behind me. I turn to see Mrs Dagnall, who's clearly divined where I'm going. Her plump feet crammed into even higher than usual patent leather stilettos, she's peering out from her office, her cheeks flushed. Behind her is a clink of glasses and the sound of female giggling.

'But my essay's due at the end of term.'

'That's unfortunate, Miss O'Shaunessy, because Dr P has just gone.'

'Then I'll slip it under his door,' I say, trying to hide my disappointment, 'so he can pick it up tomorrow.'

The secretary's now so close I can see the flecks of lipstick on her teeth, and smell the sweet sherry. 'That's impossible, I'm afraid. He's gone to Prof's shooting lodge for a Scottish Christmas – with Mr and Mrs Fothergill.' She extends a hand with nails like icing-sugar petals. 'I'll put your essay in his pigeon-hole for the start of term.'

The Baby Jesus

Columba is watching me put the finishing touches to the paper rocks surrounding the stable – orange and black splodges to look Middle Eastern, and a giant cactus at the door. 'That's really artistic.' She stares at the bright pink flower. 'You must have learnt a lot at university.'

My term has finished a fortnight before the high school's, so I've taken over the cleaning while the tired Choir nuns mark their end-of-term exams. Glad of the change from brainwork, I don't even mind when the electric polisher breaks down – just vent my frustrations on the chapel floor which is the shiniest it's ever been. On Christmas Eve the air's still thick with the smell of polish, the remains of which are lodged beneath my nails.

'I know that Easter is the high point of the Church's year,' says Mother Wilfred as she lifts the Baby Jesus out of his cardboard box. 'But Christmas is more hopeful somehow.'

An owl calls through the frosty air and the branches of

the pear tree rattle against the chapel window. Bertilla has coaxed Sisters Pious and Placid down from the infirmary for Midnight Mass, and the two old nuns are propped against their zimmers in the front row, with shawls draped over their shoulders. Caught in the air of expectancy, the rest of us line up behind them.

Unto us a child is born, intones Mother Wilfred from the back of the chapel, her old voice cracking. *Unto us a Son is given.*

She picks up the Baby Jesus and cradles him carefully in both arms, his pottery head against her heart. The rest of us watch from either side of the main aisle as she bears the Christ child towards the waiting crib. *O sing unto the Lord a new song,* we carol as she reaches the altar rail, boosted this year by the gospel-singer's voice of Bertilla. *For He hath done marvellous things.*

Mother Wilfred lays the boy child in a manger made years ago by Columba from a sewing-box. There he will be watched over by his new family – Mary, Joseph, the shepherd boy, the ox and the ass, until the Feast of the Epiphany and the arrival of the three wise men.

On Christmas morning Bertilla goes out early to distribute toys in Toxteth, so Gonzaga and I cook dinner. After I've dished up the tomato soup and chicken, Wilfie lets me sit in my old place with the lay sisters at the bottom of the table. Bertilla returns bearing a bottle of VP sherry from a grateful grockle. It's too sweet for most of the Choir nuns, so I pour extra glasses for Bertie, the lay sisters and me while listening to Wilfie read Maria Goretti's Christmas message.

'*The seventies,*' writes our Mother General, '*was a turbulent decade for the Catholic Church with brave priests and nuns fighting for freedom the world over. We must pray especially for those killed in Poland, El Salvador, the United States, South Africa —'*

'*Amandla!*' shouts Bertilla, raising her fist.

Ignoring Wilfie's icy glance, I pour the African nun a third glass of sherry. Wilfie continues to read, her voice heavy with disapproval – but whether of Bertie, the sherry or the pastoral message I can't tell.

'*What with a new Polish pope, the Nobel prize for Mother Teresa and the spread of feminism throughout the world, this is an inspiring time to be a nun. Now, at the start of 1981, I hope my nuns far and wide will carry the spirit of our Blessed Foundress into the future.*'

Then Mother Wilfred adds a few words which are, she says, of very special relevance to us at St Cuthbert's. 'It is not necessary,' she stuffs the blue airmail letter into its envelope, 'for nuns and priests to take to the streets. Convents should be fountainheads of prayer, with every moment offered up for those in the outside world. Didn't St Thérèse of Lisieux convert many souls on the missions without ever' – this last with a meaningful glance at Bertie – 'straying beyond her cloister?'

Then we open our Christmas cards. I have twelve: one from Mam, Dad and Lorraine, ten from uncles, aunts and cousins, and an unsigned card of a Dutch interior which I guess is from Dr Palfrey. Columba's little face grows flushed and Xavier claims to feel warm for the first time since coming to England. She looks quite animated as she unpacks some *biltong* sent by her brother in Johannesburg.

'It's ostrich!' she exclaims, brandishing it at Bosco. 'You chew on it – like this.' As her long jaws pump up and down a look of ecstasy crosses her horsy features.

Bertilla ties a napkin under Placid's chin, then cuts up Pious's chicken. 'Let's drink to Maureen and Elisabeth,' she cries. 'They're through their first term at the uni.'

'*Gesondheid!*' says Xavier. 'Help yourself to *biltong*, everyone.'

As my sisters raise their glasses, my thoughts dart to my essay waiting in Dr Palfrey's pigeon-hole while he tramps the heather with Mrs Fothergill and the shadowy Mr Fothergill. I've never been to Scotland so my picture of what they might be doing depends mainly on whisky ads: shooting grouse or nursing tots of Johnny Walker by a log fire while the wind whistles down the glen. But who cares, I decide, looking up and down the refectory as my sisters pull Christmas crackers. I prefer ordinary people. Except that my sisters aren't ordinary: they're worth ten times the trio of snobs in a shooting lodge. For a few seconds I feel tearfully grateful to Wilfie for letting us drink all the sherry at one sitting, to Bertilla for proposing a toast, and even to Xavier for wanting to share her *biltong*, and I wonder if the alcohol's gone to my head. And then I think, no, these feelings have nothing to do with the sherry. I've always known I belong at St Cuthbert's.

After Christmas Columba starts knitting the Baby Jesus a vest against the cold of St Cuthbert's. He's wearing it twelve days later when three jewelled eastern kings arrive at the crib: Caspar, Melchior and Balthazar the black king who, as Bertie is quick to point out, stands in the rear holding the camels. The wise men glare with fierce eyes at the presents that have arrived before their gold, frankincense and myrrh: a fresh mango, some winter pansies and a jar of honey brought by Bertie from Liverpool 8.

After Compline that evening we gather round to contemplate the new arrivals. Mother Wilfred kneels down first, clasps her hands in prayer and then begins to make an odd lowing noise. As the rest of us turn to her in alarm, she stands up, gropes in her pocket for her handkerchief and clasps it over her mouth.

She's upset by the woolly vest, I think, waiting for Columba to take it off.

But no, Bertilla's eyes have followed Mother Wilfred's, and she too is looking appalled.

'The manger! Look at the manger!' croaks Xavier.

'Where's the baby?' Columba's voice is loud with disbelief.

'The Infant Jesus has gone.' Mother Wilfred's cheeks are red as though they've been slapped.

We rise to our feet and leave chapel in a gaggle – apart from Bertilla who stays behind to help Pious and Placid with their zimmers.

'What is it?' Blind old Pious turns her milky gaze on the infirmarian. 'Where are we going now?'

'Time for bed,' says Bertilla. 'That's right, Sister, lean on my shoulder. Placid, you come round the other side.'

'Who could have done this?' moans Mother Wilfred, her hand against her ribs.

'The same person that took the secateurs from the garden shed,' says Columba.

'It's the first time he's come into the house,' says Ursula.

'Heather March knocked at the back door today, asking for food,' says Gonzaga, pulling her shawl tighter. 'Perhaps she took a fancy to him.'

'Heather would never find her way through the kitchen, up the steps and along the main cloister,' says Mother

Wilfred. 'It must have been a professional burglar.' She gazes up at the window-clasps, which are all intact.

'This is a matter for the police,' says Bosco. 'I suggest you call them straightaway.'

'No!' The Superior looks agitated. 'We don't want them poking round the enclosure.'

'All they would do is take a few fingerprints.'

'I'll go and have a look outside,' says Bertilla, grabbing a broom from the sacristy. Five minutes later she returns to say that the moon is bright and the soil under the windows undisturbed. A fox has been sniffing round the dustbins and the only tracks on the frosty lawn are his.

'Why would anyone steal a pottery baby?' asks Ursula as we move down the corridor to the front hall.

'Because he was so lifelike,' says Mother Wilfred, her voice hoarse. 'The most beautiful baby ever seen in a crib.'

The next day Mother Wilfred still refuses to call the police, so I go to the chapel alone and dismantle the manger. Hoping the infant might still be recovered, I stack his cardboard box on top of the rest. But the days pass and the box remains empty.

Jogo

I got a ß++ **very good work** at the end of my essay on Rembrandt – the highest mark in my group. Elisabeth, who's decided it's vulgar to talk about marks, has started to dog my footsteps, popping her head into my seminars at odd moments and sitting in the back of my lectures whenever she's free. Bostik is what Toby Smart calls her, because these days she sticks to me like glue. Encouraged by the Archdeacon, who wants me to mix, I dodge into the coffee bar whenever I can give her the slip. Nathalie Steen, the ex-St Cuthbert's girl, sometimes gives me a funny look and Sasha still treats me with disdain; but Hannah, Toby and Vicky are not nearly as snobby as I thought; and now I've grown less aggressive they're starting to treat me like a human being.

On a sunny Monday in Lent we climb the attic stairs for our first workshop. According to Dr Julia Mulcahy our colour sense has been ruined by theory and it's time to get back to basics.

'It'll be a waste of time,' grumbles Toby, his earring bobbing, 'messing about with scissors and paste.'

'You'd better look out,' says Vicky flicking back her red hair. 'She's rumoured to have a temper – especially with men.'

I remember the ringless left hand and the way she said *Mz.*

The door opens at the top of the stairs, and a shingled head sticks out. 'Come and make yourselves at home.'

We troop into the sunny roof space and choose our easels. With its white walls, varnished floorboards and sparkling, seaborne light, the studio is like nowhere else in the building. 'You have each been given two sheets of coloured paper, a sheet of white paper, a swatch of material, some glue and a pair of scissors,' says Dr Mulcahy, hooking her thumbs in the waist of her jeans. 'I shall watch how you use them.'

'Just like primary school.' Vicky stares in dismay at her easel. 'I'd rather write an essay.'

'When can we learn to use oils?' asks Toby, scratching his curls.

Dr Mulcahy opens the skylight with a window-pole. 'That will come later – when you've learnt about space and colour.'

I haven't messed about like this since I was a kid, and my hand on the scissors feels thick and nervous. I choose blue because it's Our Lady's colour, and begin to trace Hannah's profile on the blank sheet. And then I think, no, why bother with what I can see? Better to draw what I've lost, and keep it as a reminder.

While I cut out a tower block lit by its yellow squares, Dr Mulcahy wanders among the easels, pausing now and again to make a comment. Amazingly my scrap of cloth is the same brown wool as my habit, so I cut out a row of Choir nuns crossing the courtyard to Matins, and me at the window with a scrubbing-brush in my hand. I've just begun a blue paper cloister when I become aware of the tutor standing behind me. Knowing my little nuns look desperately clumsy and homespun, I pray that she'll pass on to the next easel.

'That's St Cuthbert's,' she says, sounding pleased.

'Dr Palfrey called it a Gothic monstrosity.'

'You have a nice sense of colour – carry on.'

I would like to say thanks but my lips clamp shut of their own accord.

Compliments, according to Mother Wilfred, can be dangerous. 'But the other students are being kind to me,' I told her recently, 'and my studies are going well.'

The Superior's face stiffened as she quoted *The Imitation of Christ*: 'The highest and most profitable form of study is to understand one's inmost nature and despise it.'

But can that be right, I wonder, with a glance at my tutor's back. Praise for my work, the friendliness of my fellow students – they're boosting my self-esteem and making me happy.

'This is baby work.' Hannah's bullet head rises from the drawing-board. 'I've seen my kid sister do better.'

'Naturally, because she hasn't been ruined by a bunch of theorists.' Dr Mulcahy digs her hands in her pockets. 'We should all return to baby work now and again.' Turning, she looks again at my cloister. 'Unlike other blues that cobalt is a warm colour. If you want it to be explosive, juxtapose it with orange.'

Before I can reply there's a knock at the studio door. For

a second I think it's Elisabeth but to my relief Dr Palfrey appears, dressed in white like a tropical bird. 'Am I interrupting?' When Dr Mulcahy fails to reply he adds with a glance in my direction, 'I want to make an appointment with Sister Maureen.'

'If you must,' she says offhandedly.

'Teacher's pet,' whispers Vicky.

'I like all students who work hard,' says Dr Palfrey who has overheard. 'Come and see me after your workshop, Sister.'

I nod, hoping to make it without Elisabeth in tow.

Dr Palfrey flaps a hand at the pile of firewood in the corner. 'I'll get Erskine to take that to the tip.'

'Oh no you don't,' says Dr Mulcahy. 'I've been gathering that driftwood for weeks.'

'What for?'

'For *natures mortes*,' she replies as though it's obvious. Then she turns her back on him, pulls out a pair of pliers and prises a nail from a piece of timber.

'I do think you're brave,' says Dr Palfrey.

'I've just had my anti-tetanus jab.'

'I meant brave to take such aesthetic risks.'

Dr Mulcahy continues to rummage in the timber. I admire her self-possession but I like Dr Palfrey too, and think she's rude to ignore him in front of us students. After watching for a few more seconds he smiles ruefully and picks his way towards the door.

The moment he's gone Dr Mulcahy straightens up and addresses the class as a whole. 'It's time to pack up,' she says, all traces of irritation vanished. 'You may take your work home but please bring it back next week when you'll learn how to combine it with newsprint and found objects.' Her face once again is looking familiar – a memory trace, perhaps, from one of the many reproductions I've gazed at this term. I'm putting her in a Florentine headdress when her eye catches mine. 'Professor Canterville has given me money to employ a model. Are you allowed to attend life class, Sister Maureen?'

'Why ever not?' I ask, sliding my half-completed collage into my bag.

'She's trying to spare your blushes,' says Vicky. 'In a life class the model has no clothes on.'

Once I was a number one striker and now everyone treats me with kid gloves. I spring to my feet and look Dr Mulcahy in the eye. 'If it's part of the course, I'll do it.'

'That's good,' says Dr Mulcahy with a smile of satisfaction. 'My plumber is a part-time model. I'll bring him along in a few weeks.'

'You mean the model will be a man?' I say, already regretting my daring.

The workshop has finished early so there's time for a coffee with the others before I see Dr Palfrey. We're at the top of the basement steps when a voice calls my name.

'Watch out,' says Toby. 'It's Bostik.'

'Where have you been?' Elisabeth hurries towards me. 'We were meant to meet in the cathedral.'

The Forty Martyrs! Too busy thinking about my workshop, I'd forgotten their special service.

'She's been with us,' says Hannah.

'Where?' Elisabeth asks me.

'In the studio – we were learning to make collages.'

'It's the first I've heard about it.'

'Bloody hell,' says Toby to no one in particular.

'Are you coming for a coffee, Sister Maureen?' asks Hannah, pointedly ignoring Elisabeth.

Elisabeth's eyes are fixed on my face.

'No, thanks,' I reply, trying to sound as though it's something I'd never do. 'I have to see Dr Palfrey.'

'I don't think that will be possible.' Elisabeth plucks at my sleeve. 'You'd better come home with me.'

Instead of carrying on to the coffee bar as I'd hoped, Hannah, Toby and Vicky are listening with interest. 'You mean you'll get her into trouble?' says Hannah, her cheeks pink.

But Elisabeth's not a player to be fazed by the terraces. 'I mean that you should mind your own business. This is between Sister Maureen and me.'

Embarrassed by her bossy manner, I start walking towards the door.

'I'll save you a seat in the Tuesday lecture,' calls Hannah.

'I'm only doing my duty,' cries Elisabeth as I stalk ahead of her to the bus stop. 'You know that I have no choice.'

'You made a fool of me – and just when I was starting to make friends.'

'It will be good for you in the long run. Those students are growing over-familiar.'

'But last term you wanted me to meet people.'

'I meant people like Sasha and Nathalie; not ones who'll distract you from your studies.'

'It's you who's distracted me from my studies, because you've forced me to miss an appointment.'

'You're not allowed to visit your tutor unchaperoned – as you know already.'

I stare in silence at two kids defacing a street sign, knowing that Elisabeth will report me to Wilfie if I don't knuckle under. But I also know that she's changed her views, and I wonder why.

When we reach St Cuthbert's Bertilla is whistling her way across the front hall. 'What's up?' she says with a glance at our faces. 'Have you two fallen out?'

'I've tried to put things right,' says Elisabeth, 'but Maureen won't talk to me.'

'Will you flippin' well get off me back?' I shout. 'I've just about had enough.'

'Take it easy, uMoey.' Bertie glances down the corridor. 'Wilfie's in a bad mood and ready to bite.'

I follow her gaze to the Superior's study door. Since the loss of the Baby Jesus Wilfie's grown withdrawn, giving her form, 4Y, to a lay teacher and leaving Bosco to run the convent day to day. Each night she checks the locks on the doors and windows three and four times before bed – and later if she happens to wake up.

'I'm on my way to collect the eggs,' continues Bertie, her eyes berry-bright. 'Let's sort this out in the garden.' She pulls down her colander from the top shelf. 'That means you too, uLizzie.' Ignoring Elisabeth's martyred sigh, she marches us towards the hen run built from orange boxes, old window frames and some spare shelving donated by Miss Vavasour, the gym teacher. 'OK, you two – what's up?'

'Maureen forgot to meet me in the cathedral.'

Bertilla looks disappointed. 'Is that all?'

'Because she went to a workshop without permission.'

'It's part of my course,' I burst out. 'All my friends were there.'

As Bertie pushes open the gate Jogo, the little cockerel given her by Mr Gopal in exchange for three novenas, sprints forward to greet her, followed by his six hens. 'Hau Lizzie – you underestimate our Moey. At twenty-seven years old she can judge for herself.'

'Particular friendships are forbidden among nuns,' says Elisabeth, her face set.

'I don't see the point of that rule,' I butt in. 'Nobody's friends at St Cuthbert's – or ever has been.'

'That's what *you* think.'

Bertie digs in her pocket for corn. 'Steady on, Lizzie – you're over-reacting.'

'Over-reacting? When this community was torn apart by a Particular Friendship?'

'When was that?' I ask incredulously.

'Before your time.'

But not, it seems, before Elisabeth's – who entered five years before me. And yet I've heard nothing about it. I turn to Bertie, expecting her to press for details; but to my surprise she picks up Jogo and starts to caress his comb.

'Why does nobody tell me anything?' I cry. 'Is it because I'm the youngest – or because I used to be a lay sister?'

The little bird closes his eyes and croons as Bertilla speaks. 'Those sad days are best forgotten,' she says. 'They have nothing to do with the present.'

'Yes they have,' Elisabeth drills on, 'because the rule against PF's includes lay people. Maureen is getting too close to her fellow students.'

Still carrying the cockerel, Bertie leads us towards the makeshift veranda and sits on the little bench where she entertained Mr Gopal and Heather March to mugs of tea and chocolate biscuits until Wilfie found out. 'Nobody likes informers. In my country we call them *impimpi*.' Her eyes sparkle with mischief. 'That means pimps.'

Instead of listening, Elisabeth steps up to me with her face stiff. 'Promise you'll keep your distance.'

'Hey, Elisabeth,' says Bertie before I can reply, 'I think there is an egg under that hawthorn. Pertelote has been there since Matins.'

As an attempt at deflection this is a failure because Elisabeth's scared of birds and will dodge collecting the eggs. Bertie sets Jogo on his feet and slides her hand under the wing of Pertelote, who moves obligingly. 'And now you must have a look at the site of my butterfly farm,' she says with a wink in my direction. She picks up the colander, goes out through the door of the hen run and strolls towards the beginnings of a large cage by the herb garden. After a second's hesitation Elisabeth follows.

'Mr Gopal gave me the wood,' says Bertie, 'and Miss Vavasour helped me make the frames. I'm going to paint them this week. Red, white and blue, eh? Like your Union Jack.'

'Certainly not,' says Elisabeth, her tone lightening a little. 'What we need are quattrocento colours, burnt siennas and umbers – like the Palazzo Pubblico.'

'There's some gloss paint in the old shed. We'll get busy tomorrow.'

'The paint should be eggshell, not gloss,' says Elisabeth in a horrified voice. 'Gloss is too bathroomy.'

'Does it matter, Sisi?'

'Of course it matters – it's part of our convent ambience.'

Feinting and dodging like a good player, Bertie's solved the immediate crisis. But my future doesn't look good. Elisabeth could sneak on me to Wilfie at any moment, and I'm hurt by her spiteful behaviour; hurt too that even a newcomer like Bertie has been told about a past scandal while I've been kept in the dark. I remember Heather's sly hints at the back door, and Gonzaga's angry face as she chased her down the steps, and wonder what it was all about, and when my sisters will see I'm as grown up as them.

I've shut the door to the hen run and am wandering towards the grotto when I notice a shadow floating over the wet grass – and then a clucking from the bantams.

Bertie and Elisabeth are outside the netting, looking at the frames to be painted. 'What is it?' calls Bertie as she swings round, shading her eyes against the sun.

While she runs towards the cackling bantams I hear a cry from Elisabeth, then see a big bird skim past her head. It has dropped so close I can make out the chestnut feathers on its strongly angled wings and the cruel eyes set in a whitish head. Elisabeth cries again as it swoops back, its wing feathers brushing her face. The bantams race towards their orange-box house.

'*Suka wena!*' Bertilla grabs a spade while Elisabeth darts to the veranda, shielding her head with her hands. The bird soars to the topmost branch of the pear tree and emits a high, piercing mew.

'*Suka wena, skebenga!*' shouts Bertie again. But instead of going away the bird floats down to the hen run, bounces on to the bare earth then hobbles towards Elisabeth with a weird, prancing gait. Her mouth wide open, she is about to dive under the bench when Jogo stands on his toes and flaps his wings three times in the face of the giant invader. And then, as the big bird lurches past him, he runs squawking for cover under the hawthorn.

'*Basoba!*' shouts Bertie and flings her spade over the top of the wire netting. It narrowly misses Jogo to land at the feet of the intruder who, emitting another piercing shriek, flaps its wings once more and rises out of the hen run.

'What was it?' I ask as it disappears beyond the tree-tops.

'I think it was a kestrel,' says Elisabeth, wiping a dribble of spit from her chin.

I shake my head. Only last week a kestrel flew into a plate-glass window during a lecture. The unconscious form on the pavement was far smaller than that great bird of prey.

'It might have been an eagle – or a hadeda,' says Bertie who is trying to coax Jogo from under the bush.

'A what?'

'iNkankane,' says Bertie as though that explains everything. When Jogo begins stepping slowly towards her she scoops him up and holds him under her arm. 'You should have run into the hen house with your wives, you silly fellow,' she scolds him, running her finger along his comb, 'instead of standing up to birds three times your size.'

'He'd make a good goalie,' I say.

'All the same, Moey,' Bertie kisses Jogo on his beak then stoops to set him on his feet, 'those birds of prey can be dangerous.' She fixes me with a gaze both bright and quizzical. 'In future he may need some wire netting over his run to protect him from his own rashness.'

Good Friday

O my people what have I done to thee? sings the community, with Bertilla's bluesy voice soaring above the rest. *Or in what have I grieved thee? Answer me.* Then we file one by one to the altar to kiss the holes in the feet of the crucifix, Choir nuns first and then the two old lay sisters. It's over an hour before the Good Friday liturgy is complete and we can close the chapel door on the bare altar, purple-shrouded statues and empty tabernacle.

It's been a Lent of hard frosts and no money for central heating, and everyone looks tired and ready to gripe. There's an awkward gap between now and supper because we're forbidden to work, read or hold recreation. Stripped of their sense of purpose, the Choir nuns gather for once in the kitchen, the only warm room in the house.

'How can you call this detestable weather spring?' twangs Xavier, tugging her shawl round her shoulders. 'Give me a Jo'burg winter any day.'

'You are not in Johannesburg now,' says Mother Wilfred

imperiously, 'so will you please stop grumbling?'

Looking round the ring of pinched faces, I wish I was a lay sister again and could escape to a far corner of the convent. But I must fight down my fidgets and stand with the rest.

Gonzaga shuffles out of the larder in her bedroom slippers. 'There's nothing much to eat,' she announces.

'Let us remind ourselves that today is Good Friday,' says Mother Wilfred to the space above her head. 'It is a time for mortification.'

Bertilla pauses on her way through the kitchen, a carrier bag in her hand. 'I'll make us a curry,' she offers, nodding at her pestle and mortar.

There's a rustle of anxiety. Bertilla's curries are fiery affairs demanding a strong will and an iron gullet. 'I'll help you chop the onions,' I offer, glad of the chance of some work.

'What sort of curry?' Xavier fingers a cold sore.

'You wait and see,' says Bertilla whose favourite recipe begins with the words: Take everything you have in the vegetable rack . . . 'The best cooks work with what the Lord has provided – like artists, eh, Moey?'

'We can't have curry on Good Friday,' protests Bosco who needs three large handkerchiefs to mop her eyes and nose. 'It's undignified, all that gasping and spluttering.'

'We always used to have fish on Fridays,' says Gonzaga.

'Fish is getting too risky,' says Bertilla who's been given back copies of the *Echo* by Mr Gopal. 'They've been catching some funny ones in the Mersey. So it's lucky we have a leftover cauliflower.'

'You shouldn't give curry to Pious and Placid,' says Xavier.

'If you don't like it, my sisters, you can offer it up,' glints Bertilla, 'and sweat out your impurities in time for the Resurrection.'

'*Noli me tangere*,' says Mother Wilfred. 'It is spiritual purity that matters.'

'Why have the Last Supper if it's all spiritual?' asks Bertilla. 'Bodily things matter too. Perhaps I'll add more pepper water,' she adds with a touch of menace. 'It's all the old ones can taste.'

'This has gone far enough,' says Mother Wilfred magisterially. 'You may make us a curry, Sister Bertilla, and the rest of us will offer it up.'

'I have twelve bantam eggs to exchange for some tamarind pods. I'll need to visit Mr Gopal.'

'Isn't it rather selfish to court danger?' asks Bosco. 'Mrs Tarn's just been mugged outside an Indian restaurant.'

'And the Archdeacon's windscreen's been smashed in Gambier Terrace,' adds Columba.

'Bertilla must take someone with her,' says Wilfie. 'Toxteth's a bad area.'

'Can I go?' I ask Mother Wilfred. I'm longing for some fresh air, and the houseful of crotchety women is getting on my nerves.

Wilfie sniffs and stalks off to her study. Taking that as a yes, I put on my cape while Bertie packs a dozen bantam eggs and a jar of honey.

It's been a week of rain and quick-running tides but this morning the weather turned and a warm wind is nudging the clouds out to sea. Bertie's the only other nun who walks as fast as me, and we swing companionably across the park with its new blades of grass still sodden underfoot.

'I'm glad it's you who volunteered,' says Bertie as we pass

the aviary with its old eggshells and long-captive gulls, 'because I'm going to see Heather March.'

Heather the down-and-out with her nosy nature, chased away from the back step by Columba. I've heard from Columba that she's never been back, but have been too taken up by the uni to ask any more questions.

'Wilfie's forbidden me to visit because Heather's an old gossip. But she hasn't long to go, Moey. Do you mind?'

I'd rather stay out in the air but we've just been recalling the Passion and Death of Our Saviour. The visit to Heather can be a Good Friday penance, my own private way of the cross.

Though some boys are playing football by the café the afternoon has a subdued air, as if mindful of the three hundred and fifty-three gaping tabernacles in the Archdiocese of Liverpool, the three hundred and fifty-three altars stripped bare and the three hundred and fifty-three purple-shrouded crucifixes waiting for the bells to ring out for the Resurrection.

At the edge of the park we pass under an oak tree bursting into leaf. *Sweet the wood and sweet the nails, laden with so sweet a load*, hums Bertie as we walk past houses I usually see through the bus window. She cuts down a street with bulging bin bags and boarded-up windows. Grown used to the expensive fabrics worn by art history students, I'm struck at once by the shoddiness of the women's clothes, and the men who are taking a martyr's pride in going without their jackets. Like most of us at St Cuthbert's it's years since I've owned an umbrella or a pair of woollen gloves, and my winter cape is shabby and thin. But at least I have a Vow of Poverty to sustain me, while these people have no choice.

A gang of kids is throwing stones at a street lamp and

two young men are changing the tyre of a red Ford Mustang while a third tinkers under its bonnet. They stop and stare as we approach, then one of them cracks a joke and starts striding towards us. He's well over six foot, and made to look even taller by a hat like a huge woollen halo. As he raises his spanner I realise I'm the only white person around, and that no one from St Cuthbert's knows where we are. But when I turn in alarm to Bertilla, I see to my surprise that she's smiling broadly. 'Howsit, Wayne? Still trying to fix that old car?'

Wayne waggles the spanner in salute. 'Hi there! How ya doin', Sister Bertie?' Now the other two have wiped their hands on their overalls, and are smiling down at the African nun. 'Where you rushin' to?'

'Mr Gopal's.' Bertie plants her feet on the pavement and laughs. 'Have you three boys been to church?'

'We go Easter Sunday,' the one next to Wayne says easily, 'in time for the Resurrection.'

But Bertilla's attention has already been caught by a woman in a jump-suit the colour of sunset pushing a baby buggy. One child is slumbering under its plastic canopy and another clutches the handle with a small brown hand. 'Sister Bertie,' the woman cries. 'You've got to help me.'

'Mary Element,' says Bertie and puts down her bag.

'It's my Tom,' explains Mary, her voice high with anxiety. 'The heat are on to him. They barged in at four in the morning and dragged him out of bed.'

My legs are itching to stride out – break into a run, even. This is not so much a Way of the Cross, I think, as a Way of Standing Still.

'I don't know what to do next,' Mary's saying to Bertilla. 'He's been in twenty-four hours on suss.'

While I try not to shift from foot to foot Bertilla listens intently to the rest of the rambling tale. 'We nuns are supposed to be holy,' she says as Mary Element moves off at last, the toddler trudging in her wake, 'but wives and mothers are the real saints if you ask me.'

'Maybe,' I reply, suddenly ashamed of my own opinion: that married women are cage birds, trading their freedom for regular birdseed. 'The Archdeacon's afraid there'll be a riot,' I add in an effort to change the subject, 'and we'll be at risk because our convent's on the edge of Toxteth.'

'He may be right. People are growing impatient.'

As though to prove her point two thick-set lads start smashing the stained-glass panels on either side of a big front door. I hope that she'll tell them to stop it, but to my disappointment she says nothing. 'My mam and dad longed for a place like that,' I remark as we pass the fancy façade.

'I'd rather live in a new one,' says Bertie, raising her voice over a police siren. 'Half these houses had black slaves.'

'That's a myth,' I shoot back, feeling nettled. 'No slave ever set foot in Liverpool.'

'There were auctions on the Goree Piazza – it says so in the history books.'

'But this street was built in Victorian times – when slavery was long over.'

'So how come branding irons were being sold in Hardman Street?' asks Bertie, looking pleased at scoring a point.

I'm searching for a reply when a flock of pigeons clatters into the air about our heads. 'Leave that bird alone!' shouts Bertie, slinging me her bag.

I swing round to see a boy with angelic blond hair and blue eyes grasping a pigeon by the throat.

'Let it go, *skebenga*,' thunders Bertie.

Mouthing a swear word, the boy squeezes the pigeon tighter and whirls it above his head.

Bertie lunges at him and grabs his elbow. 'Now will you drop it?' Not until she winches his arm behind his back does he let the pigeon thump to the ground.

'If I catch you doing that again, sonny, I'll give you a klap.'

The boy gives Bertie a blank look then darts off as the bird flaps its wings a few times before managing to get airborne.

Bertie takes back her bag and checks the eggs one by one. 'Boys!' she exclaims, pitching a cracked one into the gutter.

'In three years' time I'll be teaching them,' I say, wondering what they'll make of art history. The pigeon is now fluttering round the crucifix on the wall of the Methodist chapel – a building I've never gone into. Wild-haired and emaciated, the Saviour is thrusting upwards and outwards from His cross, straining towards the Resurrection. Beneath Him a pile of rubbish is burning untended.

'I prefer Him to our convent Jesus,' says Bertie, reading my glance, 'because He won't stay crucified.'

The pigeon lands on an upraised arm then tumbles down to peck at a rancid fish-and-chip paper drifting away from the flames. '*Gijima!*' says Bertie. 'It's bad for you.'

'Columba says pigeons only have thirty-seven taste buds.'

'Just as well,' laughs Bertie, 'given the rubbish they eat.'

We walk on to a small, brick-built estate of two-storey houses near the Rialto. Although they're no more than thirty years old, many of the windows are boarded up and judging by the smell the main drain's blocked. A group of weary-looking men avoid our eyes as we make our way to the end house, while the women all wear the stigmata of poverty – down-at-heel shoes, and bare legs mottled from sitting too close to the fire.

'We were poor in the Holy Land,' I say to Bertie, 'but we seemed livelier, somehow.'

'They're leading their lives, Moey,' she replies as we march up a weedy path. 'You can't judge them from the outside.'

Though impressed by Bertie's local knowledge, I'm beginning to feel niggled. Am I not a scouser born and bred, who's lived in the inner city all her life? I watch in silence while Bertie pulls out her keys and opens a battered front door. In the small room beyond, Heather is lying on a tattered divan. A bunch of withered grasses is crammed in a jam jar by a statue of the Immaculate Conception, and pinned to the wall above is a crayon drawing of St Cuthbert's, its colours crude like a child's. Down the side is a list of all our names and the date each one of us entered. The room smells fetid and chunks of plaster litter the rotting lino.

Bertie puts down her bag of eggs on the window-sill, then heads for the corner sink unit.

'Hello, Heather,' I say, wondering if the only chair is too rickety to sit on.

'Look what the cat's brought in.' Heather's face has lost its ruddy, outdoors look, and the skin is grey as though it's been scumbled. 'Too posh to talk to me now you're a student.'

'That's not true,' I mutter as she raises her head from the grimy cushion.

Heather's lips open and shut in their mask of pale flesh. 'I hear Lady Nevershit's got herself a job.'

I pick up the fallen eiderdown and slide it back on the bed, trying not to breathe in the smell of stale urine.

'I dare say she's setting her cap at you now.'

'Who are you talking about?'

'The ex-Sister Julian – I hear she's got a job in the uni.'

I glance at Bertie who's switching on the kettle, her broad brown face impassive.

'I can hardly remember her,' I tell Heather. 'She left the High School when I was a second year.'

The watery old eyes peer up at my mine. 'I seed her the other week – whizzing down the Bouly in her posh blue car. Nearly knocked me down on the zebra.'

Bertie crosses to the window, but the handle is painted over, and after thumping it a few times she gives up. 'What's that horrible smell?' she asks Heather.

'Upstairs flat. Their toilet leaks whenever they flush it.'

Bertie opens her mouth to speak but I cut across her, eager to show I'm on the ball. 'You should inform the landlord.'

'What do you mean, landlord?' says Heather. 'It's a corpy flat.'

'Can't you all band together and write to the council?'

'Why don't you put her right?' Heather swivels her eyes to glare at Bertilla. 'She's starting to get on me nerves.'

'It's a bad situation,' Bertie says to me kindly. 'We've complained for months but nothing gets done.' She wipes Heather's face with a towel, like an African St Veronica. 'The council is overstretched.'

'I once wanted to be a nun,' says Heather, going off at a tangent, 'but they wouldn't have me because I'm half-cracked.'

'That's no obstacle.' Bertie goes to fetch the teapot. 'Not at St Cuthbert's.'

I smile at the black nun's joke, warmed by her good humour and her refusal to put me down when goaded by Heather.

'It's not fair,' continues the old woman to neither of us in particular. 'If Brigid can still be a nun, why can't I?'

'What's she talking about?' I ask.

'Take no notice, Moey.' Bertie keeps her eyes on the tea she's pouring. 'Come on, darling, you'll have to sit up while I take your pulse.'

'If you would nurse me in your infirmary,' persists Heather, 'you could see that I took me tablets.'

Bertie consults her stop watch. 'I'm sorry, *ntombi* – our infirmary's only for nuns.'

I think of the Son of Man who had nowhere to lay His head, and wonder what He'd make of all our spare beds. 'It doesn't seem fair,' I whisper to Bertie.

'Don't think I haven't tried,' she replies, 'but Wilfie won't hear of it.' She puts a jar of honey on the bedside chair. 'We have to go now,' she says as she picks up her bag. 'Take a spoonful of this now and again.'

Heather slops a little tea on her blanket. 'How's mouldy-arsed Pious and podgy old Placid?'

'Sister Pious's cataracts are worse and Placid's blood pressure is sky high.'

'That's good,' says Heather nastily. 'When will they kick the bucket?'

'I don't know, sweetheart,' says Bertie as she follows me to the door. 'That's in God's hands.'

'Don't know? Don't know?' Heather caws after us in derision. 'It's the only thing to know, if you ask me.'

'Poor Heather,' I say as we head down the path. 'It's sad to see her rambling like that.'

'I don't understand the way old people are treated in this country. In Zululand she'd be respected and wouldn't have gone mad.'

We track across some waste ground towards Granby Street, which is changing for the worse, with more litter, more rusting cars at the kerb and more shop fronts boarded up. Mr Gopal is standing on the pavement, watching a gang of lads fight outside the offy.

'Sister Bertie!' His face brightens. 'And Sister Maureen! What can I be doing for you?'

'I've brought you some bantam eggs, my friend,' says Bertilla as she follows him into his shop.

Mr Gopal places the egg-box reverently on the counter. The wall behind him is stacked ceiling-high with vegetables made known to me by Bertie: blood-red chillies, yams, Lent-coloured aubergines and star fruit with spikes like the nails of the Cross. Still queasy after Heather's room, I breathe in deep lungfuls of the aromatic air.

'And what can I be giving you?' says Mr Gopal.

'Tamarind pods,' says Bertilla.

'Take them – take the lot.' He scoops up a double handful and scatters them over the floor. Shocked by his wasteful gesture, I stare in silence at the strewn pods while Bertie lays a hand on his arm.

'Eh, love, I wouldn't do that if I was you,' says a fellow customer in pink rollers. 'They're fetching fifty pence a pound.'

Mr Gopal ignores her. 'I have had a demolition order.' He leans against the counter with his arms folded. 'This is the end for Amira and me.'

'Demolition?' Bertie stoops to pick up some pods. 'But you're doing so well.'

'We are making way for a supermarket. This is not the type of shop they want here any more.'

'Of course it is, love,' says the woman in rollers. 'We'd be lost without you.' Ignoring both him and Bertilla, she turns to face me. 'They're over-sensitive, you know.'

Before I can reply, Bertilla has cut across her. 'We'll get up a petition to the council.'

'I do not think so.' Mr Gopal crams a handful of fresh tamarind pods into Bertie's bag. 'The neighbours are not liking my wife and me.'

'Of course they do,' protests Bertie while I wonder what to say.

'Then why do they send us death threats and dog dirt through the letterbox?'

'There's no need for that sort of talk,' says the woman in rollers as she shuffles out of the shop.

Bertie picks up her bag. 'And I used to think there was apartheid only in South Africa.'

'You are getting prejudice everywhere,' says Mr Gopal, giving her an aubergine. 'People who do not wish to work hate those who do.'

'Don't you believe it,' says Bertie as she opens the door. '*Sale Kahle!* I'll see you at Sunday mass.'

'What is the point of Sunday mass?' Mr Gopal calls after us. 'God is turning his back on the people of Toxteth.'

'Can't the police protect him?' I ask as Bertie and I move away.

'The tension is mounting between black and white – and they don't know what to do. Half the time they make things worse by over-reacting.'

On entering the park we strike across the grass in the direction of St Cuthbert's. 'I've lived here all my life,' I remark, 'yet you seem to know more about the place than I do.'

'I've joined the campaign for a new health centre,' replies Bertie as the convent spires appear through the trees. 'People like it when you get involved.'

'Does Wilfie know?'

'Oh yes,' says Bertie with a chuckle, 'and she tried to ban me. As far as she's concerned Toxteth is full of *tsotsis* and *skollies*. So I wrote straight to Maria Goretti, telling her I had to join the struggle.'

I remember all the times I've obeyed Mother Wilfred without question, not letting the down-and-outs into the kitchen to warm themselves by our Aga, nor unbolting the door after Vespers even when the weather was cold. 'I used to feel like Francis of Assisi,' I confess, 'when all I did was dole out the odd sandwich.'

'There's no easy way forward in Britain. How many of the Choir nuns could work in Toxteth – or deal with Heather March?' Bertie pats her bag of tamarind pods. 'They can start learning about the place tonight with an extra hot brinjal dahl.' To the surprise of a mounted police-woman she waves her bag in the air, making the horse shy and skitter across the road. 'I've brought them a present from Toxteth.'

Life Class

My pencil hesitates at the penis, sketches in a twist of pubic hair then swerves away down the inside leg. The heating is on high for the sake of the nude model, which is fine for the students in T-shirts and jeans but almost unbearable in a habit. My hair is clammy under my veil and I'm more nervous than I'd have thought possible outside the penalty area – so nervous I wish I'd followed my instincts and stayed away.

The trouble began at lunch, when Elisabeth quizzed me about my timetable. Thanks to Bertilla she's agreed to say nothing about the workshops – but drawing a nude man is another matter.

'Not another workshop?' Elisabeth's voice is edged with suspicion.

'Er – just the one, to finish our collages,' I lie, thinking of the Archdeacon. 'Nuns are more sheltered than priests,' he warned me last week in Confession, 'so you'd best say nothing to Sister Elisabeth. And besides, Julia Mulcahy is one of us – Catholic to the core.' He cleared his throat delicately. 'If you want to – um – feel prepared, why not take a look at a few Michelangelos?'

Though I did as he suggested, nothing in my book on the Sistine Chapel has prepared me for the naked model, or the huge roll of sausage-coloured flesh lolling on his thigh.

'In Ancient Greece small penises were considered beautiful,' says Dr Mulcahy, as though reading my mind. I'd like to ask more but daren't. To me even the word penis sounds rude, as though not meant for speaking aloud.

She stoops to change the model's pose, grasping him by the shoulders then crossing one leg over the other. I wonder how the skinny young man can sit unembarrassed before six female students, one of us a nun, under a skylight revealing every pimple. 'It was the same in the Renaissance,' the tutor continues, stepping back to survey the pose. 'Male genitalia are unrealistically tiny because of neoclassic aesthetics – so real-life penises look huge by comparison.'

I look at the model to see if he's listening, but the eyes behind his granny glasses are as pale and expressionless as a goat's. Glancing again at his penis I note that it isn't straight but curved upwards as though trying to peer through the skylight with its tiny eye. Then a single magpie flutters across the glass and I know for sure that Elisabeth will burst in at any moment. This is what Mam calls my second sight.

The tutor pauses by Hannah's easel. 'The more essays you write, the worse you get. And as for your colour sense —'

'What do you make of Dr Palfrey's colour sense?' asks Hannah slyly. Since discovering I admire him she's started peppering her talk with cheeky remarks.

'Minimalist.'

'His neckwear isn't minimalist. Paisley cravats and Yves St Laurent ties – I wonder who buys them.'

'Stop gossiping, Hannah. This is a workshop not a fashion house.'

After a grin in my direction, Hannah bends her bullet head to look for her charcoal. Glad of the silence, I get on with drawing the model's arm which stays obstinately puny-looking no matter how thick I make its lines. Looking up from my easel I catch the eye of the fox-faced Vicky, who smirks and carries on sketching. At the end of the first hour the model slips on his jeans and sweater and goes out on the fire escape for a smoke.

'Where's Toby?' Dr Mulcahy asks Vicky.

'Perhaps he's got stuck down a pot-hole – or else,' Vicky giggles, 'he can't stand the competition.'

I'm not surprised by her flippant tone. Vicky is rumoured to be having an affair with a tutor called Rex Harries, known to the students as Sexy Rexy, a plump man with a snub nose who hangs round the foyer eyeing up the First Years.

'I feel like Auguste Renoir in reverse,' says Hannah, surveying her thumb-nail sketches. 'It's powerful for a woman, drawing a naked man.'

Feeling anything but powerful, I start shading in the model's elbow. The sweat trickles down my back and I still have a sense of foreboding – but when the door bangs open at mid-afternoon it's only Toby, his blond curls tangled and his Adidas bag in his hand.

'Wherever have you been?' asks Dr Mulcahy.

'My car broke down so I hitch-hiked from Page Moss.'

'Very dedicated.'

'I didn't want to miss this,' says Toby with a wave at the model.

'You'll have plenty more life classes,' says the tutor as Toby goes to his easel. 'Use the last twenty minutes to sketch this pose.'

As he settles down to work Dr Mulcahy continues to move round the studio, stopping now and then to correct a line. 'The model's leaning on his elbow.' She points at my drawing of the biceps which still look ridiculously feeble. 'Exaggerate the thickness of the upper arm then you'll show that it's bearing his weight.' She takes my charcoal and shades in a muscle before adding, 'There's something else missing, Sister Maureen.'

It can't be the penis, I think, staring at my easel where it's boldly portrayed in all its monstrous size.

'He's a man not a gelding,' she laughs when I've gazed in vain for a few more seconds. 'You've forgotten his testicles.'

I wait till the tutor's moved on then take another look at the model. The two tiny coconuts nestling behind his penis prove so fiddly to draw that I almost fail to notice when the door opens a second time.

'Oh no,' mutters Toby. 'It's Bostik again.'

Elisabeth is taking in the whole scene – me, the naked model, Toby, Hannah, Vicky – everyone that is except Dr Mulcahy who's hunting for charcoal in the corner cupboard.

'Sister Maureen,' says Elisabeth in an icy tone, 'you must leave here at once.'

I cast an embarrassed glance at Dr Mulcahy, but far from looking annoyed by the interruption, she calmly closes the cupboard door and saunters to the front of the class. 'Sister

Elisabeth,' she cries. 'I was wondering when you'd drop in.'

To my relief Elisabeth has turned her attention from me to the tutor. But instead of explaining her mission she stands staring at her far beyond the point where it's polite. 'Sister Julian,' she croaks at last.

I too am staring at Julia Mulcahy. At last – that nagging sense that I've known her before is explained. Now I remember who she is – the nun who taught English in high school, and vanished in odd circumstances. Besides being softer and more lined, the face is now framed by auburn hair instead of a wimple, and the slim-waisted figure is shown to advantage in silk shirt and jeans. But how could I have forgotten those green-grey eyes and the imperious, almost impious air?

'Why didn't you tell me who you were?' I burst out from the back of the room.

'You'd have been forbidden to come to the studio,' she replies easily. 'I wanted to spare you a crisis of conscience.'

As Dr Mulcahy returns her attention to Elisabeth I step back to my easel, suddenly aware of curious glances.

'I'm surprised you haven't called in earlier,' the tutor is saying, a hint of menace beneath the friendly tone.

The two women seem oblivious to the rest of us.

Elisabeth eyes the tight jeans and shingled hair, then gives a glance in my direction. 'I should have known you'd wangle your way in here.'

Between the two women I can see the model, his eyes at knee-level, following their conversation like a tennis match.

'Wangle? According to the Archdeacon, that's how *you* got into the English Department.'

'So the Archdeacon's in on this!'

Seeing that the students have all stopped drawing, the model gets to his feet, stretches then leans against the attic door with his arms folded.

Ostentatiously averting her eyes, Elisabeth turns back to me. 'I've come to collect Sister Maureen.'

'You talk as though she's a piece of left luggage,' says Dr Mulcahy.

'And you, I see, are up to your old tricks – corrupting a young nun.'

'And how might I be doing that?'

'By sneaking her into a life class.'

'Sneaking? How apt that is coming from you,' says Dr Mulcahy, looking like a cat who's extending her claws. 'I take it you do remember our last meeting?'

Elisabeth shrinks back a little. 'I – yes – it was – er – before you left St Cuthbert's.'

'You sound thirsty. Vicky, make Sister Elisabeth a cup of coffee.'

Her eyes sharp with curiosity, Vicky spoons some Nescafe into a mug and fills it with water from the geyser. 'Were you once a nun,' she asks the tutor, 'like Sister Maureen and Sister – er – Elisabeth?'

'Like Sister Maureen, perhaps, but not like Sister Elisabeth. We had different notions of duty, didn't we, Sister Elisabeth?'

'I must go now,' says Elisabeth, her face set. 'It's time for my petit examen.'

'Oh yes, overhauling your conscience,' nods Dr Mulcahy, handing her the cup of coffee. 'Very important. As it happens I can help you with that.'

'You? Never!' Elisabeth slams down her coffee untouched on a nearby chair, makes for the door, balks at the sight of the naked model and turns back to me. 'Are you coming or not?'

Gripping the sides of my easel with both hands I stare at Elisabeth without moving. It's the first time I've ignored the command of a Choir nun.

'So now what will you do?' calls Dr Mulcahy. 'Sneak on Maureen like you sneaked on me?'

'You did that?' I gasp at Elisabeth.

'She most certainly did,' cuts in Dr Mulcahy. 'Didn't you, Sister Elisabeth?

'But why?' I persist, my pulse racing.

'She never gave me the chance to find out,' says the tutor, 'which is why I'm asking her now.'

Silence falls on the studio as Elisabeth raises her eyes. 'Because you're a disgusting woman who does disgusting things.' For a second she looks as though she's going to carry on but she shuts her mouth and makes a gesture which sweeps round the room till it reaches the model, whose penis has shrunk to the size of a garden snail. Then she elbows him out of the way, yanks open the door and darts off down the stairs.

The Red Card

The model bends over, picks up his granny glasses and stumbles towards his clothing. As if released from a spell I snatch up my drawing and jam it into its folder.

Dr Mulcahy follows me on to the landing. 'Please don't go. There's something I've been meaning to tell you.'

'I must catch Elisabeth – or she'll run straight to Mother Wilfred.'

'Don't I know it.'

I hurtle downstairs two at a time and nearly knock over Mrs Dagnall who's standing in the front hall with her chest stuck out. '*Miss* O'Shaunessy, if you could remember where you are—'

Elisabeth must already be on the bus because the street's empty apart from a bin bag which flops down the pavement towards me like an injured crow. My impulse is to run down the Boulevard but that would take far longer than the bus ride so I force myself to wait at the stop. In an effort to be calm, I grope in my pocket for my rosary but all I find is

Lol's lucky black poodle. Then a bus speeds round the corner and I climb on.

I should be worrying about Mother Wilfred, but my head's too full of what I've just heard. So Dr Mulcahy used to be Sister Julian, my old English teacher, who corrupted a young nun – whatever Elisabeth meant by that. Slumped in the nearest seat, I let my mind whirr like a bacon-slicer through all the things that have puzzled me in the past: the sly questions of Heather March at the back door, Gonzaga's brusque response, and Heather's nosy remarks in her flat. Wishing I was a lay sister again with nothing on my conscience but listening to the sports news, I lean my head against the window and pray that God will make Wilfie hard for Elisabeth to find.

There's no sign of Wilfie in the front hall. Desperate for advice, I glance at Bertie's shelf by the back door. Her colander and cape are on their hook, which means she's probably in the infirmary.

As I reach the top of the stairs Wilfie's entering the corridor from the far end with Elisabeth in tow. On seeing me they both pause – then Elisabeth dives off in the other direction.

'Well, Sister Maureen,' says the Superior, her eyes like stones. 'What do you have to say for yourself?'

She obviously expects me to apologise straightaway but too many questions are pressed against my lips.

'I'm waiting.'

'Elisabeth's a sneak,' I say, remembering the words of Julia Mulcahy. 'She has no right to tell tales.'

'She has every right, because I myself made her your keeper. She was fulfilling her trust.'

Watching a whisker waggle on Wilfie's chin, I think of all the O'Shaunessys who've never grassed anyone up and never will. 'It was you who made me go to university in the first place,' I say, conscious of speaking more loudly than usual. 'Life class is part of my degree.'

'Unlike you, Sister Elisabeth does not lie. She has told me it is an option.'

'It may not be compulsory,' I say stubbornly, 'but it's still part of the course – and the rest of my group was going.'

'You should follow the Rule, not the rest of your group. And that means asking permission.'

I glance over her shoulder at the red-faced baby Jesus. 'But I did ask permission – I asked it from the Archdeacon.'

'When?'

'Last week in Confession.'

Brigid enters the corridor and then, after a glance at Wilfie's face, slides past with her eyes down.

'The Archdeacon is undermining my authority,' says Mother Wilfred, her voice hoarse, 'perhaps even our order. And you, Sister Maureen, are playing into his hands.'

'But Dr Mulcahy was once a nun —'

'A nun, you say? A misfit and deviant, more like.'

'The Archdeacon said she was one of us and Catholic to the core.'

'While tempting you to leer at a nude man?' Mother Wilfred gives a tight smile. 'You are the same as you were in the fourth form – silly and impure.'

My eye's caught again by the baby Jesus tweaking his mother's nipple. 'Then why did you make me pray to a naked baby boy?'

Turning to follow my gaze, Mother Wilfred stares for a second at the baby Jesus, then her mouth sags open. 'You are wicked and – even more corrupt than I had thought,' she gasps. 'Those are devotional paintings.' She snatches my folder from under my arm, unzips it and claws at the paper inside. 'Whereas you are bringing the devil's work to St Cuthbert's!'

'Please don't look!' I cry in panic. 'Those are my drawings.'

As though by instinct she plucks out the nude and holds it at arm's length. As we stare at it in silence I remember the condom I brought into school as a girl, how she bore it to her study with stiff fingers and dropped it on to her desk.

Underneath, I know she has cause to be angry but I'm too pumped up with indignation to draw back, even if it means a red card.

'You were wrong to expel me from school,' I shout, aware of having wanted to say these words for a long time, 'and maybe you were wrong to expel Sister Julian.'

At that Mother Wilfred drops the folder, takes my drawing in both hands, shuts her eyes and rips it down the centre. Then she crams the pieces into her pocket and wipes her hands on the skirt of her habit. 'You don't know what you are talking about.'

'Then why won't you tell me?' I shout. 'Everybody else knows what happened.'

Columba appears at the bottom of the corridor and gives a shocked glance in our direction. Mother Wilfred waits until she's disappeared, then carries on. 'Have you ever asked yourself why we've all tried to protect you?'

'Yes – but I get no answers.'

'If I'd had my way you would not have gone to university.' Mother Wilfred is breathing heavily, and her face is grey. 'Then your naïvety might have remained a blessing.'

I think of my lay sister's life – willingly offered up for the sake of St Cuthbert's. 'But I didn't want to go either.'

'That is true, you did not.' To my surprise Mother Wilfred's tone has grown almost calm. 'Mother General telephoned just now,' she continues, watching me intently. 'I felt obliged to tell her about your behaviour.'

Her sad, low voice is more troubling than her anger and I stare at her in dismay, knowing that the Superior's will is the will of God, and that what I've said and done today can never be put right.

'Mother Maria Goretti was surprised to hear you are reading Art History,' continues this new, quiet Mother Wilfred, 'a pointless subject, in her view. Business Studies would be of more use to the order.'

I stoop to pick up my dropped folder. 'But I'm getting good at Art History.'

'That last remark confirms my belief that study has worsened your character.'

'I can't do Business Studies – I haven't got the right A levels.'

'Mother General has summoned me to Rome. If we find time to discuss your future, I shall explain that I too think Business Studies the wrong choice.'

'Thank you, Mother,' I say with a sense of relief. Today has been terrible – too much to take in – but Mother Wilfred is right. I've been deceitful and disobedient, and should apologise at once. From now on I'll be a model nun.

'You fail to understand me, Sister Maureen. Your behaviour at university has been at best irresponsible and at worst evil – and Miss Julia Mulcahy has deliberately endangered your vocation.' Mother Wilfred takes her rosary from her belt, and starts walking away down the corridor. 'I shall recommend to Mother General not that you continue with Art History, but that you leave university altogether.'

Pious and Placid

Knees shaking, I lunge at the infirmary door. It flies open with a crash to reveal Sisters Pious and Placid sitting up in bed with their tea trays. After flinching in feigned alarm, Pious trains her twin cataracts in my direction. 'What the hell do you mean, barging in here like this?'

'Where's Bertilla?' I ask her.

'Putting wire-netting on her hen run.' Pious puts on a mock-African accent and flaps her skinny elbows. 'To save her bleddie bantams from de big red bird.'

Placid, who's deaf as Pious is blind, looks up from her tray with a shy smile. Big-boned, red-faced and nervous, she suits her name no better than Pious.

Sensing I'm on my way out, Pious raises a freckled hand.

'What do you want?' I ask reluctantly.

She extracts a shred of cheese from her dentures and slides them back in her mouth. 'Tell me what the bloody row was about,' she whispers, her small face avid.

'That's my business.'

'Not any more, my dear – not after yelling like that.'

Placid has stopped chewing her sandwich and is sitting with an air of strained attention. I feel a prickly heat rise up my body. Where did I read that young nuns don't become saints, they turn into old nuns? Heaven preserve me from turning into anything like these two.

'I can't eat this bloody cheese,' complains Pious, pointing at a lump of Cheddar. 'It's high fat.'

'Why not wait for Bertie?' I say, halted in the doorway.

'Will you shut that door?' begs Placid. 'I'm in a draught.'

'Take this muck away.' Pious shoves at her plate so hard that it flies from the tray. 'My mother died of a fatty heart.'

Luckily the plate doesn't break. As I trail across to pick it up my mind's eye pierces Pious's breastbone to where her heart lies red and sore as the Sacred Heart's on the wall.

'Too much cheese is bad for an old woman,' she says. 'The darkie should know better.'

'Watch what you say, Pious,' warns Sister Placid from the next bed. 'Bertilla might be a witch doctor.'

'Coloured people's voodoo. It don't scare me.'

'My tea's stone cold.'

Desperate for an aspirin, I tug at the door of the medicine cabinet. 'She keeps it locked,' snaps Pious. 'You'll have to mortify yourself.'

'I'm going to get the key.'

Pious's nose, shaped like the blade of an axe, seems to grow larger as she grows blinder. 'We shouldn't be left on our own,' she sniffs, 'we should be in Yorkshire —'

'— and would have been,' Placid takes up the refrain, 'if not for Mother Maria Flibbertigibbetti.'

She means Mother Maria Goretti, who closed down the

old nuns' retirement home on the Yorkshire coast when it stopped being cost-effective.

'Farmed out!' warbles Placid.

'And cruelly neglected by that damn, damn darkie,' adds Pious. 'Doesn't it make you sick?'

'I've been in a draught for the last half-hour,' complains Placid. 'Will you shut the window?'

'It shouldn't have been open in the first place.' Pious's blind head tracks a squadron of microbes abseiling towards her nostrils. 'Liverpool air is full of germs.'

I close the window, step backwards, then bang into something hard and sharp. 'What's that?' I cry, rubbing my ankle.

'It's Pious's treasure chest,' says Placid.

Bending down, I see a big black trunk protruding from the hem of the counterpane. It has brass corners and a huge padlock. 'What's in it?'

The bobbles on Pious's shawl shiver in indignation. 'Mind your own bloody business.'

'She waits till she thinks I'm asleep,' whispers Placid, 'then drags it out.'

'You should ask someone to move it for you,' I say to Pious. 'It's far too heavy.'

Pious turns her blind eyes to the door as though I'm leaving already.

'If I was Mother Wilfred,' says Placid, 'I'd make Pious give me her key then check what's in the trunk. She keeps me awake half the night with her rummaging.'

Pious is still gazing at the door when it opens and Brigid slides in.

'Sister Maureen,' she says in a low voice, 'I'd like a word.'

And I'd like an aspirin, I want to cry back, but her tone is so pleading that I let her draw me through the door beside the medicine cabinet. It leads to an empty room that used to be the infirmary annexe in the days when St Cuthbert's was a large community. I can tell from the musty air that no lay sister living or dead has been here for a long time.

Brigid shuts the door behind us and we track across the dusty floor to a bed on the far side. She beckons me to sit beside her and smiles awkwardly.

Go on, Bid, spit it out, I want to say but am stopped by a glance at her wan face.

'I heard Wilfie shouting at you in the corridor,' she whispers after a few seconds.

'So what?' I retort, wondering if there's anyone who didn't.

'Please, Maureen, don't be cross. It was about Sister Julian, wasn't it?'

'Partly.' Avoiding Brigid's shamefaced smile, I stare through the grimy sash windows at the trees thrashing in the May wind. It's an unlucky month, and for the second time today I know something desperate is going to be said.

'It was because of me that Julian got expelled,' says Brigid, reddening.

I stare into her troubled face.

'We grew too close,' she explains, turning redder still.

Is this what Dr Mulcahy was wanting to tell me? 'What do you mean, too close?'

'You're so naïve.' Brigid sounds on the brink of tears. 'Naïve and difficult to talk to.' And then when I say nothing she sighs and says in a low voice, 'Julian and I were lovers – lesbians.'

'Lesbians!' It's the first time I've ever said the word out

loud and it slithers horribly across my tongue, its s's hissing to one another in unholy communion.

'She tempted me,' mutters Brigid. 'I must have been bewitched or something.'

'Not here in St Cuthbert's?'

'Only for a few weeks,' says Brigid defensively. 'Then Elisabeth found out and went to Mother Wilfred.'

I feel as though I've slipped out of the convent day into a place I never knew existed. While Brigid mumbles on about it being a long time ago and not caring for Julian any more, I struggle to find my bearings. Lesbians are women who do weird things to each other in bed; but Brigid's from the Dingle like me, so where did she learn how to do them? My mind whirling, I try to square my image of the cool and assured Dr Mulcahy with squirmings and fumblings in a tangled bed.

Trying to avoid Brigid's eye, I stare at the twin tracks of our feet. I always thought I knew about St Cuthbert's – its beggars, its ghosts, and all the secret life of its building. Now I see that its real secrets have been kept for years in rooms like this with stale mattresses and faded curtains. I wonder how Brigid and Julian managed to set up their meetings in the Choir nuns' regimented day – with a pluck of the sleeve, perhaps, or a shamefaced glance from beneath the lashes like Brigid is giving me now?

'Don't look so shocked,' she says pleadingly. 'I can see you think I'm disgusting but I had to tell you because Julian's after you now, I know she is – otherwise she wouldn't have arranged that life class. She's trying to corrupt you like she did me.'

'She can try but she won't get very far.'

'Don't you like her?' Brigid sounds half-anxious, half-hopeful. 'I thought I didn't in the beginning, but she charmed me.'

Her thin lips make an O of pain as I spring to my feet and track back across the floor, leaving her on the bed with her head hanging.

In Trouble with God

On a rainy Monday morning the community gathers in the porch to wish Mother Wilfred God speed. She's told no one why she's going to Rome but Bosco, puffed up with her own importance, is escorting her to the airport. The two old nuns step into the taxi while the rest of us wave. Pale and tentative, Brigid smiles at me from across the hall. I know that God Himself forgave Mary Magdalen, and that Brigid conquered her shame in order to protect me, but the thought of her sin makes me too uncomfortable to meet her eye.

As the taxi chugs off to the M62 we turn back to the dark old house. Looking bright but tense, Elisabeth catches me up in the cloister. 'How I envy Wilfie going to Rome,' she says with a little smile.

Her words land on my skin like hives and begin to itch. 'Don't pretend everything's normal because it isn't. You grassed me up and I shan't forget it.'

'Sisters! Sisters!' says Ursula. 'This is a place of silence.'

Elisabeth waits for her to disappear through the chapel arch. 'You're the sneaky one, Maureen.' Far from being abject she sounds resentful. 'You should have told me about that life class but you said nothing.'

'Are you surprised,' I hiss back, 'when you keep telling tales?'

'Because of you I had to face Julian in front of all those students.' Elisabeth's voice begins to tremble. 'It was the worst humiliation of my life.'

'Lucky you,' I reply, thinking of my sister Lol and all the other people I know who've been shamed for years by social workers and the dole. 'Your tale-telling got you a pat on the head from Wilfie but for me it means the end of art history – and just when I was beginning to enjoy it. So will you just shut up and leave me alone?'

I'm pursued through the cloister by her high little voice, begging me to be reasonable. Though I cock her a deafie I know I'm not being totally honest. She may have spoilt my chance of a degree but I, who come from the Dingle, should have known the long reach of authority. Why, I wonder as the chapel door swings open, did I so recklessly go to life class, throw away my education for a second time, and let down Mam, Dad, my sisters and the Archdeacon?

Flopping into my pew, I wonder if something went wrong with my training. I was Gonzaga's first new lay sister in forty years and instead of going by the book she formed me in her awkward, intractable image. What the eye don't see, the heart don't grieve about. It was her favourite motto, and from her I learned to ignore the bell whenever possible and the Holy Rule as a matter of course. While the Choir nuns were at prayer Gonzaga and I would toast our feet at the Aga, tune into the Curran and make bets with each other on the next race – a decade of the rosary on Springtime in Paris who always fell at the last fence.

When she grew too old to work I took over her chores with a glad heart, listening to Radio Merseyside as I peeled the potatoes, and stealing meat for the tramps – like St Martin halving his cloak with the beggar, or a female Robin Hood. What with my command of the kitchen, the rheumy thanks of the down-and-outs, and Wilfie getting older and less observant, I had soon grown unruly as a briar rose from our back garden.

Prickly and wild as I was, in those days I lived in God's presence, and His love for me flowed through my broom, making every brushstroke a blessing. The convent building was my life and I lived at its heart, cleaning its windows, sweeping its flues and thriving like a weed in the cracks of convent routine.

Now I'm starting to think housework's a waste of time, and feel sorry for women like Mam and Gonzaga who've spent their lives cooking and cleaning. Unlike the female painters I've discovered at the uni, they never got the chance to use their talents. Because life class is over I've managed to avoid Julia Mulcahy – but thanks to her show-down with Elisabeth the students have lost their reserve, and now talk freely in my presence. Art, travel, politics – they all of them know more than me, even the most naïve. And when they start on sex I feel a divvy because I've never been to bed with a boy and can't help wishing I had – just once, to see what it was like.

I stick to my vow of chastity by not dwelling on what I've missed; but I've grown obsessed by the human form, its bones, joints and muscles, all so personal and expressive. In lectures I sometimes find myself studying the slim shape of

Piers Palfrey and wondering what he'd look like with no clothes on – and then bend my head in shock. To undress a tutor with my eyes – it's disgusting.

In my head I know my future's in God's hands, and that if He allows Wilfie to withdraw me from university it's for my own protection. But I'm sure to go mad with boredom, and would far rather use my degree in the new comprehensive to help other girls escape the Dingle. That longing too is a sin – a vanity of vanities – but it's what I feel.

'You've become an intellectual,' grumbled Gonzaga the other day as I swabbed half-heartedly at the Aga. Like Columba she's out of patience with me, and no longer invites me to chat in the kitchen. Officially I'm a Choir nun, but the Choir nuns don't trust me either so I drift round the convent like a lost soul.

What's worse, I'm in trouble with God – or rather with His absence. To work, says St Benedict, is to pray, and once my devotion to cleaning reached up to the convent rooftop and down to its cellars. Yodelling 'Love Me Do' as I swept, I would feel like King David singing and leaping before the Ark. But without my housework I've lost all sense of God. Kneeling in chapel is useless as the silence is overpowering and the thin polite air won't let me ever forget myself. Ranged in two straight rows, the Choir nuns sing through their noses to the tick of a metronome. On seeing their pale absorbed faces I wish that I too could tune in to God's presence, but for me He's to be found in the eyes of a tramp on the back step or the sheen of a well-scrubbed floor – not on a snowy white altar.

As I wait for the end of the Divine Office my straying eye is caught by the crucifix and I begin to anatomise the Saviour's body – a nineteenth-century Italian woodcarving, I decide, and rather sentimental. The artist would have done well to attend life class, because the delicate palms would be torn by those over-large nails and the legs are too short for the torso. And surely that loin cloth in brutal reality would not stay so neatly in place. In my mind's eye I twitch it away as though the crucified Saviour was an art school model. For all the frozen prawns of the Baby Jesuses, we never see the penis of the grown-up Christ. Then, shocked by my corruption, I make a fervent act of contrition.

And yet I long to gaze my fill. How else, I ask myself, can I learn to draw? As Mother Wilfred would say, I'm possessed by the powerful devil of curiosity.

'Sweet sixteen and never been kissed!' Lorraine used to taunt me. 'You're a case of arrested development.'

My only reply was to toss my head, sure that God had called me to better things than marriage and motherhood.

'Bollocks, girl!' Lol would shout back. 'You're unplugged at the mains.'

Now life has plugged me in and I wish it hadn't. Once so scornful of sex, for the last few nights I've lain feverishly trying to blot out images of Brigid and Dr Mulcahy: images that come back no matter how often I whisper a Hail Mary or will myself to sleep; of knowing smiles in recreation and eager touching behind closed doors. When Brigid first told me I was stunned into disapproving silence – but an ugly desire for details of her sin is growing inside me.

As the bell sounds for the end of prayers I glance round my fellow Choir nuns and wonder if any of them have ever had such thoughts. I decide not, then notice Brigid with her face in her hands. Who would have thought her capable of passion – and for another nun at that? I think of Sister

Julian the English teacher, haughty and austere, and then see her as Dr Mulcahy, moving about the art room in her tight black jeans and clingy T-shirt, and wonder if she thinks I'm more attractive than Brigid, and if she's ever considered making a pass? And if so, when would she do it and how?

I make the sign of the cross at once and rise to my feet, appalled that I've dwelt on this thought for a split second. And then I feel a stab of regret that life class is over. Our exams start in a fortnight, so instead of joining my sisters in recreation I take advantage of Wilfie's absence to slope off to the library. There I blot out all contradictions by reading for three solid hours, going to bed with my head full of the Dutch Renaissance.

But I wake before dawn out of a dream about Brigid and Julian kissing naked in a room I've never visited, a room overlooking a full grey sea with sailboats on the horizon. My nipples are swollen and my breasts tingling, and painfully pleasant contractions are subsiding in my womb.

Unable to get back to sleep, I lie and wait for the clock to chime three and the blackbird outside my window to start serenading the false dawn of the street light.

The next day I force myself to recount my dream in Confession. It's the first time I've ever mentioned a sin against the flesh, and there's silence on the far side of the grille. Then the Archdeacon clears his throat and assures me that not even Aristotle holds us responsible for our dreams.

I sense that I've fallen from grace, with no available point of return.

The Number One Striker

It's our last tutorial before the exams and as we gather up our books at the end Dr Palfrey asks me to stay behind. He waits patiently while the others leave the room, then shuts the door.

'Wouldn't you like to tell me what the matter is?' he says, drawing up an armchair.

For a moment I'm tempted to pour out my troubles. I've grown to trust him over the year and, since finding out about Brigid and Dr Mulcahy, have decided I prefer his relaxed but courteous manner to her sharp and sardonic one.

'Nothing's the matter,' I reply. Even though I've brought it on myself, I know he'd think Wilfie's decision ignorant and petty-minded. 'It's just that the exams are coming up and I haven't started to revise.' The last bit is true enough. No matter how hard I work the result will be the same: no more study. So revision is pointless.

'Then why not look at some genre paintings?' he asks with a smile. 'They have a very calming influence.'

It's a hint as to what's coming up on my first paper and I should feel grateful – but I can't face more black and white floor tiles.

'Borrow this,' he plucks a hardback from his shelf, 'then come back and tell me what you think.'

Gerrit Dou, Gerard ter Borch, Pieter de Hoogh – I flip through his book that evening and then, anxious to have done, shove it back into my bag. As I make for his room next day I catch sight of Dr Mulcahy on the top landing but turn away when she starts to speak. At least, I think as I knock on Dr Palfrey's door, I won't be seeing much more of her.

Though clearly surprised I've returned so soon, Dr Palfrey invites me in and explains the merits of one reproduction after another while I try to stop fidgeting. The afternoon is, thank goodness, nearly over when he jumps to his feet. 'What an idiot I am,' he exclaims, 'not to have thought earlier.'

He pulls down yet another hardback then sits on the arm of my chair so I can look at it with him. Unlike Dr Mulcahy, who often sets out to shock, Dr Palfrey seems rather reserved. But my nostrils are filled with the lemony scent of his after-shave, and his sleeve's so close that my vision is filled with tweed. Then my attention's caught by a servant girl in a white-walled kitchen. 'Who did that?' I cry.

'Vermeer,' he replies, as smug as a schoolboy who's taken a wicket. 'I knew you'd like him.'

I stare at the maid's white headdress and unruffled brow. She's like a picture of myself as a nun – not as I am now, with so many acts of disobedience on my conscience, but as I used to be, safe in the heart of St Cuthbert's.

Dr Palfrey leans forward, accidentally brushing my

cheek. 'Vermeer always begins with the ideal.' His manicured nail traces the light from a window high in the left-hand corner of the painting. 'From there he goes to the real – unlike most genre painters who do the opposite.'

I sit back and stare at the girl's beefy hands which are cradling an earthenware jug. The trickle of milk from its lip is so lifelike it could be moving.

Dr Palfrey turns to Vermeer's picture of a seamstress, then on to another of a serving-girl. 'Note the light on the white walls,' he says, 'and the moments of perfect equipoise.'

'You'd have made a good monk,' I say boldly.

He twists his neck to look down at me. 'And why is that?'

'Because you prefer the visionary side of painting – its serenity and stillness.'

'And you, Sister Maureen – what do you prefer?'

'I like the women when they're practical – and living at the centre of their own lives.'

'Just as you do.' Dr Palfrey snaps the book shut and rises to his feet. 'Unworldly, pure and reticent,' he adds with a little bow.

Though I smile at his compliment I also feel a tug of regret that he still doesn't know me, and that now it's nearly too late.

'Why not take the book home to enjoy at leisure?' he's saying. 'That is, if you nuns ever have such a thing.'

I want to say he's wasting his time because I'll soon be gone from his course. But he's already fastening his bag so I pick up the heavy volume. 'I'll bring it back soon.'

He flaps his hands in the air. 'Why not have it for keeps?'

I glance at the jacket with its £25 sticker. 'I couldn't,' I say to him reluctantly. 'I have a Vow of Poverty.'

'Then put it in your convent library. I have dozens of books on Vermeer.'

When I get home that afternoon I smuggle the volume up to my cell. Soon I'll put it in the library as Dr Palfrey suggested – perhaps when my exams are over, and Wilfie's back from Rome. But it feels too early to part with it yet, so I hide it beneath my towels with my little pink mirror.

Next day the temperature soars into the eighties and the grass in the Georgian square is littered with students in shorts, T-shirts and even bikinis, smearing each other with Ambre Solaire and pretending to revise at the same time. Swaddled in my habit I thread my way across the lawn, trying not to stare at the glistening patches of white, brown and reddening flesh.

As I reach the pavement Lorraine whizzes past in her brand-new Fiesta then skids to a halt in the middle of the road. Mam told me a few weeks ago: Lol's got a new job with the Corpy and is renting a flat in nearby Gambier Terrace. 'What's the matter?' she calls as she backs up.

I gaze at my sister's strappy T-shirt and think how nice it must be to feel cool. 'What do you mean?' I ask, wondering if she's heard about my life class.

'I hardly recognised you – trailing along with your head bowed.'

Life, I reflect, has many twists and turns. Only a few months ago it was Lol who was down while I jollied her along from the convent parlour – and now she's brimming with energy while I'm wiped out by worry and sleepless nights. I long to pour out my troubles, but Lol's hated Mother Wilfred from school and would only rail against her. 'It's my exams,' I say feebly.

'Just make sure you pass,' she says, pressing in the cigarette lighter. 'Mam and Dad are depending on you.'

I dump my bag of books on the pavement. 'You of all people shouldn't have said that – because you *know* what a pressure it is.'

As the pain flickers in her eyes I rush on to the next subject. 'Do you remember Sister Julian?' I lower my voice instinctively though Dr Mulcahy's room is on the top storey.

Lorraine makes to open the passenger door. 'Why don't you hop inside?'

'I have to go to the library. Answer my question, Lol.'

'Of course I remember her. Snotty cow.'

'Do you know why she left?'

Lorraine fishes in her bag for a cigarette. 'Everybody knows that.'

'Knows what, exactly?'

'Knows she's a lezzy – her and Brigid.'

'How did you find out?'

'It was the talk of Catholic Liverpool, Dumbo.'

I plant both hands on the hot metal roof. 'Then how come I never heard – not from Mother Wilfred or you or the Archdeacon or Mam and Dad, not even from Brigid herself until a few days ago?'

Lol expels her smoke into the wing mirror. 'Have you ever asked yourself why no one ever tells you anything?'

'It's because I'm the least important person around – so I always get overlooked.'

'Bollocks, kid.' Lol flicks the ash with a small fingernail which is painted, I notice, to match her T-shirt. 'It's because you're so ignorant and girlish. You were the same in your teens – as if you didn't want to grow up.'

It's unfair, I want to wail. She sees me as sexless but I'm tortured by wicked dreams I can't even tell her about.

'Perhaps student life is an eye-opener?' Lol is watching me closely. 'I must say I've been hoping so.' She waves her hand in the direction of Gambier Terrace. 'You should pop in for a coffee sometime, and no, don't tell me that Wilfie won't let you. It's high time you thought for yourself.' Though Lol's words sound harsh her smile is not, and she gives me a cheery wave as she revs up the engine.

Despite the hot weather most seats in the library are taken, and rows of brown, black and chestnut heads are bent over their books. I'm just about to give up and go home when I spot a single desk on the first floor overlooking the car park.

Slumped on the hot vinyl seat, I gaze down at the rows of shining roofs, thinking of Mam and Dad and how choked they'll be when they hear my news. I remember my boast to Mam on the eve of my interview: once I was a number one striker, and good strikers know how to chase lost causes. How arrogant it sounds now, and how little I knew of the world. But at least it was fighting talk and spoken like an O'Shaunessy.

On the desk in front of me is my precious book on Vermeer which I've carried into the uni in case Bosco does a spot check on my cell. It has opened by chance at the picture of the maid pouring milk in her kitchen. Perhaps it's a good omen, I think, my spirits rising a little. By studying hard I might do well in my exams and then who knows? Mother General may change her mind – or I could write to the Archdeacon and beg him to work on Mother Wilfred. Anything's better than sinking without trace.

Recalling my bungled drawing of the model's biceps in my only life class, I copy the milkmaid's outline into my jotter, divide it into six sections then begin to work on the detail. The foreshortening of her right forearm is so cunning and complicated that soon I've lost all sense of my surroundings.

'Still enjoying Vermeer?'

Startled, I stare at the manicured hand on the edge of my desk. 'More than ever,' I reply.

'Well,' says Dr Palfrey after a pause, 'I just wanted to give you this.' As he slides an invitation card across the desk I glimpse the words dinner and 7.30 and an address in italics. 'For the year's most promising students,' he explains. 'Every year I invite a small group before their exams. Will you be able to come?'

Nuns do not attend social events but this may well be my last chance to talk to my fellow students so it doesn't seem a lot to ask – especially, I remember with a surge of hope, now that Wilfie's away in Rome. 'Of course I can come,' I tell him.

I wait till he's disappeared into the stacks and then, my weariness vanished, gather my books and hurry to the bus stop. Back at the convent there's no sign of Bosco, who's acting as Wilfie's deputy. Too restless to think of revising, I wander down to the herb garden where, in defiance of Mother Wilfred and the English summer, Bertie and Columba have planted beds of ragged robin, honesty, herb robert and yellow archangel where once there were roses and begonias.

'Howsit, Moey!' says Bertie. 'Not at work?'

'I need some fresh air.' I pick up a trowel and then pause, not knowing where to start. With everything growing in such profusion it's impossible to tell where the flowers end and the weeds begin.

'It's hard, Wilfie pulling you out of the uni,' says Columba, her small head cocked to one side, 'though us lay sisters will be glad when you're back.'

'And so will the people of Liverpool 8,' says Bertie. 'You can give me a hand in the Health Centre.'

Columba starts weeding the spinach while Bertie tugs at a stem of the Rambling Rector. I smile down at both their backs, the broad and the narrow: two women in love with their jobs, their skirts kilted up round their hips and their nails black with soil – while I couldn't care less about the old lay sisters or the new Health Centre. All I seem to want these days is to show off to my tutor and moon over books.

'I wonder why Wilfie hasn't written,' says Columba, straightening her back.

'Too busy jolling,' chuckles Bertie.

'What's yolling?' asks Columba.

'Going out on the town – having a good time.'

Columba shakes her head. 'Maria Goretti might want to close us down, like she did with the Scarborough home. She might be breaking the news to Mother Wilfred.'

'Not her,' says Bertie. 'On her trip to Jo'burg she spent all her time where the action was. There's work to be done in Toxteth and she knows it.' She yanks at the Rambling Rector, already becoming a briar rose, and trains it round the trunk of the pear tree. 'Eh, Moey, you're daydreaming.'

Through the window I can see a bulky shape trotting into the community room.

'Sorry – must go.'

By the time I get inside Bosco's busy writing a letter. I tell her the dinner party's a sort of revision session and my attendance is vital.

'When is this seminar?' asks Bosco, looking worried. It's

the first time her Superior's been absent and for all her bluster she's not enjoying her new role.

'Friday evening at 7.30.'

'And where does your tutor live?'

'Aigburth Drive – on the other side of the park.'

'I must ask the Archdeacon,' she says, her face even redder than usual. 'Your request has no precedent.'

On Friday morning Bosco calls me to the community room. 'The Archdeacon says you may go,' she says, looking more harassed than ever, 'and that I must collect you at the end of the evening.'

'Thank you, Sister.' It's a sneaky way of getting what I want – but then most games are sometimes dishonest, and it's my last chance of playing in the outside world. There's no doubt in my mind that the match is already lost. At least I've got into injury time.

Injury Time

As Dr Palfrey answers the doorbell his eye lights on the bunch of roses in my right hand.

'Sister Maureen! How very kind.'

Bringing flowers to the dinner party was Bertie's idea, and a bad one I see now. Knowing I couldn't afford wine she told me to pick some roses from the back garden. Careful as I've been not to joggle them across the park, some of the blooms have already lost their petals and others look a bit mildewed. Rambling Rector, Ena Harkness, Golden Shower – they've all gone down through lack of pruning. Embarrassed, I stick them under Dr Palfrey's chin like a microphone.

'Ah! Thank you.'

To my disappointment Dr Palfrey doesn't seem especially pleased to see me – just vague and preoccupied. Wishing he'd carry my flowers more carefully, I follow him through a book-lined hall into a room with big sash windows overlooking the park. In the corner is a table set with a startling array of cutlery, and I head for it straightaway. Then Dr Palfrey stops me with a polite cough, and yet more petals flutter to the floor. 'Make yourself at home.' He flaps my flowers at the other end of the room where some students are sitting in silence.

It doesn't look the least bit like home – acres of fawn carpet, magnolia walls and groups of pernickety little pictures hung too close together. Instead of telling me where to sit, Dr Palfrey hovers at my elbow for a few seconds then dumps my roses on the coffee-table to rummage for a vase in a distant sideboard.

Vicky is lolling in an armchair beside a revolving bookcase. 'Where's Toby?' I ask her.

'Got 'flu,' she shrugs, her eyes tracking Dr Palfrey who has drifted away from the sideboard to fiddle with the knobs on his stereo. So sure in his movements at work, he's like a stranger in his own home. From an oak pew by the window Hannah catches my eye and grins. At the sight of her candy pink and white striped dungarees and matching pink boots I wish I'd had something special to put on, something to make Dr Palfrey stare admiringly like he's turned to stare at Elisabeth's friend Sasha in her midnight-blue silk.

'Sit down, Sister,' says Hannah, nodding at the only free chair, an aggressive chrome structure with a backward sloping seat. I slide down the shiny black leather so my knees point at my chin like a garden gnome's. Sasha's eyes are fixed on my roses which are still lying on the coffee-table wrapped in the *Echo*. Dr Palfrey messes with a row of glasses while I wish we were crammed into the O'Shaunessys' front room in Moses Street where it's easy to break the ice. I'm rehearsing a remark about the exceptionally warm weather when Sasha starts to comment on the age of the pew.

'The good fathers of St Boniface wanted to burn it,' Dr Palfrey says to her over his shoulder. 'Pure vandalism.'

Sasha is wearing a plum-coloured lipstick, the better to form her luscious vowel-sounds. 'And what,' she asks next, 'is that wooden stand?'

Abandoning a bottle of sticky-looking fruit juice, Dr Palfrey wanders to the lectern. 'Every morning I turn the page of a treasured book. That way I always have something beautiful to look at.'

Vicky is wearing a slippery apricot dress under her usual denim jacket. Not to be outdone, she slinks over to join Sasha who's staring at the day's illustration. 'Where's it of?'

'That's the view from my window in the thirteenth century. Sefton was a royal deer park in those days.' Back in his role of tutor Dr Palfrey looks more composed until his eyes stray to Vicky's eighteen-hole Doc Martens protruding from the slithering rayon. 'That – er – figure beside the hunting lodge is presumed to be Edward the First, on the site of what we now know as Lodge Lane.'

Vicky steps a little closer, ready to ask another question, and I wonder if she's abandoned Sexy Rexy in the hope she'll get Dr Palfrey.

'Ah! The doorbell!' says Dr Palfrey.

While he drifts towards the hall we compete with each other to be useful. Vicky darts to the forgotten stereo, Hannah mops up some spilt fruit juice, I search for a vase and Sasha begins passing round some olives and gherkins. The wooden dish between her pale hands reminds me of the platters we used at St Cuthbert's till Wilfie gave them to Oxfam because they couldn't go in the new dishwasher. Now the dishwasher's broken and there's no money to repair it, so we have to wash the plates by hand anyway.

'So we're all girls at our little soirée.' Bulkier than ever in a ruby-red sari, Mrs Fothergill trots into the room. Pausing theatrically halfway, she takes us all in: Vicky frowning at the knobs on the stereo, Hannah with a dish-cloth in her hand and my roses moulting on the coffee-table: a second-division team, says her smile, if ever I saw one.

'For heaven's sake, pour us all a drink.' Her tone to Piers is bossy and proprietorial, like a wife's. 'We're dying of thirst.' Looking relaxed at last, Dr Palfrey hurries to the sideboard while Mrs Fothergill hitches up her sari and opens a cupboard door, locating a vase at once. Then she snatches up my flowers which leave an embarrassing ring of petals on the coffee-table. 'What's that dirge?'

'It's the Kyrie from Josquin's *Missa Pange Lingua*,' I tell her, recognising the music from St Cuthbert's. Then I see her derisive smile and know that I've missed whatever point it was she was making. As she bends over the vase her sari flaps open to reveal a well-filled lacy black bra cup. I'm wondering if Mr Fothergill was invited too when I become aware that she's talking to me.

'I didn't know nuns were allowed to attend dinner parties.'

'Sometimes we are,' I blurt out, stung by her air of disdain. 'It depends.'

She waggles a battered Rambling Rector. 'Depends on what, Sister Maureen?'

On one's Superior being conveniently called to Rome, I think, watching Mrs Fothergill jab its remains into the vase.

'It depends on whether it's educational,' I say out loud.

Mrs Fothergill raises her eyebrows. 'Educational isn't quite the word I'd choose for one of Piers's DP's.'

She parks the vase on the mantelpiece and trots over to

the sideboard with a sigh, a perfume like dolly mixtures hanging in her wake. She pours a little fruit juice into each glass while Dr Palfrey sits on the pew with a bemused smile, as though wondering how all these people found their way into his front room.

'Does your dispensation stretch to include kir, Sister?' calls Mrs Fothergill.

Too proud to admit I don't know what kir is, I nod non-committally.

Dr Palfrey glances at the carriage clock on his mantel-piece. 'I wonder what's happened to Julia.'

'The mordant and mysterious *Ms* Mulcahy,' says Mrs Fothergill while my heart gives an extra thump. It had never occurred to me that she'd be invited.

Mrs Fothergill hands me a glass of pink liquid. 'Tell me, Sister Maureen, what was she like as a nun?'

'She was very clever and – er, radical.'

'Perhaps dinner parties are too bourgeois for her?'

I take a gulp of kir. It's already an hour and a half past my normal meal-time, and the other students are rising uncertainly to their feet or clustering awkwardly in the middle of the room. I take another sip of my kir, which is not the harmless fruit juice it looks, and my pulse rate rises as the wine speeds through my veins.

Dr Palfrey is putting on a blue and white striped butcher's apron. 'Cynthia, will you show people where to sit while I go and see to the soufflé?'

I first learned to make soufflé in the days when my cook-ing was like my football – fast and fearless with a bravura touch. My confidence boosted by the wine, I dump my glass on the sideboard and step forward. 'I'll do the cooking – then you can stay with your guests.'

'It's perfectly all right, thank you,' says Dr Palfrey. 'I adore making soufflé.'

Hurt by the rebuff, I try to ignore Mrs Fothergill's smirk. Dr Palfrey disappears into the kitchen, where he stays for twenty minutes while the rest of us wait round the table. I'm wondering why anyone prefers all this fuss to a night in the pub, when a pinger sounds and he appears in the doorway. '*C'est au point, tout le monde!*'

To my relief the soufflé has risen well, and I'm so hungry I start eating the moment I'm served. But Vicky is ignoring her food to lean towards her tutor.

'I do so enjoy your lectures.'

Dr Palfrey looks flushed, whether from praise or from cooking I can't tell.

Vicky leans further forward so her dress slithers down her skinny chest. 'Which of us First Years is the cleverest?'

Naïve as I am, I can tell from his response that he would never be drawn to Vicky. Averting his eyes from her grubby-looking bra strap, he picks up a serving-spoon while I take another swig of wine. After all, it's my first and last dinner party, and soon I'll be stuck in St Cuthbert's for good.

'More soufflé, anyone? Sister Maureen? Cynthia? No?'

As Dr Palfrey disappears into the kitchen Mrs Fothergill removes our white-wine glasses and pours us some red. 'Cheers, everyone!' I say, raising my glass, and when they all respond with embarrassed smiles I know I've said something naff. But I couldn't care less, because they're only a load of stiffs who've never learnt to enjoy themselves.

A few moments later Dr Palfrey hurries in with a large casserole. 'Can you put out a place mat, Cynthia? Thank you.' He lifts the cast-iron lid. 'I've found a local butcher who's actually heard of *osso buco*. That is, oxtail,' he adds with a glance in my direction.

I've only used oxtail for soup and wonder why such a normally generous man should be so stingy. Glancing at the watch borrowed for the occasion from Bosco, I see the frowning black hands are already at nine. Dr Mulcahy must have forgotten, I think, surprised by a sting of disappointment.

'What time must you leave?' asks Dr Palfrey who has followed my glance.

'A sister will call for me at ten.'

'How nice – she must stay for coffee.'

Hannah is staring at the ring of bone on her plate. 'I told you I was a vegetarian,' she says accusingly.

'Does it matter?' sings Mrs Fothergill, her sari flopping dangerously close to the gravy. 'After all, the moo-cow is already dead.'

'It's a matter of principle.'

'You're right to protest,' says Dr Palfrey, going back to the kitchen. 'You told me and I forgot. Let me make you an omelette.'

'I'll do it, Piers.' Mrs Fothergill heaves herself to her feet. 'You've done quite enough cooking for one night.'

'Nonsense – it will only take a few minutes.' Dr Palfrey gives an anxious glance from the doorway. 'Cynthia, will you pass people the endives?'

Hannah takes a vegetable dish from Mrs Fothergill. 'It's nice when a man knows how to cook.'

Mrs Fothergill nods. 'They do it so much better than we do.'

Hannah picks a mange-tout from the serving-dish with her fingers, eats it and swallows some wine. 'I meant from the feminist point of view.'

'The feminist point of view fails to interest me.' Mrs Fothergill's smile is like an Aga burn. 'Feminism infantilises women.'

'Infantilised by our wish to be equal?' Hannah's voice rises. 'That's impossible.'

Mrs Fothergill's make-up has worn off in the heat and her face looks flat as a burgomaster's. 'You feminists are a boring lot,' she says, staring coldly at Hannah's candy-pink dungarees. 'Even your fashions are infantile. And for God's sake,' she sniffs pointedly, 'stop using Johnson's Baby Powder.'

I've been staring muzzily at the pottery dishes and austere white walls, wondering why they look familiar. 'I agree,' I say, taking a sip from my wine glass which has been topped up without me noticing. Although I've missed the first part of the conversation, I know that Mrs Fothergill and Hannah are discussing motherhood. 'Sensible women don't want children.'

Dr Palfrey hurries in from the kitchen. 'More endives, anyone?'

Mrs Fothergill's cheeks look like crumpled linen. 'And what do you know about children, Sister Maureen?'

I'm burning to answer back but feel sorry for Dr Palfrey who's beseeching everyone to stop bickering.

Hannah takes no notice. 'Sister Maureen has chosen a life without men,' she says, joggling him with her elbow as he slides the omelette on to her plate. 'I admire her independence.'

'Independence,' says Mrs Fothergill with an angry twitch at her sari, 'when she can't even walk home alone?'

Dr Palfrey goes round the table topping up our wine glasses without, I notice, touching his own. 'She's right not to,' he says. 'The streets are getting dangerous.'

'That's because of the warm weather,' says Sasha. 'Gangs of yobbos are hanging around.'

As though to check what season it is, Dr Palfrey stops pouring to gaze out of the window while I think of Wayne and Mary Element and all the other people I met on Good Friday. 'They're not doing any harm,' I retort, bugged by Sasha's know-it-all tone.

'All the same,' says Dr Palfrey after a pause, 'we should be careful. A crowd set fire to a corner shop the other night.'

The tick of Bosco's watch is tut-tut-tutting round my head. Although it's after nine-thirty no one except me has finished their main course. Used to the swift and silent meals of St Cuthbert's, I didn't foresee how people would chatter over their food. Soon Bosco will be ringing the doorbell, Dr Palfrey will invite her in and she'll see the row of empty wine bottles on the sideboard, the tipsy Mrs Fothergill and the absence of anything like a seminar.

The exposed brickwork over the fireplace is beginning to scroll like film credits and for some reason Mrs Fothergill is drumming her fingers on the table. When she rises to her feet I see she has tears in her eyes.

As Dr Palfrey follows her into the kitchen Hannah begins whispering in my ear. 'You put your foot in it with that remark about babies – La Fothergill's been trying to have one for years. She told us in our last seminar.'

I stare at Hannah's mouth opening and shutting out of synch with her words which follow each other at random.

'Bread and butter pudding,' says Dr Palfrey who has miraculously reappeared. 'My speciality.'

Mrs Fothergill sits down beside him. 'Piers adores nursery food,' she says, stabbing at a sultana with her dessert fork while I gaze at the earthenware dishes, the polished floor, the lectern and refectory benches tilting round me in a headachy dream. And then I realise what it is – that they're like a convent only more so. Although my throat is dry and my tongue's grown too big for my mouth I feel an urgent need to tell Dr Palfrey but can't be making much sense because instead of listening he picks up the serving-spoon and looks round the table.

'Is no one hungry? Vicky? Hannah?' He sounds so forlorn that I hold out my plate.

'Where did you get the recipe, Piers?' asks Vicky.

'I've never followed a recipe in my life.' Dr Palfrey looks startled at the use of his first name. 'My nanny showed me how to make this.'

Mrs Fothergill impales another sultana. 'I prefer fresh fruit at this time of year.'

Someone has opened the windows, and the smell of my briar roses drifts across on the night air. Suddenly I remember it's June 2nd and – 'It's my birthday,' I cry out.

'We must drink your health,' says Mrs Fothergill. 'No, don't pull your glass away – I insist.' She slops a little on my habit. 'Many happy returns.'

'Don't drink it!' Hannah's voice rings in my ear. 'It's South African.'

'How do you celebrate birthdays in the convent?' asks Vicky, her fox-face sharp in the candlelight.

'We don't. It's our feast day that's important . . . it's just that I suddenly remembered . . .'

'We would have bought you a prezzie,' says Hannah.

'I have had a present, actually.' I look at the ring of surprised faces. 'Not a very nice one. My Superior says I'm to leave university.'

'Leave? When?' says Vicky, not looking too concerned about it.

'After the exams. She thinks Art History is – not doing me any good.'

'You poor thing,' says Hannah. 'No wonder you seemed down.'

'Your regime is archaic,' says Mrs Fothergill, 'and you shouldn't submit to it.'

'Why oh why has the Catholic church grown so *philistine?*' says Dr Palfrey. 'I shall complain to your Mother Superior.'

'Please don't – it won't do any good. And besides, I should never have told you.' The brickwork is scrolling faster now and my chair scrapes noisily on the floorboards as I rise from my seat.

'Second on the left,' carols Mrs Fothergill.

I bolt the bathroom door and lean my forehead against the tiles. My features have dwindled to pins and tucks and red blotches have appeared in unlikely places – across my forehead and the bridge of my nose. I splash my skin with cold water, open the medicine cabinet and stare at a row of brown bottles. Unable to focus on their tiny labels I take two tablets from one that I think says migraine and swig them down with water from Dr Palfrey's white china tooth mug. Then I smooth my veil and glance at my watch. Quarter to ten and Bosco will already have set out from St Cuthbert's. I'll say goodbye to the others then wait by the front door.

The babble of voices fills the hall, with Hannah's angry tones rising above the rest. Then Mrs Fothergill's voice cuts in, followed by Dr Palfrey's calming them both down. Disorientated, I gaze round the cream-painted doors then open one at random. In the half-light from the hall I make out a double bed and a pile of glossy magazines on the carpet.

Someone has left the dinner table and is standing behind me. 'Looking for something, Sister?' It's Dr Palfrey, but instead of rebuking me for snooping he cups my elbow in his hand and steers me across the hall.

We are just passing the front door when the bell rings. Before Dr Palfrey can move I dart to open it, then draw back. 'Dr Mulcahy!' I cry, discomfited. Her skin is fresh from the night air, and her clear-eyed gaze makes me feel like a Brueghel peasant.

'My car broke down on my way back from London,' she apologises to Dr Palfrey who's hovering at my side. 'I couldn't find your number.'

'I'll ask Cynthia to reheat that *osso buco*.'

'Maureen, what's happened?' Dr Mulcahy steps forward and brushes my cheek with her fingertips. 'You look quite flushed.'

'I'm fine,' I gasp, stepping back. Though she used to be a nun, I feel far more at ease with Dr Palfrey who is calmly putting on his jacket.

'Sister Maureen isn't well,' he explains. 'I'm about to walk her home.'

I nod, keeping my mouth closed so that Dr Mulcahy won't smell the wine.

At that moment Mrs Fothergill trots into the hall. 'That's impolite, Piers, when you're the host,' she protests. 'I'll give the oh-so-independent Sister Maureen a lift.'

'You don't want to risk your licence.'

'Then you should ring for a taxi.'

For the first time I realise that Bosco is about to bump into Sister Julian that was. 'That's impossible,' I say wildly. 'My sister will have already set out.'

'Then we'll meet her on our way across the park,' says Dr

Palfrey, 'and you, Cynthia, can look after our new arrival.'

For a moment it looks as though Mrs Fothergill will rebel, then she turns towards the kitchen with a shrug. 'By-ee!' she calls with an angry clash of coffee-cups. Vicky is laying an extra place at table and Hannah is flat out on the pew. Only Dr Mulcahy follows us to the front door, her face concerned.

'I'll take you home, Maureen,' she says, running her fingers through her hair, which smells of French perfume.

'I'd better go with Dr Palfrey,' I reply awkwardly.

After ushering me through the front door he pauses on the top step to breathe in the cool night air. 'What a catastrophe,' he groans. 'Why oh why do I think I can entertain young people?'

'It wasn't your fault.'

'Yes it was. I'm an incompetent ass.' He gives the last word a long vowel so it sounds as though he's saying *arse* – a word I haven't heard for ten years.

'I enjoyed myself,' I lie, trying not to sound surprised.

'I was hoping your chaperone wouldn't turn up,' says Dr Palfrey, gripping my arm as I stumble on the bottom step, 'so that I could leave them all alone for a few minutes.'

The moon has risen high over the park and the sky is clear apart from a solitary plane droning homewards to Speke. 'I drank some sherry at Christmas,' I tell him, 'but it didn't affect me like this.'

'Cynthia has a heavy hand with alcohol.'

'It's kind of you to walk me home, Dr Palfrey.'

'I do wish you'd call me Piers – now that we're getting to know one other.'

'All the same,' I say, too embarrassed to obey him, 'I've been undignified.'

'You're not undignified,' he says as though in absolution. 'You're open, candid and innocent – everything a woman should be.'

I've never thought of myself as a woman – only as a girl, and then as a nun. This fresh idea, which I try for fit as we walk, feels smart and snug as a new glove, and I carry myself more proudly as we stroll on towards the Palm House. Its glass dome glittering in the moonlight, and underneath it a hare is loping across the dew.

'And what's more,' Dr Palfrey carries on in the silence, 'you have a talent for Art History. The way you've come to love Vermeer . . . it's barbarous to make you give it up.'

I smile, flattered by his concern. Now we're out under the summer sky it's hard to believe anything horrible will happen. 'Perhaps they'll change their minds,' I say peaceably, 'if I get high enough marks.'

'I hope so,' says Dr Palfrey. 'You could become a good scholar.'

'Like Mrs Fothergill?'

'Cynthia's an extraordinary person and a very good teacher. But not, I'm afraid, a first-class brain.'

We're in sight of the other side of the park and there's still no sign of Bosco. 'I thought you were close friends.'

'We are,' says Piers, 'but that doesn't preclude telling the truth – and besides, there are things about Cynthia that drive me mad.' As we pause under the street lamp outside the convent he strokes me lightly on the shoulder. It's the first time it's been touched for years and the shock runs down to my fingertips.

I could move away but instead I stand motionless, waiting for him to carry on talking. 'Those high heels, for instance,' he says. 'They make her look like Mrs Dagnall.'

It's a mean and snobbish remark but I know he's doing it to make me feel better – and what harm does it do Mrs Fothergill? As his hand tightens on my shoulder I turn my head towards him like I've watched actresses do in old films. It might after all be the last time I ever see him, so I tilt my chin and look into his eyes which, I notice for the first time, droop aristocratically at the outer corners, like the Duke of Wellington's in a famous portrait. Then the door of the convent opens behind me and footsteps crunch on the gravel.

'Happy birthday,' says Piers.

'Is that you, Sister Maureen?' comes Bosco's voice.

Before I can reply, Piers bends and kisses me lightly on the lips. Then he steps back across the pavement, raises his arms as if in apology and crosses the road into the park.

Vermeer

Bosco is looking agitated, with her veil askew and eyes puffy. 'I'm so sorry, Sister Maureen. I sat down at nine o'clock just meaning to rest and must have fallen asleep.'

I glance over my shoulder at Dr Palfrey disappearing down the path to the Palm House.

'When I came to it was 10.30.'

'My tutor brought me home,' I tell the blunt, anxious face under the street-light.

'How very kind. I shall write to thank him on Monday.'

'There's no need.' Still conscious of the wine on my breath I edge past the old nun. 'He wanted the fresh air.'

'You look tired. Have you been working hard?'

I'd hoped to retreat to the back garden but Bosco is dogging my footsteps. Shamed by her kindly concern, I turn towards the dormitory stairs.

'Your habit smells of cigarettes, dear,' says her voice at my back. 'You should give it an airing.'

Trying not to stumble, I cling to the banister. Columba is

on the top landing, taking advantage of Wilfie's absence to work late on the angular garden birds she likes making from pipe cleaners.

Bosco bends to pick up a stray tail feather. 'Will you please sweep up this mess? It's time for bed.'

'Did you have a good seminar?' whispers Columba, pasting on a jay's crest.

Feeling guiltier than ever at her innocent welcome, I dart into my cell without a word and close the door.

Our dormitory is high above the traffic and even the noise of what Sasha calls yobbos sounds faint through the summer air. My pure and blameless sisters are preparing for the night. I can hear Gonzaga splashing water into her tooth mug, Ursula dropping her rosary beads and, at the far end of the dormitory, Columba tweeting at the newcomer in her aviary. I take off my cape and remove my veil.

I've been sinful, I think, sinful and shabby. By pretending it was a seminar I finagled my way to a pointless dinner party where I drank wine when I should have asked for water, then lacked the self-discipline to stop at one glass. Drunk and vainglorious, I lost control of my tongue, was rude to Mrs Fothergill, then blabbed about leaving university.

And that was before Dr Palfrey caught me peering into his bedroom. No wonder he thought he could kiss me on the way home. Even then I could have backed away, but instead I turned my head and looked at him invitingly, lustfully even; and in the moment when his lips brushed mine I relished my sin.

Still feeling the print of his mouth, I rub at my lips with the back of my hand and when that doesn't work I scrub them with a soapy nail brush. If only I could confess my sin at once, or go on a long and punishing run. My skin feels dry and blotchy where I've scrubbed it, and far from being erased, the print of my tutor's lips now burns like a brand.

Too unsettled to pray, I pitch my nail brush back into the washbasin and, in defiance of the Holy Rule, slump on my bed fully dressed. The furniture of my cell stares back in reproach. Shoddy and second-hand, it's closer to Moses Street than my tutor's flat: the battered locker, wardrobe and utility bed under its florid, fifteen-year-old bedspread bought after the Vatican Council. You pay for cut and you pay for colour, my mam used to say. Like the people of the Dingle, we nuns can afford neither.

'Father, into Thy hands I commend my spirit.' Bosco's voice floats across the roofspace. It's the signal that lights out is in five minutes so I reach for a clean towel from the top shelf of my wardrobe. Dr Palfrey's book on Vermeer is hidden under the pile, along with my little pink mirror, and my fingers stretch automatically for the shiny spine.

But they encounter nothing but towelling. Thinking both mirror and book must have been misplaced, I grope to the back but feel nothing but wood, an old veil and some darned stockings. Then I climb on my chair in a panic, fling everything on to the bed and stare at the empty shelf.

I took down the book this evening while the others were at dinner, and sat on my bed admiring the blues, pearls and luminous citrons. The little pink mirror was there too, because I took a look at my face before leaving for Dr Palfrey's. Then I hid the mirror on top of the book and replaced both under the towels.

Someone has been in my cell while I was out.

I remember showing off about Vermeer to Ursula only the other day; but how would she have known about the book? Ursula's one of the old school and would never enter another nun's cell, let alone pry into her wardrobe. The daring Elisabeth wouldn't think twice about slipping in; but though a sneak she'd disdain petty theft, and I don't suspect her for a moment.

At the other end of the dormitory Columba starts stowing her feathers in a plastic bag and Bosco turns in her bed with an exasperated sigh. Perhaps Bosco got wind of the dinner party and removed the precious book to prompt a confession. Far from falling asleep, the old nun might have looked tired from lurking in the bushes; and her threatened letter to Dr Palfrey was an attempt to catch me out.

At the thought of such trickery my penitence begins to melt. What right, I ask myself, unbuttoning my habit, has Bosco to poke around in my cell and to spy on Dr Palfrey and me? I may have done wrong but it was mean-spirited to treat me as an overgrown teenager – when out in the world I'd have a husband and children by now.

As Brigid gives a cough from the opposite cell I wonder what she'd say if she knew about my kiss. Frigid-Brigid, Lol used to call her, because like me she showed no interest in boys. Yet she too has broken her Vow of Chastity – and not with a man but another nun. If she can be forgiven so can I because it's natural to respond to the opposite sex. I think of Mrs Fothergill fussing round the dinner table and Vicky leaning across it in her low-cut dress. Even the old nuns aren't immune: Columba beaming at Mr Gopal when he delivers the vegetables, Bosco bantering with the Archdeacon; even Gonzaga turning coy when he praises her cooking – we're all of us women beneath our habits. Only Mother Wilfred is immune.

I picture the stocky Baby Jesus with the bald head, his

starfish hand on his mother's breast. Although his eyes are narrowed and his cheeks a shade pinker he doesn't look entirely displeased. You're twenty-seven today, I hear him say. Soon you will be old like Wilfie, with a whiskery chin and whistle marks round your mouth and nobody will want to kiss you again ever.

'Dr Palfrey fancies you,' Hannah said once, her eyes navy with mischief.

It was a flattering thought but I knew she was talking nonsense. 'Dr Palfrey is no Sexy Rexy,' I said indignantly. But now a tumble-dryer turns in my belly at the thought of Dr Palfrey – Piers – kissing me, the ex-lay sister from the Dingle, and I wonder what Hannah would say if she knew – let alone Vicky and Mrs Fothergill.

When the dormitory lights go out I yank the blankets to my chin and gaze at the sky through the clear glass pane. I wasn't allowed to beat men at football but now I've found other ways to conquer. For once in my life I've used feminine wiles, and far from feeling sorry I want to shout with joy across the dormitory, making Gonzaga leap out of bed, night-cap adrift, Bosco drop her rosary beads in fright and Columba's pipe-cleaner birds flutter to the rafters.

Degas

'You get on with your revision,' Bosco says to me the next morning, 'and leave the housework to us.'

I look at her square, brick-red face, and wonder what she made of my book on Vermeer.

'Can't I just clean the refectory?'

It's Saturday, and after a restless night trying not to think about Dr Palfrey, I long to tire myself out with scrubbing.

'Certainly not.' Usually so keen to see me at work, Bosco now seems bent on thwarting me. 'We've divided your chores between us, dear. So off you go.'

I trail along to the convent library and open a book; but the words refuse to sink in and by mid-morning I'm too fidgety to read any longer. I wander to the window and stare across the park, but Dr Palfrey's house is screened by sycamores. I wish I could help him with his washing-up because it's easy to talk over housework, and tactfully not mentioning his kiss I could thank him for being a good tutor, and for seeing me home, and explain how I'd like to write to him from time to time, just to keep in touch.

But I shan't be seeing him till Monday, and between now and then are forty-eight long hours. Desperate for some activity, I wait till Bosco's in chapel then charge along to the infirmary. But the beds are already made, the old ones propped in their armchairs, and Bertie herself gone to Toxteth. I decide to catch up on my washing.

The convent laundry is a long low building tacked on the side of the kitchen. The meagre light struggles through frosted windows, and the damp grey air is laden with sweat and effort. St Cuthbert's has no washing-machine, but a vast copper stands in the corner, heated by Columba every Monday. Next to it, like an instrument of torture, is an iron mangle, and on a pulley overhead hangs the old nuns' underwear, long johns and woollen vests with sleeves, night-caps and flannel petticoats, put by Bertilla to dry in what air there is.

The room is empty apart from a Choir nun bent over the far sink. Moving closer I see that it's Brigid, her sturdy fore-arms plunged in the water. A Dingle girl like myself, didn't she help me write the essay which first impressed Piers? My spirits rise at the thought of spilling my woes, and my breath begins to come in short bursts.

But instead of pausing to greet me Brigid keeps scrub-bing at a grey-looking garment.

'You look like a washerwoman by Degas,' I say to her after a few silent seconds.

Brigid keeps her eyes fixed on the scummy water. 'And you sound just like Elisabeth.'

I jam a plug in the next sink, turn on the taps and tip in the contents of my laundry bag. 'I thought you were keen on study.'

She straightens her back and turns a sour face towards me. 'Then why didn't you let me help you?'

'But I did,' I protest, shocked by her angry tone. 'You helped me with my very first essay.'

'And when I'd shown you how to write it?' Brigid yanks her washing out of the water, then flings it back with an angry slap. 'You never asked me another thing.'

I glance at her downcast face. 'I would have done but . . . I thought you were too busy.'

'That's a lie. You know very well that I wanted to help.'

And I also know I intended to ask her, but then Dr Palfrey – Piers – began coaching me himself, and I had no need of Brigid.

But even though she's right, I'm in no mood to admit it. 'Then you must be made up that I'm leaving the uni.'

'At least you had a year.' She swabs amateurishly at a wet vest. 'I've had nothing.'

I resist the impulse to pluck her washing from her hands and give it a good scrub. 'A year is worse than nothing. I was just beginning to enjoy myself.'

She lifts the woolly vest to her nose, sniffs doubtfully at its underarms and drops it back in the scum. Knowing I've lost all chance of confiding, I start on my own washing.

'I've been meaning to ask you—'

Caught up in my thoughts I've scarcely noticed that Brigid has now stopped work altogether and is standing upright, her reddened hands dangling.

'— if you ever see Julian?'

It's the first time she's mentioned Dr Mulcahy since her confession, and I wish she hadn't. Though I've struggled to blot out what she told me, my cheeks flame up all the same, so I hide them by rummaging in my laundry bag. 'Not since the end of term.'

'I don't suppose you'd take her a letter?'

A few months ago I'd have said yes, all innocent and trusting, because in those days I knew nothing about Julia Mulcahy; nor had I been kissed by Piers, or lain awake trying not to think about him. Now I know how dangerous people can be, and how on Monday I should go to my tutor and tell him his kiss meant nothing; and how I should also help Brigid to keep away from Julia.

Brigid's still standing with her chapped hands hanging and a look of hope in her eyes. 'You suppose right,' I say, my embarrassment gone in my urge to explain. 'Any sin against chastity is a mortal sin, but worst of all is a sin with another woman.'

I make a dash for the mangle and crank the big wooden handle while Brigid stares into the scum as though her future is written in it. 'It's not that sort of letter,' she mutters.

Trying to ignore the desperation in her voice, I feed my best habit through the rollers. It comes out the other side squashed flat like a cartoon nun. Tonight I will iron it, ready for Monday morning and my final meeting with Piers.

'Please, Moey.'

At the sound of my childhood name I swing towards her; but instead of my Number One Dingle girl I see the woman she's now become: weak of mouth and doubtful of chin, humbling herself before me, six years her junior. 'It's my very last chance,' she says with a shaky smile, 'now that you're leaving the uni.'

As I meet her troubled brown eyes I see us in thirty years' time – two dotty old nuns from the Dingle with no young

ones around to cheer us up, and only our memories to survive on.

'I've changed my mind,' I say to her. 'Of course I'll
deliver your letter.'

A smile curves across her face which is brighter than it's
been since she helped me with Rembrandt. 'Thank you,
Moey.' She touches my elbow with her big red hand. 'I'll go
and write it at once.' And leaving her vest in the scum she
rushes out of the laundry, drying her hands on her habit as
she goes.

Palm House

But Monday doesn't prove as easy as I hoped. Instead of revising at St Cuthbert's, Elisabeth decides to come with me to the university library, where she lodges herself in the next desk.

I try to make good use of the time, but my legs have developed a will of their own. Whenever they start twitching, Elisabeth gives a sigh and looks up from her notes. They'll never make her a saint, I think, with a glance at her downturned mouth. She wouldn't look right on a holy picture. So why, I wonder, does she act the martyr? My marks are better than hers, and Brigid is brighter than both of us – yet she'll be getting her BA while Brigid and I are banged up in St Cuthbert's.

'How long are you going to stay?' I whisper after an hour.

'All day, I suppose.' Her eyes are hard with suspicion.

Sliding my hand into my pocket, I touch Brigid's letter. I have to find a way of delivering it to Dr Mulcahy, and also of speaking to Piers. As Bostik drops her eyes to her book, my gaze strays for the hundredth time through the library window to the pavement in front of the department, empty now the term's ended. And then I see a figure in a pale suit picking his way up the steps. I wait till the door's closed behind him then rise to my feet.

What I'm about to do is risky and even stupid, but if Elisabeth's going to hang round all day I have no choice.

'Where do you think you're going?' Her eyes, red-rimmed from late-night revision, X-ray my pocket.

'Nowhere.'

'Tell me at once – or I'm coming with you.'

'I'm only going to the notice-board.'

'Why?' Elisabeth looks set to grab up her books and follow.

'Because I need to check my exam timetable,' I improvise, 'so for pity's sake don't come with me – or we'll look more like a pair of half-witted penguins than ever.'

Ignoring her angry stare I cap the fountain-pen bought by my mam and dad with such high hopes. Elisabeth stays put, and I draw a relieved breath. Outside, the midday sun is glinting on the roofs of parked cars, and the Georgian square has a sleepy, out of season look. On the department steps I pause and look over my shoulder in case Elisabeth has changed her mind; but the pavement is deserted and so is the front hall, where the only sound to break the summer stillness comes from Mrs Dagnall's electronic typewriter. The keys fall silent as I run upstairs.

Dr Mulcahy first, I decide, and then Piers. After a year's desk work I'm so unfit that my heart is pounding when I reach the top floor. There's no need, I remind myself, to answer any questions; just hand her the letter and go. After a calming breath, I pull it out of my pocket and knock. To my relief there's no reply so I shove it under her door and hurry down to the first floor.

The unstained summer sunshine is pouring through the cupola, brightening the eau-de-nil walls and Georgian moulding. From inside Piers's room I hear the sound of footsteps, and the clink of a cup and saucer. My heart thumps harder than ever and the blood sings in my ears as I walk towards his door. A familiar scent is lingering on the landing – sugary sweet like dolly mixtures. I lift my hand to knock.

The perfume grows more intense. Then, from inside the room, comes a high-pitched giggling. Mrs Fothergill. Why, I wonder, can't she see that Piers doesn't really respect her? It's time she learnt to concentrate on her husband. Angry and disappointed at my lost opportunity, I stamp downstairs past the smirking Mrs Dagnall.

Though I focus on my revision for the rest of the afternoon, everything is sliding out of my mind; and how can I prepare for the question on genre painting without my book on Vermeer? That evening I ask Bosco if I can be excused from my exams; but she tells me that she's heard nothing from Mother Wilfred, and I had better complete the year.

Next morning, bent over my first exam paper, my neck aches and my skull feels huge and ready to shatter, like the Palm House dome. I fight to pick up marks where I can but the paper is difficult and I run out of time. My only consolation is it makes no difference.

The Choir nuns I once thought so frosty go out of their way to be kind. 'Even though He slay me, yet will I trust in Him,' writes Kevin on the back of a holy picture, while

Bosco places a jam jar of briar roses by my place in the convent library and Ursula, her face smudged with fatigue, rises early to iron my veil before I've even reached the laundry.

The following day Elisabeth has an exam, so I go again to Dr Palfrey's office. On finding it empty I return to my seat in the library and wait for him to appear now Bostik's out of the way. But he fails to turn up and I waste the rest of the day and the three after that in gazing out of the window. Mrs Fothergill, I decide, must have turned him against me – or maybe he's overtired at the year's end.

But I see him after my next exam, when far from looking tired he's relaxed and tanned. After scooping a pile of scripts from the podium he scans the hall with its crowds of departing students, sees me standing at my desk and smiles. Abandoning my script I dart towards him; but instead of waiting to speak he turns away to join a group of invigilators.

Feeling a wally and a divvy and every other kind of fool I stop dead in the middle of the aisle. There's no Elisabeth to blame this time, or bossy Mrs Fothergill – just a crowd of tweedy academics who are drifting with him out of the hall. I can tell from his wry little smile that he thinks he shouldn't have kissed me, and is too embarrassed to talk.

'Mind out the way, love.' The porters are straightening the desks for the afternoon, so I grope for my pencil case, collect my bag from the back of the room, and blunder out of the door.

Hannah and Toby are waiting for me at the bottom of the steps, and it's plain from their sympathetic faces that they've witnessed my come-uppance. 'Would you like a cup of coffee?' says Hannah.

Too embarrassed to reply I shake my head, bent only on

getting away. I've messed up every bit of my new life: the academic work, my dealings with tutors and students and, worst of all, my vows of chastity and obedience. Why ever was I let loose?

I'm loping along the street so deep in these miserable thoughts that I barely register the royal-blue Renault drawing up at the kerb.

'Where are you running to?' Cool and summery in a linen jacket, Dr Mulcahy leans across the passenger seat to wind down her window. 'You look as though you've committed a crime.'

Resisting the impulse to admit that I have, I tell her I'm going back to St Cuthbert's.

'Hop in and I'll give you a lift.'

'I don't want a lift – I want the exercise.'

'I have a message to give you.'

I bend towards her window. 'Then give it to me now.'

'It's not as easy as that,' says Dr Mulcahy. 'It's for Brigid.'

In my self-absorption I'd forgotten about my sister – and yet last night she asked me for the third time if there was any reply to her letter, the hope fading from her eyes when I told her I'd heard nothing.

'So you're leaving university,' says Dr Mulcahy as I climb in.

'How do you know that?'

'From the Archdeacon.' She revs the engine. 'He's far from pleased.'

Wondering how much he knows about Dr Mulcahy and Brigid, I turn my face into the warm wind as we accelerate down the Boulevard past Vicky walking hand in hand with Sexy Rexy, who looks plump and overdressed in his corduroy trousers and long leather jacket.

'Where are you going?'

'To the Palm House. I've been commissioned to paint a water colour — by a rich old bore, as it happens, but the money's good.'

The needles on her dashboard are rising and falling like weather vanes. 'Take care where you drop me off,' I say as we swing through the gates into the park. 'The Palm House is opposite St Cuthbert's.'

'I know that,' she says dryly.

'If they see me they'll want to know why I accepted the lift and then —' I can feel myself yammering from nerves.

'And then the whole Spanish Inquisition bit. Things don't change in that place.'

'Whoa! Stop!' I cry out. 'We're too close.'

Dr Mulcahy slews the car into the kerb. I hop out and slam the door. 'Now will you give me that message?'

'I'll tell you when we reach the Palm House. I need a hand with my gear.'

I look at the tract of grass, nearly deserted in the mid-afternoon quiet, and the windows of St Cuthbert's staring over it. 'I can't walk across there.'

Dr Mulcahy opens the boot. 'Yes, you can — by putting one little foot in front of the other. Then, when I'm settled, I'll give you the message.'

Knowing I'll never meet Brigid's eye if I refuse, I stand feeling eerily self-conscious as Dr Mulcahy drags out some boxes of paints, along with her sketch pads and a folding stool. Then, sharing the load between us, we track across the grass to the giant dome. From time to time I glance over my shoulder at the convent but its windows are mercifully blank.

I wish we could get into the Palm House and out of sight

but Dr Mulcahy, who is whistling a little tune, pauses before the main entrance, puts down her equipment and takes off her jacket. With her neat waist, lime-green T-shirt and designer jeans, it's hard to believe she was ever a nun.

'This should be fun.' She gazes at the triple lantern rising out of the granite. 'It's a miniature Crystal Palace.'

'I'm going inside.'

'Look at those giant acanthus leaves.' Dr Mulcahy is stalking round the exterior, peering here and there through the glass. 'The department frieze has the same motif.'

I run up the steps and, thankful for the shelter of the porch, occupy myself with a notice on the door: The century plant, *Agave Americana*, is in here.

'Have you never been to see it?' Dr Mulcahy has re-appeared at my elbow.

I shake my head. One of the Palm House gardeners tried to grope Lol and me when we were schoolgirls. Lol found it funny and continued to smoke her Woodbines behind the giant cactus; but I obeyed Sister Ursula who on hearing about the incident forbade us ever to enter the Palm House again. Even as an adult I've never thought to go back in.

'How very incurious of you,' says Dr Mulcahy as we open the door. 'The century plant is flowering for the first time in a hundred years.' She stacks her equipment inside, then follows me down a concrete path to the centre.

We pass the same cactus once favoured by Lorraine, then stop beside a clump of paddle-shaped leaves. The air is hot and moist, and Dr Mulcahy is now standing so close that we're almost touching. The long slim trunk of the plant springs from the middle of the cluster, to finish in a froth of yellow flowers against the glass ceiling, like something bubbling out of a test tube. Feeling gawky and out of my depth, I concentrate on the label, *Euphorbia Abyssinica*, then wipe my face with my sleeve. The temperature must be in the nineties.

'Now that it's flowered it's going to die,' says Dr Mulcahy, her eyes narrowed against the sun.

Tongue-tied, I follow her past a bank of predatory-looking green and magenta plants shaped like trumpets, tubas and flutes and then, still unable to think of a comment, stretch out my right hand towards a freckled tube.

'They're carnivorous!' she says as the frilled horn begins to close, then smiles as I snatch away my finger. 'They eat insects, silly, not people.'

I turn to a tiny plant with a lime-green cleft and spikes like a miniature hairbrush. Venus fly-trap, says the label – and yes there are the insects glued to its viscous interior. 'These things are revolting,' I say. 'Give me the message and I'll go.'

'Sit down first,' says Dr Mulcahy. 'It's complicated.' She leads the way down an alley to a bench beside a pond covered with water lilies: *Victoria Amazonica*, shaped like a three-foot flan dish, Taiwanese leaves with veins in a blood-red web, *Nymphaea Caensis* with white flowers and centres thick as egg yolks and, growing round the edges, *Pistia Stratiotes*, or water lettuce, next to *Salvinia Molesta* with a tear drop on every leaf: all have been lovingly labelled in neat handwriting. Apart from a gardener hoeing on the other side of the Palm House, we are alone.

Dr Mulcahy trails her hand in the water where microscopic fishes dart between her fingers. 'Blood heat!' She wipes her hand and pulls Brigid's envelope from her jacket pocket.

'Do you know what's in it?' she asks, her pupils shrunk to two black dots.

My veil is growing damp against the back of my neck. 'Of course not.' I stare through the glass to where a child is learning to ride a bike, and a Jack Russell is cocking its leg against a bush. The Choir nuns will still be in school.

Dr Mulcahy takes the letter out of its envelope and places it on the bench between us. Looking down I catch a glimpse of Brigid's writing, touchingly plain and square. 'You may as well know,' Dr Mulcahy twiddles a solid-looking silver bracelet, 'that she wants to leave St Cuthbert's and live with me.'

I snatch up the letter and crumple it in my hand. 'I should never have delivered it – we can't spare her – she mustn't be allowed to —'

Instead of snatching the letter back, Dr Mulcahy gives an amused smile. 'That's exactly what I think.'

'You mean you're saying no?'

When she nods her head I stare down at the crumpled letter. *Tired of it all,* I read in words smudged from the heat of my palm. *Missing you.* Poor Brigid: to know what she wants and not get it. I put the letter back on the bench, and drop my gaze to the moss agate water where I'm startled to see a reflection of Dr Mulcahy surrounded by steel girders.

She tucks the letter in her jeans pocket. 'Brigid had her chance years ago and didn't have the guts.'

For a second I'm tempted to beg her to give Brigid a second chance, then decide that delivering the letter was bad enough. Brigid's my sister in Christ who's just been saved from mortal sin.

Dr Mulcahy plucks a leaf from the edge of the pond. 'The Archdeacon says St Cuthbert's is in a state of collapse. Wilfie can't cope, apparently, and there are no more vocations.'

I focus on the small fingers now shredding the bright green leaf. 'It's not as bad as all that. Bertilla – that's a new African nun – is working in Toxteth and then there's Brigid and Elisabeth —'

'Brigid's a dead duck and Elisabeth got you sent back to wash dishes while she becomes Sister Elisabeth Bavidge, BA.' The atmosphere's more humid than ever and in the background a spring is dripping mesmerically. 'Brigid couldn't hack it in the outside world – but you could. Have you never thought of leaving?'

Technicolor pictures start exploding in my brain: me chatting to Piers in my favourite clothes – a T-shirt and jeans rather like Dr Mulcahy's – then going back to life class, finishing my degree, and even driving a car.

'If you left now you could have quite a future. Why lock yourself away in that mausoleum?'

My gaze falls on St Cuthbert's across the grass, its Jacobean chimneys orange in the sunlight. Only an ex-Choir nun could call it a mausoleum. 'I can't possibly leave,' I say to her sadly. 'It would be letting down my sisters and Mother Wilfred would —'

'Wilfie's done nothing for you and never has.'

'She allowed me to study.'

'Don't be so naïve.'

'I've grown up recently.'

'Then you'll have guessed why the Archdeacon chose Art History for you.'

'Why did he?'

'He's always been a fan of mine – and he wanted me to be your mentor.'

The heat's so intense I'm beginning to feel dizzy. 'You mean he knew you were a tutor?'

'Of course he did.' Dr Mulcahy rolls up her sleeves to the pale skin at the top of her arms. 'Whew! It's hot in here. Why do you wear that ridiculous old habit?'

'Poverty,' I reply, my speech turned flat by resentment. I thought my fate was determined by God but other people, it seems, have been twitching the strings.

'Unlike most nuns you've kept your figure.' Dr Mulcahy's eyes flick over me like a lizard. 'It's a pity you're so muffled up.'

Across the grass I can see some Fourth Formers swarming around the bus stop. 'School's out,' I gulp into the clammy air.

'Remember to get in touch if you change your mind.'

'Yes,' I croak, knowing I never will. 'And thank you for the lift.'

'Any time,' she says, following me to the door. 'You can depend on me.'

As I step on to the grass she kisses me lightly on the cheek, then disappears into the Palm House. My legs are shaking a little as I track back towards the road and my skin feels as though it's soaked in warm tea. On reaching the pavement I push through crowds of schoolgirls jamming on their panamas at the sight of a Choir nun. Only on passing through the main gates do I glance up at the windows, wondering if I've been spotted; but the afternoon sun has turned them to squares of molten gold, and each one looks equally empty.

Losers

I look first in Brigid's classroom, and then in the chapel and the convent library. But she's nowhere to be found and her place is empty at supper, which is, says Bertie, because she's got a migraine. Later that night I hesitate outside her cell for a few seconds, go to bed without seeing her and have a restless night of it, chased till dawn by flesh-eating plants and Venus fly-traps.

When she fails to appear at breakfast I run upstairs and tap on her door and then, on hearing no reply, poke my head into her cell.

Although our attics are baking in the summer heat the skylight is shut and the air musty as a pet-shop cage. Brigid is in bed, staring at the ceiling as though some dire message is written across it. Her face is sallower than usual and her hair thin and lank from its years under the veil. On her locker I see with a shock the little brown bottle of Valium all too familiar from the bedsides of women in Moses Street.

'How are you feeling?'

When Brigid says nothing I move closer, ask her again and then, like an out of condition athlete, take a lumbering run at the ten tricky little syllables: 'I saw Julia Mulcahy yesterday.'

'Julia Mulcahy?' The words sink through the stale air till Brigid lifts her head from her pillow. 'Gerrout of 'ere.' Her lips are cracked and have a crust of white at each corner. 'Just gerrout.'

Can this be starchy Sister Rigid with her elocution vowel sounds? Her accent is scouse like before she was a Choir nun but coarser than I've ever heard it, and throaty and rough as a drunk's. Too frightened even to obey, I shrink back from the bed in the hope she'll stop glaring, but she keeps her burning eyes fixed on mine.

'Is there anything you want?' I whisper.

'Not from you there isn't.'

'I could get you something to read – or a glass of water if you're feeling ill —'

The bridge of her nose is thickening, and the skin on her cheeks is dry as an old woman's. 'Just gerrout of me room, will yer? How many more times do I 'ave to say it?'

The watery eyes, sagging mouth and spatter of crude words – it hits me like a punch in the stomach. Brigid is speaking in the voice of her mam who died years ago from a larynx thickened by fag ash and Guinness, a mam that Brigid disapproved of and tried to escape by becoming a nun.

'Are you sure you don't want me to do anything?'

'You've done enough already, you sneaky bitch.'

'What do you mean?'

'Stop being so frigging smarmy. I bloody well saw you from me classroom window.'

I stare in guilty dismay as Brigid, uncannily greasy and old, hoists herself on to one elbow.

'I didn't mean to go to the Palm House,' I begin babbling. 'I was just walking home when Dr Mulcahy stopped her car and asked if I wanted a lift and then she said if I didn't get in she wouldn't —'

'Shut yer face, will yer?'

'I didn't mean to upset you.'

Brigid has lain back down and shut her eyes tight. 'Julian's a cow,' she rasps in her aged, crude voice, 'and I frigging well don't want to hear what she said.'

I'm staring in panic at the blotchy skin when her eyes snap open again and she starts to scream. 'Stop gawping at me! Just bloody well stop gawping.'

'I only went to the Palm House to hear her message,' I bleat. 'Otherwise I wouldn't have —'

'You were in there for thirty-five bloody minutes.' Brigid hacks out a cough and then squints at me as though through cigarette smoke. 'I thought I could trust you when I gave you that letter but I couldn't because you're a little tart.'

'Julia didn't mean to hurt you, she just wanted to say —'

'Why don't you go to her yourself if you're so damn keen on her?'

'She asked me to,' I blurt out, 'but I said no, I want to stay here at St Cuthbert's.' I stretch out a hand and rest it on the hump in the bedclothes.

'She asked *you* – when she wouldn't fucking have *me!*' Brigid turns her face to the wall so her voice sounds thicker than ever. 'I've thought of her every day since she left – every single bloody day. And then, when I finally write her a letter, she snogs you in full view of the convent.'

'She was kissing me goodbye – it meant nothing.'

243

'A bloody long goodbye kiss! She knew I was looking out that window – she fucking well knew.'

'She can't have done. And even if she did – then you're better off without her.'

'What the fuck do you know about it?' Brigid buries her face in the pillow and pulls up the blanket.

'Please don't be so upset, Bid – we need you in St Cuthbert's. Soon we'll be going comprehensive and —'

'I bloody well loathe teaching,' croaks the new-old Brigid. 'My pupils bore me shitless and I bore them right back because I've nothing left to say.'

'But you're a great teacher,' I lie feverishly.

'I'm not and you frigging well know it, and if I had a home in the world I'd go to it today. But I haven't, so that's that. Now will you bugger off?'

Though her words burn in my mind for the rest of the day I say nothing to the others, scared that news of her coarseness will reach Bosco. After supper Bertie leaves Brigid's cell with an untouched tray – but she too stays silent. Though the door remains shut for the whole weekend, Brigid's despair seems to seep through her keyhole so that on Monday it's almost a relief to go to the uni for my last exam.

Dr Palfrey, as I now make myself think of him again, is invigilating with two tutors from the French department. I try not to let his presence put me off but the paper's on my worst subject, the care and treatment of water colours, and I only manage two and a half sides. When the time's up at last I spring to my feet and gather my pens, unable to help glancing in his direction. To my surprise he steps down from the podium and starts walking towards me. But why make a fool of myself twice running? I hurry from the hall at once and by the time I'm across the road I've convinced myself he wasn't smiling at me at all but at somebody standing behind me.

That evening I wander round the convent for the first time in months, and see from the dry wood and dust balls that the Choir nuns have fallen down on the cleaning. To give my new life a kick start I ask Bosco to be excused from the Divine Office. She says yes if I'll say my rosary while I work, so the next morning while the Choir nuns are in chapel I put on my old serge habit and apron.

First I tackle the roof space next to the dormitory, where broken chairs are stacked ready for mending and out of favour statues huddle in a corner like frightened pygmies. Before the Vatican Council they each had their own plinth in the high school and were prayed to before every lesson. Then the Pope decreed them to be apocryphal, and Wilfie told me to take them down, smash them into small pieces and bury them in the garden. With a whispered apology to each I lined them up in the shed and raised my hammer; but something in their noble and resigned faces made it impossible to obey, so I smuggled them up to the attic when Wilfie wasn't looking, in the hope that one day they'd be recalled.

Looking at them now, I know that day will never come. St Agatha balancing her poor blancmangy breasts in a dish, Sebastian stuck full of arrows, and the brave curly-headed Lawrence trapped for ever on his grid-iron – what a bunch of losers. We've been martyred in vain, they seem to say, and will never ascend to heaven. I fetch a bowl of hot water from the kitchen and sponge them down. Through the partition which divides the roof space from the dormitory I hear the odd muffled moan from Brigid, whom I mention to each saint as I soap the sorry mouths and resigned noses.

Released from the chilly chapel air I'm able to pray again, and while my hands work on I murmur one decade of the rosary after another in the hope that both God and Brigid will forgive me. Ignoring my aching muscles I turn next to the cloakrooms, tugging crisp packets from the radiators and scraping chewing-gum off the floors.

At the end of a fortnight I'm back in my old routine, pleased to have conquered my disappointment. I even start to hear the boots of the Holy Army.

At the weekend Mam and Dad come to see me in the parlour where I tell them I've left the uni, and will never get a BA. When their faces fall I remind them I'm not the academic type, and am happier by far at St Cuthbert's where big changes are underway. I feed them so much detail about Bertie's new health centre and her plan for a people's dispensary that in the end I almost believe what I'm saying myself, and they go away looking satisfied.

But sometimes, when the morning sun flames on the Palm House dome or the high clouds are ribbed like the roof of a cathedral, I think of all the great painters I shall never now discover. Then the thought of Hannah and Toby and Vicky and Elisabeth graduating without me makes me turn away from the window, shut my eyes tight and gabble my old motto like a mantra. *Those that are first shall be last; and the last shall be first.*

I only wish I could believe it. My life is not, any more, the one I'd have chosen, but for God's sake I'm going to put up with it.

De Profundis Clamavi

My dreams last night were mingled with the sound of partygoers shouting to each other on the way home. I've always liked street noise, so jump out of bed feeling energetic and cheerful. Alone in the early morning quiet I start sweeping the cloister, pausing as usual to watch the Choir nuns tittup across the courtyard to Matins. My convent life, it occurs to me, has come full circle.

After breakfast I wake Pious and Placid, help them wash and clean their dentures, and start cleaning the infirmary windows while Bertilla makes their breakfast. It's a warm July day and the limes in the park are glowing green. Using my mam's recipe of warm water, malt vinegar and back copies of the *Echo*, I rub the inside of the glass and then raise the sash and look down on to the street. Someone has smashed the bus shelter during the night and a drift of milky stones lies on the pavement. Inner-city opals, Mam used to call the broken glass. A working woman's jewel box.

Over the Palm House a cloud is sailing, soggy as a new-done water colour. I'm wondering if Dr Mulcahy finished her painting and, if so, how much she got paid for it, when an angry hum comes from the cloud's centre – as though the Lord's about to rebuke me for my money-grubbing thoughts. Then six helicopters fly out in close formation and skim over the tower block, drowning out our chapel bell.

'Those bloody machines ruined my sleep,' grumbles Pious, tossing her rosary beads down on the counterpane. Her hands are shaking and her skin's the colour of under-cooked pastry. 'I thought one of them was perched on the chimney.'

I nod, in too good a mood to be bothered with Pious, who should be used by now to inner-city noises. Down in the park a dozen policemen are waving their batons as they run across the grass. Thanks to my first-year lectures I now understand the laws of perspective, and know that my retina has registered the figures as pin men. But my brain has adjusted the information to tally with past experience, so I perceive the men as life-size. When I remember the workings of the eye the figures stay small: funny little matchstick men running in single file.

'Close that sodding window,' says Pious. 'I'm in a draught.'

'People were screaming out there all night,' adds Placid, the bobbles on her shawl shivering in anxiety. 'This is a bad area.'

'Hey, but it's just like Soweto.' Bertie swings in with their breakfast tray. 'There's trouble in the air, you mark my words.'

She pours the old nuns' milk while they shove in their dentures and say grace. Leaving them to chomp and splash their way through their Coco Pops, I follow Bertie down to the kitchen.

'Those were nothing but drunks rolling home from Lark Lane,' Bosco is saying to a worried-looking Xavier. 'And as for the helicopter, the police have bought themselves a new toy and want an excuse to play with it.'

'Ag, you're out of date,' says Bertie, tipping some potato peelings into a bucket. 'The Liverpool police don't have time to play – they're under too much pressure.'

'Will you get that hen food off the table?' says Xavier. 'It's unhygienic.'

Bertilla's reply is drowned by the roar of another helicopter, this time flying so low it rattles the crockery on the tray Elisabeth's placing on the table.

Bertilla eyes the untouched toast and marmalade, 'Hau! So Brigid's still not eating. That worries me.'

'Not eating!' Elisabeth rolls her blue eyes heavenward. 'She's not even speaking – just lying there moping with her eyes closed.'

Bertie casts a meaningful glance at Bosco. 'She needs to see a specialist.'

'What's wrong with her?' I ask anxiously.

'There's nothing wrong with *Brigid*,' snaps Bosco, who's a martyr to her high blood pressure. 'Dr Reilly has said so.'

'I don't mean that sort of doctor,' says Bertie. She picks up the plate, tips Brigid's toast and marmalade into her bucket and is lugging it through the back door when she bumps into Columba.

'A man's come over the back wall in the night,' she pants, 'and he's crushed our ragged robin with his great boots.'

'There you are,' crows Xavier. 'It's the scallies.'

It's a word she's picked up from me and I can't help

smiling in recognition, glad I've left my mark on the Choir nuns' language as they've left their mark on mine.

'Calm down, Sisters,' says Bosco. 'Ragged robin is only a weed.'

'It's not a weed.' Columba turns for support to Bertie. 'It's an important part of our —'

But Bertie's taking no notice. 'I'd better get down to the hen run.'

'Bertilla is too attached to those bantams,' says Bosco, her voice raw with fatigue. 'If I had my way she'd be made to—' She's stopped from developing her point by a ring at the front doorbell.

We never have visitors on a Saturday, so stare at each other in surprise before I dart across the hall with Bosco in my wake telling me to put on the security chain.

I peer through the six-inch crack at Miss Vavasour's leathery face, which is smeared with blood above her eyebrow.

'Sister Maureen! Thank goodness you're safe!' Her red Mini is parked in our drive, and her Yorkshire terrier is yapping at her heels.

'You've got a cut on your face!'

'Someone chucked a lump of concrete.'

'What's going on?'

Bosco pushes me out of the way, undoes the chain and pulls Miss Vavasour inside. Her dog scampers across the hall and cocks its leg against the fireplace.

'Take a look through the window,' says Miss Vavasour as a police car roars past. 'They've been rioting all night long.'

Hordes of men are streaming past the convent towards the city centre. Some of them have shaven hair and big boots, and others are wielding iron bars. I run back to the kitchen, whisk the tea-towel off the transistor and tune into Radio Merseyside. 'The Rialto is burning,' says a newscaster's voice, 'and the number of wounded has risen to thirty-two, most of them policemen and —' His next words are drowned by a crash from the front of the house. By the time I arrive in the parlour the parquet is strewn with broken glass, and Bosco and Miss Vavasour are staring at a jagged hole in the window. 'It's just as well I came round,' says the games mistress, clasping a handkerchief to her forehead. 'I've got a tool-box in my car.'

Elisabeth's leaning on the window-sill, watching a group of hard-faced boys march past with lighted tapers and pieces of iron railing. 'The proles are revolting.'

'Go and get Bertilla from the hen run,' snaps Bosco. 'Miss Vavasour needs first aid.'

'What the hell's going on?' calls a voice from the next floor. Through the parlour door I see Pious in her nightdress, her grey hair spread on her shoulders, groping her way downstairs on blue feet. 'Will somebody tell me?'

Placid is hovering behind her. 'We're frightened, really frightened. Will one of you come and sit with us?' On seeing Pious she lurches forward, grabs the banister which I've polished that morning, and slithers down to the next step.

'Get them back to bed,' shouts Bosco, slamming the parlour door on Miss Vavasour. 'And will somebody come and patch up this window?'

I coax the old ones back to the infirmary while Bertilla starts bandaging Miss Vavasour's forehead and Columba looks for some hardboard. There are more people than ever outside, all of them surging towards the city centre where a fairground noise of grinding machinery rises every now and again to a roar. As I run to the kitchen to make Miss

Vavasour a cup of tea, a thumping sound comes from the direction of Lodge Lane, like the banging of sticks on dustbin lids. Then somewhere out of sight a horse starts whinnying, and a row of policemen run past the window into a hail of bricks and stones. Inside the convent, Columba brings Bertie some chipboard from the hen run, and together they cover the parlour window.

'I'm off now to Julia Mulcahy's.' Miss Vavasour drains her cup of tea as the crowd on the pavement begins to thin. 'Her flat's right in the firing-line.'

Bosco's eyes bulge. But rather than reveal her surprise to a laywoman, she smiles politely from the top step as Miss Vavasour reverses her Mini down the drive and roars off into the traffic.

'Rather her than me!' says Elisabeth as we unplug a black and white telly from one of the classrooms. 'It's a jolly good job it's not term-time. We'd have got stuck in the university.'

I nod, but as we lug the TV upstairs I'm aware of feeling cheated and out of touch. How is it that I, who was born here, didn't have a clue about the riots? I wonder who the rioters are and where they come from; not the Dingle, I'm sure, where people bear their troubles stoically, and would never dream of wrecking their surroundings.

We settle Pious and Placid in bed while Bosco tunes in to a news flash and the others gather round to watch. 'You can see more from the window,' I tell them, raising the frosted glass and looking down to where a policeman is trying to put a black man in a neck-lock.

'Shut that window,' begs Placid, 'or they'll be throwing more stones.'

'If only Mother Wilfred was here,' says Bosco who is watching the jumping blue screen where a Black Maria is mounting a pavement, its engine straining.

'That set's impossible without an aerial,' says Elisabeth. 'I'd rather read about it in the papers.'

'Those people are nothing but common criminals,' cries Xavier as the camera pans to a man in Granby Street felling a policeman with a mallet. Then it swings away to an Asian man with a sad face and blurred edges, running across the road in front of a Land-rover.

'Mr Gopal,' shouts Bertie as the man's intercepted by a baton-wielding policeman.

The shot changes to firemen in front of the blazing Rialto.

'Sister Bertilla! Come back at once!'

But Bertie is charging down the stairs.

'They're professional agitators.'

'The government should ban the Communist Party.'

'What about the Labour Party? I blame that godless Michael Foot.'

'It's their own district they're messing up – that's what I can't understand,' says Xavier, staring at the screen where a rioter is attacking a lamp post with a sledgehammer. 'Why don't they march on Sefton Park?'

'Please don't tempt Providence!' says Bosco. She drags down the blinds, switches off the television, drops heavily to her knees and pulls out her rosary beads. There's a burst of gunfire close at hand and then a thump in the back garden. 'Let us pray that this disturbance may end quickly so that our policemen may return in safety to their wives and families.'

She's making the sign of the cross when an agitated-looking Columba puts her head round the door and beckons her from the room. Desperate for more news, I sit up on my heels and switch on the TV, which is showing a house blazing in Granby Street. From the next-door off-licence people are running with crates and bottles.

'The devils have started looting,' says Placid, making the sign of the cross.

The façade of the house wavers and falls into the street, like a giant buckling at the knees. As smoke belches up from the ruins Columba comes back, this time for Ursula.

'What's wrong?' I ask her.

'On no account leave the infirmary,' she gasps when I rise to my feet. 'Just look after Pious and Placid.' Before I have time to protest she's out of the room with Ursula and off upstairs.

A few moments later Ursula comes back and stands with her arms folded just inside the door, as though on guard. 'What is it?' I ask again.

Her reply is drowned by a siren wailing down the street, so I wait for it to pass. But instead of speeding on to the city centre it must be swinging into our front drive because I can hearing the spray of gravel against the step. I move to answer the door but Ursula pushes me back against the bed. Startled by the rough gesture, Placid cowers against her pillows while Pious, who can see nothing, is staring at the television. Then Bosco's voice comes from the hall, louder and higher than usual, followed by the tramp of boots.

'The buggers are robbing us,' says Pious.

'It's nothing,' says Ursula through pale lips, 'absolutely nothing.'

But the boots pound up the first flight of stairs, past the infirmary door and on to the dormitory where no man, not even Dr Reilly, is admitted. Then we hear the noise of a bed being dragged from the wall, and rough male voices, and something bumping down from the attic and knocking against the banisters. Ursula stands grim-faced all the while, only moving when Columba comes back into the room to turn up the television even louder. She's on the brink of tears. Mystified, I stare at the screen where policemen are vizored like inter-galactic warriors – and then the front door slams shut and the room is lit with a swirling blue light.

'Will you please stop treating me like a baby,' I beg, 'and tell me what's going on?'

At that Ursula draws me into the little room that leads off the infirmary. Closing the door behind us, she tracks across the dusty floorboards to that same bed where Brigid told me about herself and Julia, and signals me to sit down beside her. Fixing my eyes on the frosted-glass sash, I wait for her to speak.

'This will come as a shock to you, dear, because I know you've always admired Sister Brigid.'

The room's at the side of the house so the noise of the riot is muted, but away on the far wall a bee is buzzing against the frosted glass. It's Ursula's silence that tells me what's happened, a silence so full of meaning that it parts the air between us and creeps into my brain, where a picture is forming of a figure lying alone and unaware.

'Has Brigid been taken ill?' I whisper as the silence freezes in my skull.

'No, Maureen, not exactly.' Ursula touches my sweating palm with her disciplined hand. 'None of us remembered her at first – then Bosco went up and found her unconscious, and the empty pill bottle on her locker. It's a terrible thing, dear. Sister Brigid has tried to commit suicide.'

Purgatory

I race downstairs and open the front door. A pall of brick dust hangs over the city and the light is low and sickly as though the sun's worked loose from its socket. A man with a crowbar stares as I dash into the road where the flashing blue light is edging through the crowd; but just as I start to run the siren sounds and the ambulance disappears.

'Sister Maureen! Come back.' Ursula runs up behind me, clutching her side.

'Brigid needs me,' I cry into her taut face. 'She's all on her own.'

'Bosco's gone with her to the Royal. Come back inside – it's dangerous.'

I shake off her hand and run down the street, but the crowd has closed round the departed ambulance. I try to push through them but the ground turns to sponge and silver spots start spinning before my eyes. People are fighting and shoving all round me, and at the end of the street I can hear the clatter of hooves.

'Mind out of the way, Sister,' yells a burly man in a donkey jacket. 'You're going to get hit.'

My breath ragged, I blunder back to where Ursula waits on the pavement. She grips my elbow and propels me up the path and into the convent, not letting go till we've reached the community room where the others are saying the rosary. She clearly expects me to kneel down beside them, but my throat's too dry to pray out loud. Slumped on a chair, I struggle to grasp what's happened – that Brigid, who's been in my life for as long as I can remember, has tried to kill herself.

Holy Mary Mother of God, pray for us sinners . . . The others have finished the Agony in the Garden and are whispering their way through the Crowning with Thorns, but for once the familiar words seem pointless. While the rest of us were worrying about the riots Brigid reached for her bottle of sleeping tablets, crunched them down and prepared herself for what might be her final voyage.

If only she'd called me beforehand, I think, fighting back my tears, I'd have made her change her mind, told her how I'd loved and admired her since girlhood, and how much I needed her at St Cuthbert's.

Dear God, I keep muttering, please let her recover. I'll do anything for You if You let her recover.

When the phone rings at last the others are on to the Crucifixion. Someone has switched off the television, and the only sounds to puncture the silence are the stutter of gunfire, Ursula's strained voice in the hall, and then the click of the receiver.

'That was Bosco from the Royal.' Ursula hurries back in, her voice breathy with distress. 'By the time they got there it was too late.'

'Too late?' croaks Columba.

'The accident suite was full of injured policemen.'

'If only you'd told me,' I burst out. 'I once did first aid – I could have saved her.'

Bosco ignores me to make the sign of the cross. '*Eternal rest grant unto her, O Lord.*'

'*And let perpetual light shine upon her,*' we respond in a scattered chorus. Gonzaga is blowing her nose, and Columba is crying openly.

'*May she rest in peace.*'

'*Amen.*'

We're gathered in the kitchen when Bosco rings the doorbell an hour later, having cut through on foot from the Royal. We make her a cup of sugary tea while she phones Mother Wilfred in Rome. Then she sits down and tells us how the ambulance raced along Lodge Lane till it was stopped by a barricade of blazing cars. Next it tried to force its way down Upper Parliament Street but that too was blocked by rioters. In the end it had to go round by Edge Lane.

'If it wasn't for those troublemakers,' twangs Xavier, 'Sister Brigid would still be with us.'

'It's terrible to think of her lying alone.' Columba wipes her eyes. 'Why can't we lay her out in St Cuthbert's?'

'Because of the inquest,' says Bosco harshly. 'She'll have to stay in the mortuary for a couple of weeks.'

Columba tops up the teapot with boiling water. 'When she comes home I shall decorate the coffin with chervil and feverfew from our herb garden.'

At that Bosco puts down her cup and looks round the kitchen. 'Where's Bertilla?'

'Not back yet.'

'She should be here with us,' says Bosco, blue eyes bulging. 'Not traipsing round Toxteth after Mr Gopal.'

'I agree,' says Xavier. 'She had no right to go charging off like that.'

'Do you think Brigid meant to kill herself?' says Elisabeth, her voice cold and clear as a bell.

'No, dear,' quavers Columba. 'It was an accident.'

'Or maybe a cry for help,' suggests Kevin.

'She'd been depressed for weeks,' adds Ursula. 'Teachers often get off-balance at the end of the school year.'

'I think it's our diet,' says Xavier, pulling her shawl round her arms. 'We don't get enough red meat.'

'You may think what you like,' snaps Bosco, 'but if Bertilla had been here she might have revived her.'

'Let's not get into a dispute,' says Elisabeth, dumping a pile of scores on the kitchen table. 'We need to decide on the funeral music. I vote for a Bevernôt mass – restrained and aloof, just like Brigid.' She gives Bosco a garden-party smile. 'And some Pergolesi, don't you think?'

Hostility is clogging my veins like sludge. It's not Bertilla who's to blame, but Elisabeth and her tale-bearing. If she hadn't reported Brigid and Julian, they would both be here today and our community would be intact.

Elisabeth starts leafing through a requiem mass while Bosco sits staring at the dresser and the rest of us drift off to our separate tasks.

The shouts and explosions continue throughout the day, but it seems disrespectful to switch on the news; and after the shock of Brigid's death the risk to our building seems nothing.

But when the others have gone to bed that night I creep

into the kitchen and turn on the radio. Although nobody felt like supper the draining-board is piled with cups and saucers which I wash while listening to a news flash. The rioters have been brought under control but the Rialto is still blazing. Nearby housing estates are in danger of catching fire.

After drying the crockery I go upstairs and get undressed. A few seconds later I hear Bertilla come in, and Bosco's raised voice in the hall. Then the front door opens again and I hear footsteps marching down the path then the click of the garden gate.

Feeling lonely and insecure, I lie and stare through the skylight at the reddened clouds, listening to the shouts in the park and trying to think of anything but the lonely figure in the mortuary.

But when the convent clock strikes two and the thirtieth siren wails down the road I can blot out the image no longer. Columba and Kevin meant well when they said that Brigid killed herself by mistake, but in my heart I know better. Brigid did it on purpose and I was wrong to blame Elisabeth. Brigid chose death over a miserable life, and we're all of us to blame for that. And me most of all.

I've joined it without noticing: the starchy St Cuthbert's of the Choir nuns, down on anything secret or spontaneous. I remember how Brigid swallowed her pride and told me about her and Dr Mulcahy. All she'd done was show someone a bit of love but instead of putting my arms round her and telling her it was OK, I stalked out of the infirmary with my nose in the air.

And worse, knowing exactly how she felt, I went with Dr Mulcahy to the Palm House and let her kiss me in full view of the convent – enjoyed it even, smugly aware that I too was attractive, though too pure to be tempted. And then, without thinking how Brigid might feel, I told her all about it in my stupid heedless way, too obsessed with my own problems to notice her suffering. Lorraine was right, I decide as a siren wails in the distance. I'm unplugged at the mains and always have been.

I think of the future I'd pictured for Brigid and me – how we'd be like Pious and Placid but nicer, two daft old nuns with a childhood only we could share. Now there'll be just me – or, I realise with a chill, me and Elisabeth. And in between are the lonely years at St Cuthbert's with no one to share my thoughts except Bertilla – and she's too caught up in the outside world to be bothered. The only other person I could talk to about Brigid is Julian – alias the wicked and worldly Dr Mulcahy – but now I've left university I shall never see her again.

Over the rest of the weekend we try to come to terms with what's happened and get back into some sort of routine. By Sunday night the rioting is over but the streets round the convent are strewn with rubble, looters are rampaging through the city and the buses have stopped running. A few days later the Archdeacon comes to see Bosco by taxi, not wanting to risk his new Cavalier. After half an hour I hear the ring of the tasselled bell pull in the parlour – his usual signal he's ready for tea.

When I enter the room he's mopping his face with a large white handkerchief that must have been ironed for him by my mam. Though the weather is hot the windows are shut to keep out the smell of burning. I've been too distraught to do any baking and his face falls when he sees the near-empty tray. Then he rallies and lumbers towards me. 'I'm so sorry to hear about your little friend.'

When my eyes fill at the show of sympathy, he pulls out his handkerchief again and flaps it in my face. Then he draws up a chair and watches me lay the table. 'What a tragedy,' he sighs. 'It seems only yesterday that I baptised her.'

'Will you please give the news to me mam?' I ask him, taking off the tea-cosy. 'I can't get through because their phone line's down.'

'I'm telling no one till I've briefed the Coroner.' His eyes stray to the teapot, which I'm clasping by the handle. 'Luckily I know one who's a good Catholic.'

'Why do we need a Catholic coroner?'

For once, the Archdeacon seems reluctant to spell things out. 'Because he's sympathetic to priests and nuns,' he says after a pause.

I begin to get his drift: suicide is a mortal sin for any Catholic, and doubly shocking in a nun.

'Sister Brigid endangered your convent's good name in life,' he carries on, his eyes still fixed on the teapot, 'and she's done it again in death.'

'It was a moment of weakness,' I cry. 'Surely God won't send her to Hell.'

He holds out his cup and saucer. 'My business is to stop this scandal from spreading. The parents won't like it, won't like it at all.'

I think of Brigid's poor grey soul, judged wanting so often in life and waiting to be judged yet again. 'But I need to know what you think.'

'Well, really – I'm not sure that I can . . .'

He's expecting me to pour but I won't lift the teapot until he's answered.

'It's true that suicide is a mortal sin,' he intones, 'but the good God is merciful.'

I fill his cup right up to the rim. 'Do you really believe that, Father?'

He takes a long draught of Darjeeling. 'If our beloved little sister felt one flicker of regret after swallowing those tablets, then God in His infinite compassion would absolve her that instant.'

While he pops in an extra sugar lump I remember Brigid's doubtful chin. 'She always had second thoughts – so she must have changed her mind at least once.'

'Then that settles it,' says the Archdeacon heartily. 'She will now be sitting on God's right hand, talking to Him about her dear little friend from the Dingle.'

His tone was so confident I'd started to believe him – but with that he went too far. Brigid may not be in Hell but I'm doomily aware that she's just the type to have a long and tortuous Purgatory.

'And remember this,' the Archdeacon continues unaware. 'Now you, Sister Maureen, have your very own patron among the Blessed.'

I try to picture Brigid on high but her face under its halo is as sallow as ever and her eyes are full not of love but resentment. And who can blame her? She preferred death – maybe even Hell – to community life and might ignore my prayers out of revenge. She might even join the Holy Army and jeer at me as I clean – but she never did like the company of lay sisters, so it seems unlikely.

I ponder these thoughts in silence, too intent on my vision of the afterlife to concentrate on the Archdeacon. Despite his attempts to turn the conversation to more earthly topics such as how he must muzzle the *Echo*, his talk soon falters and he asks me to call him a taxi. The moment he's slammed the door I make my way to the garden, wanting to cheer myself up by the only way I know: hard work.

I go first to the little graveyard where Brigid will soon be buried, and start picking up the tinnies and chewing-gum wrappers scattered among the headstones. Though Brigid hated manual labour I can sense her presence as I fill my barrow and wheel it towards the grotto. Our Lady's nose has got another chip and the niche where she stands has been rifled by rioters grabbing stones for ammunition. The kneeling figure of St Bernadette Soubirous has been tipped on its side, and I wonder as I right it what she thinks about the riots. In a single summer in Lourdes she had eighteen visions of Our Blessed Lady, so she might just feel at home in these apocalyptic times.

I spend the rest of the afternoon plugging the gaps in the grotto and when my arms start to ache I sit down beside Bernadette and watch the leaves of the pear tree stirring in the sunlight. Some dirt is clinging to the saint's brown dress, which I notice is the same shade as our habit. 'I'm sorry,' I whisper as I wipe it away, 'really sorry.'

I've always thought insomnia was a Choir nun's luxury but I haven't slept for nights and my world is starting to blur round the edges. The air is still thick with the smell of burning, and the outline of the convent building is wavering a little in the heat. Then the pear tree starts to shimmer and its leaves dissolve in a green cloud while the tower block behind is rocking as though in an earthquake. I know I should run and warn my sisters – but my limbs are too heavy to move and my gaze is fixed on the topmost flat and the clouds that are swirling past its windows. Then I hear a strangled croak at my side, and my eyes are dragged downwards to the sallow face of Bernadette.

'What is it?' I ask her as the blood in my ears starts to sing.

She's struggling to speak but the words which are winding through the singed air are dark and clogged with earth.

'Jaaahhh.'

I search her troubled brown eyes which, I see with a shock, belong not to the saint but to Brigid. 'What is it?' I cry again.

The lips of the statue part in distress, and there's a lump of soil on her tongue. 'Jaaahhhh.' The words come again, more clotted and dark than ever.

I sit as still as I can till the noise in my ears dies down and the tower block stops swaying. The smell of burning has faded, and the leaves on the pear tree are their usual greyish green. As soon as I've stopped feeling dizzy I rise to my feet and look down at the pottery face, now blunt and impassive as ever. Even though she's on the other side, I think sadly, Brigid is still too proud to beg a favour.

But her meaning is clear all the same, and as I totter across the lawn to the back door I know beyond a shadow of doubt what it is that she wants me to do.

The Message

Thanks to the Archdeacon, the Coroner returns a verdict of accidental death, and Bosco rings Mother Wilfred in Rome while I wax the chapel floor, Ursula orders a headstone and Columba combs the garden for the few white roses that aren't worm-eaten. I wish that Elisabeth wasn't choosing the music, but as Bertilla points out it doesn't much matter, because uBridgie was tone deaf.

Moving briskly for the first time since the suicide, Bosco hurries into the sacristy to tell us that Mother Wilfred's flying home for the funeral.

'Thank God for that,' murmurs Columba, clasping her hands. 'Now she can pay her last respects.'

Ursula looks up from her flower arrangement, her horse face mild. 'Dear Brigid will be glad. They were like mother and daughter.'

I give an extra hard rub at a candlestick, knowing that if dear Brigid had a grave she'd be turning in it now. She and Mother Wilfred seldom saw eye to eye, and if she was like a daughter it was a very slack and surly one; as for Wilfie, she was often heard to complain that Brigid was unstable and lacked staying-power. Her suicide must have confirmed the Superior's worst suspicions.

I picture the tall and critical figure looming over the coffin. Disobedient girl, it snaps. How dare you kill yourself without permission?

But at least Wilfie will be an extra mourner. Brigid's real mother died years ago, and apart from an uncle in London she has no relatives. I sent a message asking Mam to invite all in the Dingle who remembered Brigid Murray, but Mam wrote back to say Brigid's a long time gone and there won't be many. Nor can we march in her pupils to swell the choir, because the school holidays have begun. That leaves Dr Reilly and a few of the secular staff. Not an impressive turnout for a woman born and bred here.

But Brigid herself couldn't care less about the absence of pupils, and of people from the Dingle. She wouldn't mind if Wilfie stayed in Rome and none of her sisters showed up. She told me so in her thick dark voice: Dr Mulcahy's the only one she wants at her funeral, and it's my job to get her there.

If only she'd asked for something easier, I sigh, after the operator has told me that Dr Mulcahy is ex-directory. Miss Vavasour knows the address, but she's away on holiday. I ring Mrs Dagnall who says that staff telephone numbers are confidential, and she is not at liberty to disclose them; which means that I'll have to catch Dr Mulcahy in her office.

But when I ask Bosco for permission to go to town, she refuses at once. It said so on the BBC: the city's still unsettled after the riots. Over the next few days I beg her to let me visit the shops, the library and even the Archdeacon. I'm lying, I know; but when I think of Brigid's poor grey soul floundering around the afterlife, I'm happy to commit so small a sin on her behalf. But Bosco refuses each request, and I'm back where I started. Nor can Bertilla deliver a message because Bosco's told Wilfie about her disobedience over the riots, and she's facing a disciplinary. Until then, she's been ordered point blank to stay indoors.

Remembering that the best goals are often scored in the closing minutes, I try not to lose heart. Then the undertaker rings to warn us that he's bringing Brigid home to St Cuthbert's, and Bosco remembers that the Sisters of Mercy have borrowed our trestles. No sooner has she left for their convent in the next parish than Mother Wilfred phones to announce that she's flying in this evening.

'We must make a funeral banquet, Soweto-style,' says Bertilla as Ursula puts down the phone. She gives me a smile. 'It's time we had a bit of life in this place – and uBrigid won't mind, eh, Moey?'

'It's nice of you to cook – given the way you've been treated.'

'Good things can come out of bad.' Bertilla lifts down her pestle and mortar. 'There are going to be some changes round here – big, big changes.' She crosses the kitchen and opens the larder door. 'Hau, no vegetables. Lucky that Mr Gopal is out of hospital.'

'Has he not been evicted?'

'Not as far as I know. But I'm under house arrest and can't visit him.' She gives a chuckle.

Luckily there are no Choir nuns left in the kitchen. 'I'll go,' I cry, ever quick to get possession of the ball.

'Are you sure that's wise?' quavers Gonzaga. 'Bosco said that nobody should —'

'Of course it's wise,' says Bertilla. 'Moey was born in Liverpool 8.' She stops me as I'm shooting through the door. 'Why not pop in to see Heather when you've been to Mr Gopal's? You can take some clean sheets and change her bed.'

With no buses running, a visit to Heather will add at least half an hour to my morning. 'I won't have time.'

'That's not like you – and Heather is failing fast.'

There's no way I can ignore a dying woman, so a few minutes later I'm loping down the garden path with a bag of clean sheets and a jar of honey for Heather, and some bantam eggs for Mr Gopal. Though I'll take any blame that comes my way I'd like to be home before Bosco, so once I get into the park I break into a run. Apart from its trampled grass and extra litter it looks nearly back to normal – even including the tramp who's reeling towards me down the path, swinging his bottle of Thunderbird like a censer. I try to dodge past him but on seeing my habit he steps forward to bar my way. 'Want a fuck?' he says, fumbling at his fly. 'Go on, Sister, give us a fuck.'

Usually I'd ignore him and slither past, but I'm too pumped up by my errands. 'Mind out the way,' I say to him.

'Have you never seen a cock before?' he snarls.

I struggle not to laugh out loud. Mother Wilfred's Baby Jesuses, Piers's Michelangelo and a male model in life class: all the world, it sometimes seems, wants to acquaint me with the male form – but how to tell that to the tramp? 'Of course I have,' I say to his pock-marked old face. 'We've got a bantam back at the convent.'

'This is no bantam.' Planting himself in my path, the old man wiggles his varicose worm.

'Better put it away, Dad,' I call as I step past him, 'before a pigeon gets it.'

At that he pulls up his zip with an air of pique, spits sourly and shuffles off.

Eager to make up for lost time, I hurry on to the Boulevard where the gravel is strewn with broken glass and ornamental railings. In Granby Street an upturned Ford is lying in the gutter and the street signs are covered in dust. Most of the shops are boarded up, and all unprotected windows have been shattered. A smartly dressed man is selling shirts from a clutch of hangers, and Mr Gopal is standing behind a makeshift stall in front of his burnt-out shop. With most of the supermarkets shut he's obviously doing good business.

'I'm sorry to be hearing about poor Sister Brigid,' he says as I hand him the eggs. 'When is the funeral?'

'Tomorrow morning at eleven.'

'Was it a nervous breakdown?' he asks, his brown eyes avid and concerned at once.

'I think she'd been overworking,' I say, then try for a change of subject. 'We saw you on television.'

He fingers the bruise on his cheek. 'I am telling the police that my property was on fire, so they hit me with a baton. It was good that Sister Bertie came round – got me out of the cells.'

I wonder if Wilfie knows all this, and if she does, why she isn't impressed.

'First the Council gives me an eviction order,' continues Mr Gopal, 'and then the rioters fire my shop. I say to Amira, What next?'

'May I have two pounds of tomatoes, please? And three pounds of carrots? And nine grapefruits.'

'Nine?' says Mr Gopal, stepping neatly over a cracked paving-stone. It's years since a St Cuthbert's nun has asked for so much fruit.

'We're preparing for Mother Wilfred's homecoming.'

'Who is cooking?'

'Sister Bertilla.'

'Then I give her some extra carrots and avocados. No, please do not thank me.' Mr Gopal glowers at the Caribbean man next in the queue. 'All the less for them to steal.'

'I'm on my way to see Heather March,' I say, hoping to divert his attention.

'You will take her a mango. This one is ripe – must be eaten today.'

I put the soft yellow fruit in my bag, not wanting to tell him that Heather's been unable to eat since the Rialto burned to the ground only yards from her window.

'And tell Sister Bertie to come back soon,' adds Mr Gopal. 'We miss her, I and my wife.'

Puffs of low-flying grime are smudging the sky, so that I long to rise on high and scrub it clean. Apart from the gush of water from a burst main, the road to Heather's flat is eerily silent, with TRESPASSERS WILL BE PROSEC-UTED notices sprouting where there's nothing to protect but rubble. Littered with old tyres and milk bottles, the land round the estate is like a bombsite. The only sign of life is some men planting saplings by the children's play area.

'Who is it?' A red eye is applied to a crack in the door.

'Sister Maureen.'

The door slams shut. Then a chain clanks and I slide inside, and follow the shrunken figure into the front room.

Although Bertie warned me that Heather was failing fast, I didn't expect the brown-blotched face, the skin dripping like gauze from the old woman's arms and the smell of rotting bananas.

'Where's Sister Bertilla?' she caws, climbing back into bed.

'She's preparing a meal.' I put down my bag and start pulling back the curtains. 'Mother Wilfred is —'

'Leave them curtains shut.'

'But the looting stopped days ago.'

'If the robbers see you inside they hang on your doorbell wanting to dump their knock-off.'

'Just say no.'

'The old feller next door said no. Next thing was a fire bomb through his window.'

'I'm sure things will soon get back to normal.'

'The 8 will never be normal because it's run by crims.'

'I've just seen some men planting trees.'

A smell of ammonia pervades the room as Heather shifts to the other side of her bed. 'The scallies will soon see to 'em.'

'Do you want to drink your soup in the armchair?' There's no point in asking her if she's wet the bed, Bertie told me, because she won't tell the truth. If in doubt just change the sheet. But that's easier said than done with Heather defending her foul nest like an angry pigeon.

'Here,' I hand her a mug, 'drink your soup.' While she brings her cracked lips to the rim, I take a clean sheet from my bag, noting that the mango has burst and stained the white linen.

Heather spits out her soup. 'I won't be needing them sheets because I'm not drinking.'

'I'll leave them anyway,' I tell her, picking up my bag with a sense of defeat. There seems no point in leaving the mango.

'I want to be nursed at St Cuthbert's.'

'Sister Bertilla will be back to see you soon,' I reply, hoping it's the truth. Her disciplinary will involve the Superior, the Archdeacon and two senior community members, and no one knows what they'll decree.

As I recross the waste land I shout at the lads yanking branches from the newly-planted saplings but they take no notice. Then, praying that the Sisters of Mercy will have asked Bosco to stay to lunch, I march on to the university.

My worn shoes have blistered my feet, and I'm struggling not to think of them as I slip past Mrs Dagnall's office and up to the attic, where to my relief, Dr Mulcahy's door is standing open. Her room looks much the same as it did before, with the clutter of books, the jar of sharpened 3B pencils and the poster of a poppy by Georgia O'Keeffe. There's even a half-empty cup of herbal tea on the desk. With her door unlocked she can't be far, so I write a note with one of her 3B's: 'Brigid has died very suddenly. Her funeral is tomorrow at eleven in St Cuthbert's.' And then I add my signature and the date, followed by the words 'Brigid wants you to be there' which I underline twice in the thick black lead before propping the note against the cup.

Although the china is still warm I have a sudden hunch that Dr Mulcahy either won't read the message, or will fail to come to the funeral. Discouraged, I leave the room and trail downstairs, thinking how difficult Brigid can be, and the vengeance she'll wreak from the spirit world if her Julian doesn't show up.

Working-class Feet

As I reach the first-floor landing Dr Palfrey is coming upstairs with an armful of books. 'Sister Maureen! Why so bleak?'

I could never explain my thoughts of the last few moments, so I search my mind for the next truest thing. 'One of my sisters has killed herself,' I blurt out, knowing at once I've disobeyed the Archdeacon.

'Not Sister Elisabeth?' Dr Palfrey's gaze is part shocked, part quizzical.

'It's someone you've never met.' The waste and shame of Brigid's death surge through me. 'And will you please not tell anyone it was suicide, because we're supposed to keep it secret?'

'Why not come and have a cup of coffee?' Dr Palfrey rests his hand on the small of my back while my legs walk of their own accord to his open door. 'You're clearly very upset.'

My feet are still throbbing in my worn-out shoes and my arm aches from the bag of vegetables. Slumped into a chair

I catch sight of the After Eight clock on the mantelpiece. Ten past two. I've already been gone three hours, and have no hope of getting home before Bosco. I would like to rest here all day, looking over the square while Dr Palfrey fusses over his coffee grinder and blue and white cups. It's the first time we've met properly since the night of his dinner, but I've lost all traces of hurt pride. Compared with riots and death a rebuff from a tutor seems nothing, and I wonder how I could have been so petty-minded.

'It's always a shock,' Dr Palfrey pulls up a chair, 'when someone important disappears from our lives.'

'It's just that – I could have helped her and didn't. I was prim and disapproving —' My eyes begin to smart.

He takes hold of my hand as though about to read it, then caresses my palm with his thumb. 'I find that hard to believe.'

My hand, still sore from carrying the bag, burns as though laid on the Aga. Then he takes out a handkerchief and wipes my face like Mam used to do when I was a kid; which makes me cry all the harder.

'It's just that I feel so lonely,' I try to explain, 'without Sister Brigid and – Art History.'

'I tried to tell you after your last exam.' He rises to his feet and pours two cups of coffee. 'I've written to your Mother General.'

'To say what?' I gasp.

He hands me a cup and a small plate of biscuits. 'To say that you should be here with me, developing your mind.'

The coffee is sweeter and stronger than any I've ever tasted. Dizzied from a scalding gulp I see myself in three years' time, a first-class honours graduate.

'Mother General will say no,' I tell him. 'She thinks Art History's useless to a nun.'

Dr Palfrey sits down beside me and sighs. 'I don't know how you can bear it.'

'I can't bear it – not any longer,' I say to him. 'The way of life's too hard for me.' I've never thought of it like this before, and my faithless words set off a shrilling in my head. I should have confided in the Archdeacon, or Bosco, or any one of my sisters – not a university tutor. But the moment the words leave my mouth I know they are true. 'I'm going to get out.'

Dr Palfrey sits up straight. 'My dear Sister Maureen, do you think that's wise?'

'I can't stay on in that dark house – with only old nuns for company.'

'But why do you wish to re-enter the world? Not for marriage and a family, I hope. Those are conventional aims for conventional people; which people like us can afford to ignore.'

On his use of the word 'us' I feel the temperature rise in the little room.

'But I can't ignore them any longer. I'm the same as other women and want what they want.' I hesitate for a moment then force it out. 'I want ordinary things like work and holidays and friendship and —' my voice falters '— I want love and sex.'

He leans back in his chair and presses his fingertips together. 'Love is a romantic delusion and sex is a poor thing compared with the monastic ideal.'

I remember how elated I felt after his dinner party, when I found out that I too was attractive to men. 'Then why did you kiss me?' I ask, my voice unexpectedly loud in the quiet room. 'Was it just to churn me up?'

He gazes into the little cathedral he's made of his hands. 'It was a moment of indiscretion – the wine, the night and the music.'

'Is that all?'

'I'm not sure.' He looks up and smiles uneasily. 'I kissed you out of pity, I suppose. You seemed so vulnerable – like an overgrown child among adults.'

'I might have been then – but I'm not now. I've started to grow up.'

'Then you'll understand what I'm saying.'

He takes another sip of coffee while I wonder why he's denying what happened, and the current of feeling between us. Then it strikes me that he can't do otherwise. As a tutor he risks being charged with bad behaviour, losing his job even. 'I'll never tell anyone what you did,' I say to him. 'It was partly my fault, because I looked at you so —' I would like to say invitingly, but it sounds too crude.

'You're a sweet and innocent person and you mustn't blame yourself.'

'I'm not innocent,' I cry out, fed-up with being patronised. 'I want to be kissed again, kissed and touched.'

He stirs uneasily in his chair. 'You don't know what you're saying, Sister.'

'Not Sister – just Maureen.' Draining the last of my coffee, I think of Brigid and her love for Julian, and how she lost her only chance of passion. Then suddenly I know I'll lose mine if I leave this room without doing something; that I'll rush straight back to St Cuthbert's, and stay there for the rest of my life.

But what should I do? Hoping for inspiration, I rise to my feet and begin to unhook my habit.

He clatters down his cup and saucer. 'Sister – er – Maureen! What on earth are you doing?'

I want to do with him what Brigid did with Julian, and feel as she felt. Drawing in a lungful of air, I step out of my habit then drop to my knees in my underskirt, like a travesty of St Bernadette. My face is level with the crutch of his black trousers, and my eyes are fixed on the mound at his fly. 'Make love to me, Piers,' my words tumble out in a rush.

'But you're one of my students.'

I think of Vicky, who claims to have had passionate sex with her tutor Rex Harries on the carpet under his desk, and hear the familiar drumbeat of competition. 'I'm no ordinary student.' I rest my hand on Piers's knee. 'I'm older than the others – older and cleverer.' I must be going mad, I think, then a second thought follows on its heels: it's now or never. Dazed by my own daring, I put my hand on the bulge and begin stroking.

His hand covers mine, attempting to still it. 'This is all very pleasant – but I'm not making love on my office floor.'

Staring down at his slim white hand on mine, I'm overtaken by the need to know him better; to see him without his clothes on, bared to my gaze like a life-class model. 'Why not?' I ask boldly.

When he fails to reply I continue my caresses while he sits motionless. Seeing that I'll have to lead the way, I stand up, pluck off my veil and, ignoring his curious glance at my hair, begin fumbling with my suspenders. 'Please,' I say to him. 'It won't do you any harm – and to me it's a matter of life and death.'

'Very well,' he says, lying back in his chair like a dental patient.

I pull off my stockings and turn the key in the lock in case Mrs Dagnall comes trotting upstairs on her return from lunch. As I slide down my knickers Piers is sifting the air with his nostrils. Then I notice the smell myself, sharp and pungent. The scent of my body, I think, dizzily, enjoying its first taste of sex. A fruity smell, fizzing and lush.

'Whatever can it be?' Piers springs to his feet and begins rummaging in his wastepaper-basket while I stand awkwardly in front of his chair. Then he notices my abandoned bag.

'Mango,' he cries, extracting the dripping fruit with forefinger and thumb. 'And overripe, too.' He drops it in the wastepaper-basket and sits down again.

I take off my blouse. Piers's eyes slide away from my woolly vest while I drop to my knees once again, embarrassed but determined to carry on. As I unzip his fly he lowers his gaze to the white underpants beneath the black corduroy. 'My spoilt priest look,' he murmurs as I slide my hand inside. 'I must have known you were coming.'

His penis feels soft and warm as I tug it out and let it hang over the elastic like a drugged cobra, even thicker and fleshier than the life-class model's. Encouraged, I slip out of my vest and stand before him, conscious of my swollen nipples. He remains seated, though breathing a little faster.

'Aren't you going to get undressed?' I ask him.

'In a moment, perhaps.' He pauses, then adds with a self-conscious smile. 'Look, this may sound strange, but I should love to suck your breasts.'

Wishing he'd asked for something else, I sit on the arm of his chair and bend over him.

'We men are such babies at heart,' he murmurs, then his

lips clamp themselves on my right nipple, like Mother Wilfred's favourite Christ child.

Wishing I hadn't thought of my Superior, I feel a tugging sensation inside, as though my womb's been hitched to a wire. Glancing down I see Piers stroking his stiffening penis. At last, I think with relief, and grow aware of a responsive quickening of my own desire, and a wetness between my legs.

There's an imperious knocking at the door and a tug at the handle. 'Piers, are you there?' comes the voice of Cynthia Fothergill.

I hold my breath as Piers freezes at my breast like a naughty cherub.

'Are you there?' calls Mrs Fothergill again. After a silence she raps harder. Withdrawing his lips, Piers pushes me away with his hand.

'Oh, fuck.' Mrs Fothergill's words are followed by a sigh and then the noise of clattering stilettos.

But when I lean again towards Piers he stands up and pushes his now drooping penis back in his underpants. 'I never saw Cynthia as an angel of virtue,' there's a sense of relief in his voice, 'but she rescued us that time.'

'I didn't want to be rescued,' I say dully, dragging my vest over my tight breasts. The habit of confession, so desirable in a nun, is, I now see, useless in a seduction scene. I embarrassed Piers by telling him what I felt, whereas a more experienced woman would have coaxed him along.

'But later you will be glad,' he says, inching up his zip.

'I doubt it.'

'You seem rather forward for a nun.' He rises to his feet. 'Do you often do this sort of thing?

I feel as though he's tweaking my heart with a pair of

pliers. 'Can't you see that I didn't know what to do?' I'm unable to stop my voice from trembling.

'Please don't start crying again.' He puts an arm round my shoulder. 'In future, my dear, it might be better to let the man make the first move.'

'What man would approach a nun?'

'You'll find one quite soon if that's what you want,' says Piers, his mood lighter since he's fastened his trousers. 'Convents often feature in pornography – as you'd have found out,' he adds, with another tweak of the pliers, 'if you'd stayed on to take my second-year course on the eighteenth-century satirists.'

He unlocks the door while I pick up my stockings. 'You mean some men find the habit attractive?' I ask, wondering if Mother Wilfred knows this.

'I, for one, have always been stirred by self-denial – and your figure is that of a Greek athlete. If only,' he adds sadly as I pull on my stockings, 'you didn't have working-class feet.'

I stare at him in puzzlement, wondering if he finds them disproportionately large.

He points to my big-toe joint, bent inwards by cheap shoes when I was a child, and reddened by today's walk. 'Cynthia's feet are deformed too. Those stilettos, you know. Such a pity. I've always wanted a woman with feet like a Raphael Madonna's.'

The uncalled-for criticism, the link with Mrs Fothergill . . . why is he bent on hurting me? 'Perhaps you should advertise,' I snap.

He remains silent, fiddling with a paper clip and staring out of the window while I finish getting dressed and stalk out.

At the bottom of the stairs Mrs Dagnall's crossing off names from a list on the notice-board. 'Dr Palfrey tells me you're leaving us,' she says, a drawing pin between her teeth.

'I may just decide to come back,' I reply, my voice shaking with pent-up anger, 'so don't start celebrating yet.' And then, ignoring her startled face, I bang out of the door and into the street.

Hell

Sick with shame, I barge across the square with my head down, wanting only to get off campus. A horn blares as I dive across the main road, a car swerves to avoid me, and I glimpse the angry man at the wheel, and a woman's frightened face beside him. My limbs are shaking as I pass the parade of shops, and my hands feel weirdly unencumbered, as though I've lost some vital ballast. As I stall in the middle of the pavement a Caribbean woman with a shopping trolley bangs into me from behind, dislodging some of her parcels.

'Watch what you doin', sunshine.'

Only when I stoop to pick up her bananas and mangoes do I remember Mr Gopal's vegetables, still lying on Piers's floor. Soon Mother Wilfred will be back from the airport, with no special dinner to welcome her. But that's too bad, I decide, blundering on down the street. Bertie will have to go to Mr Gopal's herself, or else cook something different, because I'm never going back to Piers's office.

Only when a man at the bus stop stares curiously do I realise that I'm making a lowing sound, like a sick animal. Turning my face into the wind, I see a flock of gulls over the cathedral, white feathers on the breath of God. Every weekday for the past year I've examined my conscience under that great lantern. Keeping my eyes on the gulls, I start walking down the pavement towards it, and then up the cathedral ramp. At the concrete porch I pull out a square of Irish linen I hemmed as a novice and embroidered in pale blue cross-stitch: *Sister Maureen O'Shaunessy*. Then I soak my name with spittle and swab at my face, trying to get rid of the lemonish scent of Piers's aftershave. But no matter how hard I scrub, the teasing sickly smell still prickles my flesh.

There must be a special service, because a priest in white robes is pacing down one of the aisles. Staring through the glass doors at the congregation, I remember listing my smug little faults in a notebook, while the worst fault of all was growing inside me like a cancer. Wasn't I an ex-lay sister, exempt from the Holy Rule and closer to God than any Choir nun, closer even than Mother Wilfred? And now, after bringing disgrace not only on myself but on my sisters, I cannot make myself re-enter that bright and holy space. After a last glance at the altar I track back down the ramp.

If I wasn't a nun I could punish my sinful body with an hour's circuit training followed by a ten-mile run. As it is I can only keep tramping the streets till the ache in my heart grows less and I think of somewhere to hide. The river gleams at me dully in the gap between two buildings, and on it is an oil boat nosing into the docks. For a second I consider walking to Moses Street – then Dad could phone

Mother Wilfred and tell her I've lost my vocation. But Mam's been boasting about me for years – her joy in my holy way of life, my dedication to God – so I can't turn up without warning. Her daughter the failed nun – the neighbours would gossip for weeks. If only Brigid hadn't killed herself but found a flat in the Dingle instead. Then she'd have been there to help me, starchy but sympathetic, and I could have stayed with her overnight and broken the news gently.

The sheen on the slate roofs promises a storm and a headache tightens round my temples. Believing we were soulmates, I poured my phial of perfume at my tutor's feet like a would-be Magdalene. I was stupid to fling myself at him like that, stupid and wanton. A vocation is a pearl of great price, my best and greatest treasure, and instead of mourning its loss I'm tramping the streets in a fret of embarrassment and pride which makes each memory a fresh torture: my insistence on getting undressed and locking the door, his refusal to take off his clothes, his condescending glance at my woolly vest, chopped hair and unshaven legs, gross to his fastidious eyes right down to my clumsy feet.

Ahead of me the tower of the other cathedral – the Anglican one – shines pink against a backdrop of storm clouds. It's so much bigger and better than ours that I've never wanted to go inside, and am already drifting down the hill towards China Town when my feet turn round of their own accord and bear me towards the façade. It's the heart of the Church of England, and I half-expect the ground to shudder and tilt beneath my Catholic feet. But I pass like a fly between its two huge pillars, then on up the six sandstone steps.

Two high thin windows above my head are concealing who knows what secrets behind their wire mesh. No one I know would dream of entering that Gothic portal, so I could hide away for ever in the dark interior. Then my eye is drawn to the statue over the porch. Its head is round and bald and its hands spread as though addressing a rally: not a God who sits and eats with publicans, but a thin-lipped God with an unforgiving stare. Sinners like Mary Magdalene and me could never clutch at those thick, self-righteous ankles.

To the side of the iron gates is a gap in the railings, and a narrow path lined with tombstones. Still desperate to keep moving, I sheer off down a tunnel hacked through the rocky foundation. The slope's so steep it hurts my legs, sodden fish and chip papers are glued to the floor and sides, and the air smells dankly of piss.

Gulping in the air at the bottom , I step into a deep gorge lidded by a pewter sky. This is the ravine at the cathedral's base, the great quarry from which Liverpool was built. I remember peering into it as a child when my dad lifted me in his arms so I could look down on the graves of all the dead Proddies. The tombstones have since been banished to the sides, and tramping past I see one or two Catholic names – a Conlon and a Duffy – and feel sorry they've been left to moulder in such an alien place.

A lawn has been laid on the ravine floor, now day-glo bright in the gathering gloom. Petrol cans from the riots litter its surface, and on either side are the great ramps down which hearses were once drawn by coal-black horses with nodding plumes. The place is deserted apart from a man throwing a stick for his Staffordshire Bull. When he stops and stares I think that he's going to approach me, but the dog lays another stick at his feet and he picks it up.

My headache binding my temples like a crown of thorns, I zigzag across the grass for a few more minutes and then, unable to think of anything else to do, toil hopelessly up the far ramp and back along Rodney Street. White-coated receptionists are switching on the chandeliers, and two young consultants are sharing a joke in a Georgian doorway; which makes me wonder if Piers can be trusted not to gossip to his colleagues or, worse still, write to Timothy Bavidge.

The only person I know who's suffered shame like mine is Brigid, so as I pass the parked Mercedes and Porsches I pray that she'll shut him up.

I'll do nothing of the sort, you stupid fool, says her voice in my ear. You flung yourself at his head.

I lean in shock against a red BMW, accidentally starting its alarm.

I did it partly because of you, I say into the ringing noise. Because of you and Dr Mulcahy.

Nnnnnnn. A receptionist rushes down the steps with a car key in her hand, so I skid away down the street.

Nnnnn. Nnnnnn, goes Brigid – in a creepy, meaningless voice I can't shake out of my ears even when the alarm has stopped.

I've done my best, I tell her. I left your message on her desk.

Nnnnn. Her voice is softer now, but I know from its bossy tone that she's giving me further instructions. Startled by the speed of the traffic, I stand at the junction with Leece Street and wait to cross the road.

Soon the sky will go dark with storm clouds, intones Brigid as the noise level drops mysteriously, *and —*

What are you on about? I cry, dodging in front of a lorry.

Nnnnn, she goes again as I halt by the white line. *I'm the saint of the inbetweens.* And then, when I still don't get it, *NNNNNNNNN.*

It's only then that I catch her meaning. You must be mental, I yell, my voice even scouser than hers.

A double-decker is bearing down on me but that doesn't bother Sister Rigid. *I killed myself without telling them why,* she carries on, *so I cannot ascend to Heaven.*

But I'm *not* going to kill myself – and I'm never going to tell them what I did.

If they can't understand their young nuns their order will wither on the vine.

Too bad, I yell back. It's myself I've got to think about.

You're upsetting Our Blessed Lady, replies Brigid. *She wishes the order to continue.*

You should have thought of Our Lady before you topped yourself.

Brigid's angry now, and as usual when angry she starts to withdraw. *Nnnnnnnnnnnnn.* At last the noise is growing fainter and by the top of the hill I've shut it out altogether. But inside I know that she's right, and I'll know no peace for the rest of my life unless I face up to my sisters.

By now my headache's so bad that my vision's blurred, and my blisters are weeping through my stockings. Trying to ignore them I tramp past the burnt-out Rialto and Heather's estate, then a few drops of rain hit the pavement and I wish that I owned a mac. By the end of the Boulevard the drops on the gravel are large and round as communion wafers.

Soon the rain's coming at me from every quarter, so fierce and cold that it pierces the skin of my soul. The grass of the park is a mire of beer cans and torn newspapers, and the mud oozes into my shoes after only a few paces. Then the tower block comes into view and the convent spires beneath it, and I think of Columba, her bird eyes sharp with worry, and Gonzaga waiting patiently at the kitchen table.

At the thought of telling them I'm leaving, the ache in my heart grows hot and I stand stock still, unable to face their relief at my return.

Keep going, girl, says Brigid. *It's now or never.*

With her voice in my ears I plod on across the mud. Soon the convent is just fifty yards away, and I see a row of shadowy figures at a first-floor window, with a taller figure at their head. The stern eyes of Sister Carthage are fixed on mine as she points a warning finger at the gate. But the street lies empty in the glancing rain, and what her meaning is I cannot tell.

Maria Goretti

Scarcely aware of the black, humpbacked taxi roaring past, I hurry across the road. Although the rain is easing off, my shoes are squelching at every step.

The taxi pulls in as I reach the gate, and the cab door opens on a stout, black-clad calf. Longing to dash up the path, I hover reluctantly at the kerb while Bosco levers herself out of the back.

'That's right, Sister Maureen, hold the door,' beams Bosco, clearly delighted by the Superior's return. 'I'm going to call the others.'

Forcing my face into a smile, I bend forward to greet Mother Wilfred – but the woman climbing out is not her. Though unknown to me, she looks vaguely familiar: young, olive-skinned, and wearing the first suit with shoulder pads to be seen in Liverpool. Signalling to the driver to carry the suitcases, she plucks two brown bags of groceries from the arms of Mother Wilfred on the back seat. Then she straightens her tight skirt and fixes me with such a frank and confident stare that whoever she is I know she's not British.

'How do you do, Sister Maureen,' says the newcomer who has obviously learned her English from an American. 'I have in my handbag a letter from your tutor.'

'Ask Mother General's blessing,' snaps Mother Wilfred, climbing out after her.

Maria Goretti! Remembering the laughing face on her logo, I drop to one knee before her soft leather loafers.

'Get up,' she says, holding out a French loaf and two bottles of wine. 'The sidewalk is soaking.'

Clutching the groceries to my chest I gaze at the shining face and uncovered curls. On the very day I decide to leave, Mother General appears. It's too much to cope with.

'Get up, please,' she repeats with a touch of impatience. 'These customs have gone out of fashion.'

'I was supposed to bring back some vegetables,' I volunteer, forgetting my intention to be honest, 'but I left them on the bus.' This is not just a lie but a stupid thing to say and I can only hope Mother General won't find out that the buses aren't running.

She runs her tongue round her red lips. 'And then you went for a long walk in the rain?'

Mother Wilfred's eyes are fixed on my twisted stockings.

'We stopped at a supermarket near the airport,' continues Maria Goretti after a pause, 'so please stop worrying about your absent vegetables.'

'Mother Maria!' Elisabeth bounds down the path and flings both arms around Mother General. 'What a surprise.' Behind her hover Columba, Gonzaga and Ursula, all looking equally startled.

'Mother Wilfred has told me about the sad death of your

Sister Brigid,' says Maria Goretti to the row of faces, ' so I have come in time for the funeral.'

'Have a rest before supper,' urges Mother Wilfred. 'Columba will bring you a nice cup of tea.'

'I will join you for a drink in the community room,' says Maria Goretti, not looking at all as though she needs to rest, 'but first I want a word with Bertilla.'

'She's gone to buy vegetables,' says Columba with a puzzled glance towards me.

'How you British nuns love your vegetables.' Mother General reclaims the bottles I'm still clutching to my chest. 'Now you, Sister Maureen, must go and change. And you, Sister Ursula, can carry these – and hurry up, please – it is almost time for an aperitif.'

'How does she know all our names?' asks Columba ten minutes later, when I appear in the kitchen in my dry clothes. 'No Mother General's been here for twenty years.'

'Mother Maria has a degree in psychology,' says Elisabeth from the larder, where she's opening a bottle of wine. 'She's said to be very astute.'

Remembering the bold brown eyes fixed on mine, I wonder what she'll say when she hears my story. I swallow a couple of aspirins, then help Columba unpack the groceries. 'What's this pasty stuff?' she asks with a sniff.

'Houmous,' says Elisabeth, dipping in a forefinger. 'It's a Greek starter. You can eat it with pitta bread.'

'Which is here,' I unwrap the next package, 'along with black and green olives, tomatoes and a funny kind of cheese.'

'That's feta,' says Elisabeth while I find our few remaining earthenware dishes and begin to arrange the olives.

'The old ones won't like it,' said Columba, surveying the

piles of green and black grapes, 'but it certainly looks festive. I only wish Brigid was here.'

'Where's Bertie?' I ask Columba as we carry two trays into the community room.

'Gone to fetch Heather March.'

'Here to St Cuthbert's?'

Columba dumps her tray on a desk and imitates Mother General's shrug. 'Why not?' Looking roguish and Continental she spreads her small hands. 'With your *grrrreat* big convent so very empty?' Then she picks up a glass and adds in her normal voice, 'That means all the more for us to look after —' then halts as Maria Goretti saunters in on her soft leather soles.

The others trail in behind her – apart from Ursula and Kevin, who are watching over Brigid. 'We thought you'd come to close us down,' confesses Columba as we gather round the empty hearth.

'To the contrary,' says Maria Goretti, 'I have come to put you back on your feet.' She dashes some wine into a glass, takes a sip and rolls it round her mouth like an expert. 'Carignan grapes,' she pronounces. 'One of our ancient *cépages*. See, I have brought you the best from our Mother House vineyard.' She raises her glass and smiles round the community. 'To rejuvenation.'

Rejuvenation! It'll take some doing, I think, as the circle of tired faces turns guardedly towards the wine. After so many years of poverty followed by the stress of the riots and Brigid's suicide – what chance can there be for St Cuthbert's, washed up on the edge of Toxteth in a wrack of beer cans and used condoms?

Bertilla enters the room supporting Heather March, whom she settles in an armchair to scowls from Pious and

Placid. Then she pours a glass of wine for each of her three charges. At the sight of the ring of faces growing pinker with every sip I think: this might be the way forward.

Heather flashes a V-sign at Pious and Placid then squints at the bareheaded Mother General. 'Light me a fag, luvvie.'

Maria Goretti pulls a disposable lighter from her handbag while Bosco coughs ostentatiously, then starts at a ring on the bell. Looking puzzled, Columba trots off to answer it. No one calls at St Cuthbert's after six.

A few seconds later she puts her head round the door. 'Sister Maureen's tutor is here.'

My heart clenches in my chest as I remember my prayer to Brigid. Far from muzzling Piers, my dead but vindictive friend has brought him right to our front door – and just in time to meet Mother General. Desperate to head him off I jump to my feet, but Maria Goretti motions me to sit. 'Please invite him in,' she instructs Columba. 'I so enjoyed reading his letter.'

'I hardly think —' Mother Wilfred looks at her community, each with a glass of wine.

'Nuns have been a mystery for too long,' says Maria Goretti. 'It is time we were a little more open.'

'Piers is a friend of my brother Timmy,' says Elisabeth as he appears in the doorway. His jacket is damp and creased and a hank of hair flops into one eye.

'Dr Palfrey,' says Columba. Stepping sideways she urges him forward. He is clutching the now disintegrating bag of vegetables and for once, faced with a roomful of strange nuns, he seems to have lost his poise.

Maria Goretti rises to her feet and extends a manicured hand. 'How good of you to call in person. You will have a glass of wine?'

Piers's eyes swivel over her expensive haircut then on past the spiral of smoke from Heather's cigarette till they meet mine and skid away. 'No, thank you,' he says. 'Must dash.'

'But we have not discussed your letter.'

'Er – another time,' he stutters, thrusting the carrier at Maria Goretti.

'This is very kind of you,' she says, peering at Mr Gopal's carrots and grapefruits, 'but we already have some —'

'Sister Maureen forgot them after her – tutorial,' says Piers, backing out of the room.

'Thank you very much for returning them.' Maria Goretti's eyes are bright with amusement. 'And even though she does not say so, I am sure Sister Maureen is grateful too. And now, if you will not stay for a drink, Sister Columba will show you out.' As the front door slams she hands me the bag. 'So at Liverpool University you have your tutorials on the bus?'

'That must take some doing,' Elisabeth puts in as I study a bunch of carrots. 'The buses haven't run since the riots.'

'I have been watching the events on Italian television.' To my relief Maria Goretti has turned her attention elsewhere. 'Another reason to come here and see for myself.'

'You'd better be careful, Mother,' says Wilfie. 'It's a dangerous place, Toxteth.'

'Not if you wear a habit.' Emboldened by her wine, Gonzaga stares pointedly at Mother General's waspwaisted suit. 'People round here have a lot of respect for nuns.'

'If it is dangerous I shall take a taxi,' says Maria Goretti. 'That is, if your cabbies will run the risk.'

'No Scouse taxi driver has ever declared a no-go area.' In

298

the presence of this foreign visitor Heather has regained all her pride in her native city. 'You'll be safe with one of them, love.'

'The Archdeacon says that the Pope's coming to Liverpool next year,' adds Gonzaga. 'He'll travel from Speke to the city centre in his Popemobile – even though he's just been shot at.' She turns to Placid who's sitting on her left, and repeats the news loudly.

'He'll pass within yards of this convent,' boasts Pious, unaware of Mother General's grimace. 'We're going to kneel outside the Cheesecake Factory.'

'I hope His Holiness looks at us and not the people in the pub opposite,' whispers Columba.

'Why not come back for his visit, Mother General?' persists Gonzaga.

'It might spoil his day,' laughs Maria Goretti. '*Il Papa* and I don't see eye to eye.'

Bosco looks scandalised. 'The Holy Father is Head of the Church on earth.'

Maria Goretti runs her hand down her ten-denier shin. 'I know he is, and when he speaks *ex cathedra* I am bound to obey him. But I pray he will stop laying down the law for women all over the world – when he himself is a lifelong celibate.'

As Gonzaga, Placid and Columba smile uncertainly, Mother Wilfred stirs in her chair. 'So are we all, I hope.'

'Sure – but it is a problem for us nuns.' Mother General takes a sip of wine. 'Life with other people is a great education.'

'That is why we must love our sisters in Christ,' says Mother Wilfred, frosty-faced. 'But not, of course, to excess.'

'I wish the Holy Father would call at the convent,' says Placid, who's lost the drift. 'I'll never get down the road on me zimmer.'

Maria Goretti opens her mouth to speak then closes it. In the silence that follows I wish that she'd been here all along – then I mightn't have got into such a mess. 'Who's for another drink?' I ask, rising to my feet and seizing the bottle of wine.

After dinner I leave the table to help Bertie make up a bed for Heather. But before I've reached the infirmary Mother General steps out of the chapel and draws me to one side.

'So,' says the Italian nun with a stare, 'you were surprised by your tutor's visit, yes?' She must have renewed her lipstick after the meal because her lips are still coral-red. But her face close up is older and softer than it first appeared, with shadows beneath the eyes. Not knowing what to reply, I fix my eyes on her right shoulder pad.

'I see from your face he has hurt you in some way.'

'It was my fault, not his,' I say, taking a deep breath. 'I went up to his room and – um – tried to tempt him.'

Despite Mother General's worldly ways I'm half-expecting her to faint, or else summon Mother Wilfred to have me cast out at once. But she moves forward a pace and pats me on the shoulder. 'There are worse sins than impurity, Sister Maureen.'

At the sudden invasion of my body space I step awkwardly back, joggling the frame of a Madonna and Child. 'And so,' says Mother General, 'at supper you look exhausted when everyone else is happy. Why is that?'

By now I can smell her perfume, headily mixed with travel and sweat. 'I think I've lost my vocation.'

'A vocation is not a bag of carrots to be left on the floor of a man's office.'

Remembering Brigid's decree, I struggle to tell the truth. 'I was impure and unchaste,' I babble, pressing my palms against the wall behind me. 'I took off my —'

Mother General holds up her hand. 'I do not wish to learn the details. Those you must confide in your confessor.' She smiles a little sadly. 'Middle age will dim your passions in due course. No, Sister Maureen, your sexual failings do not worry me.'

My thoughts turn to the cold figure now lying in our chapel, and I wonder if she really could have admonished me in Rodney Street – or was it just my own bad conscience?

'Like many lay sisters you were young when you entered,' continues Maria Goretti, leaning against the chapel door, 'but our recruitment process has changed. These days you would be told to come back when you'd grown up.'

Even though I'm going to leave, my cheeks flame up at her hint that I'm substandard. 'I'm grown up now,' I croak.

'Then you have a chance to prove it. The next few days will be a test of your maturity.'

So will leaving St Cuthbert's, I want to cry out. It's high time I took on the world. But the words won't come.

'You must ask Our Lord for guidance.' Mother General's face turns dark, like Our Lady of the Sorrows'. 'Whatever you decide, know that my thoughts and prayers will go with you. And now,' as she opens the chapel door I glimpse Brigid's coffin on its twin trestles, 'Sister Bertilla is waiting. Go and help her make a bed for the unfortunate Heather.'

Epiphany

Pious has refused to speak, even to Mother General, after learning that Heather's sleeping upstairs. But Placid, sensing an ally, has taken the newcomer under her wing and donated her spare dressing-gown and bedroom slippers. Now the two of them are sitting by the infirmary window while Pious sulks in the corner.

'I've been telling Sister Placid about the burning of the Rialto,' says Heather, 'less than twenty yards from me front door.'

'We'll put your bed next to hers,' says Bertie, 'so you can keep on chatting. But first we'll move Pious to the far corner.' She seizes the headboard and begins dragging the bed across the room.

'What's that?' Heather points a knobbly finger at the trunk that was hidden underneath.

'Pious's treasure chest,' says Bertie, picking up a clean sheet. 'For Heaven's sake don't touch it.'

Ignoring her, Heather stands up and totters across the room.

'She'll smother you in your sleep,' says Placid.

But far from protesting, Pious stays hunched in her corner while Heather, panting a little, tugs at the latch.

'She's forgotten to lock it,' crows Placid as Heather yanks up the lid.

'What's all this?' shouts Heather.

Too startled to answer, Bertie and I stare at the objects inside the box: the secateurs, gardening gloves and twine from the shed, the wooden rosary beads given me by Brigid that once belonged to her Irish nan, a pair of sheepskin gloves, Piers's book on Vermeer, my little pink looking glass, a copy of the *Catholic Herald* . . .

On top of this magpie's nest lies the Baby Jesus. Ignoring a recently chipped forefinger He smiles chubbily at the three startled women, one black and two white, who circle his makeshift crib.

'What an Epiphany,' says Bertie.

'You mean it's all knock-off?' asks Heather.

'Pious can't see,' I whisper, 'so how could she find her way down the chapel corridor, then up the aisle to the sanctuary?'

'She waits till everyone's asleep,' explains Placid. 'The dark makes no difference to her, being blind.'

I imagine Pious scenting her way to my cell with her nose like the blade of an axe, then groping up to my wardrobe and under my towels to seize on my hidden possessions.

'Thieving cow,' says Heather as Pious sits immobile behind her cataracts.

Bertie helps Heather out of her dressing-gown and into bed. 'It's a pathology, so there's no point in blaming Pious,' she says. 'That's right, Placid, drink your cocoa.'

'Mother Wilfred will be pleased,' says the old nun.

Bertilla laughs as she tucks her in. 'She's praying in front of her favourite Madonna and Child – so she'll think it's a sign.'

It's a sign all right – but what of, I wonder at ten o'clock that night as I make my way to the chapel. Mother Wilfred has given me the second watch, which lasts till two in the morning. It's a privilege to keep company with the dead, so I've no intention of backing out – even though the aspirins have failed to banish my headache and every ligament in my body feels torn.

The chapel is unlit apart from the row of tall candles on either side of the coffin. When I approach the prie-dieu at its head, Ursula makes the sign of the cross and rises to her feet. Not until she closes the door behind her do I lower my eyes to the still figure.

Instead of her brown wool habit, Brigid is wearing the bridal dress that, like every nun, she wore at her Clothing. The hair beneath the white net is not lank like I saw it last, but shining and softly curled, and her skin in the candlelight looks pink and young. The lilies of the valley round her forehead are far too waxy and white to have come from our garden, and her nails, in life often chipped and broken, are manicured and lightly varnished.

She looks more like Snow White than a troubled young nun, and it's hard to believe that she isn't at peace with God.

Her rosary is imitation mother-of-pearl, and not one I've ever seen her use. Pretty and ladylike, it belongs in a gift shop not a convent. As though planning a crime, I look round the dark chapel, my eyes half-blind from the candlelight, then prise it from her icy fingers. Then I take out her nan's wooden beads.

After saying five decades, I wind them round Brigid's clasped hands. Though the rough wood looks out of place against her manicured nails, I sense that she'd like to have them with her.

It's dark now outside the chapel, and a barn owl is calling on the roof. Soon Xavier will be arriving to take up the vigil.

'I left a message on Julian's desk,' I whisper on bending to kiss Brigid's forehead, 'and I'm sure that she'll get it in time.'

Requiem

I hang round the front door until the community is in chapel and the Archdeacon waiting in the sacristy, but Dr Mulcahy doesn't appear. I keep hoping against hope that she'll stalk in halfway through the funeral, but Brigid is laid to rest in the graveyard beyond the grotto with only her sisters to mourn her.

There's plenty to take my mind off my grief. St Cuthbert's is in chaos, with Heather polluting the air with swear words and cigarettes, and Bertie setting up a Well Women's clinic in the infirmary annexe. Out in the back garden Mother Wilfred is attacking her Rambling Rector with the newly restored secateurs, and Pious sits in the sunshine beside a frizzy-haired counsellor who specialises in kleptomania, in this case caused, she has assured us all, by a lack of love in Pious's youth. Next week the old nun will be having an operation on her cataracts.

Meanwhile Maria Goretti is liaising, as she calls it, with local businessmen. Mother Wilfred says nothing at first, but when a group is shown round the enclosure she wonders out loud if their presence is strictly necessary.

'You must maximise the use of the plant,' explains Maria Goretti, then sees Mother Wilfred's puzzled frown. 'These men will show you British nuns how to make money.'

'That is not our vocation,' says Mother Wilfred, clearly angry at being called British. The old ones look at her round-eyed, alarmed by her challenge to the Mother General who has so changed their lives for the better.

Maria Goretti makes a square with her hands and looks through it at a damp-stained pillar. 'Your beautiful cloister could be a tourist attraction.'

As usual with Mother General's suggestions, Elisabeth looks enthusiastic. 'Oh yes, Mother Maria. We could use some of your photos for the brochure.'

But Wilfie is still doubtful. 'Victorian buildings are ten a penny in Liverpool. Why would people pay to see ours?'

Maria Goretti is taking her camera out of its soft leather case. 'You have something to sell to them, Mother – and people who are rich love to part with their money.'

'That's not what it says in the Bible.'

'Your Archdeacon has still not given you any funding. Can you not see that he's using his wealth to keep female religious in check? You must start making money for yourselves.'

'I hardly think —' says Mother Wilfred in a shocked voice.

'I know, I know – you cannot serve God and Mammon.' Maria Goretti nods at Elisabeth's neat figure, framed in a Gothic archway. 'Good for vocations,' she smiles, clicking the shutter. Then she lowers the lens and turns back to Mother Wilfred. 'We are too old to beg money from our priests,' she says, her American accent stronger than ever. 'All that is past history.' And off she trots down the corridor, her Nikon swinging from her hand.

For Maria Goretti, it seems, there are two kinds of past history. The first is that of the Gothic cloister and stained-glass window, which she plans to turn into a marketing tool; and the second is the past of our shabby old habits – soon to be swapped for Marks & Spencer separates – and of the plaster saints in the attic, already consigned to the tip.

I struggle to agree because I admire Maria Goretti and know that she's good for the order. I also know that she wants young nuns at St Cuthbert's, and is praying for me to stay. I too pray daily for my lost vocation, but can't help hoping my prayer won't be granted. The housework has been taken from my hands and a team of joiners is hammering in the cloisters, fitting new sashes and mending the draughty skirting-boards. No sooner have they gone than a gang of young men from Mrs Mop is revolving down the corridor in their matching pink Mao suits, finishing in one week what I'd never manage in a lifetime. Where I used dustpan and brush they use pine-scented cleansers and lots of electricity, scaring the Holy Army with suction machines bigger than lawn mowers. Already some painters are priming the dank distemper and plastering the cracks through which the ghosts once materialised. When Wilfie asks where the money's coming from, Maria Goretti tells her not to worry – she's found us a sharp accountant. The painters have long ladders and loud transistors and, as Bosco points out, most of them aren't even Catholics; but even she's won over by Maria Goretti's mix of money and optimism, and starts taking the men tea and biscuits far oftener than is strictly necessary.

I thought I'd have liked this energetic new life but the banging and yodelling gets on my nerves. Like my mother and my nan before her, I'm drawn by nature to the difficult and the illogical, and can't find a niche in this new, labour-saving world. Only the chapel remains untouched, with the tabernacle draped in its usual green for the long uneventful season after Pentecost, and the light of a grey August pouring through the open windows. With no housework to do and no new term to prepare for I've got time on my hands, so I sit there hour after hour, watching the bees buzz round the worm-eaten roses Columba has rescued for the altar, and struggling to find my lost form.

Then one day they appear before me in the sanctuary: two architects in double-breasted suits, ushered in by Columba. They tell her to roll up our old floral carpet, and without lowering their voices, start planning to refurbish the chapel. Not wanting to hear any more, I go to finish my rosary in front of the grotto. But two more men have got there before me, men with big muscles and sledgehammers levelled at the rocks.

'Stop that,' I cry. 'Stop it at once!'

But the men can't have heard me because they carry on hammering until the wall behind Our Lady falls in a great slab, exposing her narrow back to the tower block.

'Stop it!' I cry again, knowing the men are committing a sacrilege, a crime from which St Cuthbert's will never recover.

The older man lowers his sledgehammer. 'I'm only doing what I'm paid for.'

'It's your Mother General's orders,' adds the second, lighting a roll-up. 'We've got no choice, love.'

Shutting my eyes in the middle of the lawn I sense the

sun going in, the day turning dark and cold and the convent falling into ruin. Then I open my eyes on the sun shining as normal, and a workman bringing down his hammer on the head of Bernadette.

I spring forward and grasp at the wooden shaft.

'Steady on, queen,' he says, swinging it high in the air.

I grab his forearm which is tattooed red and indigo, and yank it down towards me. The flesh feels warm and sinewy, and his eyes, which are looking into mine, are brown and knowing.

'This un's cracked,' the man says to his mate as I let go of his arm to wipe my hands on my habit. 'They should have warned us about 'er.'

All I can do now is appeal to Maria Goretti, so I start running across the lawn towards the convent.

'Eh, Moey! What's up?'

A well-known voice is calling me but I haven't time to stop now.

'Will you slow down, you cracked mare!'

It's Lorraine, barring my way in a tight red jump-suit and stiletto heels.

'How did you get in here?'

'From the street.' She jerks her thumb at a yawning gap in the wall. 'Since this morning you're open to the public.'

'I must find Mother General. Those men – at the grotto —'

'I know – she's just told me. It's being dismantled.' She grabs my wrist and pulls me towards her. 'Calm down, our Maureen. It's only plaster.'

'I know – but it's a sin. Things'll never go right after this.'

'Wipe your face, for God's sake. It's covered in muck and snot.'

A pigeon whizzes overhead, its wings spread in an aerial cross, then swoops down past my face. 'I can't stand it any more,' I sob. 'I really can't stand it.'

Lorraine hands me a Kleenex. 'I'm surprised you've stood it so long.'

'I don't fit here any more – but I've nowhere else to go.'

'Mam and Dad would be made up if you came home.'

'I'd feel so ashamed going back to Moses Street.'

'I wouldn't worry – no one'll recognise you. The Holy Land's been colonised by Yuppies.'

I blow my nose on her handkerchief. 'Yuppies?'

Lol draws me to a nearby bench, obviously placed there for the visiting public. 'Young Urban Professionals,' she says patiently. 'Meaning trendy solicitors who double park their Porsches.'

The sun that dazzles through the pear tree is hurting my eyes. 'I don't know what you're on about.'

'They keep their Filofaxes in their Gucci bags,' carries on Lorraine, then adds when I continue to look blank, 'You're clearly not ready for the eighties, our Moey. What you need is halfway house.'

'But where?'

'Number 22 Gambier Terrace. I'm off to Corfu for a holiday.' Lorraine rummages in her handbag, yanks out some keys and jangles them above my head. 'My flat is yours while I'm away.'

I stare at them without moving. 'I'm not ready, Lol – I mightn't make it on my own.'

Lol drops the keys in my lap. 'Of course you can.'

I stare doubtfully down at the heavy bunch. 'What are they all for?'

'These three are for the door to my flat, which is Number

12, and this one is for the street door. The rest are from work. I live on the edge of a red-light district, so you'll have to wise up. But there's space, a hi-fi, and a good spec opposite the Anglican cathedral.'

I close my hand on the keys. 'How did you know to come here this morning?'

Lorraine shuts her eyes and waggles her hands in the air. 'I had a dream,' she announces in a quavery voice, 'a dream that you needed assistance. Then Our Lady came down in a cloud and pointed me to the convent.'

'You're kidding.'

Lorraine opens her eyes. 'Of course I'm kidding, you stupid eejit.'

'I'm still not ready to leave, Lol.'

'Of course you are.' She springs up from the bench and shakes down the legs of her jump-suit. 'I want you there in my flat when I return.'

'But what about my sisters? And Mother General – she'd be so disappointed.'

'Then why did she ring and ask me to come over? She may just have had enough of you and your cracked ways.'

Limbo

The Pope must have failed when he tried to abolish Limbo, because it's still there and I'm still in it, drifting from one day to the next, forbidden by the Holy Rule to confide in my sisters, and too undecided to speak to Maria Goretti. By day I potter round the garden, feed the bantams, help in the infirmary and avoid close conversations with my sisters, especially the friendly, curious Bertie and the nosy Elisabeth. At night I dream I'm an old nun trapped in a bed between Pious and Placid, and wake at dawn believing I'm stuck here for life.

Then one day in early autumn Maria Goretti calls me into the study she's taken over from Mother Wilfred. 'The public can see through your kitchen window,' she says, eyeing me thoughtfully, 'and all that old Pyrex is out of keeping. You must buy some decent casseroles — earthenware or Le Creuset would look good.' She hands me a wodge of notes. 'But whatever you choose, make sure it's microwave proof!'

*

Though no longer interested in cooking, I relish the thought of a few hours' escape. It's a sunny September day with clouds like topsails floating above the Mersey. I run upstairs to my cell, put on my new rubber-soled shoes and then, almost without meaning to, pop the keys to Lol's flat in my pocket.

Wilfie's in bed with flu, so my errand can take all the time in the world. On my way to the city centre I drop into Mr Gopal's to buy Bertilla some okra. 'Please give her my news,' he beams at me from behind the counter. Bertilla had raised a three-hundred-strong petition but the council ignored it and were about to send in the bulldozers when the riots started. Now the councillors have changed their minds, because they see at last it's the sort of shop that's liked by the locals.

'A much-needed facility in the area.' Mr Gopal waves a letter from his MP then turns to his boxes of vegetables. 'All those stupid old shelves must go. We are going to modernise.'

After leaving Granby Street I cut across some waste ground towards the kitchen shop, where I buy three matching Provençal casseroles in glazed earthenware. Then I walk on to Gambier Terrace and, feeling like a criminal, climb the three flights of stairs to Lol's flat. It takes me so long to fit the right key into each of the three separate locks that I half-expect a neighbour to come rushing out. But no one appears on the landing, so I shut the door behind me and dump my carrier on the settee. A card bearing my name is propped on the coffee-table. *It's time you made up your mind, girl*, it says in Lol's writing. *See you on the 22nd.*

It takes only a minute to inspect the flat: living room, kitchen and bedroom joined to the bathroom by a tiny corridor. Used to the high ceilings of St Cuthbert's, I wonder if I could ever live in such a shrunk-down space.

I would like to pray for guidance but my chest's hollow as a cored apple and I'm far too restless to kneel down. Lol must have got Dad in to decorate because the wallpaper dazzles my eyes after years of white distemper, and the few small pictures are lost among the poppies and tulips. Collapsing on to the settee, I see that every flat surface is littered with knick-knacks: a whole pack of glass dogs, a miniature Blackpool tower, dolls in flamenco dress and holiday snaps of Lol in a night-club and sitting on a beach in her bikini.

After the noise of Maria Goretti's workmen the stillness of the flat seems unearthly, as though preparing me for a message – a message I mightn't want. Desperate to break the silence, I hunt for Lol's transistor, but she must have taken it on holiday, so I turn to her records instead.

She's pitched out all her old favourites – The Beatles, Gerry and the Pacemakers, Cilla Black – and their place has been taken by pouting male stars with spiked hair, flaunting their women's dresses: Queen, Adam and the Ants and David Bowie, leering with panstick faces from sleeve after sleeve. But I don't feel up to songs from their shocking-pink lips, so search on till I spot a John Lennon LP, his last, so it says on the sleeve, before he died. I plonk it on the turntable and fiddle with the knobs on the tuner. But none of them turns on the power, and after a few minutes I flop on to the settee feeling defeated and out of touch.

The two giant speakers are pouring silence into the air, thick and unsettling. I could pick up my carrier and run back to St Cuthbert's, but I'm still half-waiting for some sort of sign. Flicking through a back copy of the *Echo*, I see news of the riots, of Heseltine's visit to Liverpool, and page after page on the royal wedding. I look at the princess swathed in her ivory silk. At twenty, Diana's found her place in life with husband, family and happiness guaranteed. And here's me at twenty-seven with my future still in doubt. Thrown by so many pictures of her success, I toss the paper back on the table.

Yet Lol, like me, made a mess of her first year – and now she's back on her feet. I've been too self-absorbed to ask her how she did it – but now I want to know her secret. Drifting into her bedroom, I gaze first at the pile of love stories on her table, then at the stilettos under her bed, then finally open her wardrobe door. Her skirts are, as I expected, skimpy and tight and her tops even worse than I remembered – clingy and see-through with plunging necklines. The only modest one is stuck at the back of the wardrobe – a pink nylon relic from the sixties, with ruffles round wrist and neck.

I could learn courage from Lorraine, I think, fingering the gossamer sleeve. Perhaps if I tried on her clothes like I did as a little girl . . . it might help me see my way. Gazing in her wardrobe mirror, I wish my figure was showy like hers, and not lean as a peeled parsnip. Outside the window a church clock strikes one, which means my sisters will be filing into lunch. How shocked they'd be if they could see me now, gazing all alone into a bedroom mirror.

If only I could get free, I think as I struggle out of my habit: free of my sense that I'm letting down my sisters; free of my love for St Cuthbert's, a place now changed beyond recognition; free not to end up like Pious and Placid, and free to re-enter the world. I raise my hand to the silky skin beneath my vest and stroke it, then gaze at the tracery of veins on my inside arm. Free to look at all the paintings I want, no matter what their subject. Free to touch, smell and investigate, to look at my body as much as I please, and the bodies of other people: their musculature and tell-tale nerves and skin, all so expressive and unique.

But if I was free, what would I wear?

I slip into Lol's blouse, and spend the next five minutes trying to button it up. Then I pull on the longest pair of jeans in her wardrobe, which are still too short for me. A row of lipsticks like cartridges is on the shelf: Flamenco Red, Orange Fantabula, Frosted Mocha Cranberry. Shocking Hot Pink seems the colour closest to my blouse, so I part my lips and daub it on. With my long betrousered legs, ruffles and garish mouth I look like Adam Ant.

When the doorbell pierces the air, my face in the mirror looks like a cartoon; the mouth and eyes three alarmed Os, and my hair sticking up in fright. And then I see the intercom, lodged by the hall door like a secret weapon. A visitor down in the street can't possibly know that I'm here.

The bell rings again – followed by a blessed silence – and then by three long peals, and a tapping at the flat door. Whoever it is has got inside the house and climbed the stairs.

For an absurd moment I scrabble at the buttons of my blouse, afraid Mother Wilfred has risen from her bed and trailed me through Toxteth. And then I realise it's probably a neighbour worried about burglars. I hurry to open the door before they call the police.

A figure is standing on the step in white canvas trousers and blue sailor top.

'Dr Mulcahy!' I gasp.

'For goodness' sake call me Julia,' she says, crisp and calm.

'How did you know I was here?'

'The Archdeacon phoned. He saw you climbing the front steps.'

I open the door wider. 'Come inside.'

Julia's face is tanned and her hair slightly tousled, like a woman on a yacht's. As she saunters into the flat her eyes grow wide at my frilly pink blouse, and jeans too high around the ankles. 'What on earth have you got on?'

'I just wanted to see – I didn't know you'd be —'

Without waiting to be asked, Julia's sat herself down on the settee. 'The Archdeacon spotting you just now was pure chance. Divine intervention, you might say.'

I suddenly realise how panicky I've been feeling, how glad I am to see a familiar face. 'I don't think God's intervening in my life at the moment.'

'Of course he is.' Julia sounds indignant. 'Leaving isn't a crime.'

Yes it is, says a voice inside me. 'I wish you had come to Brigid's funeral,' I say to Julia out loud.

'I didn't get back from London in time. And even if I had, I wouldn't have come. Brigid opted out, and I can do nothing to help her. We must leave the dead to bury their dead.' She narrows her eyes as though I'm a studio model. 'The gamine look for you,' she pronounces.

'What do you mean?'

'You look great but terrible, if you understand me. I must introduce you to Norman.'

'Who's he?'

She runs her hand through her shingled hair. 'My stylist.'

'I don't want to have my hair cut – I'm still a nun.'

'But you won't be for long,' says Julia.

I think of Brigid being lowered into her grave, and Dr

Mulcahy very much alive and jaunty in her car on the motorway out of London. 'I've no money,' I snap.

She dips in her bag for a plastic card. 'This one will be on me.'

I continue to prevaricate. 'Er – my hair's too short as it is.'

'A decent cut will give you a boost – and stop you moping about the past.'

'I can't go now,' I lie. 'I'm due back at St Cuthbert's.'

'Get into your habit,' she says. 'We can take off your veil once we get to Norman's. Then you can go home to St Cuthbert's, ready to leave when the moment comes.'

I walk into the bedroom in a dream and unbutton the frilly blouse. And then, while pulling off my jeans, I become aware of Julia leaning against the doorpost. 'You're still in good shape,' she says, eyeing me up and down. 'You'll be a hit when you've learnt how to dress.'

My hands shake as I scramble into my habit. 'That day may never come.'

Julia shrugs. 'Let's wait till you see your new haircut.'

I lock the door with the three different keys and follow her down the stairs. In the street a woman with blonde bouffant hair is eyeing the traffic. Her short, tight skirt and leopardskin top would fit well in Lol's wardrobe. 'I don't want to look like her,' I say to Julia.

As she laughs and shakes her head, a Vauxhall Cavalier stops beside the woman, who leans forward to direct the driver. Though Lol warned me her flat is on the edge of a red-light district, it's only when the woman climbs into the front seat that I guess her trade. I glance at Julia to see if she knew all along, but she's hurrying in the opposite direction. 'Luckily it's a Tuesday,' she says as I catch her up. 'Norman might fit you in straightaway.'

We push our way downtown through the crowds of early-afternoon shoppers. Hairdressers seem to have changed since I last went to Maison Gwladys with my mam. Gone are the rows of dryers like space helmets and the eye-watering smell of perms. Norman's is unisex, with male customers on one side, women on the other, surrounded by pale cream walls with mirrors and giant pot plants. The energetic young men wielding hair-dryers pause for no more than a second when they notice my habit. Then I'm shown to a huge leather chair where I pull off my veil and hand it to Julia so Norman can tilt my head this way and that as though I'm in life class. 'I could make her look like Debbie Harry,' he says.

As long as it's not Adam Ant, I think, glad when he beckons a junior to cover my habit with an overall.

Julia sits by my side while Norman snips. Soon my shoulders are covered in mousy down and, embarrassed by all the attention, I let my eyes roam the salon. But I can't escape my reflection – first the front view then the back view, brilliantly lit, and beside it a three-quarter face, and my left and right profiles, and even the top of my head. Up and down the room there are dozens of oddly angled Maureens, all hovering on the brink of this weird new world. I'm trying to explain this to Julia when my eyes stray to the backwash in the mirror, where a blond man is being shampooed. His eyes are shut and his leant-back profile angled at the ceiling, like the head of John the Baptist on a dish.

'Please don't jump about,' says Norman. 'You'll ruin the cut.'

'It's all right,' says Julia, following my gaze. 'Piers Palfrey is still on holiday.'

I watch Norman's scissors flash round my nape till Julia catches my eye. 'Piers has told me all about it,' she says. 'Or rather, he told Sexy Rexy.'

'And Sexy Rexy told you,' I add dismally.

'You're making her blush,' says Norman.

'You've no need to blush,' says Julia. 'Piers Palfrey is a cold fish.'

'At least,' I reply lamely, 'I shall never see him again.'

Julia stares at me in the mirror. 'He'll be there next term!'

'He will – but I won't.'

'Why on earth not?'

'I can't ever go back to that place – with or without my habit – when everyone knows what I did . . .'

For a second Julia looks like the nun I once feared in first form – austere and over-demanding. 'Letting a man run your life!' she snorts, then adds more gently, 'He's the one that should be embarrassed, not you.'

'It wasn't his fault – I took my habit off in his office.'

'Lucky fellow,' murmurs Norman.

'It can't have been all your fault,' says Julia, ignoring him. 'Piers had been flirting with you all term.'

I think of my tutor, high-minded and austere. 'But why?'

'Because he thought you were safe. He must have had a heart attack when you took your clothes off.'

I see I've been playing a game without knowing the rules – like the swots in school who couldn't do sport.

'Piers prefers married women,' says Julia with a glint, as though not entirely sorry to be telling me the truth.

I remember the giggling from behind his door. 'Like Cynthia Fothergill?'

'Exactly. You remember that dinner party – when he fussed over you to hurt her.'

I think of the thick, slack penis and the thin lips clamped on my nipple. 'I just can't face seeing him.'

'Nonsense. You have to live down the shame like I did – or go under like Brigid.' She lays her hand lightly on my wrist. 'Remember I'll be here to support you.'

I look at her face under the spotlight, knowing, poised and self-assured, and the sight gives me hope for the future. As I am now, so she was once – pondering a new life, uncertain and insecure. And as she is now, so one day I might be.

'Do you really think I could do it?'

'Of course you could – and do it with style.'

I turn back to my reflection and watch Norman rubbing in mousse. The cut makes my Mersey-grey eyes look bright, and my expression bold and worldly; an impression I spoil by gasping at the bill, which is well into double figures.

'You're like a fairy godmother,' I say to Julia as she hands me my veil. 'I'm almost sorry to put this back on.'

'And now,' says Julia, 'you may go to the Walker and look at the exhibition of new sculpture. It will get your eye in for the start of term.'

I'd rather have rushed back to Lol's and stared at myself in the mirror, but as a way of repaying Julia I go straight to the gallery after saying goodbye, and spend the rest of the afternoon wandering round the semi-abstract shapes. My favourite is a granite mother and child by a famous woman sculptor, and I can't help wondering what Wilfie would make of them. The hole in the mother's body is not carved, it says on the label, but wind-eroded: nature's way of working with stone, and so big it lets the light shine through. Wondering if one day I might have children, I look at the mother who reclines on her massive elbow while the baby, not suckling but still closely connected, balances on her hip.

At the end of the afternoon I buy a cup of coffee and sit watching the other visitors. Though I'm still in my habit my hair feels light and feathery under my veil – a secret self known to no one but Julia. To my surprise, that self feels at home in the gallery – but how, I wonder, would it feel in the Dingle?

After collecting the casseroles and my bag of okra from the cloakroom, I cut through the streets to the river, then turn south towards the Holy Land. On the opposite shore is the tunnel shaft and its twin vents, two giant versions of Lorraine's speakers and both pointing at Everton. Ahead of me is the Dingle. Glad of my soft new shoes, I pick up my pace along the prom.

After a week of gales the Mersey is hushed at low tide and for once the air over the city is still, its lavender haze ruffled only by the piping of oyster-catchers down by Mother Redcap's. On drawing parallel to the Holy Land, I stop and gaze up the hill towards the cobbled street where I was born, and where even now Dad will be waiting for his tea, and Mam will be pottering round the kitchen.

'Good evening, Sister.'

A black-suited figure is scuttling down the hill towards me: Father Gorman, Mam and Dad's parish priest. Lifting his black trilby, he approaches me sideways like a crab. Now there's no chance of my visit remaining a secret – and I'm too proud to beg him to keep his gob shut. Rather than ask outright why I'm loitering on the prom, he prefers to grumble about the failure of his amnesty scheme for looters. Hoping to see colour TVs and microwaves handed in by the rioters, he advertised his church hall as a collection point and persuaded the police to turn a blind eye. But the looters have boycotted the scheme and at the end of the week the church hall is still empty.

'This city will never get on its feet,' he grumbles, splaying his fingers.

Yes it will, I think, turning away to the Pier Head. The city will and so will I.

The day begins to wane as I walk back to the city centre. Soon the sunset is blazing, flamingo-coloured, over Perch Rock Battery and Formby Point opposite. Nearer by, two tugs are racing round the bows of a container ship like anxious sheepdogs, chivvying it into Seaforth docks while a pilot boat chugs past them to Port Authority.

With the Holy Land at my back, I think of all the other ships that have sailed this same river: the monks' coracles from Birkenhead Priory and, many centuries later, slavers returning from the tropics with copper-sheathed hulls heading for the Narrows, three-masted schooners laden with coffee and tobacco, and Irish boats bringing immigrants like my great-grandparents, Tom and Margaret O'Shaunessy, to live in their terraced houses by the docks.

I was always one for black and white, good and bad – but at last I'm learning the importance of grey, of the in-between things that can't be called right or wrong. Slackening my pace a little, I stare with new eyes at the grisaille that is taking shape before me, a ghostly end-of-summer hue, its separate and subtle tones yearning for recognition. Never before have I noticed so many shades: the pewter grey high above the Atlantic and beneath it the seal grey of the Mersey; the gunmetal wings of the gulls perched on the stones, and the dun of the shoreline where they walk, searching for clams beside the men digging for lugworms. And above it all rises the granite walls of the Liver Building. Liverpool, a city built from grey stone, rising out of the grey water.

When the container base gantries spring floodlit out of the dusk I quicken my step. The city lights are already switched on, so the buildings are reflected in the still water, as though stood on golden stilts. As the evening breeze flutters my veil I think of Lol, who learnt to survive failure, and Brigid who didn't. Soon Lol will be back from holiday, expecting to find me in her flat; and Julia too will be waiting, ready to give support. Then at the beginning of next month the students will arrive for the new term, flocking into the city like the first Barnacle geese of autumn, now beating their way upriver in a perfect chevron.

I've been grounded for too long, I decide, turning inland towards St Cuthbert's. It's high time I got myself airborne.

Ave Alma Mater

If Lol was right and Maria Goretti wants me to go, she disguises it well. When I enter her study she invites me not to kneel in front of her desk but to sit in an armchair near her own, and smiles kindly as I stammer out my news.

'You are not yet a full Choir nun, Sister Maureen, so your vows are not binding.' She gives a glance at my new fringe, which I've tried to slick back beneath my veil. 'Though you are free to leave any time, please know I would like you to stay. The Church needs women like you who are young and belong to the people.'

I shake my head. 'It's impossible.'

'It may help you to know that St Cuthbert's is getting a new Superior.'

A retired Superior is never allowed to stay on in the convent she once ruled. I sit in silence, wondering where they'll send Mother Wilfred and how she'll adapt to yet another upheaval.

'Don't you want to find out who it is?'

I shake my head, knowing it will be either Bosco or Xavier or some other old Choir nun who likes bossing people about.

'It's Sister Bertilla.'

'She'll be good for Toxteth,' I say, 'and good for St Cuthbert's. But as far as I'm concerned it makes no difference.'

'But I thought you'd like it.' For a second Mother General looks like a disappointed schoolgirl. 'A Superior you get on with, money to work among the people —'

I stare through the window at the hole where the grotto once was, and Maria Goretti follows my gaze. 'Mother Wilfred has told me about your fortune-telling and convent ghosts – and in Italy too there are many superstitious peasants. But we in the modern church have had miracles enough. What we need now is reason and progress.'

I remember the clump of the lay sisters' boots, and their sisterhood of sweat and effort stretched across the centuries. 'It's the ghosts that've kept me going.'

'But your ghosts are not real.'

My eyes take in the designer suit with its minuscule crucifix on the lapel. They're more real than you are, I want to say, but I know that she'd never believe me.

'Mother Wilfred should never have made you a lay sister. The way of life is too limiting.'

'But I loved cooking and cleaning.'

Mother General ignores me. 'I was hoping the university would broaden your mind. Then you would see your . . . apparitions for what they are: a consolation prize for the have-nots.'

By have-nots she means people like my mam who saw Our Lady in the blue of her kitchen Formica, and my nan before her, writing to City Spooks in the Mersey Mart before saying her rosary; and before them both, St Bernadette Soubirous, bullied to death by her convent Superior.

'You do not have to stay with such people,' Maria Goretti cuts across my thoughts. 'You are quick-witted, Sister Maureen, and can if you wish lead a fulfilling life.'

I remember Bosco's elocution lessons and my Choir nun's training and the way I can hardly speak to Mam and Dad any more, and wonder what else I would have to do to be acceptable. 'St Bernadette had visions – and she was canonised.'

'St Bernadette was canonised for her obedience, not for her visions,' says Maria Goretti. 'Soon, Sister Maureen, your life will grow more satisfying. Then your hallucinations will cease.'

From outside her door comes the crash of a workman's ladder, and then the buzz of an electric drill. Alert and encouraging, Maria Goretti's eyes are fixed on mine as I try to explain how I feel. 'Now Brigid's gone there's nothing left for me here.'

My words must have had the ring of truth because she rises from her armchair. 'The order has never kept anyone against their will, Sister Maureen, and it never shall.' She crosses the room to her desk, opens a drawer and counts some notes into an envelope. 'I take it you will continue your studies. This money should support you till your student grant arrives.'

Hurt by her cool tone, I reach for the envelope. This convent has been my home for nearly ten years, and I've poured my heart and soul into it.

Maria Goretti pulls out a paper carrier and passes it

across her desk. 'Those are your secular clothes,' she continues while I peer doubtfully into the bag at the jeans, T-shirt and gym shoes folded inside. I'd forgotten that a nun leaves the convent in the same clothes she wore to enter it. 'I have spoken to Lorraine. She assures me you have somewhere to live.'

'Her flat's in Gambier Terrace, by the Anglican cathedral.'

'You may leave tomorrow morning during Matins. I myself will break the news to Mother Wilfred. As for you, please remember the Holy Rule and say nothing to your sisters. There are changes enough in the air, and I don't want to start a stampede.' And with that she locks her drawer, follows me out of the room, and turns with a smile to the taller of the two workmen.

Hiding the carrier bag under my cape, I scurry straight to my cell. Already feeling like an impostor, I shove the clothes to the back of my wardrobe and go downstairs for my last few hours as a nun.

'Are you all right, dear?' asks Columba, who as a lay sister is quicker than most to sense a change in atmosphere.

I smile uncomfortably. 'Why do you ask?'

'Because you don't seem quite yourself.' She nods at the gaping hole in the enclosure wall. 'You're taking it too hard.'

I stare at her small frame worn down by a life of service. Since I was a novice I've taken pride in saving her legs, running her errands and making her cups of tea. What will she say when she finds that I've gone – and without even saying goodbye? 'Don't worry,' I say, feeling like a double agent. 'I'll be better by the morning.'

Evening recreation is spent as usual in the community

room. Maria Goretti has had the frosted glass replaced with clear panes, so I can see the pear tree shiver as a breeze creeps up from the river. Too on edge to share in the talk of the alterations, I gaze at the face of one nun after the other: Wilfie, Bosco, Ursula, Kevin, Bertilla, Xavier, Elisabeth, Gonzaga and Columba. I had thought I'd only miss the lay sisters, but I was wrong. The Choir nuns too have been part of my family since I was a novice, and it chokes me to let them down. We've been so beleaguered over the years, so out of date and poverty-stricken. Not trusting myself to say goodnight I slip out of the room and go early to bed.

I close my cell door and open the roll of money. It's a lot – more than a month's housekeeping – and I hope it comes straight from Rome. After tucking it back in the carrier, I slide out of my habit and into my T-shirt and Levis, which make me feel skinny and insubstantial. Luckily they still fit after all these years, but the flared bottoms look odd even to my non-fashion-conscious eye. I've just crammed my feet into the gym shoes when I'm startled by a tap at my door. For a few seconds I hesitate, then skid forward and open it an inch.

'I knew something was up,' whispers a voice through the crack, 'but I didn't guess what till this evening.'

I open the door to Bertilla, whose berry-bright eyes take in my T-shirt and jeans, and linger for a second on my new haircut. 'We will miss you, uMoey.'

Columba appears in the corridor behind her. 'This is sad, sad news,' she whispers. 'I haven't dared tell Gonzaga. It'll break her up.'

'Will you ask her to forgive me?'

'Of course I will – it's just that we'll miss you, dear Maureen.'

'Moey's only going to Liverpool,' Bertilla tells her, 'so she'll come back and see us.'

'But it won't be like the old days,' says Columba, 'with all of us under one roof.'

'Times change,' says Bertie, her voice thickening, 'and so do all the best people. Maureen must do what she thinks right.'

'You will always be our sister,' says Columba, her eyes brimming, 'no matter where you travel.' She hands me one of her pipe-cleaner birds, a fork-tailed raptor with an orange feather glued to its pate. 'Take this little fellow as a keepsake.'

'I'll remember you always,' I cradle the fragile creation in my hand, 'and I'll never live among better people.'

The only other person I see that night is Xavier, who appears at my cell door long after the rest have gone to bed. Unable to sleep, I'm sitting in my dressing-gown, watching the full moon sail through the sky.

'I overheard what the others were saying,' whispers the lanky South African, 'and I want to tell you something before you go.'

I stare at the pale blob of a face in the gloom.

'I know you and I have never been friends,' she continues, 'but be sure of this: you are making the right decision. I'm fifty-one so for me it's too late; but at your age I'd be doing the same.' And with that she flat-foots her way down the corridor.

When the clock strikes two I climb into bed where I lie for the rest of the night with my eyes open, listening to the sighings, rustlings and snorings across the partitions, and wondering if I'll ever share a sleeping space again, or if I'll be like Eleanor Rigby and die an old maid. At the first stroke of the rising bell I spring up automatically, then flop back on the edge of my bed. Even though no one can see me, I feel too self-conscious to put on my jeans. Clutching the mother-of-pearl rosary I took from Brigid's coffin, I start begging God to see me through the next hour and then stop, because it hardly seems fair to ask Him to help me leave Him.

I put the beads in my plastic bag along with Lorraine's keys, the envelope of money, and my luminous shrine of Our Lady of Lourdes, which I wrap in tissue paper along with Columba's pipe-cleaner bird. My little pink mirror is already in the waste bin, and Piers's book on Vermeer is in the school library. Having accepted it in disobedience, I felt it wasn't mine to keep. This morning Xavier will find it on her desk, and label it in her neat hand.

When the community leaves for chapel, I pack my toothbrush, face cloth, night-dress, lecture notes and essays, and then get dressed, leaving my habit on a hanger in the wardrobe. Not a lot to show for all those years, I think, picking up my bag.

For a moment I imagine that Wilfie has come to say goodbye but it's only the creak of a board as I cross the front hall. Which is just as well, I tell myself, not wanting to be seen in my skimpy casual clothes.

Drawing back the bolt on the front door I let myself out into the pearly morning light. Blinds are going up in the tower block, and from the chapel comes the sound of the Choir nuns' chanting. The familiar tones halt me in my tracks, and I gaze at the beautiful old building, knowing I've been happier here than I'll ever be again, and that I'm throwing God's best gift back in His face. And then I see the

Holy Army at the window – a row of pale faces with Brigid at the end looking mopey. I wave but she doesn't wave back – just stands there watching my departure, but whether to bless or to curse I cannot tell.

'Forgive me for leaving,' I whisper. 'It was now or never.' At the front gate I turn again but their faces have gone ugly and menacing. Then, as I stare at the jagged shapes, I see that they're only splashes of paint left on the glass by the decorators. Hoping against hope that I'll still catch a glimpse of my ghosts, I drop my bag and look from one window to the next while the orange bricks brighten in the sun, serene and silent as a Dutch master. Only when all the windows stay blank do I accept that I'll never see the Holy Army again.

But as I turn my back on the house I know my future will be haunted all the same – not by the ghosts of dead lay sisters but by my life as a nun and my sinful decision to leave it.

Out on the dual carriageway the rush-hour traffic is roaring into life. As the convent gate clicks shut behind me I dodge between cars across the road and into the park. The ground is still wet with dew, and my flares are flapping awkwardly round my ankles. But the mist has vanished from the hollows and the dome of the Palm House is glinting in the sun. My new haircut feels crisp and feathery, and my gym shoes are cushioning my feet. Tucking my carrier under my arm, I take a deep breath and start to run.

Epilogue

On her last morning at St Cuthbert's Mother Wilfred woke early and wandered into the middle of the lawn. The wind had howled all night: the first of the September gales, and more forecast for the week to come. The light, shining yellowish and gloomy through the low-slung clouds, fell on the rubble the builders had piled over her favourite rose bush. Not that it made much difference. Despite her attempt to prune it, her beautiful Grace Abounding had turned into a briar, its suckers entangled with stitchwort and couch grass.

A movement in the hen run drew her attention from the ruined garden. The bantam cockerel, comb crumpled, was flapping his wings in a sea of mud. He stretched his neck as though to crow but gargled hoarsely instead.

Bertilla had netted the top of his run against marauding kites but hadn't noticed the hole under the wire. A fox had slipped in and carried off all the hens in the same night. Everyone thought the cockerel had gone too –

until Columba noticed him two days later, cowering under a fuchsia bush. He'd been unable to crow ever since.

Yes, the new Superior was too wrapped up in her Well Women's clinic to worry about her garden and her bantams.

'Why do the women need a clinic if they are well?' Mother Wilfred had asked her resentfully.

'These folk need amenities,' replied Bertilla. 'We must make better use of the plant.'

Out on the street, a man was staring curiously through the gap in the garden wall. Mother Wilfred glared back and then, when he failed to move on, went inside the convent and shut the door. In the old days she could have retreated to her study but Bertilla had already taken it over and was turning it into a dispensary. Instead of an office of her own, the new Superior would have a work station in one corner of the community room. It had arrived yesterday in a flat-pack from Habitat, which Mother Wilfred had thought was a religious supplier until the worldly-wise Elisabeth had put her right.

Staring now at its stripped-pine surfaces, Mother Wilfred knew that her life had been a failure – had known it for months, even before Maria Goretti saw fit to tell her.

'One of your young nuns grew so desperate she committed suicide. As a Superior you should have had better inter-personal skills.'

'But the religious life is meant to be lonely,' said Mother Wilfred, harking back to the days of her own formation. 'I had to keep my distance.'

Maria Goretti sighed. 'You should have given Sister Brigid some positive reinforcement.'

Mother Wilfred stared at the slim young Italian. She'd

thought she'd known better than her Mother General, discounted her, even: a terrible sin of pride – and now she was being punished.

'It's too bad,' cooed Maria Goretti, 'that the balance sheets have forced us to close our retirement homes. But never mind – we'll find you some place nice.'

Today Mother Wilfred was leaving for an old people's home in Leicester, a place she knew nothing about, leaving Mother Bertilla to fill the cloister with shoplifters and drug addicts.

But Bertilla's got a shock in store, thought Mother Wilfred with a slight rise in her spirits. The Archdeacon, turned into an ally by his dislike of Maria Goretti, had phoned yesterday.

'So, St Cuthbert's has fallen on hard times.'

From his breathy tone Mother Wilfred knew he had bad news up his sleeve. 'We'll soon be open to the public,' she stalled, 'and we've already applied for partnership money —'

'Then you haven't been told!' sang the Archdeacon. 'Mother Maria Goretti has just telephoned the Bishop. Your convent and high school are going on the market – too run-down, it seems, and expensive to maintain.'

Mother Wilfred had gasped and groped dizzily for a chair. Though the receiver was clamped to her ear, she could scarcely follow the Archdeacon's drift.

'The convent will be advertised as business premises,' he was saying, 'with the chapel as its marketing point.'

'That is Mother Bertilla's problem not mine,' said Mother Wilfred. 'She is the new Line Manager.' She invested the last two words with all the scorn at her command: a deliberate act of disloyalty.

'So your Mother Bertilla will be presiding over a council flat,' intoned the Archdeacon.

'And going out to work each morning like any other woman.' It was hard for Mother Wilfred not to sound vindictive.

'If she can find work,' replied the Archdeacon. 'I can't support the idea of a Well Women's clinic so she may not get those diocesan funds she's after. And now,' he added, clearing his throat, 'what news of young Maureen?'

'I have no idea,' said Mother Wilfred frostily. She was telling the truth because none of the community ever mentioned Maureen O'Shaunessy and so far Maureen hadn't returned to see them. But they thought about her, Mother Wilfred knew. On the first morning Gonzaga had cried at the sight of the empty breakfast place. And instead of burning Maureen's holy habit, as instructed by the Rule, Columba had washed and aired it, and returned it to her cell, as though hoping she'd reappear any moment.

It was unfair, Mother Wilfred thought sadly. Even though they didn't say so, the old ones blamed her for letting Maureen go. Because the wayward, unworldly Maureen had a vocation, of that Mother Wilfred was sure. After forty years as a nun she knew the signs, not all of them likeable: the unstoppable determination, the refusal to deny her visions, and the utter devotion to St Cuthbert's.

The old ones thought she was glad to see the back of Sister Maureen, not knowing how hard Mother Wilfred had prayed for her to stay. Soon Maureen O'Shaunessy would be one of those ex-nuns with frumpish clothes and dissatisfied mouths of whom they saw more every year, hanging round convents, perpetually striving for a sense of importance, searching for something as grand as that which they'd betrayed.

The love of Our Blessed Saviour for each individual soul: that was what Mother Wilfred had tried – and failed – to teach the young nun.

And now the only young nun left was the vain, self-centred Elisabeth who thought she was Mother Wilfred's favourite because she was the least rebuked. Only the other day she'd been flicking through a fashion magazine left behind by Maria Goretti.

'Don't you wish you were young again?' said Columba, smiling fondly.

'No,' said Mother Wilfred, trying not to look at the stupidly exaggerated styles. 'I wouldn't be young again for the world.' She turned to Columba and looked her straight in the eye. 'I haven't got long to go and I'm glad of it. The best is past and the great days of the religious life are over.'

In an hour's time the taxi would arrive to take her to the station, and she could put off her packing no longer. If only they could have banded together against change, she thought as she plodded up the stairs. Then she could have told the Archdeacon to keep his funding, Maureen would not have gone to university, and Toxteth could be left to its own devices. And Maria Goretti, already gone to set up new cost centres in Latin America, would soon have forgotten all about them.

But now their holy community of women had been broken apart, and nothing would ever be the same again.

Mother Wilfred dragged her suitcase from its place on the top of her wardrobe beside the golden-haired baby Jesus, recently rescued from Pious's trunk.

'Politically incorrect,' Bertilla had said when Mother Wilfred had tried to return him to the chapel. 'Next year we'll be having a multi-cultural crib made in Peru.'

Mother Wilfred took him down from the wardrobe, opened her suitcase and put him inside.